Into The End

Ψ

Book #1
Into the End Series
B.R. Paulson

B.R. Paulson

Captiva Publishing, LLC
B.R. Paulson
www.brpaulson.com

Captiva Publishing , LLC
Copyright © 2012 Bonnie R. Paulson

All rights reserved. No part of this book may be reproduced in any form or by any means without the prior written consent of the publisher, excepting brief quotes used in reviews.

This book is a work of fiction and any resemblance to any person, living or dead, any place, events or occurrences, is purely coincidental. The characters and story lines are created from the author's imagination or are used fictitiously.

This book is licensed for your personal enjoyment only. This book may not be resold or given away to other people. If you would like to share this book with another person, please purchase an additional copy for each recipient. If you're reading this book and did not purchase it, or it was not purchased for your use only, then please return to the purchase-point and purchase your own copy.

Thank you for respecting the hard work of this author.

ISBN: 10:   1470142465
       13:   9781470142469

B.R. Paulson

Acknowledgments

To My Husband – Thank you. I love you.

To my critique partner: Maggie Fechner. Thank you.

To my beta readers: Connie (mom), Kammie and Gary Roylance, and Chelsea. Your input has been invaluable. Thank you.

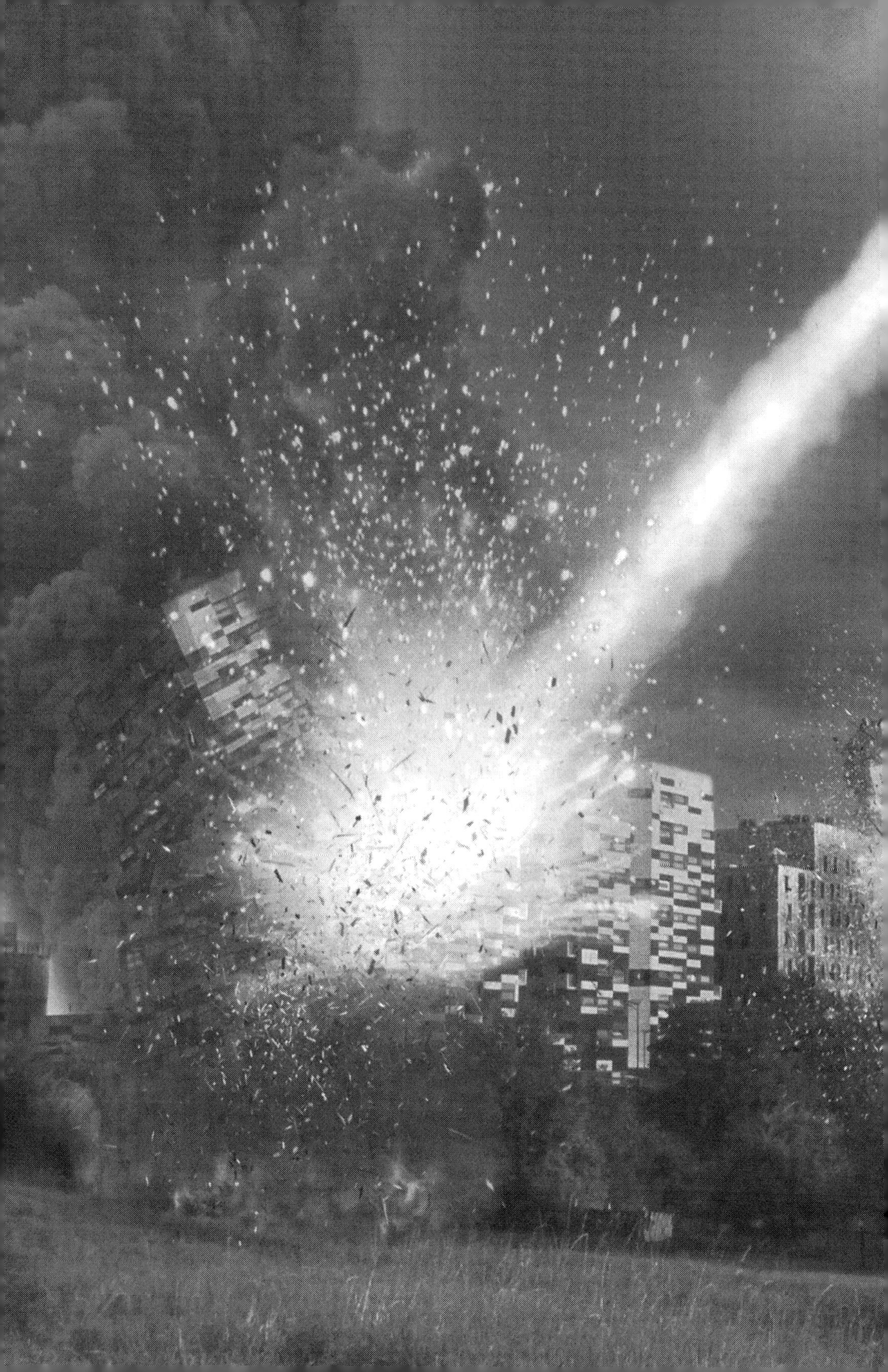

Chapter 1

Rachel

The end of the world had come.
Finally.

Rachel hadn't had a solid night's sleep in twenty-three months, three weeks and two days. An hour, maybe two a night for the last two years. Twenty-four hour news flickered on the TV.

Crisp May air breezed through the open windows. Rachel tucked the blanket tighter under her chin and readjusted her legs on the couch cushions. Restless leg syndrome would be a perfect excuse for her sleeplessness, but couldn't be further from the truth. Her legs weren't restless. She was.

The news anchor returned from commercial. Rachel turned up the volume. A squared picture flashed of burning buildings and gaping crevices. The older woman on screen sighed, weariness covering her lack of surprise. "Another earthquake in the string of disasters to the west coast struck an hour ago in Ellensburg, Washington. The Washington coastline has now been decimated to the middle of the state. Experts project a following tsunami to the new islands created from the Cascade Mountains should manifest in the next few hours."

Ellensburg? Mere hours away. Andy had been right.

The camera shifted to the man who shuffled paper. Lifting eyes desensitized to the horrors from recent days, he continued below a new popup screen. "In other news, after almost ten years of closed, high security airspace, the president has released a statement declaring that the airspace over the States is now open. He has requested assistance from other countries. The White House sent his formal request yesterday morning and has yet to receive answers from the NATO countries. The open space is an invitation for any help we can receive. Do not be alarmed if you spot airplanes or helicopters in the air."

A muffled thud sounded from the roof. Rachel muted the TV. And waited. At least she thought she'd heard something. Maybe… Well, maybe she'd slipped into that place between sleep and awake. Or maybe she was finally ready to sleep. It might be the mentioned assistance dropping food and supplies.

Rachel closed her eyes, smiling at the image of care packages dropping to the ground.

Thump! This time from the roof above her. Rachel snapped her eyes open and followed the sound with her gaze until it dropped off the steep grade. An orange glow drifted past the closed vertical blinds. Another. A new thud. Care packages didn't glow… did they?

Rachel escaped the pull of the blanket and knelt at the window. A burnt umber shone around the edges of the blinds. Faded in and out. Maybe young neighbors played with fireworks.

She pushed a few of the slats out of the way and gasped.

Falling debris, some on fire, catapulted from the sky. Large pieces hurtled to the ground while other materials and paper rode the calm May air to settle wherever it wafted. Flames burned out on contact with the grasses and streets, but here and there a small ember took hold on a tree or roof top. Smoke billowed black and white with different fuel.

A scream rent the air.

Rachel scrambled from the couch and shot down the stairs. Out the door, she landed on the grass and froze. Where had it come from? A second shriek slashed from the house next door. Bob and Martha. Rachel ran to the front door and pounded.

The retired gentleman flung the panel open, his white hair tufted here and there. "Rachel. What's going on?" He stuck his head out the door, the fire light revealing his absent hearing aid. "Where's Martha?"

Crackling from the back yard and another scream led Rachel through the gate, Bob trailing behind. Both dodged the increasing onslaught of fiery remnants. A paper bag, the corner curling with flame, slid off Rachel's shoulder. She stepped over a yellow charred chunk of foam in the shape of a small seat. A doll's head, or half of one anyway, rolled on the grass when it landed.

Rounding the corner of the house, Rachel tripped over the cement patio. Damn. Every time she came over, she stumbled over the same protrusion. Good thing she hadn't changed into her robe. The last thing she needed was to fight terry cloth tripping her up.

Finding Martha took a moment with vision limited through the falling debris. By the side fence, behind the rhododendrons, Martha chased her dog, whose tail and lower back had caught fire. Yips filled the air. Burning hair and flesh permeated the smoke trailing from burning paper and wood. The dog's water dish sat on the edge. Rachel picked up the bowl and dumped it on the burning animal.

"Oh no." Martha caught and patted the whimpering lump. She raised her eyes to her husband, tear filled. "Sparkles. He's…"

Bob couldn't hear her, but the pain on his face declared complete understanding.

Andy, Rachel's husband, had a gun. He could put the poor animal down. The kids needed to get up and get out of the house. Speaking as calmly as possible, Rachel approached the woman and touched her shoulder. "Martha, we need to put Sparkles out of his misery. I'll grab Andy. He can do it."

Gray hair, matted at the back, shook as Martha nodded. Rachel's heart ached for her friend. She struggled to keep from sobbing. "I'll be right back."

Sprinting, she returned to her house and bounded up the stairs. "Andy! Wake up. You need to get up." She powered through their bedroom door and grabbed Andy's foot. Hand over hand in the darkened room, she followed the lines of his sheet-covered, toned body and shook his shoulder hard. "Andy!" She yelled. "Andy, wake up! Hurry!"

Her husband didn't open his eyes but brushed her hands from him and rolled over. Rachel glanced toward the doorway. "Wake up, damn it." She grasped his shoulder tighter, ratcheting him back and forth until he turned to face her.

Andy yanked his ear plugs out and sat up. "What? I just fell asleep an hour ago." Bleary, he blinked hard to wake up. "The house better be sinking." He yawned and rubbed his face.

"Andy, things are falling from the sky. Martha's dog caught fire. He… They need you to put him down. Please, hurry." Rachel reached underneath the bed and pulled out Andy's Glock. Snapping the clip into place, she palmed the butt.

Mouth agape, Andy climbed from bed, his boxers low on his hips. He slid his jeans on and his t-shirt followed. Rachel grabbed his arm as he bent to retrieve his socks. "No, you don't have time. We need to go now. They need you." She pulled him to the door and handed him the gun. "Here. I'll get the kids ready. It's time."

"Time?" Confusion gave way to understanding, the softness of sleep hardened to the angles of his masculine features. "Got it. I'll be right back." He snagged a quick kiss, pressing his lips to hers like the world's end had paused just for them.

Andy pounded down the stairs.

Rachel turned to the kids' room. All three shared a room because Andy had opted not to spend any extra money on finishing the downstairs and instead had invested the surplus on supplies which he'd packed for speedy transport.

Cole stood in the doorway, watching her. "Mom? Where's Dad going?"

Hugging her oldest to her, Rachel breathed in deep. Innocence would be shattered. Even as a psychologist she didn't have the tools to prevent it. She pushed his unresisting form from her and looked into his eyes. "We have to go. Now. I need your help."

Squaring his jaw in perfect imitation of his father, Cole nodded. "Tell me what to do."

"Get dressed. Grab Beau and get him dressed. I'll get Kayli." Further into the bedroom packed with bunk beds and dressers, Rachel ignored the rush of fear. Adrenaline, pure and simple. She didn't fear the end. She didn't fear anything. Not since Rhode Island. She repeated her mantra. Nothing scared her. Not anymore. She had Andy.

Cole leaned into the bottom bunk. "Beau, we need to go. Grab Blanky. Hurry up."

"Kayli, honey, you need to wake up. We need to get out of here." Rachel rubbed her daughter's arm.

The lightest sleeper, Kayli, a smaller version of Rachel with her dark brown bob and blue eyes, sat up and threw her blanket on the floor followed by her stuffed doll. "Is this the emergency you and Daddy talk about?"

Rachel opened her arms and helped the six-year-old down. "I think so. Either way, we're going to pretend it is. I need you and Beau to get dressed and follow Cole to the backyard. Remember the drills?"

Solemn, Kayli and Rachel's tow-headed, four-year-old boy nodded. "Yes, Mommy."

Rachel nodded at Cole. The fourteen-year-old had plenty of experience watching the other two. They followed him like baby bears to peanut butter. She left the smaller kids in Cole's capable hands to gather last minute papers and memory items. The majority of the necessities had been packed months ago.

A gunshot pushed its way through the walls. Rachel paused on the landing between the flights of stairs and hung her head. Martha loved Sparkles almost more than her grandchildren. Almost.

Poor Andy. He loved domestic animals. But he was strong. Stronger than most men. And he was hers.

Anxious whispers flitted down the stairs from the kids' room. She'd have to hurry. The last thing she wanted was to have the kids outside by themselves, but she didn't want them in the house too long either. What if it caught fire?

A few pictures from the walls downstairs topped the pile she accumulated on her walk through the house. Climbing the stairs, Rachel dodged around the opening door. "Sorry."

Andy steadied her, his fingers warm on her elbow. "I didn't know you'd be right here, sorry about that." She met his solemn gaze. "I had to put the dog down. Martha is pretty upset, but Bob got her to go inside out of the fire. I asked them if they'd like to go with us."

Rachel exhaled. "Oh, good. Are they going to ride their quads? When can they be ready?"

His hand on her back, Andy followed Rachel up the stairs. Even after all the time they'd been together, his touch still tingled. "No, they want to get to Spokane. The news reported the Red Cross stations are open and ready for thousands. I'd like to see if that's changed. Bob is leaving in the next few minutes. They aren't even packing." The couple stopped mid-level. He reached up and brushed a strand of hair from her cheek. "Are the kids up?"

Beau appeared at the top of the stairs. "We're here, Dad." Backpack straps darkened his shoulders. Kayli bobbed behind him.

The electricity shut off. Darkness enveloped them. Kayli and Beau whimpered. Rachel searched with her hands and feet for the stairs and grasped their arms while offering sounds of comfort. Utter blackness greeted their eyes. Even the streetlamps fell victim to the blackout.

Andy moved around the living room, his steps padded on the carpet and stilted on the linoleum. A slight sticky sound indicated he stood in front of the fridge where Kayli had spilled grape jelly the night before. A moment later, a scratching and the flare of a match glimmered as the sun. Kayli, Beau and Cole followed Rachel down the stairs to the living room.

"I guess watching the news is out." Andy lit a decorative candle from the centerpiece on the dining room table. "You guys have your packs? Rachel, is that everything you need?"

He led the way to the sliding door, his light a beacon as they left their home. Maybe for the last time. Or maybe just a drill. Rachel's heart pounded.

Caboosing her family train down the deck steps, Rachel opened her mouth to stop Andy, beg him to reconsider. Spokane had Red Crosses. They'd be around others, know where their friends were. Sometimes being with the crowd was more than people gave it credit for.

Miniature meteors fell from the sky as far away as the river, over thirty streets away.

"Let me take that." Andy set the candle on the lowest step and removed the pile from Rachel's arms. The kids stared into the sky. Fire streaked the night sky, blocking out the stars. Andy pointed at the stairs. "Rachel, can you grab the radio? It's in the box under the deck."

Radio, radio. Rachel hated the Tupperware boxes under the steps during the daylight. Night time was worse. Maybe the bugs and spiders would know the sky was falling and leave her alone.

Locating the small wind up box required Rachel's complete focus. She taught fighting fears and overcoming obstacles. A spider was not something that created fear. No, instead it was disgusting. All those legs.

Something brushed her arm. *Crap, was that a spider?* She shivered. Yuck. Her fingers closed around the box and she yanked it out, scratching her arm where the tickle had been. "Got it." She banged her shin on the trailer tire, shapes blurred shadows against the white vinyl fencing.

Andy's hand found her arm, his angled jaw and firm lips illuminated by fluttering flames. A thump on the tarp covering the trailer behind Andy's quad startled Rachel. Andy took the radio before she could drop it. The spiders had bugged her more than she'd realized. "Beau, Kayli, Cole? You guys down here?"

Cole stuck his head up from the trailer behind the four-wheeler Rachel would drive. "Dad has us in already, Mom. Kayli and Beau are under here, too."

"Thanks, Cole." Her kids. Her husband. She needed them. Maybe that was a fear she had. Losing them. Tools to face fear made it hard to accept any. Focus on the moment, on the now. Not on what has happened and not what might happen. Focus. She wouldn't lose them. Andy was too prepared.

A car honked from the front yard. Three houses over a roof caught fire, lighting the area like a large torch. Every moment more urgent than the last.

"Let's see what we can get." Andy pushed the buttons and messed with the antennae. Static. "There's nothing on FM." Garbled murmurs cleared little by little as Andy pressed the button.

Rachel leaned forward. "Wait, what's that?"

"AM." Andy bent the small antennae and a harried voice fought through the static.

"… end it there. I'm not sure where they went. Hold on, here comes something." Muffled rubbing followed by sounds a phone makes when it's dropped. The voice couldn't belong to a guy older than high school, and he returned, hushed and frightened. "For those of you able to hear me, this is Tom Mason. We are under attack. I repeat, we are under attack." Shuffling followed by quickened breathing. "Fairchild was targeted this morning and multiple bombs have made contact, annihilating the base. Spokane hasn't fared any better, having received ill-aimed missiles."

Rachel stared at Andy. She recognized the boy's name. But… he'd said…

This was it. What they'd prepared for, Andy'd warned her of.

Tom Mason… She couldn't grasp the familiarity. Where had she heard that name before?

But Andy had assumed, hoped, the end would happen in their children's children's lives. Not in their own. Prepared or not, the reality was jarring.

Tom continued, his young voice assuming a level of maturity well beyond his years. "Moments before the television was cut, the news said to get to the relief shelters in town. I wouldn't do this as there is more danger in numbers. Get out of town, but be careful. I repeat, do not go to the relief shelters. Something isn't right. I'll sign back on once my position has stabilized."

Static.

Palms sweaty, Rachel clenched her sweatshirt in her hands. "What do we do?"

"Exactly what we're doing. Let's get out front and see if we can warn anyone else." He grabbed her hand. "We're ready for this.

Rachel, tell me you remember the way to the property." A falling flame reflected in his eyes.

Rachel inhaled, focused on steadying herself. If the area was attacked, they'd planned on getting to their property in the national forest northeast of Coeur 'd Alene, Idaho. He'd drilled her like their lives depended on it. Because they did. "Yes, I do."

Andy nodded. "Good. We won't get separated, but in case we do, get there. That's where you'll be safest. I will meet you there, just like we planned. ATVs are ready and packed. Let's leave." He pulled her into a hug and caressed her back through her shirt. "I'm sorry. I know you're scared. We can do this."

Rachel clutched him, hard. But time was of the essence. They separated and he gave her hand one final squeeze. "Did you get the documents?" The red container held their documents – birth certificates, Social Security cards, titles, immunizations, deeds, anything they might potentially need to prove who they were and where they belonged.

She had added the small file box full of the important paperwork and unhooked the external hard drive of the computer the day before. She'd scanned every document months ago and saved everything to the memory bank. When the hard drive had blinked, indicating it was full she'd added it to their cache of survival items.

Rachel tossed one last glance at the slider doors glowing with the reflection of bright orange flames from the burning house. One fleeting moment donated to the memory of her dark glossy hardwood California king bed. A folded open romance novel on the side table. Socks and underwear piled at the foot of the bed from laundry the day before. Rachel tightened her jaw. She had to do this. If she wasn't strong for the kids, who would be?

The falling objects were more irregular, testifying of passing time. Rachel and her family wouldn't be there much longer and who knew if they'd ever return.

Chapter 2

Brenda

Nothing pissed Brenda off more than when Rachel or her husband were right. Seriously.

She pounded up the stairs to the master bedroom and pushed the door against the pile of dirty clothes mating on the floor. Her husband was a slob. That was the nicest word she had for him.

Boots on, she tromped across the floor to stand beside the bed. Face up, he lay with his arms splayed. With his mouth open and his longish hair matted on the pillow case, he had an almost insane look to his normally hard and twisted features. Nothing about Lee spoke of a kinder, gentler side. Especially when he was awake.

Asshole.

But he was her husband and Brenda owed him at least a warning before she went. Disgust smoothed from her expression, she reached out and prodded his shoulder. Once. Twice. On the third one, he snapped his eyes open and grabbed her forearm, yanking her on top of him.

"Waking me up, Brenda?" His breath blew across her cheek and she closed her eyes against the stale alcohol mixed with pepperoni stench.

Brenda bit back her whimper. She swallowed. "But we're under attack, Lee. There are bombs going off all over the place. Don't you want to get out?" *Please, please, let me go,* she begged behind eyes that betrayed none of her fear or anxiety.

He ignored her, laughing at her situation instead. He rolled her to her stomach, ripping her thin scrub pants and shirt from her skin. "Just back from your trip and you can't wait to get in bed with me. I'll oblige you this time, Brenda, but next time you know the rules."

Teeth gritted to prevent her screams from escaping, Brenda counted in her head. He never took longer than the count of three hundred. Never. Never. Never.

At two-hundred-and-fifty-seven he slapped her rear end and pushed off her. Brenda didn't say a word but waited as he left the room for the connected bathroom – that her job paid for.

Asshole.

Karma would be a missile or bomb taking out Lee while he showered. But Karma hated Brenda. Not that she gave a damn.

Chapter 3

Andy

Thirteen years of marriage, five years together before that and Andy couldn't believe his fortune. When Rachel held his hand, invincibility coursed through him. The effect hadn't waned over the years.

Rachel checked on the kids in beds Andy had built in the trailers for just such an event. She whispered something to each one and kissed their heads. Two steps brought her to the oversized quad where she climbed onto the kickboard and swung her leg over the seat, settling in for the ride. Andy patted her hand and climbed on his.

The trailers would work well. He'd custom built the axle-free wagons when rumors of attack on American soil had filtered around the web over a year ago. Many people had scoffed at the possibility – who would dare to wage war with the Great US of A? Andy hadn't needed more than a rumor. All too vividly he recalled the terror and loss of September 11, 2001. It didn't take much to bring to mind the stories his grandpa had told of Pearl Harbor and the horrors there.

The earthquakes in California, Oregon, Nevada and southern Idaho had followed the whispers of foreign attack, smothering the warnings of invaders in the wake of the abysmal destruction. But Andy had ordered pieces for the trailers and upgrades on their four-wheelers, also called quads. He'd special ordered the ATVs to have engines as big as a car's.

Two pairs of riding gloves rested across his gas cap. He tossed Rachel hers before yanking on his own. "The gate's unlocked, we'll just ride through. I want to double check on Bob. He might change his mind, if I tell him what we heard on the radio. Point to the street and the prairie. I'll push through first." He clenched his jaw and continued, "Your pistol is in the box zip-tied to the handlebars." He hated that she might need the weapon, hated he'd made her take a hunter safety course and practiced how to use her gun. In fact, she could use all of the guns he owned and so could Cole. But she hated weapons. Something from her work with the government.

Andy started the engine and Rachel followed his lead. They gave the motors a moment to warm up, but couldn't spare more. Andy pushed the throttle and all four wheels inched forward. He powered through the gate and Rachel followed. He tossed a glance over his shoulder. All three kids peeked over the side of the trailer from under the tarp Andy had placed to protect them from the falling debris, big eyes and little hands the only things in view.

Outside the semi-serenity of their backyard, chaos was building. Neighbors stood on their lawns, shouting to each other. Two more houses had caught fire, flames running along the roof line and in the windows. Five men stood by the mailboxes as they watched the sky.

Andy slid from the seat. He motioned at Rachel to stay put. Bob's open garage door showed an absent car. Andy poked his head through the man door and called out. No one answered.

Anticipation tightened his shoulders. Another neighbor, two doors down, drove by in a truck, stopping to lean out his window. "Andy? Is that you?" The headlights sliced through the night, highlighting Rachel and the ATVs.

"Yeah, you guys heading out?" Andy walked alongside the rig, talking to the man while his wife drove.

"Yeah, news said to get to Spokane. Air Force is supposed to be helping with casualties and shipping people further east. First wave is leaving in four hours." He looked at the four-wheelers. "You guys heading to Spokane in that?"

"No. We're going into the mountains. Heard on the radio Fairchild was attacked. Spokane got stray bombs. I'm not sure the city is the safest place to be, you know?" Andy reached his driveway and stopped. Two more cars lined up behind the truck.

"Spokane is the safest place right now. You follow us. We'll watch out for you." The man waved to the other cars who responded with honks. He looked at Andy. "Bob and Martha left a bit ago. We're going to try to catch them."

"Okay, good luck. I'll talk to Rachel. Don't wait for us." Andy studied his neighbor's face. He wouldn't see him again. Odd. He patted the hindquarter of the truck as it passed and waved at the passengers of the cars. A small girl, eyes wide, watched him from the back seat of a four-door sedan.

"Andy, we need to go." Strength and weakness warred in his wife's voice. She called her fears insecurities, hadn't admitted to real fears since she'd gone east two years ago. She always overcame her "insecurities". Taught others how to face their fears, define them, but never claimed her own.

Protecting his family took precedence over his neighbors. Safety. He had to get them to the ranch. "Let's go." He climbed on his quad and motioned Rachel across the street and up the embankment to the prairie plateau.

Metal creaked and rattled with each rotation of the tires as they moved forward. Eerie quiet allowed the crackle of hungry flames to drift across the field from bordering neighborhoods on fire.

Rachel revved over the curb, bouncing and tossing, picking up speed. Andy followed and sped up the incline to the plains.

A truck and a station wagon pulled from their driveways. A sports car followed suit and the three cars sped into the night. Toward Spokane.

Rachel stopped and waited for Andy. He pulled abreast of her and they turned to watch their neighborhood. Tail lights disappeared in the falling flames. His wife shook her head. "Do you think we'll see them again?"

Reaching across the distance between them, Andy grasped Rachel's hand. "No."

A shudder ran the length of her body. She nodded and sniffed.

He wanted to take the burden from her, shoulder anything for her. "Leave the lights off until we get further from town. Something doesn't feel right."

She whispered, "Andy, nothing about this night feels right."

He squeezed his wife's hand before letting go. "At least we're together."

They revved away from the residential areas of Post Falls to the upper regions of Coeur d'Alene. They needed to make it through one city before they reached the wilds of the National Forest and the potential moderate safety.

Falling debris lessened south of Rathdrum outside Hayden. Dark evergreens sliced into the pre-dawn sky. A plane passed about three-hundred yards overhead. Rachel and Andy ducked from the thunderous noise. Cole poked his head from beneath the tarp only to retreat a scant second later.

Deeper into the trees skirting subdivisions and strip malls of Coeur d'Alene and Hayden, Andy motioned Rachel to stop. "Let's take a quick break. If we see more cars, we'll need to go the back way which will take longer."

They cut their engines and slid off the quads. Andy stretched his arms over his head and bent down. The sudden quiet relieved the constant pull on his hearing. Without having to strain, he easily picked up the sound of car engines, horns honking, and shouts filtering through the thin protection of trees between Rathdrum and Coeur d'Alene.

The population wasn't large in the Idaho towns. Spokane was the largest metropolitan area on the east side of Washington but nothing worth attacking if American domination was the goal. What was the goal? The result had never been hinted at, merely the attacks. Even the "who" had always been undefined in Andy's findings.

Andy rolled his head on his shoulders and sat down on the edge of his trailer to think. Rachel joined him and placed her hand in the crook of his elbow. "What do you think is happening? Do you think Brenda is okay?" She murmured the last.

She hadn't said that name in months. Andy wished he had answers for her. Something or anything to make her feel better, give her some staying power. "I don't know. If it's the Chinese, they have the numbers to attack by foot, but I'm confused why they would attack Spokane. I would have used my fire power on New York or Dallas, heck D.C. but Spokane? Kind of farfetched."

"Do you think something will be on the radio? Are you sure we shouldn't go to the shelters? She might be there…" Her voice trailed off with the shake of Andy's head.

Through the lightening dark, the sight of Rachel lowering her face tugged at Andy's reserve. "I'm sorry. I'm worried about your sister, too, Rach, but we can't risk the kids. Maybe once we get up to the property and settle them in, I can leave for more information, maybe even retrieve her." He forced lightness into his voice. "Who knows, we may be wrong and it's just a freak accident and we'll be home by Friday." His wife nodded, clutching the false hope in his statement, though unable to let go.

"It's a great idea to check the radio. Let's see if Tom Mason is back on." Andy stood and unstrapped the radio from the front rack. He pressed power and the lights lit up.

Whispered urgency crackled from the speakers. "...worry. There are a lot of people rushing toward town. I think the Arena is where they're setting up shelters. I can't tell you more because I'm not going into town." A shuffling and heavy breathing and then, "After the first few bombs at Fairchild, I think we had a break, but a few planes have been circling and I'm not sure, but something else is going to happen, I just can't figure out what. Get away from Spokane. Don't go west. I repeat do not go west."

As if in a cave or somewhere underground, his voice would rub in and out, clear and then not-so-much. His gasps suggested he might not be stationary, but the lack of background noise created a vacuum as they searched for signs of where he might be.

Rubber screeched on asphalt and the tear of metal on metal colliding ripped through the clearing. Andy pushed Rachel toward her quad. "Get on. Hurry!" Would they make it? His wife, he watched her. He couldn't take his eyes from her.

They started the engines and pummeled deeper into the forest. Lights catapulted into the clearing off the side of the freeway. Cars piled up behind the accident. The new break in the trees and brush displayed the stop-and-go traffic.

A hundred feet separated Andy's family from the next neighborhood. A straight path shafted through the jagged foliage line. Rachel followed him as he rolled along the fence perimeter. House silhouettes rose into the sky.

Relatively quiet engines were the selling point of the quads. Smooth rumbles disrupted the assumption the large beasts would roar when started, but Andy had added after-market mufflers which silenced the putt of the sound. He'd put them on in case looters or rioters were a risk as he shuffled his family to their cabin.

Homes in the cookie cutter neighborhood had an abandoned air. From the back yards at four in the morning people could be sleeping. Or maybe they'd noticed something was happening and they'd evacuated as well.

Andy slowed as he closed in on the turn of the vinyl fence, the street beyond empty.

A scream rent the air. He spurred forward.

The fence ended and the street opened to a Y leading left and right. In the crux of the split a house sat with a garage on one side and a large veranda off the other, giving the impression of arms welcoming each person into the neighborhood.

Flames grew from the garage roof and engulfed the lower portion of the house, except the far side of the deck where a lattice crept up the side. Another scream followed, sending chills up Andy's spine. He didn't want to put another living thing down because of burns. Or listen to its pain.

He climbed off his idling quad and rushed to Rachel's trailer. The tarp was cool where he grasped the edge. "Cole."

His son sat up, pushing the tarp from him. "Yeah, Dad?"

"I need you to sit on my quad and wait with Mom." Andy swallowed and held back the blue covering while Cole climbed out. The boy's awkward movements hid a grace he displayed on dirt bikes and on the football field. Growing fast, Cole would soon be able to hold him down in a play wrestling match, a fact that saddened Andy.

Rachel climbed down and joined Andy. Cole swung his leg over the seat and settled where his dad had been.

Andy grabbed his wife's hand. She had to make it, no matter what. "Rachel, get back on the bike. Listen, I'm going in. If I'm not out in five minutes you have to go."

A plane, its outline a mere shadow in the dark sky, zoomed overhead almost as close as the last one. The closest airport was thirty minutes away. They had no reason to be so low in that area. Damn. Josh had been more right than Andy'd realized. His ironclad grip matched the intensity behind his next words. Promise me." Where his fingers wrapped around her wrist, he could feel her small muscles tense.

Her beautiful blue eyes wide, his angel nodded. "But…"

"No. Five minutes. Go. I'll catch up to you, okay?" He looked once more at his wife. "Rachel, do you hear me? I'll get to you no matter what." She nodded and for the briefest moment, he doubted he'd see her adorable freckles again.

Andy looked to his son and shook the feeling of doom from his shoulders. He spoke slow in an unmistakable tone that a father used with his son. "You follow your mom." Andy used his shored up courage and forced himself to turn from his family and sprint down the short stretch of blacktop to the house.

Unreal, the heat burned his skin through multiple layers of clothing, pushing from the house in a powerful consistent wave. A few degrees cooler than the baking body of the house, the deck hooked to thin lattice. Andy gained a foothold and climbed the questionable framework, worried he hadn't heard another peep since he'd left the quad.

"Hello! Is anybody in here?" Crackling flames drowned out his words as they ate at the other side of the door. Strong heat buffeted from below.

Whimpers edged along the edge of the wall.

Andy swiped his hand through the air in front of him, back and forth. Inside, the house was darker than the forest beyond the fence. His fingers brushed something warm and pliable. A squeak said he'd found what he'd been looking for.

Two people, teenagers by their size, huddled in the corner clutched together. At least they weren't on fire like the dog had been.

"Come on." Andy tugged them toward the open window. The boy clamored out, the girl a bit more hesitant, but they both shimmied down the make-shift ladder.

A hiss from behind and Andy turned. A red line streaked through the dark. Creaking followed by pops like gunshots and sparks drifted up, or was it down? A loud crash and immense heat.

Rachel?

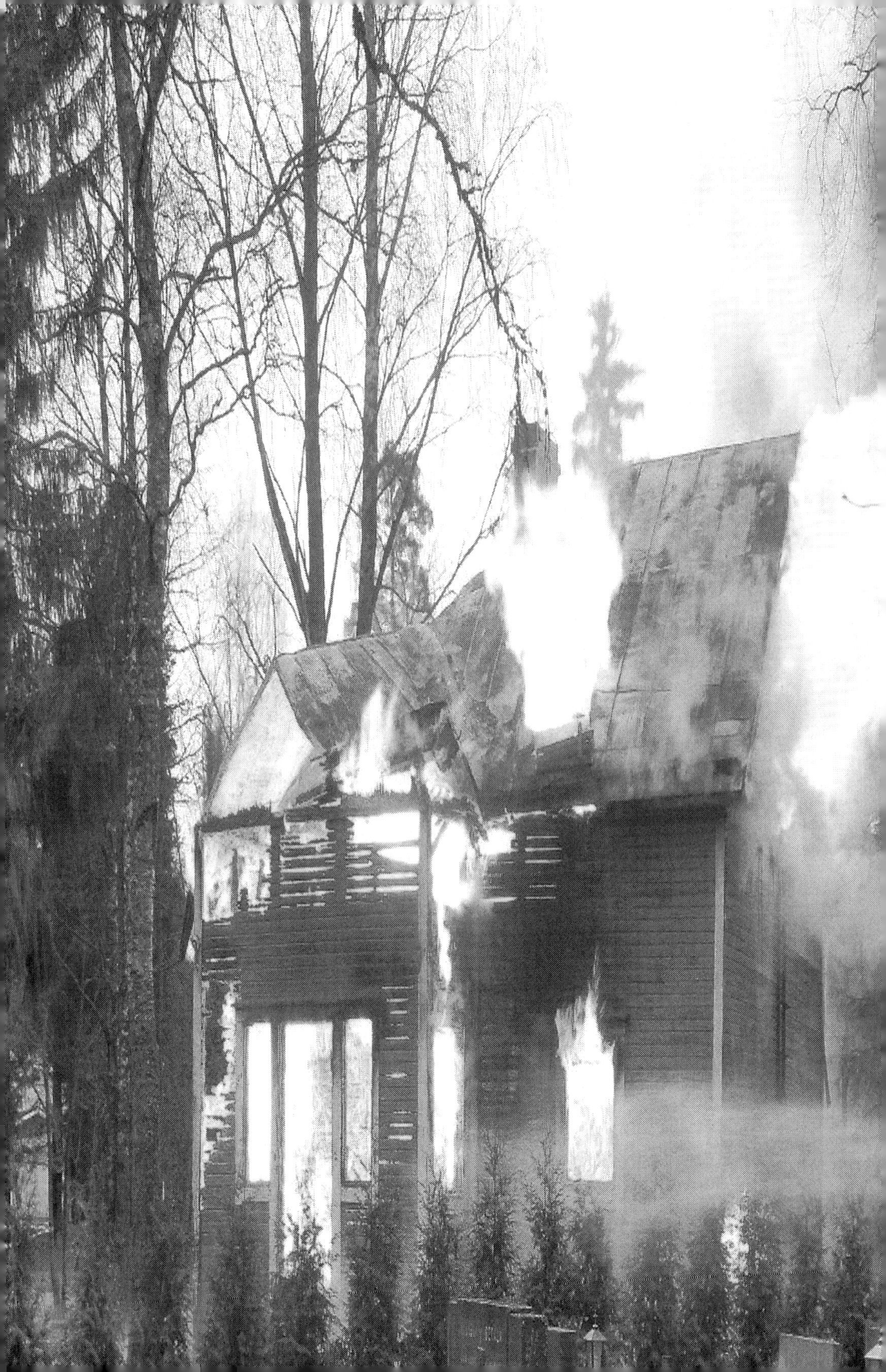

Chapter 4

Tom

Tom wiped his forehead. Notorious for cool evenings, May held true to the standard and Tom was grateful. Running in a balmy August would have dehydrated him faster and he needed all the strength he could store.

Scrambling into the crawl space between his "radio station" and the kitchen, he clutched the small mic. Transmitting equipment would run when he clicked the talk button and continue to appear in sleep mode. But his voice would carry and the men in his house listened, waiting, hoping he would slip up.

A chance to escape had come and gone, but another would slide into view. The damnable thing was, he'd been out. Three times. Yet he continued to return in case his parents made it home.

Hopefully they didn't come home.

The radio equipment had to be left behind. He'd take his portable unit, but how long would it work? Was anyone even listening? Did anyone even care? He couldn't get anyone on the ham to respond. Spokane had been hit, and who else? How many Americans were still out there? Tom had to make another announcement. Just in case.

Guttural voices thudded through the drywall. Tom closed his eyes and tried to control his breathing. He focused on a mundane memory the way his psychologist had taught him to take on fear. He'd started hamming with his buddies. Borrowing his dad's equipment until he'd paid off his own. He'd learned tricks and tips and taught his friends.

In class, his physics teacher had pulled them aside and warned them from pursuing the hobby further, something about Big Brother had Cousins outside the big 50. But Tom and the other three had ignored his conspiracy theories, certain the instructor thought everyone was out to get them. Heck, the man wrapped his cell phone in aluminum foil when he wasn't using it, missing calls and text messages on a regular basis. He wasn't the only one in the northern Idaho and eastern Washington region whose religious gospel was made up of theories conjured by men on the extremes of idealism.

Dang if the teacher's prophecies hadn't played out, one by one. Tom was the last of the original four… still alive. His friends had died in a car accident, built up as alcohol related, but Tom and his friends didn't drink. Losing control had no appeal.

Sitting in on his dad's radio conferences had added to his fear. Riding his bike and running for stress relievers, Tom had researched escape and survival, joined the Scouts and annoyed the owner of the local Surplus Store. He could tie a knot while tapping Morse code with his foot.

Pressure had built in the air, like steam in a kettle, needing release. Everyone had recognized the rush toward something, a change, but no one had understood what it was. Tom had broadcast his own ideas, but he'd been stupid. He'd never protected his location and hadn't thought of it until a few weeks ago.

Too late. Invaders in his home.

Tom closed his eyes. He was an only child. If his parents had been hit during their graveyard shifts at the hospital, he'd be completely orphaned.

If the foreign-speaking men found him, his family could be demolished. He gulped against the tears. Hardened reporters didn't cry. They listened and learned. Suck it up. He could do what was needed.

The sweat on his forehead and neck collected particles of dust, the itch unbearable in the mounting heat. Fortunately, his dad had never gotten around to remodeling this side of the house with new insulation. Fiberglass would not be welcome.

No more than eighteen inches wide, the crawl space allowed very little room for Tom to move. He stood sideways, his growing body large and awkward in the tight area. But clumsiness came when he moved… and he wasn't moving.

A door slammed, the walls shook and dust sprinkled down on Tom.

"What's going on? Why haven't you found the boy?" English but heavily accented, the voice hummed through the wall where Tom rested his head. He pulled back and stared at the studs, trying to predetermine if the man sensed he was there.

Shuffling feet, a barked command in another language and sudden quiet unnerved Tom more than the rummaging and rifling of his family's belongings. He pressed his ear to the cardboard colored backing of the drywall, the stamp in line with his nose. His stomach hurt. He desperately wanted to hold his mom and dad – but thinking about them would have to come later, when he could cry or plan or something. But he had to be alive to get to that point.

"Tom. Tom, where are you, little boy?" Sing song, the man's voice raised like he talked to a small toddler, the contrast extremely offsetting like fangs on an Easter bunny.

Tom's stomach no longer hurt – maybe it had vacated his body. He held his breath. Fingers numb and tingly. His legs wobbled. The other men would be outside or downstairs, or up, or wherever. But Tom had to get out. A promise in the newcomer's voice scraped Tom's vertebrae with ice and dread. He'd escape or the man would make him regret ever waking up.

Determination won against the impulse to flee. Tom clenched the microphone in his hand, grateful for something to hold onto. Before running, he'd need his backpack he'd left in the radio room which so far had remained undiscovered. His dad had built him a nook in the back of his closet for a private calling space. Tom would pretend to be a spy or reporter on a special mission. He'd give anything to be pretending right then.

The man's stealth couldn't sneak past the creaky floorboard in the hallway to his parents' bedroom which meant he walked in the opposite direction of Tom's room.

Only a moment's reprieve before the man would redirect toward Tom's room to inspect and maybe destroy his radio equipment. The further the enemy walked to Tom's parents' room the higher Tom's chances at escape.

A click from farther down the hall, probably the linen closet came through the plaster. Attic stairs would distract the accented-intruder for a minute, maybe less. Tom had to run for it.

The thin wooden panel slid into the wall. He waited. The rub almost imperceptible, but in the stillness of the house anything could carry. A footstep sounded overhead.

Tucked under his desk across the room sat his pack with his supplies. He could do anything or go anywhere with the items in that pack. He needed to grab it and get to the front door. And get the hell out.

Eyes trained toward the door with the occasional glance at the window, Tom darted across the thin carpet. He knelt on the ground and grabbed the bag. He didn't have time to collect anything else. Escape had to be the primary goal. Tom would find food and other supplies along the way. The weight of his and his dad's ham radio conversation pads thunked him in the lower back.

The lack of time didn't stop him from pushing the small family picture from the wall into his front coat pocket.

Who knew when, or... gulp... *if* he'd see his parents again.

Pressed against the door jam, Tom waited for the hall clock to tick ten seconds. The footsteps dragged out slow and steady across the ceiling, stopping every few feet. Around the corner would be the empty kitchen, and the hallway to an office, the master bedroom and bath, the linen closet and laundry room, with stairs making up the far wall. To the right, down his hall, was his room, another bath, a storage room and the door to the lean-to garage. He'd never make it out, if he went to the garage. His dad had covered the entire thing in plastic and sided it to eventually be made into a workout room, but he'd never gotten around to finishing the project. His mom had asked for help with the garden, then the kitchen, then something to do with patio furniture. The time to finish it came and went, lost in the busyness of the Honey-Do lists.

The lean-to exit was blocked and the front and back doors had men covering them, exact number and location he didn't know. Tom was stuck in a raccoon trap with no experience getting out. He wanted to pinch his arm, wake up in his bed, his dad yelling for him to get a move on, or rain pattering the window.

Wait a minute, he could use the window, maybe not in here, but off the kitchen. The large bay window led to the greenhouse over the deck. Hide under the wooden slats. What did he have to lose? Best not to think about that.

A footstep thudded on the narrow stairs. Tom held his breath and dashed over the tiled floor into the oversized pantry. It would have to do. The man would head into Tom's hallway next.

Tom slipped between the partially folded doors and froze amongst cans of soup and boxed pastas. Another missed opportunity because he'd waited too long. He deserved a swift kick in the butt. *Come on, Mason, get your head in the game.* Life or death now.

Heavy tread from boots scraped past his room. A moment later the lean-to door creaked. Tom poked his head around the white bi-folds. No one in sight. The window was inches away and cracked. He wouldn't have to flip the lock.

Kneeling on the cushions, Tom grimaced as he slid open the window. Angling his body through the opening, Tom rolled onto his front to wiggle the rest of the way. Maybe he'd find his stomach under the deck.

The hammer of a revolver clicked and Tom jerked his head up.

Chapter 5

Rachel

Andy. Her back hurt but the ache paled each time she glanced in the direction of her son driving their four-wheeler, the man of the family. Where her husband should have been.

She'd made them leave. The house had caved in. Rachel had swallowed her scream. Clenched her gloved fingers into the rubber of the handles and hollered at Cole. He'd stared. He couldn't move. How many times had she called his name? Five minutes? Try ten. They'd sat there for at least ten minutes but the sound of a helicopter had chopped through the haze.

Cole's name had exited on a scream. They'd tore from there with flames at their backs. Andy was behind them. How could she move away from him…

They crested the hill, dust billowing behind them. Nothing stirred down either side of the fork.

Noon had to be just around the corner. Their mouths were dry as the powdered tire ruts stretching behind them. Rachel had pushed them, not stopping for even a sip. They hadn't seen anyone after they'd passed the main highway.

Cole's eyelids drooped and his head lolled.

"Cole, we're almost there. I promise."

He rubbed his eyes and slurred, "I'm tired. I miss Dad."

"I know." But Rachel's heart whispered it hadn't been long enough to miss Andy yet, even with the loss so glaring and sharp. She did, even though it wasn't logical.

The radio hadn't given anything more than static and Rachel hadn't asked anyone if they had news. Andy had worked into her brain the importance of keeping clear of people for a while once the end began to wrap its tentacles around the world. Desperation can drive otherwise humane people to do the unthinkable. Keep going. Get to the ranch. Had Bob and Martha made it to safety?

"Mommy, I'm hungry." Beau's whines had increased until he was saying something every five minutes. Her patience wore thin, but she bit her lip.

Rachel didn't know how much more she could take before snapping. She sighed and waved Cole to drive beside her. Over her shoulder she answered in a normal voice with a hint of 'that's enough', "I know you are. We all are. Only a few more minutes and we'll be at the ranch. I'll make a big huge lunch, okay? Maybe we can have some fruit or something."

Beau mumbled, his words lost beneath the growl of the engine. Rachel ignored him. They were so close. She had to hold it together – for her kids and her sanity – until they were safe on the property. One more corner.

Across a small bridge over a deep snowpack-fed spring, the road led them deeper into the northern National Forest. Rachel and Andy had saved and penny-pinched like misers to purchase the modest ten acres in the middle of nowhere up the side of a mountain.

And like they crossed a line, the heat vanished with the dust and a chilly breeze whisked at her hair. Cole's teeth chattered and he shrugged his jacket on. Winter lingered in the deeper regions of the mountains. Gray crusts on snow burms struggled to melt in the high altitude and little sun streaming through the thick evergreens.

Creeks and springs would be glutted until mid to late-June when the real heat waves began and triple digits ate at the moisture corroding the land.

She'd forgotten the slow awakening of spring in the higher altitudes.

Just as suddenly as the temperature changed the road ended in a clearing. The only vehicles so high up would be the contracted logging trucks to preen the forests a little at a time. Cole braked and Rachel motioned for him to wait.

Off the quad, Rachel retraced their tire tread the hundred yards to the bridge past the bend and watched for anyone following them. Secrecy at this stage of the journey was tantamount to their future safety. No one could see how to get it in. Even if looters or enemies weren't following them, that didn't mean it wouldn't happen later. The stakes in the game had changed and every precaution, while seemingly paranoid, would at some point be an asset.

Rachel glanced at the swirling rivulets. Had it been just that morning her kids had slept in their beds? It felt as though decades had past. Her husband, love of her life, hadn't died in a terrible house fire saving someone else's kids. Terrible things didn't happen to Rachel. She planned for them, saved for them, but they never actually happened. Until that point, she'd been unrecognizably blessed. No deaths in her family, unremarkable work. She'd been traumatized by experiments, but in actuality she'd do the invaluable psychoses training again, if she were given the choice.

The list of terrible was mounting and Rachel didn't appreciate the load dumping in her lap. Her clients weren't the only ones who needed stress management skills. Her favorite? Listing the last names of the Presidents of the United States in chronological order. The most mundane, rote mind exercises were the best. *Washington, Adams, Jefferson, Madison, Monroe…*

One minute of grief. But not until her children were safely ensconced at the cabin, after they slept that night. Heaven knew she wouldn't be able to close her eyes without seeing the house fall in on itself in red and orange flames, her husband inside. On repeat.

Tripping over a jutted root, Rachel caught her balance. She was clumsiest when she was tired.

The perimeter of the clearing hid the entrance to their land. A tree carved with a large heart and her husband and her initials marked the start of the search. Count three over from that trunk, turn east to its mirror and count two trees to the right into the bushes. Behind the tallest brush a log led the way into the forest where halfway between a large cedar and a tamarack a hard right finally led in the right direction. Another mile in and their home-off-the-grid nestled in the protection of the trees.

Andy had loved spy novels and Louis L'Amour stories. Rachel counted and the journey continued. Branches hung low, bent from holding heavy snow throughout the winter, in their long held positions. Moss shaded the sides of bark like a child had colored on the trees with different hues of green crayons. Small patches of snow warred with the vegetation for a grip on the land.

Trees had fallen, thin trunks blocking the way of the path.

Cole stood on the foot plates of his quad and powered over them, the crunch and snap of wood too loud for comfort. Rachel winced and stayed a modest distance behind him. She couldn't let him drive in back. She had to see him, make sure he was fine. Besides, each and every one of her children had memorized the way into their land. Andy had treated it like a spy game and the kids had eaten the directions and clues like cinnamon bears, soft and chewy with a hint of danger – who knew if the next one would be too spicy for fun.

Dang, he was everywhere. She could smell him in the fresh breeze pushing pine scent through the forest.

Steam from their engines rose in the mid-day shades of the forest. The last tree marking the beginning of their land came into view and Rachel's shoulders sagged. Home, their new one and until things straightened out – if they straightened out – it would be for a while.

The tarp rustled from her trailer. Glancing over her shoulder, Rachel smiled at Kayli and Beau. Even with the circumstances surrounding their reasons for coming, their dad gone and whatever else awaited them, the magic of the land and its memories were stronger than the fear or uncertainty. They had more fun times with Andy at the cabin than anywhere else on Earth.

Rachel faced forward. Smack dab in the middle of the ten acres where a knoll jutted out from the side of the sloping mountain, Andy had built a "green" home in the land.

Living in a "cave" was the last thing she wanted, if anything should happen. Heck, on vacations, she didn't want to wake up to dirt. She wanted room service and hot baths. But her husband, her beautiful smart husband had laughed. "Rachel," he'd said, "You can and will have all that here. You just need to give me time to create it." And she had, because anywhere Andy was, she was.

And he'd given her everything he'd promised.

"Cole, stop by the door and we'll unload the stuff there. After that, you and Kayli can take the quads and trailers to the lean-to and store them behind the wood. Beau, you can help Mommy." Rachel stood and, after stretching out her lower back, turned off the engine. She rescued her two youngest from amongst the supplies packed with so much care. Beau's little legs couldn't contain his excitement and he ran around the front "yard", jumping over the white patches and whooping at each new thing.

Rachel longed to ask them to stay quiet, but they were kids and needed something to release the emotions overtaking them. A small knot of envy pushed at her heart. Beau could run and be carefree, even for the moment, the gravity of the situation too large for him to comprehend.

Rachel would never escape the images in her heart.

A small hand slipped into her fingers and Kayli's body pressed against Rachel's side. She looked down at Kayli's thick auburn hair glinting in the strengthening light of day. A sniff escaped her daughter. Rachel knelt down and placed her hands on the little girl's waist. "Honey, what's wrong?"

Everything.

Large swimming green eyes looked at Rachel, and Kayli whispered, "Daddy isn't with us. Why not?"

And the question knocked Rachel on her butt. She hadn't considered the possibility that the kids wouldn't understand what had happened right before their eyes. What did she say? How did she explain it? Did Rachel even understand herself? Her training hadn't prepared her for juvenile grief. She dealt with behaviors, mental instabilities and insecurities. Fear. Not grief.

Basics. She could remember the basics, right? Rachel cleared her throat for more time. Logic. Approach everything with honesty and logic. Even with her mate missing in a world shot to hell in a hand basket, she'd treat everything with logic. "Kayli, do you remember the house that fell down? The one with the fire?" At Kayli's timid nod, Rachel continued, tears welling in her eyes. "Daddy was inside, honey. He's not going to be with us now."

Kayli's eyes widened. Her lower lip quivered and the rest of her features screwed up in a mask of pain. She tightened her fists at her side and shook her head, never taking her eyes from her mother's face. Rachel's stomach turned. "I'm sorry."

Her daughter choked on a sob and stood frozen, trapped in her grief and unable to vocalize it. Rachel knelt down and pulled the small body into her arms. Holding Kayli with the fierceness of a mother bear, Rachel vowed in her heart to protect her children from the horrors that might come. Even if she had to steal, go hungry or kill. They'd lost their dad, she'd be damned if they would lose themselves. The kids were all she had left of Andy.

Some of her earlier psychology training had covered loss. Recalling the exact steps was impossible, but she had a copy of her psych book at the cabin for light reading. She'd check for more information on ways to treat grief in children.

Kayli's heart wrenching sobs abated and she hiccupped against Rachel's shoulder.

"Should we get things unpacked and settle into our 'cave'? Like Batman?" Rachel patted Kayli's back and looked up. Her two boys watched them a few feet away. Cole guarded against showing anything, even to his mom. Beau's confusion tore at Rachel more than Kayli's tears.

Standing, Rachel grabbed Kayli's hand and Beau's and corralled Cole with her arm to the cabin. "Come on, guys. We need to get settled before we do anything else and I think I hear tummies rumbling. Want something to eat?"

The mention of food lightened the mood. How could anyone be dead when the normalcy of eating needed to be attended to? The incomplete family pretended Andy had stepped out to stack a cord of wood while Mom made lunch. For the space of a few seconds, each one needed the situational delusion for their sanity's sake.

If Rachel let herself, she could lie until even she believed it. But could she accept the sadness that would come, if she didn't deal with the truth? She didn't know. The gravity was stilting and, maybe, if she just placed one foot in front of the other she could get her kids through it.

She'd bury her heart in the garden later.

~

"Cole, let's put the compost items on the side of the plot where Dad had it last year. Here's the remains from lunch, would you, please?" Rachel handed the newspaper bundle of orange peels, bread crust and tomatoes over and smiled at his grossed-out expression. "Just wait 'til the compost starts doing its job. You're going to wish I was changing diapers again."

Moments later, Cole returned to stand by Rachel in the circle of the kitchen. He hung his head. Setting the broom to the side, Rachel grabbed Cole's hand. Fourteen-year-olds. "What's the matter?"

He lifted his chin, eyes red. "Dad died because of me, didn't he?"

Rachel pulled Cole to her and peered into his face. "What are you talking about? Did you set fire to that house? Did you scream from inside? Did you give your daddy the inherent desire to help any and all people at every opportunity? No. There is no way you are responsible for your dad."

"Mom, you sound mad at him." Cole's eyes lowered.

She was, in a way. But not to the extent her anger could be considered step one of the grieving process. She was… upset that Cole would even consider it was his fault… a strong sense of responsibility his father had had as well. "I don't mean to be upset with your dad. But I think it's okay to think that Dad might have been more in control of the moment than you think."

Cole's longish brown hair jerked back and forth as he shook his head. "It's not his fault. He had to take some time to tell me to get on the quad. He might have made it, if he hadn't needed to do that."

Ah. "Cole, it was Dad's time. You couldn't control what happened. You had nothing to do with it. I promise. Now I think we all need to rest. We've been up for a very long time." She would have to make dinner in a few hours and the kids looked like she felt.

Their shadowed eyes and downturned lips, sunken in cheeks and slow movements testified to the fatigue of the last twelve hours.

Cole didn't argue which solidified naps. One more trailer to put away and she could lie down as well.

Rachel released her son who disappeared into the back hallway toward his and Beau's room.

Three bedrooms and one bath, a pantry, makeshift laundry room and storage area and a hidden escape hatch made up the rooms in the back portion of the hill. Closest to the kitchen, the pantry was stocked with food and supplies as well as outfitted with an in-ground icebox.

Ice wasn't involved. One day Andy had left his bottled water inside a crevice while he worked. He'd forgotten about it until later and sent one of the kids to retrieve it. Unscrewing the cap, he'd swigged a mouthful of ice crystals in the water.

Deep in the dirt, the ground never completely thawed. And with the underground spring burbling feet from the home, the cool temperature was easy to hold, ideal for the summer but would test them through winter-like weather.

Her icebox was green, never used any energy from the solar panels Andy had backpacked in for electricity.

She hoped they wouldn't need the wood fireplace Andy had set up to spread smoke into twelve different chimney pipes along the ground so it wouldn't give away the location of the house. His mechanical engineering degree had come in handier than they'd thought possible.

Outside, the air was a touch warmer, but not enough to take off more than one layer of clothing. Rachel eyed the trailer, unsure if anything made completely of aluminum and steel would be light enough to move by hand. But if Cole could do the other one, then for the love, she could, too. She crouched down and put some force into lifting the tongue of the wagon. Empty, the trailer flipped up like a misshapen teeter-totter and back down on her toe. Rachel gasped at the pain. Wow, it was turning into one doozie of a day. Could it get any worse? Andy was the one who did this crap. Not her. Andy… where are you?

Applause echoed through the trees. Rachel whirled and stepped closer to the door. Her smaller .223 was inside, loaded and ready to be discharged. Her pulse raced and she had no qualms killing to protect her babies. Heck, she had sworn it not too long ago.

Tanned skin and blonde hair spiked from under the edge of his cowboy hat. The man was familiar but too far away to see the details of his face. The distance shortened, but Rachel couldn't place him. She orbited around the door, keeping her body between him and her kids as he moved closer.

"I didn't know women could lift a metal trailer. Are you Superwoman?" He drawled the last question, hooking his hands in his front pockets.

Dang her inability to hide even the mildest emotion – according to Andy. She averted her face to check on the gun. Polite women were dead women. She didn't reply, just eyed him and stepped forward to push him back. He didn't budge.

He raised his eyebrows and looked over his camo encased shoulder. A glance tossed toward the sky and he stepped under the tree at the front of the house. "Do you mind if I come in? I'll store the trailer, but we need to get out of sight. Excessive movement could catch their eye and I don't want to do that just yet."

Come in? He wanted in her house? Where her kids rested… Who were "they"? And how did *they* know Rachel and her kids were even out this far? She and Andy had been so careful… "Who are you?"

"Rachel, it's me. Joshua Hughes? Andy's friend? I've been helping him for over a year. I haven't changed that much." He threw a furtive glance around the clearing. "Can we talk about this inside?"

His blue eyes focused on her and a jolt traveled the length of her spine. Not... "Jay? But Andy didn't mention you were up here. Wha —" She'd left him at the university. Him and all the memories, the surreptitious glances, the pangs of longing when he jogged by without a shirt, the uncomfortable shifting when he'd walk into the dorm room and interrupted a make-out session. "I don't..." Rachel cleared her throat and dug her fingernails into her palm. Andy was lucky at the moment he was dead... she wanted to kill him.

The distance between them narrowed and panic overthrew her thought process. She didn't worry about him as a stranger anymore, no, Rachel worried about what he would do with his hands if he found out Andy was out of the picture.

She backed into the doorway and reached behind the wall to grab the Glock 23. The stubby body fit her hand, an extension after the many hours in the woods and on the shooting range. And rolled her eyes. She wasn't going to shoot him.

But she was irritated and the kids were inside washing up. And dang, she didn't like the exaggerated reminder that Andy was dead by mere hours.

Two yards away, his focus shifted and he turned to back into the house, watching the perimeter, the sky, anything and everything but where he should have had his attention. Her hand rose into position and yielded little when his back pushed against the barrel. His hands popped up to his sides like flags. He froze.

"Good, you remember me." He sighed. "Do we really need to rehash everything? Andy and I got passed it, can't you and I?"

Rachel didn't answer. She'd been teasing, that's all. Playing, but the moment had lost itself in the conversation. She opened her mouth, but he cut her off.

"I helped Andy build this place. I live just up the way." Nothing moved. "He had to have mentioned that I was helping." He glanced over his shoulder, his eyebrows raised.

She'd never heard Andy mention Jay. But he had mentioned… "Hughes? Not the same Hughes who shot at loggers on his land?" Andy had spoken of Hughes every chance he could, especially after a weekend working on the cabin. He'd never mentioned Jay. But Hughes and Jay being the same person explained why Andy never pushed having her up with him to work on the cabin.

"The same. Can I come in?" He didn't lower his hands until she'd removed the pistol from his back.

"Yes." Rachel clipped the safety and tucked the piece into the waist band of her jeans. She offered a tight smile. "A girl can never be too careful. Sorry, Jay."

"It's Josh, now. I haven't been Jay since college." Turning around, Josh's smile eased her tension. "No worries. I'd be upset with Andy, if he hadn't prepared you. Seems like you can handle a gun. Where's Andy? He didn't mention me?"

"Your name didn't come up often." She left it at that. He didn't need to know about the separation and near divorce at the beginning of her marriage because of him. No guy should have that much draw.

He followed her inside and took a seat at the picnic-style table Andy had built into the wall. She avoided meeting his gaze, looking instead at her fingers wrestling each other in her lap. "Andy… Um, well." How did she speak words she wasn't really comfortable thinking? The first time had to come and why not when she was still numb from the shock? "On our way here, we stopped and he ran into a house… on fire to save some… some people and…" Rachel swallowed, "…and the house fell in on itself before Andy made it out." Not too bad, she'd made it through the initial declaration. And without tears. Maybe she was tougher than she thought.

Josh leaned away from the table. His cheeks slackened, pupils dilated. "Not Andy."

Rachel nodded. She'd done well so far, why push it? She patted his hand resting on the table. If she had to console one more person over *her* husband's death, she was going to shoot something.

Jaw tight, Josh averted his gaze to the middle of the floor. Was he crying? Oh, no. A grown man crying would break down her barriers and she'd... seriously? Rachel swiped at the unwelcome tears. She rested her head in her hands and sobbed in bursts and gasps. "What is going on? I was safe twelve hours ago and now my husband is dead, we're under attack and the world is ending. The only thing Andy talked about was the possible attacks and war and being prepared. I thought I wanted it to happen just so he'd shut up and stop talking about it, but now that it's here, I'd much rather go back to listening to him rant and rave over dinner." She gasped against the deep pain ripping through her. Odd that she'd share her grief with Jay – wait, Josh.

Silence brooked no argument and Rachel lifted her head when Josh shifted in his seat. "What? Did I miss something?"

"No. It's terrible. But I think you need to brace yourself," he leaned toward her, "it's going to get a lot worse." He moved his finger as if to etch the words on the table.

Unbelievable. Her stomach clenched. "How? Oh, crap, is this one of your conspiracy theories you worked on Andy? He used to come home freaked out sometimes and the next day go out and buy ammo or insulated sleeping bags. How much money did you fleece out of him for sky-falling-scares?" Out of nowhere her tears of sadness turned to anger.

Andy had taken out a second job to pay for items that would "green" their cabin, more gadgets and survival tools to pack in the trailers, more and more and she and the kids had seen Andy less and less. And he'd made good money with his first job.

The majority of buying sprees fell after visits into the forests and helping Josh. How much time had her family lost because of *Josh*?

Her anger was misplaced, she had enough sense to understand that, but more than enough anger to not care.

"Conspiracy theories? That suggests it isn't true. Did you happen to look around while you drove up here? Did it look theoretical to you?" He bit his words off beneath the wipes of his arm across his face. Rachel gave him a moment, pretended it was sweat and not tears he swiped at.

"You didn't come up with this one." She scoffed and shrugged off the look he shot her way. She didn't want to hear from his mouth the same things Andy had spouted. A portable gun reloader and unregistered weapons were crazy. Crazy, she'd said to Andy. The world is sinking, he'd said.

Her guest removed his hat, releasing shorter blond waves which fell to his cheekbones. Fingers through his hair, he sighed. "I can't imagine how you're feeling right now. I don't… Andy was a great friend. I'm going to miss him."

Pulling a small radio from his front flannel pocket, Josh slid the yellow piece across the table. "We'd planned for the possibility of something like this happening. Andy has a charger in the pantry. I'll keep mine on. You beep me if you need me and I'll come here to check on you. Every day at this same time, I'll come by. If you're not here by choice, tie a red towel on the door handle before you leave."

She didn't know what to make of him and his "orders". Irritation laced her tone. "Look, I appreciate your concern, but I don't need a babysitter. I'll take the radio, but please don't trouble to come all this way." Andy had talked of the whereabouts of Josh's place, but Rachel hadn't been interested and assumed one more zealot lived in the woods of Idaho, great. She hadn't listened – hadn't cared. But now, seeing who Andy had hidden, she wished she would have invested more time in checking up on her husband.

"Okay. Do you need anything? Can I get you wood?" He stood, his broad shoulders drawing her eye. He wasn't Andy. The discomfort sparked with a palpable burn between them. Rachel didn't have a reason to be uncomfortable with him... anymore... except he was the man she'd considered leaving her boyfriend for.

The tension of the attacks and fatigue combined with the loss of her husband mounted against her. The weight was enough to snap an elephant femur.

But he was Andy's friend who'd been dealt a load of bad news, too. He probably had left his college-day crush on her in the past. She had. She'd quiz the crap out of him later. He had to know more than he was letting on.

Rachel wasn't lost to the grief and disbelief. She had no excuse to be rude. She pushed away from the table and ran her damp palms down the sides of her jeans. "I'm sorry. Josh, you didn't..." A tic formed at the corner of her eyelid. "I appreciate the help. Let me settle in and we'll ease into the neighbor thing."

Josh tucked his chin and eyed her. "Did you get any news?"

She bit her lip. He wasn't taking the hint to leave. She had always been terrible at the art of subtle suggestion. "A radio broadcast, sporadic at best." Manners prevented her from telling him bluntly, but what was she supposed to say? Get the heck out, I want to mourn my husband? At least she didn't have to go through the arduous task of securing each and every entryway Andy had developed. How had she traveled so far from the profession that made up who she was – defined how she reacted? She had more training than that. She could handle it.

"Well..."

A roar followed by a long screaming whistle broke through the uncomfortable peace between them like a hammer through an eggshell. Rachel dropped to the ground, down had to be safer than up. She breathed in and out, her clothing layers working against her as the sweat collected between her shoulder blades. "What was that?" Did she want to know? She needed to get into the bunker room. Get her kids into the room where nothing could hurt them.

"I don't know, but I'm going to find out." He stood from his crouched position, confident like her Andy had been. Not willing to wait for answers but on the lookout to ask more questions. The ground shook, reverberating through the mountain. The roaring stopped.

Whimpers from the back rooms called for Rachel. Of course her kids would be frightened, but she didn't want him to leave, not yet. She turned to Josh. "Don't go. I need help. I hate to ask, but… and we're so tired. I don't know how much more we can take. We should be safe here for a little bit. Do you mind? Then we can go look."

He nodded his head, blond bangs hanging across his forehead. "I agree. Go sleep. I'll stay on the couch." His gaze sought hers with a promise. "I won't leave."

Capability to spark fear and distrust using complex riddles and puzzles was a talent Rachel had studied in college. She had children to protect and didn't need fabricated fear to collide with actual unadulterated nightmares. In an obvious upcoming war.

She didn't have anyone else to shoulder the scarier stuff. Using Hughes as another body between the enemy and her kids may not be the most ethical move, but Rachel didn't care. Andy hadn't made it which made the kids her objective and nothing more. Plus, hadn't Andy set her up for this?

Niceties no longer mattered. She'd count on Josh to maintain honorable behavior around her family because Andy's fondness for the man had saturated his words. By the tears in Joshua's eyes at the news of Andy's loss, the feelings were reciprocated. And she remembered how close they'd been. The truth of their relationship was one she may never realize.

She succumbed to the whisper in her heart that she would need help in the coming days, weeks and months. The same voice didn't want to be alone and welcomed a friend in the crazy chaos. But could she count him as a friend?

Well, she'd better make a decision – he was staying on her couch. While she was torn by curiosity to investigate the crash, her kids wouldn't make the trip, bogged down by fatigue and grief. Rachel refused to leave them alone. Protecting them included not only keeping them safe but also taking care of them. They were dead on their feet and needed sleep and more food. She'd contain her anxious wonderings about the sound until the kids were ready to go with her.

Deeper in the cave, where the noise was muffled, Rachel pushed open Kayli's door. "Kayli-bayli, do you want to come lay down with me in the bunker room?" She left the door open for her daughter to follow her. At the boys' door, she whispered the same and they followed, Beau clutching his blanket.

Nobody questioned her. Andy had run them through the same drill over and over. But just the same, her children were still kids and they had to have a breaking point. How would it elicit? Rebellion? Malcontent? Discord? Hysterics?

Small cots sprang open with the slightest touch in the master, further back in the cave. Cole climbed into his against the far wall. Kayli and Beau did the same while Rachel closed and bolted the six-inch thick lead door. Radiation, weapons, man or beast would never make it through. She'd locked Josh outside the protection and couldn't bring herself to offer. In the small space, even with her young kids, she needed a small amount of privacy to say goodbye to her friends. Her husband.

The sound would wait. In fact, any further sound wouldn't penetrate the room with the door closed. Could she imagine the world wasn't burning long enough to get some sleep?

She didn't care about any of it. Her world had already fallen apart. Screw the other stuff.

Rachel tucked each of her babies in bed. They mattered. Nothing more. Each one slid into sleep before the tears and worry about Andy could run over.

True, it was extremely early, way too early for night time, but with the small amount of sleep the night before, the trauma from leaving their home with everything they owned, their neighborhood, fire raining down on them in their flight, losing their daddy and fleeing to what may or may not be a secure place, Rachel and the kids needed rest. A chance to physically recuperate and cut out the grief as it sliced through the numbing shock.

The small light on the wall turned on and off with movement, but was dim enough to not be an issue while they slept. Rachel shoved the boxes filled with food and supplies lined up along the wall. She pulled back the sheet and climbed in. The double mattress spread out beside her, cold, immense. Andy's absence was insurmountable.

Rachel bit the corner of the pillow while she cried silent tears.

Chapter 6

Tom

Tom dropped his body weight to the deck. A shot rang out over his head, pinging through the plexi-glass of the green house. He clenched his stomach muscles, certain urine was about to stream down his leg.

Pounding echoed in the house, as fast and hard as Tom's pulse. In a crouched position, he ran to the door and out onto the lawn. Twenty feet to the woods.

Another bullet whistled through the air. Unidentifiable words chased him.

Tom threw a glance over his shoulder. He *had* to look. Two men rounded the side of the house in a dead sprint. The original gunman stuck by a plant hook, twisted, and attempted another shot from over his shoulder as he wiggled against the post the tomato plants were staked to.

Ten feet. Five feet. Three. Two. One. Even midday, the forest's darkness welcomed Tom. He'd grown up playing on the acres between their property and the State Park's campground. Familiarity would help his escape. He hoped.

Another shot zinged through the branches of a lilac bush two feet behind Tom. Adrenaline shot him forward. He reached a speed he hadn't realized he was capable of and hurdled creeks and fallen limbs. Boughs from evergreens hung much higher than his head. Game trails were clear, if one knew what to look for.

Volkswagen-sized boulders clumped together, the groups screening him for a few moments.

Another shout cut through the forest.

Tom focused on his breathing. The backpack banged against his spine. His dad's conversation book, convo to those in the "know", weighed twice what Tom's did. At the moment, Tom regretted bringing the books and taking up valuable space in his pack. Not a necessity when trying to survive in the wilderness.

If he could get to the State Park, there might be a Ranger or some Fish and Game patrol officers on duty. He'd take anyone of authority. Tom hadn't packed a gun of his own. Couple months until he turned eighteen. His dad was planning on buying him his first handgun, a necessity among the other right wing anti-gun control friends of his dad's. Who didn't know how to at least handle a gun in the area? His dad had taught him at a young age. Educated gun handlers were alive because ignorance can't be taught – Dad's favorite saying.

Tom kicked his feet harder. Don't think about Mom and Dad. The situation was better left unexplored while men pursued him, intent on killing.

The pounding of his heart, his patterned breathing, and his own foot falls on the crinkling mulch and new growth drowned out his predators' sounds. He couldn't distinguish anything. The sensation of being deaf assailed him. A bubble surrounded him. Frustrating.

A river ran south along the park, just past the campground. Snagging a patrol boat secured along the pilings to catch fish poachers would be easier than running down the first person he saw. State Park, huge. He gasped. A stitch in his side clipped into his thoughts.

Rolling his weight to the balls of his feet instead of the long strides he used for longer distances, Tom unclenched his fingers and shook them out. Loose hands, loose legs, no cramping.

He had to have lost them. No other shots — crack. Never mind. Tom ducked his head. About ten feet behind him the bullet demolished a young sapling's trunk.

His cheeks flushed with the run, the building heat and now anger over his complacency. He winged his arms and the stitch dissolved. His therapist had once told him to recite something when he was looking for control. Recite. His favorite...

Alpha, Bravo, Charlie... In rhythm with his pounding steps.

A low fence, two feet in height, lined the Sundown Campground. While Memorial Day weekend started the season off with over-packed camping spots, campers usually filled half the spots two weeks early. Tom expected multiple tents and trailers to occupy the sites by the river, but zero met his searching gaze. He'd never felt so alone.

The bullets would stop around other people, right? They had to. If only he could *find* other people.

Not breaking stride, Tom lifted his knees, taking the fence. He continued at his ankle-twisting pace. The ranger station was on the opposite side of the grounds near the river. Tom had to make it there. He would. Muscles congealed like jelly, but Tom pushed harder.

The open layout of the campground wouldn't aid his flight. Two trees per site were the maximum allowed because of dry season fire danger. Idiotic drunks often dropped the ball on controlling their own camp fires. Tom's home had been threatened more than once by forest fire due to the carelessness of a camper.

Laughter. Was that... girls laughing? Tom whipped his head to the right. He'd missed the pup tent set up along the outer circle of the sites. Clothes hung here and there. A girl, wet hair dangling down to her chin, brushed her teeth and said something to another girl sitting with her back to him. Tom had a feeling he wouldn't be safe with them. They weren't safe. They were just girls about his age. Girls who weren't safe!

Waving his arms, Tom veered off course. "Hey." He gasped. "Run. Men. Guns. Run!" He yelled as loud as his overexerted lungs allowed, which wasn't much. But the young women spun to face him and watched with disbelief rounding their mouths and widening their eyes. Tom recognized them as some girls from the rival high school.

Each girls' gaze flicked from his frantic form to a spot over his shoulder. The second they realized they were in danger came too late as a bullet hit the first one in the face, blood lining her sun-kissed forehead. The other spun around with a shot connecting below the collarbone.

Shock yanked at his legs to stop, but imminent death powered through. Changing his path had slammed him closer to his pursuers. Dang it. He pumped his arms harder. Because of him those girls were dead. The stitch in his side moved to his stomach and nausea worked at him.

He crossed through their camp, past their inert bodies lying tangled on the pinecone riddled floor and toward the solid brick restrooms further along the path. When he had a moment, he planned on bending over and vomiting in the dirt.

Heavy footfalls of his attackers receded, worrying Tom more. He could out-maneuver them, maybe, but how far would he go? How many people would he endanger before they'd catch him? Or would he surrender because of the number they'd kill for him?

The temptation to turn back with only two girls shot was strong. How weak did that make him?

Running as fast as he could, Tom catapulted himself around the side of the restrooms. Fragments of red rock showered the air as a freewheeling bullet bit into the corner of the building behind his shoulder. He grabbed at the rough surface of the next corner, the skin on his fingers giving under the grater-like texture of the bricks. He ignored the sting. A bullet would hurt a heckuva lot more.

He slammed into a petite body and they tumbled to the ground. "I'm sorry. Are you okay?" he whispered. She couldn't be more than sixteen years old. Her hair, pulled into a haphazard bun atop her head, allowed stray strands to frame her newly washed face. Yoga pants, a jacket over a t-shirt, socks and tennis shoes rounded out her relaxed outfit. Shoes she could run in.

Tom jumped up, ignoring the pull of his backpack on his shoulders. The bag wasn't getting any lighter. He clutched at the girl's hand and yanked her to her feet. He didn't want her cheeks tinged with blood for rouge and ears to have bullets for accessories. She looked up and Tom nodded. Jenny.

Her brown eyes widened and she gasped when she recognized him. He must have knocked the wind out of her. Crap, that wouldn't make for a good running partner. Where could they hide?

The surroundings didn't offer many options. The bathrooms would be too obvious. A stand of brush about thirty feet up the road might be thick enough. Dumpsters just a bit past that might work, but they'd have a hard time getting out without being caught.

Impromptu escape wasn't something he had thought he would need practice at, but his inexperience was frightening. Where would they go? Tom opened the nearest door and let it slam shut. "Go." He whispered and pointed to the brush. They needed to hide and hide now!

Confusion evident in the darting movements of her eyes and jerking motions of her head, Jenny didn't move in the direction Tom pointed. He grabbed her shoulders and turned her. Nothing. So he pushed. The shove gave her the inertia she needed and in less than a moment they trampled around the large collection of brush. Tom shoved her into the middle of the leaves and brambles where he forced her onto her knees in the dirt and dried leaves.

Kneeling beside her, Tom's breathing was ragged and fast. His companion whimpered. "Please, don't kill me."

Tom clamped his hand over her mouth and nodded toward the building. Was she kidding? Tom didn't have time for jokes. The view was a straight shot from where they sat protected by the thick canopy of bright green spring leaves.

A gun followed by a man emerged around the corner. He stopped by the first bathroom door and yanked the panel open. Gunshots resounded from inside the small room. Tom and Jenny jumped. She started shaking. He had never been this close to her.

Pressing his lips to her ear, Tom's voice was barely audible, "It's okay. Was anyone else in there?" She shook her head. Tom loosened his hand on her mouth. "I'm going to take my hand away but you have to stay quiet. Those men killed two girls at a campsite not far from the bathrooms."

Tears filled her eyes. She couldn't nod, but when Tom removed his hand, she covered her mouth with her own fingers, digging into the soft flesh of her cheeks. He watched her, wondering if he'd have to hit her over the head to knock her out like he'd seen in an old Jean Claude van Dam movie. Tom had never tried it before, but it looked painful and he didn't want to hurt her. She'd always been nice to him. And heck, if she wasn't prettier up close than he'd remembered. Stupid thing to notice when men chased him with guns… but teenage boy hormones are rarely subdued – at least his dad had always said so.

Jenny had to have been with the others in the campsite which would explain the tears. Maybe when he finished throwing up in the dirt, he'd also apologize for being callus.

More shots and the man tromped out the first door and into the second on the opposite corner. He fired more, probably into each stall rather than risk someone jumping him. Back outside, the man eyed the bush. A step forward and another, he stalked the brush like it might bolt any second.

Jenny huddled closer to Tom, her breathing shallow. Tom gripped her arms and pulled her to his chest, unable to tear his gaze from the approaching threat. Their past and future tightened into a finite moment.

Not more than three feet from the furthest leaf, the man stopped and pressed his hand to his ear. The hand with the gun pushed something against his throat and he spoke, his words short and clipped but in English, "Not yet. Do you want me to continue? No? The bodies? River's right here. The parents? We didn't see them. Okay. Meet you there." He spun on his heel, the rocks grinding into the dirt road and in seconds, disappeared into the woods.

Tom released Jenny and fell onto his rear end. If a girl hadn't been there, he'd have lost it and cried like a baby. Thank heaven for girls. Especially this one.

"What is going on? What are you doing up here and who are they?" She looked him up and down and creased her eyebrows. "I thought you were a good guy. Did you switch teams or something? Tom, are you a bad guy, now?"

Oh, great, now he was lumped in with the villains of a stupid cartoon. "No, I'm not a 'bad' guy. They're after me. I live up the way." He watched the corner of the bathroom another moment, then turned his focus to her. "Hey, what are you guys doing up here? You need to get home. What are you doing hanging out with those girls anyway? Rival school, Jenny. I didn't think cheerleaders could cross boundaries."

"Nice." Jenny rolled her eyes. "We're all on the committee for the regional cheer camp. My parents had the week off and stayed home and they suggested me and the," she swallowed, "girls go camping to pick out the best sites for the big cheer campout in a few weeks."

"Your parents let you camp by yourselves?" He dropped his jaw. Seriously? What kind of parents did she have? "Do they live in a box? There was another earthquake in Washington."

The girl flushed. "Well, we were supposed to have a leader with us, that's what we told our parents, but we wanted to go by ourselves."

Tom didn't bother responding to that. What would he say? You're an idiot? Not what you said to someone you've been stuck on for the last year. "You have no idea what's going on than?"

The fiery debris had been almost nonexistent at his house, too. He wasn't surprised she hadn't seen any at the park. Tom had only known because a running friend had called to let Tom know what was happening before the phone lines and electricity went out. Tom had grabbed notepads and pens and ridden a bike to the overhang looking over Spokane Valley.

From his position he'd been able to see the fires as far away as Airway Heights. Stray bombs had torn up the old Catholic church near the hospitals. He didn't know who or what was hit. But old alarms, remnants from for World War I and II, had wailed into the night.

The brunette looked at him with confusion in her eyes and the tilt of her lips. Her hands shook.

"Okay." How did he tell her? What and how much did he share? "Um… There's been at least one attack."

"Besides us? On who? My parents? The same man?" A quaver in her voice declared she was close to her limit on how much she could take.

"No. I don't know exactly who dropped the bombs, but it seems they targeted the Air Force base and struck Fairchild. Stray missiles and damage hit downtown." He placed his hand on her upper arm. "I'm sorry."

They sat together in the large grouping of bushes, protected for the moment, but for how long? A time table had been constructed for Tom, but he had no idea what it meant or the goal behind it.

He was stuck in the middle of calculus without a textbook or pencils and he had to define a slope without numbers. And the cute girl he'd been watching all year witnessed him screwing up.

She turned to him. "What do we do now, Tom?"

"Stay alive."

Her gaze fell past his shoulder and she stared as she took in his answer. Jenny Peterson didn't have the cheap-platinum look like most cheerleaders. Soft angles in her cheeks and jaw platformed large chocolate eyes lined with thick, thick black lashes. Her skin was pale and smooth, free of the blemishes most girls her age sported. And the lack of makeup let her real beauty show which stood out more than any other girl Tom had known before. Why couldn't he have spoken to her before the world came under attack?

Tom looked at her until she met his gaze. For a long drawn out second, they ignored the branches poking their sides and necks. Tom cleared his throat. "I need to get going. Where's your car?"

Jenny clutched his hand, her skin warm and soft. "Don't leave. What if those men come back?"

"I don't think they will for now. Hopefully, there's time to get away." Tom hooked the straps of his backpack at the waist and bear crawled out of the bush. He leaned back to offer her a hand.

But she wasn't looking at him. "Where are you going? I... I don't have anywhere to go." She stared in the distance of the campsite. "Or anyone else, now."

Oh, no. He had to watch out for himself. How was he going to help her? Looks didn't matter in war. Tom was only human and had weaknesses. And Jenny Peterson was one of them. "Come on." She followed him. They stood up outside the leaves after a long look around. "Did you guys bring a car?"

She nodded and walked around the edge of the plant. Tom stayed a close distance behind. At the corner of the bathroom, he realized where she was going and grabbed her arm. "What are you doing? Didn't you hear me? Your friends are dead. They were shot. Do you want to see that?"

Jenny stopped and looked down. Stray hair fell around her cheeks. "How can they be dead? We were just planning on going for a run and eating breakfast."

"Trust me, they're dead. And I hate that I'm the one telling you." He pulled her the other direction. Tired. He felt so tired. "We need to find your car."

Jenny was remarkably strong. She pulled against him and yanked her arm free. "Are you kidding?" She pulled at the waistband of her pants. Her eyes flashed. "Do these look like they have room for car keys? Everything's back at the camp."

Tom shot a harried look at her tight pants. Nope, no way could she fit a key in those pants. His hands might fit. He shook his head and met her gaze. She'd seen him checking the pants out a little too close. Heat flooded his face. "Sorry. Okay. I'll get the keys. Where are they? And while I'm there, do you need anything else?"

"Can you get the pink and white tie-dyed duffel bag for me? The keys are sitting on the camp chair closest to the fire." Sadness rounded her lips and faded the sparkle in her eyes.

Tom peeked around the corner and listened. Nothing seemed out of the ordinary. Dang, he'd better not be walking into a trap. That would really cramp his plans. He tossed one more look over his shoulder. Jenny watched him which bolstered his courage.

Heart pounding, in the eerie quiet, every step a boom from a bass speaker, Tom's stomach hurt. Too much adrenaline and too little sleep. He'd been scared thinking about getting himself out. Taking on Jenny would give him an ulcer or gray hair, or both.

The pup tent guarded his view from seeing the rest of the site. He slowed and each step lasted three counts. He approached from the east and a slight breeze rushed the coppery scent of blood into his face. Buzzing. So much buzzing. And he saw them, the two girls, lying face down in the dirt covered in hovering yellow and black hornets. Innocence splashed on the dark brown and black dirt.

Seconds. He'd been gone seconds.

Searching the woods, partly to check for returning chasers and partly – well, mostly – to keep his mind from registering the details of the scene, Tom edged the borders of the site. Pink and white tie-dyed duffel by the tent. Check. Keys… keys… on the camp chair. Oh no, he had to walk over the girls.

He couldn't go around, to one side he'd hit the tent and the other way was blocked by more chairs. He didn't want to make more noise than necessary. And he hated hornets. But they seemed busy with the girl laying face down on the ground. She must be the one shot in the head.

He stepped over the girl who'd been pierced by a bullet above the collarbone, meeting her eyes with his own. Her eyes flickered. Holy crap! Did she know him? Tom hadn't seen her since the last basketball game against their school. Her hair was lighter.

Tom dropped down to his knees and pressed two fingers to her throat. A thready pulse, softer than the beat of the irritated hornet wings, pushed against his fingertips.

Tom pushed his hand to the open hole at the base of the neck. She moaned, but couldn't move. Tom rolled her off the dead friend and looked at the wound in the back of her neck. Minute bone fragments laced the macerated edge of the golf ball-sized wound. Crap. Her spine. He swallowed the bile racing up his throat. Cross medical school from his goals.

He gently returned the girl to her back. Unable to move her head, she focused on his face with her eyes and another groan escaped her parted lips. Specks of red rode the shattered breath escaping her mouth. And for one more second her body was stiff, fighting for life. In the next, limp, and she was gone.

Wiping his hand down her face to close her eyelids, Tom contained a gasp. Enough. Get the keys. His fingers dripped red but he stood and clamored to reach them. His sanity held on by wisps of air.

Stumbling back to Jenny, Tom wiped his bloody hands on his pants before handing her the keys. "Run. We need to get out of here." He carried her duffel while packing his own bag on his back. Somewhere safe. But where? They opened into a run just faster than a jog. When Tom had been out that morning looking around and watching, listening, he'd seen people flocking toward the large Arena on the north side of the river. A stray bomb had disabled the bridges. Headlights and flashlights had gathered and traveled in lines toward the schools and large churches. People had collected together like mercury.

In all of his research, he'd learned initial attacks were followed by more. Kick the victims while they're down. The attacking entity would wait for the majority of people to group and then do more damage when people hoped for a reprieve.

Dry pine needles from the previous fall crunched under their feet.

Jenny pointed at a red Subaru Outback. She gasped, "There." Whipping the jingling keys into her hand, she pushed a button on the remote and the Subaru's lights lit up. A subdued beep acknowledged their arrival. She slid into the driver's seat and Tom threw the bags in the back.

"Where to? Your house? Or should we check on my parents?" Jenny shifted and peeled out of the parking lot.

"No, I'm sorry, we can't go to the city or anywhere a lot of people might be. I'm afraid it's just us for a while." Tom turned to look out the back window in case they were being followed. "And we can't go to my house because that's where those men chased me from."

"I can't go check on my parents? Or my little sister?" Jenny's lower lip trembled and real tears threatened. She swerved, missing the wooden posts lining the drive to the exit by centimeters.

"Hang on, Jenny. Calm down. We can't get into town right now anyway. Too much is going on. I promise, I don't know how, but we'll find out about our parents." He faced forward. "Mine were working the graveyard shift at Deaconess Hospital last night." If he focused on her too long, he'd let her have her way regardless of the danger.

"My parents live just up the hill from there. Nobody would attack a hospital, right? That's just wrong." Jenny steadied the wheel. The ranger toll station guarded the entryway, short and squat with the roof shaped like a mushroom. "We need to warn these guys. Hold on. It will just take a second." Pulled up to the window, Jenny rapped with her knuckles on the glass through her lowered window.

A pale-faced man brought his nose to the microphone. A sheen of moisture shined on his forehead. "Y-yes?" The heat of the day hadn't yet begun but already a fan whirred in the upper corner of the booth.

"Sir, there are some dangerous men in the campground. You need to be careful. Here, I'll write down a description for you." Jenny dug through her purse, but Tom's eyes never strayed from the man whose hand shook as he reached for the window.

A red spot of light glimmered behind the man's ear. Alarmed, Tom met the petrified man's gaze. He shook his head and the ranger's blood splattered the window. Jenny screamed, dropping her purse, hands frozen in the air.

Tom leaned across the seat and jammed his foot onto the accelerator. The front panel screamed against the metal guard rail. His leg brushed against hers, but for once, he didn't care.

Cranking the wheel, Tom kept his foot on the gas and fought to stabilize the vehicle. "Jenny! Snap out of it." His words cut through her screeching. She pushed him out of the way and replaced his hands with hers. The car barely slowed as she took control of the pedals as well. He settled into his seat and looked behind the car. "We need to find a place to stay. Head east. I know someone in Post Falls who might be able to help us."

The car responded to Jenny and zoomed away from the park. Tom leaned his head out the window. Cool air rushed past.

He vomited down the red paint.

Chapter 7

Rachel

Beau rolled over and smacked Rachel's nose with his elbow. She was covered in kids. Cole lay behind her under her legs. Kayli snuggled on the side opposite Beau.

Andy's absence was profound, even with an extra three bodies warming the bed with her. The light flickered. She rubbed at her tight eyes, gritty from the silent crying she'd done most of the night.

What time was it? Andy's degree in mechanical engineering had lent itself to the creation of their shelter, but no matter which way he turned the numbers, he'd frowned every time he'd had to tell her he couldn't get a window of glass that thick for the room deep in the mountain. Rachel had laughed. She'd considered the whole thing a joke. Never in a million years had she believed her family would actually need the land and supplies he'd worked on.

Reuniting with Josh Hughes came to mind. Had he stayed? The crash. Was it safe to go out of the room? Had he stayed? She didn't want to take any chances, but the four of them would go crazy trapped in there for long. If there had been another attack, she needed to know. She could handle anything with information… not-knowing did her in.

She lifted Kayli's leg draped over her waist and laid it on the sheet.

The door leading to the underground spring was built like the one leading to the house. Completely encased, Rachel and her kids were safe for at least three months from any external threat. The thought both relieved and nauseated her.

"Mom, do you want me to move?" Cole murmured from his spot. He rolled over and Rachel sat up.

She brushed her hand over his forehead and leaned him back on the bed. "Thanks, Cole. I'm going out the back door to see if we're safe. Lock the door behind me. I'll knock with the tuning fork when I get back, okay?" Rachel pulled on her pants and then tucked her Glock into the waistband at the rear.

Her son nodded. He'd had to grow up so fast. Matter of hours. And his growing wasn't done. Cole would be mature well beyond his years in no time. No amount of behavioral adjustment would change that.

Rachel pulled her flannel on. She smoothed her hands over her hair.

It could be morning or night. A small amount of concern for Josh grew inside her. He'd only been checking on them. Andy had trusted him enough to not tell her but continued being friends. If Andy had told her about the situation sometime in the last two years, she wouldn't remember. She'd blocked a lot from that period.

She twisted the heavy aluminum bar vertical and pulled the door open. In the dark, she turned and watched her kids disappear behind the metal shield. The damp hadn't changed. The same musty, moldy scent greeted her mixed with the refreshing briskness of spring water.

A flashlight magnetically stuck to the door, but Rachel had to find it... running her fingers across the trim and over to the corner. An odd shape, smooth on the edges, resisted her push. Two hands and a lot of work finally worked the light free.

The yellow beam shafted through the dark, more than welcome across the old mountain's fresh water hidden away like a miser-protected mine. Andy had laughed when he'd brought Rachel through the first time, and had pointed at an untapped vein of gold as thick as his thumb running in jagged angles through the cave. Splitting into two and sometimes three to come back to one, the metal shined in the walls the entire path upward.

Rachel had no idea why they hadn't excavated it, but Andy had reassured her over and over they didn't need it as bad as privacy. Some things would have to do as decoration or as a trail to the exit. Follow the yellow brick road.

Her light bounced off the wet rock and the stream rushing through the holes in the cavern. Echoing, the cacophony should have been deafening, but instead Rachel had her own symphony.

She climbed the natural rock stairs layered in silky underground flora, careful not to slip. That'd be her luck, tripping and falling into the water. What would her kids do? Rachel dug her fingers into the crevices of the wall for additional support.

A rock cluster overlapped in a zigzag pattern, left-right-left-right back and forth until the damp air faded. She sucked in the fresh air, tasting for radiation. Wait, what did radiation taste like? Fresh blooms? If so, she was done for because the pungent aroma was heady and concentrated enough to saturate her tongue. Blossoms overwhelmed the entrance and further disguised the hole. Maybe radiation smelled like pine needles, bark or dirt... Or men's deodorant? Rachel spun around, her hand to her mouth, the flashlight ready to bring down on someone's head.

Josh held up his arm to ward off the impending blow. Rachel gasped and sobbed. "What are you doing? Oh my gosh, you scared the crap out of me." Anger filled her. Every time she turned around this man startled her. Who needed to worry about radiation? Rachel would be dead from stress.

Holding out his hands, Josh spoke calmly, "I'm sorry. I haven't heard anything from your room all night. I needed to stretch my legs. Why'd you come out the back?"

How long had they slept? Rachel shook her head. "Because I didn't know if the front was safe." Unharmed, trees led away from their position on the slight hill. Radiation would damage the plants, right? A small plume of white smoke snaked into the cloudless sky in the north.

He looked the direction she faced. "I poked around a bit, but I didn't feel comfortable leaving the house for too long. It will take a good hour to get there by foot." He rubbed a hand down his face and sighed. Josh took her elbow, the warmth zingy and not-altogether-unwelcome, and propelled her down the hill toward the front of the house, about five minutes easy going. "From what I could gather, I think a plane crashed on the next ridge over. Since you're up and okay, I'll run over and check it out."

"Are you expecting anyone in particular?" Who would be up this way in a plane? There weren't any landing strips and no groups of people to attack.

"No, but if the enemy is out here, then they know about operations they shouldn't and a leak of information like that would be more significant than a bomb or two going off." He stayed beside the door while Rachel let herself inside.

"What information would be worse than a bomb going off?" She offered a laugh shrouded in disbelief. "You know where the headquarters are for the Northern Militia?"

Josh ducked his head and pulled the door shut. Rachel's chuckle died in her throat. She grabbed his arm. "Do you? Know where the headquarters are?" Impossible. The location hadn't been uncovered even by their own government. Some people didn't even believe the Militia branch existed. He walked to the kitchen. Where was her answer? "I'll grab the kids. We'll go with you." He whirled, his eyes wide. Rachel turned down the hall. Two can play that game. Maybe on the way she could get some answers.

By the master door, she pulled the tuning fork from the small slot beside the trim and struck it against the metal handle. A musical hum vibrated in her hand and up her arm. The prong, touched to the door, made the metal sing.

The lock revolved and clicked. The door opened. Cole's hair rooster-tailed in the back at the crown and a smudge under his eye plucked at Rachel's maternal nature to rub it away. He ducked from her reach. Beau and Kayli rolled over on the bed and sat up.

"Mommy, I'm hungry." Beau grabbed his belly and slid off the short bed. At her side, he buried his face into the soft spot above her knee. Of course he was hungry, they'd been in bed nearly twelve hours.

"Well, let's get something to eat. Kayli-girl, come on." Rachel herded her children into the kitchen and dining area.

Cole poked his head out the front door to Josh loitering by the opening and smiled, "Hi, Mr. Hughes. You coming in to eat? Mom's gonna make us something." Returning inside, his smile slipped a notch at Rachel's dubious expression. "He's a buddy of Dad's, Mom. When I'd come up here we'd eat over at his house or over here. He's really nice and has an Army-issued HumVee. Isn't that the coolest thing ever? The tires are bigger than me."

Rachel didn't dare update him on the true nature behind Andy and Josh's relationship and how she played in all of it.

If he stayed to eat, Josh couldn't go to the site without them and she really wanted to see what they were dealing with. "That's nice, Cole, but next time check with me, okay? I don't want guests to feel obligated."

"No, I don't have anything going on right now. Thank you for the invitation, Cole. Call me Josh, okay?" The familiarity bugged Rachel. She didn't know why.

Cole's smile widened and his green eyes squinted at the edges – like his dad's. Eh, the pain hadn't even begun to ache like it was bound to, but the little paper cuts here and there were growing larger and more invasive like butter knife cuts. When would reality sink in completely? She'd had her cry last night, but that was just loneliness enhanced by trauma and shock and fatigue. Andy had been away from her longer than two days before. She'd never blinked an eye. But the reasons were different. Business trip versus death. Comparing a worm to a snake.

Rachel offered a tight smile to Josh and nodded to the table. Anger hadn't taken effect yet. Shock and denial would be first, but was that last night and now? Or was she just barely starting the grieving process? Analyzing oneself was always frowned on at school, but it was hard having the knowledge and being unable to apply it in a personal aspect. If she'd been a biology major, she could've applied the physical information like adrenaline response and fatigue syndromes to their situation, personal or not. Maybe psychology really was a pseudoscience like Brenda said.

Pancakes and eggs would be a good way to start in their cabin of solitude. Comfort food worked wonders in improving outlooks. Plus she needed to keep her hands busy.

She whisked eggs in a large bowl and set them aside until the stove heated the pans. The mix was ready in less time. Rachel peeked over her shoulder at the table. Josh and her three kids stared at each other. Andy's loss was significant.

Rachel had never considered the possibility of losing her husband. The nightmare had been there, of course, but in her conscious thoughts, she'd never contemplated how or why or when he might go. If Andy could die, then logically so could their extended family.

Where were Brenda and her husband? Rachel had informed her not long ago that if anything happened, Brenda was to get to Rachel's place in the woods.

Rachel hoped Brenda had listened, even if only to the part of how to get to the cabin. But Brenda would do what she wanted. She always did.

"So Josh, um, do you have family at your place? Did you get married? Have kids?" Was she seriously making small talk when a plane had crashed nearby? She didn't think she wanted to know about what future he'd chosen when she'd walked away.

"No wife. No kids that I know of." He offered a stilted laugh. 'I can't believe I just said that' written all over his face with a blush and downcast eyes.

"Oh, I'm sorry. I just…" No kids or a wife? That didn't fit. She'd always pictured him married and settled. No family was hard to correlate with what she'd been told. She turned with a plate filled with eggs and pancakes and placed it in the center of the table. "Cole, syrup and forks, please. Kayli, cups and Beau, milk." The kids scrambled to do their part, comforted in the normalcy of the tasks.

"Josh, how'd you meet my dad?" Cole plunked the bottle of syrup on the table and leaned toward Josh.

"We went to the University of Idaho together. We joined the Engineer Everything club. He was mechanical and I was electrical. After school, we worked on a few projects for a couple jobs and when I found this place by me was for sale, I emailed the link to him." Josh helped distribute the utensils around the table as well as the plates from Rachel's hands. Their fingers touched and his eyes flickered but didn't move from Cole's face. "I'm surprised he didn't say anything."

He didn't sound surprised, hurt more accurately fit the bill. Rachel stifled a suspicious ache as well. Josh had been a large part of Andy's life and yet her husband had never disclosed information about him since college. Odd.

Why would her husband hide his acquaintance from her? She could have dealt with it. Especially if they were as close as Josh said. What was she missing? "Weird he never clarified you were the one up here with him." She took the seat on the outer edge of the table and cut Beau's breakfast after everyone else's plate had been filled.

Josh cleared his throat. Syrup puddled on his plate. He avoided her gaze and muttered, "Not really."

Rachel tilted her head. "What?"

Awkward. How did she engage the conversation from that point? She couldn't force the topic. If she further pursued his absence from their lives, did she damn herself or Andy or was she insinuating paranoia into the moment where there was none?

Rachel's discomfort rose three-hundred percent. She brushed it off. "Okay, guys, come on, let's get done. We need to go on a little mission."

Part of her wondered at Andy's intention. He'd kept Josh away in the normal world, but had stowed his friend away in his family's only sanctuary, but to what end?

Continuing the conversation without embarrassing anyone or shoving her foot in her mouth or being disloyal to her husband would be the test. A change in topic would be welcome, but Rachel was at a loss. No matter which way she turned, she was rude.

"I want to go to college in Boise." Cole spoke up, a stray bit of egg escaping his mouth.

College was a ways off and in their situation who knew if it was even a possibility. The new conversational path didn't bring the relief she'd hoped for, instead opened up a new wave of despair to focus on.

"What do you want to go to school for?" Josh ignored Rachel's silence. At least she had gratitude for Cole's comment in that regard.

"Firefighting and pyrotechnics. If I'd been trained, I could've saved my dad." The smaller children stared at their plates, no longer interested in their food.

Rachel swallowed the lump in her throat and put her hand on Cole's. "It wasn't your fault. The fire was too far gone. I don't think grown firemen would've been able to save Dad, if they'd been there. I can't lose you, too." Afternoon sunlight filtered past brown curtains. Forcing joviality into the conversation, Rachel laughed. "How long did we sleep, Josh? Do you know what time it is?"

Josh glanced at her and the kids. The younger two followed the exchange with eyes wide as owls. "It has to be close to two. I think after a quick scout around, we might be able to go for a fishing trip down to my pond. Anybody interested?"

"That sounds great. I'd love to see the crash site, too." Rachel sipped at her milk.

"Wha – why?" Josh rested his hands on the table, a square of pancake stuck to the spikes of his fork. "I can go while you unpack your things."

True, the cartons and bins had yet to be placed in their new home. But unpacking could wait. Rachel arched her brow. "On the quads we could get there fast and get back. You said it's just on the next ridge, right?" Was he hiding something? A crash site shouldn't be off limits, especially to her. She had kids to protect and she wanted to see for herself that everyone was dead. He didn't need to go alone and she didn't see the harm in taking the kids with them. She hadn't seen him in a long time, which meant she didn't know him from Charles Barkley. He hadn't had a chance to earn a lot of her trust, yet.

His opinion whether she went or not didn't matter at the moment. She had to protect the kids. Not him. Her gun snuggled the small of her back, a piece of security in the insanity of the situation.

She stared the blue-eyed man down. The kids, familiar with the eye challenge, lowered their gazes and shoveled food into their mouths.

Josh didn't look away.

Rachel added a long drawn out sigh.

Cole picked up his milk glass and muttered to Josh, "Man, give it up or the guilt will be next. She'll get her way. Just give in."

The revelation startled Josh and he broke the eye contact, his gaze flitting to Cole and back to Rachel. But once broken, the stare was hard to reconnect and since he'd given first, the control had been handed over. He probably didn't even know it. One point for Rachel.

"Let's finish eating and we can head out." Avoiding his gaze was the next move. Why hand over the control she'd won. If she acknowledged his stare after winning, she'd be acquiescing there might be something wrong with what she was planning.

Psychology – play the game.

~

Rachel dug her heels into the thick grass, tugging on the hitch of the trailer. Adrenaline had given her strength the day before to move the wagon like it'd been made of plastic. But chemical strength had abandoned her sometime over the night and fatigue worked with worry. She pushed the wheels forward a few feet at a time.

Cole tumbled out the front door with his sister. He handed his water bottle to Kayli and rushed to help his mom. Rachel grunted her gratitude and bared her teeth in an attempt at a smile.

The wagon jerked ahead of them and became too light too fast. She glanced over her shoulder, startled to find Josh pushing against the trailer from the rear.

"How did you do this by yourself last night?" He grunted.

"Me? Rachel wiped her chin. Cole and Kayli did the other one."

Attaching it to the quad was a cinch after that.

Kayli and Beau climbed into the well of the trailer with Cole's aid. Emptying the contents had increased the depth and the kids' heads bobbed above the edge, their napes disappearing behind the walls.

At Rachel's side, Josh pulled his work gloves from his hands. "Are you sure you want to take them?"

Her voice low, Rachel didn't look at the kids. "They'll be safer with me than here alone, worrying. We don't have to take them up into the site. But I want them with me."

"It won't be pretty. Are you certain you want to go? I don't mind going alone." Josh arched his eyebrow at her. He asked questions like Andy – subtle suggestion techniques to make her think any choice was hers but actually pointing her in the way he wanted her to go.

"I'm sure. Thanks." Andy hadn't gotten away with it, either. "Where's your ride?" The perimeter was clear and his arrival had been soundless.

"I hiked here. I don't have ATVs. I go on foot everywhere unless it's an emergency which I use the HumVee for."

"Oh." That didn't make sense. "Why?"

"Because we don't have a gas station or pump out here and I only have so much stored which has an expiration date. I go to your place and food plots. We live close enough to each other I can be here in a matter of minutes." He shrugged then grabbed at the nonexistent padding around his middle. "And then of course, I can always do with the exercise." She never would have guessed he had dimples which increased his charm. Dumb boy.

"Right." Yep, he was Andy's friend. Making jokes about his weight like a woman, even without an extra ounce of fat in sight. Maybe it wasn't such a bad thing, him being around. He reminded her of Andy and the reality of her husband's death was easier to push away. It probably wasn't the best route to approach grieving, but she could push the process off a bit longer. Well, she didn't know for sure. She was a psychologist who specialized in fear identification and its treatment. She had no clinical analysis for the steps and effects of grief. Maybe she'd research it in her spare time.

The busier she was, the less time she had for the pain. "There's room on the quad, if you want to ride with me. Since I'm already driving, it's like carpooling, right?"

Josh met her gaze. "Thanks, I'd appreciate that. Do you have a gun?"

She nodded. "Do you mind if I drive? Redistribute the weight a bit instead of concentrating it all in the back." Josh climbed on the seat and held out his hand. Rachel suddenly regretted her offer. On a bike behind Andy would be fine. He was her husband, dead or not. On a seat behind a different, *slightly* attractive man less than forty-eight hours after her husband's disappearance, Rachel wasn't sure she was in the right state of mind. She would have to wrap her arms around Josh's waist.

Her interest in the crash site waned. She should have driven. But then his arms would be around her waist.

The quad tires rolled over and under trees dripping in moss called bear hair. Lichen painted the southern sides of the trees with camouflage-floral patterns of greens, whites and grays. The fire bombs hadn't been sent this far inland. Lack of significant population combined with the absence of any military presence protected the mountains and woods for imminent attack.

The breeze bit at Rachel's face and ears. She'd been stupid not to bring a hat. Of course, she'd made the kids grab theirs, but as a mom she failed to apply the same measures to herself. Month of May for crying out loud.

They ducked under a tree resting in the forked crotch of two cedar trunks split four feet from the ground. She focused on keeping her legs skewed and grabbing the metal rack behind her for support rather than the man in front of her.

Dipping into the valley between ridges, the quad's engine held them from speeding into the thick down-slope. Rachel didn't know how to proceed into the silence with Josh. Something neutral. The wreck? "Maybe they have a radio or extra fuel on the plane."

"If it didn't burn up."

Right. The wreck had smoke.

"The white smoke tells me the heat was high. If there are any survivors, which I doubt, they'd have to make it out before the flames started and I don't think they'd have much time to grab anything."

"Radio or information of any kind would be nice." Rachel might not have believed every conspiracy Andy had dropped on her, but she'd listened and learned how to be prepared. Information and necessities would be helpful in a survival situation. Rachel, Josh and the kids had food. What they needed included who, what, when, where and how.

She leaned forward, careful to keep her mounting irritation under control. "What's going on? And don't tell me you don't know."

His back tightened, pulling him away from her. Over his shoulder, his words carried just enough. "I'm not sure exactly who it is, but I can tell you it isn't our normal enemies."

Rachel rolled her eyes. "Who is it then? Are you saying it's our friends?" Andy had never tried that one on her.

Josh shrugged and didn't answer.

The air chilled between them, stiffened in part by the upper elevation's drop in temperature. Okay, the temperature didn't have any effect on the discomfort building between them. Rachel's tendency to argue with everything he said was the problem. She leaned back. Her obvious attempts to keep distance between them on the quad couldn't be helping either.

Something about him grated her nerves. Like when they were younger. The way he looked just a little too knowingly at her. The soft scent of Dial soap curled around her and strapped her to the rack.

Knowing what was going on out in the world would help Rachel's growing loss of control. Maybe if she gained some knowledge, she'd be less cranky and wouldn't be on edge.

The quad growled up steeper and steeper, thin, rocky paths to the peak of the ridge. Rachel switched her hold from the rails on the quad to around his waist.

What if there was no world left? Maybe her little family and Josh was it. What if America was obliterated and the enemy was taking over? Radiation everywhere? Another country would be stupid to assault the US with nuclear bombs – not because the US would retaliate in kind, but because they would destroy a very valuable asset. Radiation would ruin any chance of inhabiting or colonizing the country. And isn't that what she would do? Infiltrate. She'd taught the concept in her fear training courses. One could essentially take over another's life, if they controlled it with fear.

"Mom, what's that?" Cole pulled Rachel from her musings, pointing at a large chunk of white and gray metal half-decapitating a tree near its base.

Josh interjected before she could compose a response. "It's the first part of the plane to fall off. We should see more of the wreckage as we get closer."

Shafts of sunlight sparkled off a rectangular fragment protruding from the brush, another oblong tip of a wing lie on green moss, and fingernail-size metal shards littered the forest floor in sporadic bursts. Josh slowed the vehicle. "I don't know how much further we want to take this. With the metal on the ground the tires might get ruined." He slid from the seat and Rachel's hands fell to her lap.

The kids left the trailer without urging. Rachel climbed from the seat. She stood beside the quad and looked behind them. They'd traveled far. Thank heavens, they had the ATV. The kids would have been too weakened to do a round trip. Josh walked ahead and Cole, Kayli and Beau followed.

"Watch your step, guys." Josh stepped over razor-edged debris thrown around like wedding rice. He stopped and offered an arm to Rachel, but she looked past him, like she didn't see it.

Unexpected how the glittering metal pieces added beauty to the forest in random ways – flash of white and red in a dark section of bark, the spots of light from metal as if tossed from a mirror, large pools of sunlight through the damaged treetops, and rainbows swirling in small collections of fuel on rocks and the thawing dirt.

No one spoke, as if they all understood, even the littlest one, something bad had happened there.

In the middle of the path, sudden like the appearance of an aneurysm, the body of a plane rested with its left side crumpled underneath a pile of young trees and rocks while the right side posed, ready to take off in its undamaged state. Burnt fuel and plastic warred with the spring breeze carrying the scent of melting snow and burgeoning growth. Black smoke had stained a weaving pattern over the white paint almost obscuring the red circle on the tail.

Blinking at the symbol of the Japanese flag, Rachel herded her kids into a bunch at her side. "Josh, I thought Japan was an ally. Why is their plane up here? After all the aid we've given each other over the last couple years, why would they do this?"

He shook his head and met her gaze over Cole's head. "I don't think it was Japan. I think this is a rogue plane that was sent to make people think it was Japan. I don't remember a Japanese plane ever having only the flag painted on the side – usually they have a saying or symbolic gestures included as well, but this is just the red dot." Josh pointed at the cockpit. "Japan isn't known for cowardice. They'd have attacked us as we came up the trail, if they'd been able to. I don't think there are any survivors.

"I could see the flames yesterday from your place. The wet spring prevented the fire from spreading or it was a flash burn, constrained to the fuel. I'll bet the metal is still too hot to touch." He motioned toward the carcass of the plane and stepped onto the charred grass. A crunch marked his movement.

Right. "Cole, stay with the kids." Rachel patted his shoulder and walked into the crash-made clearing on the balls of her feet, ready to flee at the slightest provocation. She glanced back at her kids. On the edge of the clearing, danger was less of a threat… she hoped.

The air warmed a degree with each step. Heat, as if the plane was the sun, radiated from the center of the circle and the ground was swamp-like under melting snow mixed with dirt. Mud sucked at her boots. The cooler air waged a battle against the plane's heat and little by little pushed against the force field created by the burned metal.

Rachel circumvented the outer ring of the wing span until she was even with the cab. The glass was black from smoke and if she wanted to see more, she'd have to get closer and wipe off the glass. Bare hands? Heck, no. She darted to a tree along the edge of the clearing and pulled down some moss, the spongy hair would protect her hands and work well to break through the black soot.

Feet from the door, Rachel looked around the hood for Josh.

A potential enemy didn't run from the plane or the woods and attack her kids. The clank of metal on metal broke the reverence they'd been trapped in. "Sorry." Josh called, his voice burning in the heat of the plane as it crested from the other side.

Rachel swiped at the shimmering glass. Heat sizzled the ends of the moss but a large enough cut through the black coating showed nothing in the front seat. No chairs, no bodies, no steering wheel, nothing.

She dropped the moss and stepped backward. No body. The heat would have killed anything, but it wouldn't have turned a body into a pile of nothing. The bones would still be there, or a pile of ash, anything, not nothing.

A twig snapped under foot and she glanced down. Long parallel drag marks led a path into the woods a few trees away from where she'd grabbed the moss. The survivor or more than one might wait in the woods. Was she stupid enough to check?

Josh called to her from the other side, but she couldn't place his words. He called again.

Rachel raised her eyes, placing her hand at the small of her back.

He rounded the mashed nose of the plane. Josh watched her every move, his gaze flitting to check on the kids. His stance stiffened and he watched the plane and Rachel for an indicator of what exactly was going on. Rachel answered the question in his eyes with a shake of her head. His jaw tightened. Her fingers wrapped around the gun and she pulled it from the band of her jeans.

He removed his own gun from some hidden place. Rachel tapped the drag marks with her toe, bringing his attention down. She moved backwards, eyes on the trail and their point of disappearance. Her kids. She had to get to the kids.

The sound of an engine turning over broke the tension. Rachel stepped toward the trail. The quad.

Running toward the path, she skidded over loose metal and rocks in her hard-soled boots. Mid-stride, she cocked the Glock, passing the kids in her flight. The thunder of Josh's steps slowed behind her and his voice carried on the mild breeze. "Cole, all of you, follow me."

Even in their haste, the small group arrived too late. The tail end of the trailer crashed along behind her four-wheeler at a terrified pace. Rachel aimed and shot at a spot above the driver's head. He only ducked and pushed the engine harder.

Son of a bitch.

Chapter 8

Tom

Tom couldn't sleep. The smoke from Spokane burning covered the night sky. Stars didn't shine through and the moon competed with the smoke and clouds. His parents. Jenny's parents. The girls at the campground. The ranger.

His stomach ached. He hadn't eaten since the day before.

Jenny tossed beside him in her seat, trying to curl onto her side. Her ponytail had loosened sometime in the last few hours and brown strands lay across her cheek and trailed down her neck. Tom had never been able to get her alone in the hallway, forget about a car overnight. His mom would freak. Jenny didn't seem overly concerned.

Watching her kept his mind off the issues at hand. For a while.

The Subaru had made it back to Trent, the highway between Idaho and Washington. Tom suggested they head into Idaho away from Spokane.

Earthquakes and tsunamis had crippled the western part of Washington. If Tom and Jenny drove west, they wouldn't find anyone to help them. They'd just run into more refugees.

Seattle was gone. Olympia gone. Spokane's hospitals were gone. All major disaster units were decimated. Four hours west and they'd hit ocean.

Give it time. Tom's dad had guaranteed Medical Lake and Cheney would soon have salty beach property.

Northern Idaho and Montana hadn't been struck with tragedy that ate half their land. Tornadoes, storms and failing economy, sure, but their mountains hadn't moved and water hadn't swallowed them whole.

Tom and Jenny hadn't made it far when they reached the constipated crux of highway. Cars sat idle as people shouted left and right. Jenny couldn't get across the line of vehicles driving into Spokane. Bumper-to-bumper terror.

"Maybe we should go into Spokane, too." Jenny had offered.

Tom had spluttered, trying not to yell. "No, we can't go into town."

"Why not?"

"Because we don't know if the attacks are over." He hoped they were, but more than likely, they weren't.

"There aren't any more bombs going off. Other people are headed into town. Come on. We might be able to find our parents, get some food." She had clenched her fingers into her flat stomach. "I'm so hungry."

He'd sighed and looked at her with sadness in his eyes. "I'm sorry, Jenny. You can go if you want to. I can get out here. But, please, think about it. The attack may or may not have been meant solely for the base. Why would they stop when Fairchild isn't completely down? Or the town? They're waiting until more people come together to get aid before they drop the rest of the missiles." He had looked out the window at the cars honking in the afternoon light, the line moving an inch at a time, faces pressed against rear windows as each vehicle was packed with possessions. "It's what I would do, so imagine what someone who wants to *kill* us would do."

She hadn't argued with him. Eventually, she'd London-crawled the car across the busy highway onto the empty lane running into Idaho. The car had sputtered out of gas just north of Post Falls. Tom had suggested they wait for dark. But once night had fallen Jenny had been too scared to leave the car.

Tom was too scared to sleep.

Jenny opened her eyes, her voice husky in the intimate setting. "Can't sleep?"

He wiped his hand down his face and moved his tongue behind his closed lips. His mouth was so dry. "No. I don't feel safe out in the middle where anyone can see us. I had men trying to kill me, remember?"

"Me, too." Oh, right, they'd shot at her as well. Guilt pushed on his stomach, or maybe that was his bladder. She glanced over his shoulder out the window and then back at his face. "Well, what do you suggest?"

"We need to move. The car isn't worth much without gas." Tom shifted in the passenger seat, resting his hands on his legs. The wide shoulder of the road led a significant distance along the highway or offered a turn down a straight stretch of road, discernible only by the pale buildings dotting the prairie fields shrouded in darkness and layering smoke.

"But we're protected." Jenny's eyes widened, showing the whites.

"No, we're not. Not only could those men find us, but if anyone wanted to rob us, we're sitting ducks." He gave her a moment to consider their position. "If I were alone, I'd go down that road until I hit a neighborhood. If no one was home and it looked deserted, I'd probably go into a house, get some food, and then head into the mountain range. I heard there's militia up that way. It'd be safer than sitting here or going west."

Her lower lip jutted out with the fervor of stubborn female salsa. "What do you mean militia? Do you think I'll slow you down or that I can't go that way?"

"I mean people with guns and some way to protect us. My dad told me they're thick up there." Tom held up his hands. "And I'm not saying you would slow me down at all. I know all about your running times in track. I'm just sharing what I would do, if I were the only one making decisions." He looked over his shoulder out the rearview mirror. The line of red serpent eyes had only gotten longer and the tail end was closing in on their location. Anger, frustration and fatigue would be the ruling factor alongside fear. People were little more than animals when threatened or faced with road rage. He swallowed. It was against everything in his survival instincts to sit there and do nothing.

The last thing Tom wanted to be around when he grieved for his town, his family, his friends and his home was someone else's loss.

A loud boom called from behind the car, close enough to rattle the windows but far enough to not damage the vehicle. Tom opened the door and jumped from his seat.

Wind from the explosion buffeted his face with gritty heat, particles heavy on his tongue as he tried to breathe. Jenny followed Tom, hesitation in the slow rise of her hand to the roof. Red and orange played across her skin.

In the space of the heartbeat between the noise and leaving the car, screams rent the air. A few cars flashed their reverse lights and squealed backward, rear-ending others behind them in a mad dash to turn around.

Whistle. Kaboom. Another car disappeared leaving a roiling ball of flames in its place. The recoil from the blast, closer than the last, knocked Tom into the open door, a handle crunching into the muscle of his thigh.

Something was dropping bombs or flying missiles at the trapped vehicles. Tom didn't know what was going on, but there were too many people in the vicinity and it most likely wasn't going to stop. He slammed the door shut and opened the back. "Jenny, we need to go. If you want to stay with the car, that's fine, but I'm leaving." Tom pulled his backpack from the seat. He didn't want to leave her but he couldn't force anyone to do anything they didn't want to. And as cute as she was, he didn't want to die.

Without speaking, Jenny copied his motions but leaned under her front seat and pulled out an item she tucked into her duffel bag.

"Do you have everything you need?" Tom swung his pack on his back and clipped the waist strap. At her nod, he glanced once more to the burning vehicles. He wanted to help the people, but urgency to get away from the site rushed him to the side of the road and across the perpendicular street.

The crush of rocks on pavement under Jenny's feet matched his pace. Ducking into the ditch on the east side of the road, they crouched behind the overgrowth for protection.

Cars squealed away from the accident, honking at each other and hurtling away into the night. A black truck, orange and yellow reflecting off the paint, pulled alongside the abandoned Subaru. Two men climbed from the cab and shot their guns into the front and rear windows.

Jenny covered her mouth to muffle a gasp. Tom's jaw dropped. Across the rough gravel, their fingers sought each other and clutched with desperation in the night.

Looking through the shattered glass into the empty interior, the men waved their hands, shouting as they proceeded to dump gas onto the car. A small flicker of light illuminated the hardened face of one of the men. A man Tom recognized from his house. Flames overtook the interior.

Jenny laid her head on her arms. Tom placed his hand on her back and patted softly, never taking his eyes from the scene. The men drove away from the explosions, headed straight for their hiding spot. Tom tensed. "Close your eyes and don't move." Jenny froze. Her silent sobs paused while she held her breath.

The truck didn't slow as it took the corner, tires squealing as they revved down the road. Rocks flew through the air and peppered the brush Tom and Jenny hid behind.

Increasing flames lit up the night. Jenny grasped his hand again and met his gaze. "What now?"

He looked down the road, pretending her touch wasn't the one bright spot in the night. The truck's lights were visible but shrinking fast. "We have to go that way. I don't know what's past Rathdrum. I need to get supplies and we won't get any in the woods. At least not yet."

Jenny nodded slowly. "Okay. Lead the way." Her white clothes and white and pink duffel had a dim glow.

"We need to get you darker clothes. I can see you like you have a light under your skin." Tom nodded at her.

"Okay." Jenny fell into his jogging step, matching his speed and artfully dodging rocks and holes that would roll ankles. They fell into a rhythm, pat-pat, breathe, pat-pat, breathe. A clump wound itself through every other step as their packs slammed onto their hips.

Tom glanced her way every couple seconds, startled to find her doing the same. He offered her a half-smile which she returned. His smile grew.

No street lights illuminated the way. A lack of stars and the struggling moon offered very little in guiding them to a neighborhood. Another car turned onto the road. They jumped from the side of the road and onto the prairie. The car sped past without acknowledging their presence.

Tom found his pattern to which Jenny continued to meet perfectly. He spoke with little effort. "Let's stay on the field. We might be able to cut across in a bit."

They fell silent. Inhales and exhales matched like the rhythm of their feet over the late-spring tilled ground. Random cars passed by on the road but Tom and Jenny had moved into the field and the distance added safety from discovery.

"Tom, are those houses?"

Hard to decipher against the night sky, roof lines slashed here and there, some with fences, some without. "Yeah, let's slow down." He needed to get his bearings. The house he wanted should be close unless he had gotten all turned around. Or she'd moved.

Post Falls, Idaho was infamous for neighborhoods planted in farm fields. Some people could look out their back window and see another house or a busy road while others saw budding grain or a combine pushing through the golden rows.

Stopping on the sidewalk before the corner, Tom didn't know which way to go. They needed food and a place to hide, at least for a little while. He needed time to rest so he could formulate a plan. He'd been up for too long and worry nipped at his concentration while fatigue crunched it in two.

Jenny couldn't be much better. She'd had two friends die and she didn't know about her parents or other family members. Like Tom.

To the left, a house looked vaguely familiar. The angles were right, but he didn't remember a fence. The color of the house was unrecognizable in the dark. Hope pushed him in that direction.

"This one looks deserted. See if the gate opens. I'll keep an eye out." Tom glanced up and down the roads. No cars had passed by in a while and he hadn't seen a soul in or around the other houses. The field was black. Minimal sounds amplified in the dark.

An angry dog barked a few streets over, but overall nothing else suggested other people were in the area.

"It's clear." Jenny called and held open the gate until Tom passed. She allowed it to click shut. The white vinyl fence glowed in the dark. As much as it could without light.

A shape similar to a deck and stairs loomed out of the sea of black grass. Tom took Jenny's hand without thinking and led the way to the steps. She didn't pull away.

First and foremost on the list of necessities was food. He didn't want to loot, could care less in fact what kind of material belongings the house held. Food. He was interested in the food. Needed the food. And if no one was there, maybe never returning, why let the food go to waste? And if the house was the one he thought it was, the owner wouldn't mind.

Jenny didn't question his hold on her hand. She squeezed and whispered, "I'm a little scared."

He held onto his macho attitude and didn't tell her he was peeing-his-pants scared.

The stairs squeaked and Tom held his breath. Up another. And yet another. At the top, he pressed his back into the cool vinyl siding, his free hand palm down on the faux wood grain.

Heck, he was more than a little scared. If a girl hadn't been with him, a cute girl at that, he'd probably cry. Well, maybe not, but he was definitely scared. He reached out and pushed on the handle of the slider, soft at first then harder. A sucking sound, followed by a quiet rub, allowed Tom to release the air on a whoosh from his lungs. Unlocked, thank goodness. He tugged on Jenny's fingers.

Warmer than outside, the house had a lived-in feel. The smell of marinara sauce and ripe peaches called to their bellies. Plants brushed their jacket sleeves when they passed.

Tom's foot connected with a dog dish sitting on the floor of the kitchen. It clattered across the linoleum, no water or food spilling from it. He and Jenny jumped and then offered a small laugh. Maybe it had just been a bowl dropped to the ground and never picked up.

Not expecting much, Tom flipped the nearest light switch without result. He reached into his pocket and pulled out a lighter. The faint glow felt like sunshine to their overtaxed eyes. Adjusting to the presence of sight was easy.

Jenny ran her fingers over her hair to smooth out strands and shifted her gaze to Tom and away again. He was suddenly self-conscious of how he looked too. "Let's get a quick lay of the land and turn the light off. We have no idea if those men are still out there and how much of this flame you can see from the road."

Jenny nodded. "Do you think the water still works?"

"It should. Do you have any water bottles?" Tom tugged his backpack off and withdrew two empty bottles. Water was essential but he'd had to flee his house before he could fill them. Dry bottles only played havoc when one was hungry and thirsty. And he could definitely use the toilet.

From inside her large duffel, Jenny pulled out three different water bottles. "I was going to fill them before our hike in the afternoon, but... well..." She looked at the elongated flame in Tom's hand. "Do you think we'll get to go back home?" Her voice was small and for the first time since he'd met her, Jenny looked really lost. She'd been scared at the campground but confident running. The situation was as wearing on her as it was on Tom.

"Honestly? I don't know how much of a home we have left. But if we get back, I'd love to take you out to the movies on Friday. We could go get a pizza and drink all the root beer we can handle." He smiled. She had to perk up. Tom was holding it together but with control thinner than a spider's thread – for her.

Swiping at her face, Jenny offered a half-smile. "I'd love to, Tom, and I'm going to hold you to it. My dad might..." Crestfallen at the thought of her loved ones missing, Jenny fell into the nearest dining room chair and sighed. "I have no idea what's going on. Is there any way we can find out something?"

A task! The job kick-started another adrenaline push. "I'll look around. You find food and we'll meet back here. We need to try to get some rest before the morning." Jenny didn't stay in the kitchen, instead she followed Tom. He looked over his shoulder. Of course she'd stay with him, he had the only light in the place. Or maybe she enjoyed his company. A boy could hope.

If Tom hadn't had the lighter, he wouldn't be able to force himself away from the back door either. The house was blacker than the night but had a horror flick feel to it. Jenny was cute enough to be the dead bombshell in the first act.

How had he had the balls to ask her out but in normal life he couldn't ask her out at school? He'd known her for years. If she hadn't been within hearing, he would have slapped his head and cursed at his idiocy.

Modest but well kept, the house had stairs leading up and down with a slight landing classic to the California split levels popular in the northwest. Tom hated all the stairs, but it wasn't his house. No, his home wouldn't greet him for a very long time, if at all. He'd never been inside the house he'd been looking for, but the picture on the wall, above the landing to the stairs, greeted him. And he sighed with relief.

He'd found it. The house. She wasn't there, but her presence was everywhere. He focused and shoved his fear from him, calmed by the thought she'd been there.

Jenny snagged a chunk of his jacket and followed him like she'd leashed a seeing-eye dog. He had no problem with her hand on his back, pressing into him if he stopped. Crap, he had no right thinking of her the way he was.

"Do you know what you're looking for?" She whispered a short distance from his neck. The hair stood up at his nape and hives ran down his spine. She had to be kidding. Who in their right mind would breathe on a teenage boy? Fatigue was messing with him. He wasn't a horn dog, had never been that close to a girl before. But he wasn't thinking straight. They needed rest and food.

Tom turned and nearly smacked her to the floor with his shoulder. "Sorry, um, you can wait here, because I have no idea what I'm going to find and I don't want you in danger or anything." As tired as he was, he didn't have a chance at staying focused without some distance from her baby powder scent and husky I-just-woke-up whisper. He tried to wipe an image of her cheering at the last basketball game from his mind, little skirt flipping all over the place with each turn of her ankles. Great.

"But you have the light and it's dark in here." All girl. Dang it. He'd never been good at holding out when a chick needed something. His mom had often said he was a long-lost knight searching for a damsel-in-distress. And this damsel had agreed to go out with him when they got home.

"Okay, but you're distracting me. Can you hang back a foot or so?" *Keep your hands to yourself? Please?* She had no idea her effect on him.

"Do you think I could use a bathroom?" Actually, she had a good idea. He needed one, too, and it would get her away from him.

"Let's get some food together and refresh ourselves before we get some sleep."

"We're sleeping here?" Jenny tightened her fingers.

Tom stopped his trek down the stairs and turned to her, enveloping them in the small circle of light. "Jen, aren't you tired? We need somewhere safe and we don't have a car. Do you have any ideas? Do you want to return to the Subaru?"

She snapped her mouth shut and shook her head. Tom didn't mean to be harsh but if she questioned everything, they would go nowhere fast. "I know the lady that owns this house. We're fine."

Tom continued down the steps. The wood trim and banisters were dark, chipped here and there from wear. A garage door to the left and various doors lined the hall to the right. What was he looking for? Someone hiding downstairs, maybe around the next corner, or in the den?

He needed to evaluate their needs. Then he could go forward making plans and picking up things they could use instead of walking around without a clue what was going on. "What's in your duffel?"

They'd left their bags upstairs, but Jenny was a girl and as a rule knew what she'd packed by heart. "Clothes, hygiene essentials, extra shoes, another coat, my purse, journal and some hair products. Why?"

"Okay, we need to outfit you with essentials. That bag can carry more than that and you need items that will help you in the long run. I don't know where we're going next." The lighter burned his thumb tip. "Just a sec. It's gonna be dark." He let it off and she moved close to him, her shoulder jutting into his arm. He had no idea what was going on outside. *Focus, Tom.*

He enjoyed her proximity for a moment longer then switched hands. Flicking another flame, Tom missed the warmth of her body behind his. The light brought safety which allowed her to back up.

She tilted her head. "What do you think I need?"

"Food that doesn't weigh much, a blanket or another coat. Extra socks. A flashlight or lighter. Toilet paper. That type of thing." He shrugged. "If you see something that would help in a survival situation let me know. Some things are heavier than they're worth and you don't want to be strapped with too much weight. You want to be able to run, if you need to."

To the left, the garage would have tools and things useful for outside. Out the door, the temperature was the same as inside.

A lantern container tucked above more boxes captured Tom's attention. He reached up and knocked it down to arm level. A tinkling noise relieved him. Still in the container. "Can you hold this?" Tom handed the lighter to Jenny and removed the lantern from the box. White gas. Sweet. He turned the knob and sparked a glow with the ignite switch on the side. Light flooded the two-car garage.

Jenny blinked and released the lighter.

Covering the contents of the house was disturbing and sad. Tom tried to ignore the pictures on the walls of smiling people and various mementos of their life. Knick knacks littered shelves inside a den. Kindling and ashes had been abandoned beside the open steel door of the fireplace. A fire. Warmth.

Viewing the family that lived there as if they were all strangers lent stability to his moment. He couldn't handle the concept another person he'd known had been traumatized in the attacks. Especially her.

Tom set the lantern on a low coffee table. "We'll stay down here tonight." A second slider behind the couch led out to the backyard. They would have two escape routes, if needed. And warmth. Blankets beckoned from a pile on the back of the sofa.

Tom didn't know if he was more tired or hungry. Did they need to set up a watch? He didn't know what to do. His survival courses covered fishing with a zipper and surviving a bear attack. Not one pamphlet he'd collected covered breaking away from men trying to kill you with a hot girl in tow. Plus, they'd be sleeping together. Well, not like that, but… he was nervous about it anyway. The car was one thing, sofas or floor entirely different.

Time for a quick decision. Jenny wasn't in a state to make choices. Tom would have to do it for the both of them. "Let's get our bags and lock the house. I'll make a fire. If anyone sees the smoke, we can deter them from getting in for a little bit, at least long enough to get away."

The den's only access to the outside was the slider and it faced the fenced in backyard. Tom grabbed a large blanket and tucked the edges around the blind frame. Light might show a little bit around the edges, but for the most part, they'd be able to pull off a blackout and blend in with the other houses on the block. "I'll grab the bags if you want to use the bathroom."

She smiled and followed him only as far as the restroom off the stairs. The lantern guarded from the table.

Chapter 9

Brenda

Enough was enough. Why hadn't Brenda recognized it months ago? Her husband had been dabbling in weird cult-like religions and groups. They'd grown so far apart his abandonment didn't surprise her one bit. Hurt her, sure, surprise her, nope. And was she really upset anyway? She'd returned from the southern Cali Red Cross mission determined to leave his abusive butt anyway. He'd used her body like she hadn't warned him. He waited until she got in the shower, then left. In her damn car.

Brenda kicked a rock from under her foot. "Humph." *Now what*.

She'd given up on the fire department four hours before. Sirens hadn't hinted they were anywhere near her neighborhood. And by the looks of things, Spokane was in worse need than she was.

Her house smoldered behind her. The trucks wouldn't be worth much at that point, but at least someone could rescue her. Lee had taken their only working car.

Brenda flipped open her cell. Still no signal. No word from Rachel. Nothing from work. No ambulance. Her landline *had* worked, but the only wall of the house still standing was the back one by the bathroom. The phone lines had run along the front of the house. Melted plastic would do about as good as her worthless cell. Even the internet wasn't working from the Smartphone screen.

Where was her knight-in-shining-armor?

Three other houses on the street resembled news coverage of the forest fires from the previous autumn. SUVs and coupes had passed by yesterday afternoon in a mad frenzy to escape the falling embers, proof that even prestigious neighborhoods weren't immune from life's tragedies.

Trapped in an M. Night Shymalan movie couldn't be worse. Brenda had no answers and her husband had left her. She'd stared out the window at the blistered buildings of her hometown. Spokane wasn't much but she'd grown up there. Her sister lived in the next town over, just across the Washington/Idaho border.

If Brenda's last few months nursing in the destruction of the quakes and tornadoes had taught her anything, it was family had more importance than things. And Brenda had plenty of things. Had.

Brenda had jumped, toweling off, when the garage door had shut. Lee hadn't told her he was going anywhere. The engine started in the garage and squealing tires explained what he had been too cowardly to discuss. What did she do? What could she do? She'd eaten dinner in the dark, tried to sleep in the abandoned neighborhood and been awakened by the smell of smoke.

He was a bastard. He never returned.

In her robe and slippers, Brenda had run to the kitchen, dialed 911 and given her information to a harried sounding woman on the other end of the line. She'd hung up and a cough attack had run her from the house.

Still in her bathrobe, Brenda watched Spokane burn. Hell, she paid taxes on the most sought after view in town which encompassed the entire downtown and much of the valley. The flames ate at the rubble of Sacred Heart and Deaconess. She was out of a job with those buildings burned down. The nurse in her ached at the thought of all the death in the walls. So many would be dead. Sacred Heart alone was filled with small ones, babies and children. Innocents. So much loss.

She turned from the scene spread out below. The house was gone. She had nothing of her own. Even her purse was in the rubble she called home.

The May sun pricked her skin. She'd be red if she stayed outside much longer.

The Hansons hadn't been home since the day before and Brenda's house was gone. They most likely wouldn't mind if she snuck in and used the bathroom. Her bladder was more annoyed than her burning cheeks. Taking care of the essentials would take her mind off the circumstances of those she couldn't help.

Stepping around landscaping rocks up the path to her neighbors', Brenda knocked before pushing the unlocked door open. Absolute silence greeted her with a cool rush of air. They'd taken the dog with them. Good thing. The yapping mutt was not on her list of tolerances.

The wife, Sheila? Sheena? whatever, was about Brenda's size. After using the bathroom and washing the soot from her face, Brenda tiptoed into the master bedroom to the closet. She wasn't going back to her house and most likely wasn't going to be getting any help this far from town. She needed to get to her sister's or into Spokane. That would require jeans, tees, a jacket in case it got cold and good shoes.

The wife was a fashion guru, but Brenda couldn't care less. Her robe was sooty and made her feel like a disintegrating chunk of burned wood. She dropped it where she stood and pulled things from the over-neat closet. Clothes and food. Brenda didn't mean to steal or trespass, but circumstances dictated her actions. What if Mr. Hanson – Curtis? – had left his dirt bike? That would be great, but her luck rarely held. Look at her house sending its last breaths of life up in gray and white swirls next door.

At the door to the garage, Brenda grabbed up a hiking pack abandoned in the corner. Inside the bag, as if packed for her, were socks and granola bars, a water bottle and a poncho. She could fit a blanket and some more food inside and maybe a few other things. Cracking open the door, she gasped. Yep, the bike was there, helmet and all. She'd grown up on two-wheels but it'd been a while.

She needed to get around people, find out what was going on. Food first.

Electricity had been out since the day before in the entire neighborhood. Brenda stayed away from the fridge. She couldn't afford getting sick and she didn't feel like digging through the contents without the light coming on. Too many memories of poor-college days when the fridge was just a cooler and she never knew if the milk would be chunky or just sour.

Half a loaf of bread, jar of peanut butter, crackers, pickles and candy bars slipped into the pack, ideal for the road. She added some apples to the cache but the bag wouldn't hold much more.

She pulled her brown hair into a disheveled bun, zipped the pack and pulled it on her back. In the next few hours she'd either be with a group of people or she'd break into another house and go from there. Survival had become the name of the game. She'd learned a thing or two the last six months.

The stolen shoes on her feet were just a bit too big, but at least they didn't pinch. She tied them tighter and looked back at her neighbors' house. Hopefully they were okay. Whether they were or not, she had to get out of there. She didn't know what was going on, but it couldn't be good. Not another soul was in sight.

In the quiet garage, Brenda crossed her fingers. She pushed the garage door opener. No electricity but maybe, yes! Batteries powered the draw mechanism as well as the light.

A light. She searched for a flashlight among the items strewn about the disorganized tool box and shelves. She didn't have time for this. Her fingers clasped onto a solid, cold cylinder. Bingo. Tucking the slim part into the strap hanging off the side of the pack, Brenda slung her leg over the bike.

Hm. She loved kick start bikes. Standing, she thrust her weight onto the protruding metal stick. The engine growled under her.

Ah. And she pulled onto the drive. With a few stutter stop-and-go's – it really had been forever – Brenda roared down the street, burned homes blurring in her peripheral vision. Where to go? Rachel's or Spokane?

The bridge across the Spokane River decided for her. Blocked by a semi-truck twisted in half and two other cars crumpled into the guard rail, the way was impassable even with Brenda on a dirt bike. Alright. She could put up with her sister. And Andy. At least she'd get to see her niece and nephews.

Smoke spiraled into the sky from different spots, a group of trees, cars, houses. Brenda wasn't the savviest girl in town but she'd been blessed with a sprinkling of good sense and hell, if she didn't head into the woods to go the back way. Desperate people would kill over a can of food, let alone a dirt bike. Hopefully she'd be at Rachel's within the hour. Rachel wore the same size she did. How perfect if her sister had an extra pair of hiking boots.

~

Brenda rolled over. Rachel must have returned from wherever they'd gone. Voices murmured from the living room, but faded like they went downstairs. How long had she slept? The room couldn't get any darker. No power in Post Falls, but she'd arrived earlier that evening and the sun had been up.

She'd ducked into the backyard and hid the bike on the other side of the house in the fenced-in hole Andy had added to the yard to store the mower.

Hesitant foot tread from the stairs to the kitchen whispered through the door. There weren't any weapons in the bedroom, as far as Brenda was aware. She'd never trespassed in Rachel and Andy's space the few times she and Lee had visited.

Rachel and Andy wouldn't trundle about the house without a goal in mind, which meant someone who didn't belong was in their home. Brenda wasn't armed, but she didn't tolerate fear in others or herself. She groped in the dark for the doorknob, twisting as silently as possible.

Her eyes burned from searching for light to focus on. It couldn't be more than a couple hours before the sun would rise, but without the street lights and moon, it might as well be an Alaskan winter outside.

She pressed her body against the wall. No one could sneak up behind her or come from the room she'd just vacated. Judging by the noises, the intruder had yet to make their way to the kids' room or the bathroom on the upper level of the disjointed three floors. Looters and gang bangers came to mind.

Rustling in the kitchen localized their position and Brenda moved step by agonizing step down the short hallway, onto the stairs. Down one, two, three, four and she stopped at the bottom, careful to breathe from her mouth without gasping. She had no idea what she was supposed to do, but she had to do something, right? Didn't she? What if she didn't? No, it wouldn't help anyone thinking like that.

Brenda brushed against a wooden frame hanging from the wall. Antlers. Andy's antlers would do some damage, but how did she get them down without being seen or heard.

In the dark, Brenda rolled her eyes. Seriously? She couldn't see her feet but she was worried that the person in the kitchen would have superhuman powers and spot her with his night vision.

Brenda blinked. And blinked again. What the heck? Was she going crazy? A white light was moving up the stairs. It turned the corner and the brightness was all she could focus on for a moment. Long enough that the person holding it could register her presence and gasp. Dang.

"Who's there?" Brenda's vision cleared and she no longer felt like a moth hovering around a patio light. Blinking, the white circle staining her view, she looked over the lantern into the brown eyes of a very pretty teenager. The sound of stampeding feet heralded his arrival before the boy came into view. His sandy blond hair flipped over brown eyes. His lips parted in astonishment.

"Who are you?" He stepped forward, his hand out to the girl.

"Brenda. Again, who are *you*?" She crossed her arms over her chest and tried impaling them with her best I'm-the-adult-here stare. They didn't react the way she'd hoped.

"You don't live here." He reached the girl and pulled her to his side, transferring the light to his hand. Protective was good.

"No, but my sister and her family do. I'm sure you understand why I'm annoyed that you broke into her home. What are you doing here?" She shifted her gaze between the young kids. They couldn't be more than seventeen or eighteen, and that was being generous. The girl had the frightened look of one of Brenda's patients – wide eyed and shaking. Not the best person to get information from.

"We needed to get out of the cold. The backdoor was open." He lowered the light to his side, but glanced over his shoulder to the windows. He looked back at Brenda. His voice lowered. "You look like the woman in the pictures."

Rachel and she had been told that growing up, even with their different coloring. Brenda ignored the poses on the walls. Waving into the living room, she nodded, "Sit down. Let's talk."

A whirring sound followed by knocking filled the middle level. He jumped and spun toward the slider past the kitchen. Orange light competed with the white as it strained through the front window. Green lights blinked the time on the DVD player a few feet from the couch.

Brenda walked to the boy and placed her hand on his arm. His wild gaze met hers. She smiled. "It's okay. The electricity came on. Sit down."

He nodded, but waited for the girl to sit first. Sitting beside her, he turned the dial on the base of the lantern and the flame lowered to barely the wattage of a small votive candle. He'd freaked and didn't appear to be coming out of it any time soon.

"What're your names?" Brenda plopped into the easy chair by the wall. Seriously, she wasn't asking again.

"That's Tom and I'm Jenny." The girl pointed at the skittish boy.

"Do you guys know what's going on? Where are your parents? Did you drive up?" Picking up the remote for the TV, Brenda pressed the power button. Static lit up the room further. "I got here this afternoon and finally fell asleep a few hours ago."

Tom turned off the lantern. "Spokane was attacked. Not sure by who yet, but the local ARRL members who were able to get through reported hostile activity. I confirmed and lost contact with the remaining handles. When I got back home, no one was broadcasting anymore. Just me. I'm the only one with AM capabilities, so I radioed out to whoever could hear me and ran."

Jenny cut in. "But who were those men? Why did they shoot at us?"

Tom shot a look that clearly said, "Shut up" her direction.

Brenda shook her head. "I'm confused. Who shot at you? What's ARRL and what do you mean attacked?"

Tom dropped his hands and looked at the ground. Fatigue seemed to pull at him and his wariness faltered. "I don't know who shot at me. Men. At my house. I think it's because I radio? Three of my friends died not long ago and they were into calling like me." He reached up and rubbed the side of his nose. "ARRL stands for Amateur Radio Relay League and is a national organization for amateur radio hobbyists, HAM radios. My dad got me into them. And attacked, as in, someone bombed Fairchild and Spokane."

No. Why would anyone do that? And right after the sequential earthquakes tearing California, Oregon and the western half of Washington into the ocean three months ago. America was as vulnerable as it could get.

Brenda's emergency nursing stint had originally been intended for what was left of Nevada and Arizona after nineteen tsunamis had torn the states apart. The flooding wouldn't go away but what did it matter when the population had disappeared into the sea? She'd been shuttled to the California island instead.

A fellow nurse had returned from Vegas a few days before that where, as she'd reported, she'd walked along the newly formed beachfront. She'd sat down to look at the water and rest from the trauma in the city when an arm, leg and small foot had washed up. Brenda had recommended Rachel for the requested therapy and hadn't yet heard if Rachel had accepted the referral. One never knew with her sister. But if it had to deal with fear, Rachel was acknowledged nationally as the best.

"Okay. Well, they probably have Red Cross set up somewhere. Let's grab ourselves a vehicle and get into town."

Brenda pressed the channel button, flipping between scenes of static. Darker, lighter, the static had no real focus. Until... "Hey, is that a news program?"

Tom jumped up and pressed his face to the screen. "Yes." He spun to Brenda as she worked on the volume and reception. "We can't go into any populated areas. They're still bombing and it wouldn't be safe. We need to get into the mountains. We'll be relatively safe there with the tree coverage."

A memory of Rachel standing on the front patio and waving her arms flashed through Brenda's mind. "Get to the mountains, Brenda. No matter what, get there and you'll find me. I promise we will find each other. Get to the mountains. Remember the trail?" Rachel had said, emphasizing mountains with an upward swirl of her hands.

"Why? What's going on?" Brenda had asked, holding her fingers up to block the bright spring sun.

"Nothing. But if something does, you get there, fast. I don't think anything will, but Andy has been ranting about this for months now and since you're my sister, you have to promise you'll meet me." Her steady eyes were betrayed by the intensity in her voice. Brenda had promised.

The memory didn't stop her from questioning the surety of the teen-aged boy. "How did you get away?"

Tom hushed her, pressing his hands behind his back as he turned from her to stare at the screen. The volume was up loud, but only a few words came through the muted veil.

"...not sure where the attacks are coming fro... when you get to the centers, hold on. You will... at the end of the line... bring food, water, shoe... leave everything else, do not gather weapons, just get to the nearest city..."

"Did you hear that? Do you know if this is a national line? Which one is it?"

Brenda pressed more buttons and a clearer picture filled the screen. The CNN logo covered the corner while a woman with unkempt hair and no makeup held herself rigid in the anchor chair. The sound waved in and out but her lips continued to move and the picture was constant.

"We can't go downtown, Brenda. Jenny and I just left her car on Trent because the line of people driving to Spokane was bombed. Men shot up her car after we hid in some bushes. We need to get some rest and then get into the woods."

The woman on the screen said one thing while the teenager professed something else. Hm. Teenage boy or professional woman? Brenda didn't hold much with age differences and the boy's passion was enough to convince her. Plus, he spoke of grit and reality. Brenda recognized that. She'd seen it. Lived it. Lived from vending machine meal to the next with blood and trauma in between mad dashes to the bathroom and shared cots in the mess tents. Nothing was as true as the harsh abrasion life offered.

The question wasn't which way to go… the question was did she take them to Rachel's or leave them somewhere once they all got to a safer location? She may be a city girl now, but she'd been raised in the woods where common sense was beat into a person who could be stung to death by bees or chased down by a bear, if they didn't know how to recognize instinct.

"I know of a place in the National Forest. Up Hayden Lake Drive until it turns into a logging road where it stops in a clearing. Rachel's up there." Details could be worked out later. Tom and Jenny looked dead on their butts and Brenda's nursing side claimed the choices. "Food. Let's eat and get some rest. Turn off the TV, Tom. If men are still looking for you, this could be a ruse to flush you out. Keep the light off, too. I know this place well enough to find my way around without the lantern. I'll grab some food and we'll stay downstairs. Let's eat, sleep and then head east. We aren't too far from the foothills as it is."

Her no-nonsense tone snapped something into the kids as if they recognized an adult had just removed their mantle of responsibility. They stood, the blurry look in their eyes fading with relief. Tom turned off the TV and led the way downstairs.

Brenda moved to the kitchen and flipped the lights off. Why was the electricity back on? She hadn't wanted to say anything to Tom and Jenny because they looked like anymore news would push them past the limit, but the national media wouldn't cover something that was strictly local. From the coverage, the nation had been bombed and everyone was getting the same information.

Brenda hadn't seen everything, but the damage heading out of town had been ugly and horrible. Houses smoldered beside untouched trees. A twisted slide the last piece of a destroyed playground outside of a cratered-in school. Abandoned cars on bridges and streets at intersections had peppered the scenery.

In town would be a hundred times worse. But the weirdest part was the fact that no nukes had been used.

The fastest and most effective way of decimating a large area would be to drop a radioactive bomb – which everyone and their brother had these days – but they'd dropped missiles. Brenda wasn't an arms specialist or even a Battleship player, but she knew what an atom bomb would do. Missiles didn't make sense. And how many other cities? Why weren't they getting any help? Did anyone know what was going on? The last she'd heard, the capitol was begging other countries for help after the tsunamis had wiped out the survivors from the latest earthquake, measured at twelve-point-two. The president had promised help was on the way.

But they'd awakened to bombs not first aid.

Brenda stood at the sink and gazed out the back window into the backyard Andy had landscaped with care, giving Rachel her raised gardens and vinyl fencing. The floodlight from the shed gilded the grass with silver. A shadow slithered over the fence and disappeared around the corner behind the light.

Brenda blinked and refocused. Trick of her eyes? From the neighbor's yard another dark shape slid over the white fence to the grass. As if made of fog, the illusion faded into the inky green carpet. Her mind played tricks on her... maybe.

"Tom? Jenny? Come up here, fast." In seconds, the teenagers joined her on the cold linoleum. "I'm sorry. It's probably nothing, but I thought I saw men or something out there." Nothing moved. Three sets of eyes probed the dark for anything that didn't belong. Brenda began to feel foolish. A minute passed. Jenny coughed. Brenda shifted on her feet.

"What did you see?" Tom nodded toward the yard. He stepped to the table and picked up a backpack and tossed the duffel to Jenny.

"In the corner, I thought I saw someone climb over and hide behind the shed. On the other side it looked like someone slid over and disappeared into the grass." Brenda's nervous laugh tinkled into the tension. She glanced into the yard and pointed. "See, something just moved, over by the raised box."

Tom turned and froze. Speaking fast, he shrugged into the pack. "Listen, I don't know who is after us, but we need to move. Now. Brenda, where are your shoes? Get them and get ready to run. We'll have to break into another house and get more supplies later."

Brenda's breathing quickened and moisture collected between her breasts. What the hell was happening? She slid into the hiking boots, bending to tug the ties together. "What do we do now?"

Tom watched something over her shoulder. His eyes widened and he grabbed Jenny's arm. "We run! Get out, now!"

Brenda glanced over her shoulder. A bright light flashed against the window and glass shattered. She didn't have time to scream.

Chapter 10

Rachel

The energetic steps had morphed into trudging. Forest highlights – a squirrel running up and down a tree trunk, a rabbit's nose poking from its burrow, early spring bird songs as they twittered about the branches – had lost their appeal. Beau slept on Josh's back, piggy-back style and Rachel pulled Kayli along by the hand, every step heavier laden than the one before.

Rachel tripped three times over Cole as he placed one foot in front of the other, careful to avoid protruding roots and overgrowing foliage.

She wanted to ask Josh all kinds of questions but the timing wasn't right with the kids there and who knew where the thief had gone. Nerves scuttled along her skin at the idea the man could have gone to her place, could be going through their things or waited to ambush Rachel's group. If Rachel had been alone, that'd be one thing, but with her three babies to guard over, she didn't feel comfortable going home alone.

Thank heaven, Josh had volunteered to walk them back and check things out.

Humid heat sweltered around them. The sun worked its way through the spindly needles to the snow beneath and warmed the air. Maybe fresh air was overrated. Moss and dirt and some other unidentifiable scent filled her nostrils and what she really wanted was to smell the coconut candle she burned in her office at home. Or had burned. Whatever, fresh air sucked. Rachel kicked a rock and it skittered to rest against a fallen rotten log.

Josh stopped walking and held up his hand. "Do you hear that?"

Rachel tilted her head. Yeah, a faint putting like an engine in idle sounded from just over the next rise. She nodded and met his gaze. Whatever or whoever it was, the kids needed to be hidden. While Josh looked to the left, Rachel searched the right. She tugged on his sleeve and pointed at a rocky overhang past a copse of trees. The kids could rest there, if Josh moved some brush in front of the opening. No one would know the difference as long as they didn't move.

Picking their way to the partial cave, Rachel whispered in Cole's ear, "You need to make sure no one talks or comes out, okay? We will be right back to get you. Do you understand?" Her son, so adult yet so young, nodded, his expression grave.

Rachel transferred Beau from Josh's back to Cole's lap. The Currant bush offered a thick blind which Josh moved easily into position. Rachel waved her fingers at Kayli who hadn't stopped staring at her mother since they'd reached the hiding spot. Rachel longed to whisper that she'd be right back and everything would be fine, but she couldn't bring herself to offer what could possibly be false hope.

Moving faster without the children in tow, Josh and Rachel hiked to the trail and beyond to take the motorist by surprise. The familiar groan of the quad grew louder as they traveled parallel to the path. Rachel would recognize that motor anywhere. One didn't ride for hours on a machine and not become intimate with the ticks and knocks of the engine. The faster, rounded out putt suggested the four-wheeler was in gear but not rolling. Were they being watched?

She shot a look around the forest. Nothing stood out. Oh, if only Andy were there, he'd grab her hand and hold on. No, wait, he would have made her stay with the kids. He had a protective side.

Rachel didn't know Josh well enough to reach out and hang onto his hand for dear life. He'd probably spook, if she did that. And what man wouldn't? She was now a single woman with three kids. That was worse than a ball and chain, it was more like a ball and dungeon. But still, the comfort of not feeling alone would be nice.

Shaking the longing for Andy's companionship away, Rachel stopped beside Josh, aware of his proximity in inches not feet. She pulled a leaf out of her field of view. The quad sat no more than ten feet away, revving into a small Aspen sapling which held it in place. Slumped over the handlebars, the driver was either dead, passed out, inebriated or playing possum. Rachel didn't care which one. She wanted her quad back and the risk eliminated.

Josh pressed on her shoulder with his hand and raised questioning eyebrows her way. Was he asking if it was okay for him to check it out? She nodded.

He slid from behind the bush and swiveled his head to encompass the area with his gaze. What would she do if he was attacked? Fight to free him of course, a small piece of her owed him something and Rachel didn't know if she could abandon him. On the balls of her feet, ready to run or spring a counterattack, she allowed the shallowest of air to pass her lips. She pulled her gun and held it, ready to fire if the man became a threat.

Josh closed the distance to the quad. His gun appeared in his hand, like magic. One step, two… he looked around ready to flee the opposite direction. Three, four, five… he waited again, watching the prone man on the machine. Tossing another look around the clearing, six, seven and eight disappeared beneath him. A foot away from the man, Josh reached out and poked his shoulder with the barrel of his gun.

Nothing. Flesh barely recoiled back into position, wiggled like ill-made gelatin under the black and brown shirt. Josh pushed harder and the body gave in to the weight unanchored to the ATV, sliding to the ground in a graceless heap. An arm and leg overlapped and the head lay at an unnatural position.

Josh knelt down and felt for a pulse.

"There's no way he's alive." Rachel left the confines of the brush. Relief relaxing her grip on the butt of the gun. "Looks like he smashed into something before driving. That little tree couldn't have done this."

Standing, Josh brushed his hands on his pants. "He could have fractured his neck in the crash but something completed the break. I've seen that before." He glanced once more at the fallen man. "He doesn't look Japanese, huh." The blond hair was most likely accompanied by blue eyes which were hidden behind closed and swollen eyelids. His size was more German than Japanese.

Rachel nodded. Germany was supposed to be an ally. As was most of Europe. Russia didn't count as an option since it had rolled into the USSR and what was left had become nothing more than a front for some people hoping to hold onto their patriotism. Great Britain? Australia? Who in their right mind would send a plane marked like Japanese property over the wilds of America? During an attack…

Having worked with Europeans, Rachel knew they had different values from Americans. They feared different things.

But did America have something foreigners feared enough to attack?

She didn't know and at the moment she didn't care. Rachel wanted her kids and to be in the relative safety of her new home. At that point, who could she trust? Maybe people of ethnicity, but how would she know who was American and who wasn't before she shot them?

Alone in the cave, Cole, Kayli and Beau waited for her, probably worried. Spinning on her heel, the thick soles of her boots crunched like bone-on-bone with her weight, like the sounds the man's neck would have made when it snapped. Goosebumps rose on her skin. There wasn't a cool breeze to be had.

Getting to the overhang seemed to take forever and a day. She couldn't get there fast enough. In reality, she hadn't been gone more than a handful of minutes, but they dragged out longer than if she'd had her hand on a hot frying pan.

The sharp peaks of the leaves scratched her hands, pricking her fingertips as she shoved the bush away. She swallowed a flood of desperation before she smiled. "Okay, guys, let's go. We got our quad back. You don't have to walk anymore." Relieving Cole of Beau's weight, Rachel mommy-ducked the kids to the clearing. Before entering the circular opening of the path, Rachel stumbled.

She'd forgotten about the traumatizing effect a dead body would have on kids. Already she was desensitizing to the traumas in the world. It wouldn't be healthy for the children to see the body, but the faster they got back to their place the better off they'd all be.

Rachel paused. What should she do? Kayli and Cole, directly behind her, couldn't see anything. Rachel searched the area for the body. Nothing. No quad. No body. No Josh. What the heck was going on? Rachel slowed her hurried pace. "Should be there in a minute, guys." If she scanned the area any faster, she'd be in danger of whiplash.

A soft whistle caught her attention. Josh waved toward him, nodding his head slightly in the direction of the bush where they'd hid before discovering the thief. He stood by the trailer of the quad.

Rachel searched his face as the kids climbed in the padded wagon. Josh didn't look directly at her, but nodded his head. He'd dumped the body behind the brush. Well, at least her kids hadn't seen it. He'd been thoughtful in that regard, discarding the dead. She wondered if he had experience doing that. If the situation hadn't been so fresh, Rachel might have laughed. What electrical engineer had experience dealing with a situation like the one they'd crammed themselves into?

Most electrical engineers had glasses on their noses and a part down the center of their thinning hair. Josh was on the opposite scale with his muscular frame and tight jaw line. He looked like he'd be more comfortable wielding an axe than pushing buttons on a calculator.

Odd how they'd mashed together and synced so well. They almost completed each other's tasks. She and Andy had taken nine years to get to that point.

~

The washcloth hung limp beside the towels already clipped to the clothes line Andy had strung up the summer before. Losing herself in menial chores helped stave off the pain of grieving. She didn't want to deal with it until things had settled down and they had more information which could be indefinitely. She was fine with that.

"Rachel!" Josh padded into her front yard, the hair on his forearms glinting in the sun.

Front yard had a nicer ring to it than clearing. She wasn't camping for crying out loud. At least she was trying not to feel like she was. "Hey, Josh." The next article was a pair of her panties. *Uh, right.* She shoved the lacy whites underneath the pile of pants and grabbed jeans. Reaching her arms up, she clipped the clothespin in place and glanced his way. Tension tightened the skin around his eyes. She dropped her hands. "What is it?"

Josh stopped in front of her and steadied his breathing. "Someone is at the dead end of the road. Every few minutes they call out your name."

And that was not what she'd expected. "My name?" She glanced in the direction of the road. "What does that mean?"

"It means, if you don't want them to start looking for you and maybe finding you, you might want to head out and meet them. I'll stay with the kids."

"What if they want to hurt me?" Rachel kicked the laundry basket. Of course, she'd go. She couldn't risk the kids.

"If they want to hurt you, use that cannon you've got in your belt." He arched his eyebrow.

Rachel's laughter spilled from her mouth, not the first time she'd laughed in the last two days since returning from the plane site. Josh had shown up whenever he'd wanted and had stayed for a few meals. The kids had liked the stories of what their dad had been like young and single. Rachel had enjoyed his company, but found herself stopping what she was doing throughout the day and watching the doorway, looking for Andy. Or Josh. For some reason she was mixing them up.

Smoothing her hair with her fingers, Rachel didn't know how to approach the stranger. Hostile? Hospitable? She settled on scoping out the situation first. Cole watched her from the window as she walked to the forest. Confidence for the kids on the outside, what-the-heck scrawling across her insides.

Each step was carefully placed. Turn here, twist there.

"Raaaachelllll!"

She jumped, ready to run back to her cabin. But the voice wasn't threatening or even very old and had a tone she recognized from what seemed a lifetime ago.

She inched closer to the edge of the clearing. Green leaves covered her view of the exact center of the end of the road. Hunching under the low hanging bull pine branches, Rachel scratched the back of her neck.

Red abrasions covered his left arm and face. He wasn't old enough to vote but to get all the way out there alone testified of his capabilities. He must have conquered his fears. She hadn't seen him in a while.

Rachel didn't move. Tom had made it that far, he could figure out what to do without her help. She'd never told him how to get to the cabin, or even that she had a place out in the forest. Three kids depended on her. Pulling a lost chick from the rubble might break her.

She'd almost convinced her heart not to care when the man-boy slumped to the ground and shoved his battered face in his hands. Sobs rolled over the matted grass and hard packed dirt, amplified by the startling quiet of the forest.

The memory of his first visit to her office crashed in around her. Pregnant with Beau, she hadn't stood but called out for him to come in. A waif of a boy. She'd eyed the fast food bag on her desk, maternal instincts begging her to force him to eat her lunch. He'd sat in her chair, the cushy one Cole jumped in when he visited.

Something different about that boy. He'd been melancholy mixed with an aura of skittishness. Every move like a second thought. The boy-Tom had stared at the edge of her desk and he'd picked at a cuticle.

Rachel had flipped through his file. The fries had driven her nuts. He didn't move a muscle but the finger picking, picking. Pick. Pick. "I have some fries here, would you like to help me eat them?"

The young face had crumpled, tears poured down his face. Fear. She recognized the emotion. She'd taught the emotion. Crying males had always been her downfall.

Tom had become a favorite. She'd cried when he no longer needed her services.

Despair and sniffles covered the sound of her cautious steps as she approached him. Mud and charcoal matted his hair into clumps. His shoulders would be broad once they filled out. Poor Tom was between gawky adolescence and masculine grace.

Rachel knelt beside him. "Tom. I'm here. What's going on? How did you get here? Are you okay?"

He fell on his butt and scuttled backward a few yards. "Wha — Rachel? I – I mean, Dr. Parker. You look like... Brenda." Tom hiccupped, his breath rushing in and out with each gasp.

What... "Brenda? When did you meet my sister?"

"Briefly. She didn't make it. We were attacked. I don't know if she's still alive or what. They got Jenny, too." His voice caught on the name and he dropped his head to his hand. "I have no idea how I made it without being captured, Dr. Parker."

Rachel's survival mode flashed her gaze around the clearing and down the road. Wind whispered to move and move fast. "Come on, we need to go." She clutched the handle on his backpack and pulled at his bicep. He stumbled behind her, falling to the moss covered ground behind the protection of the bushes. Rachel clapped her hand over his mouth.

Alarm widened the boy's eyes and he struggled with little effort. Rachel pressed her free finger against her lips. Turning from his stilled form, she watched the road, her hand still covering his mouth. What was it? Something... maybe she'd imagined the danger. But a tremor... something stirred in the air. Paranoia wouldn't create the sensation, fear would, but...

A rumble answered her doubt, shaking the ground with large throaty vibrations. A black Hummer crawled into the small circle, minimizing the area further. The tank-like vehicle stopped where Rachel and the boy had sat moments before.

Tom whimpered against her hand. Real fear diminished him to the boy he'd been in her office. Dammit. Whatever was happening out *there* was tearing apart her children. And Tom was one of her "children". She smoothed her hand across his brow and turned her attention to the clearing.

The afternoon sun failed to penetrate the dense leaves lining the periphery. A man stepped from the passenger seat dressed to match the imposing vehicle in sleek lines and crisp cuts. Kneeling, he fingered broken grass in a sea of crushed blades. His dark glasses, cliché with his dark suit, blond hair and government appearing HumVee, reflected the afternoon sun, hornet eyes searching for fresh meat. Like a cloud crossed before the sun, he'd dimmed the spring cheeriness of the woods.

Rachel strained her ears for any sound that would give away the location of her kids. Above all else, they had to be protected. Dang it, she'd been so stupid. She failed to learn. Somehow the men had found them. No one would chase a woman with a few kids. Tom might be the prey, but so young? How much damage could he do?

The man swooshed his arm to encompass the clearing and three clones with different hair colors poured from the vehicle with long electronic wands. Choreographed down to each step, the men peeled from each other to sweep the length of the wands up and down the wall of foliage. High pitched beeping shattered any remaining peaceful ambience the forest held.

Mouth close to the boy's ear, Rachel whispered, "We need to move back about twenty feet. Those are Motion Sensor Prods, MSPs. They'll be by us any second. Can you move?"

He nodded. She removed her hand from his mouth. Rachel couldn't chance returning to the cabin.

Low to the ground, Rachel led the boy behind a large fallen log. The roots reached toward the sky as if salvation lay in the clouds. She clenched her fingers into the crumbling, rotting wood.

Slumped against the trunk, Tom didn't try to see what was going on. Rachel had all but carried him and if it hadn't been for the high screeching, their cover would be blown. If they swept over her spot and she moved even a fraction, the probes would combine her heat, motion and density with wind speed and, using an advanced logarithm, calculate the likelihood of her being human versus, well, not. She'd seen tests during a few site consultations the fall before Rhode Island. The MSPs had been amazing then, imagine what technological advances had been made in almost three years. Could it locate the motion of air now?

Unable to just sit there and not have an idea of what to expect, Rachel needed coverage. The two men closest to her position were sweeping fast and closing in on each other. They'd meet right at the spot she and Tom had darted through the leaves.

A sudden breeze pushed dangling roots across her hand. Of course. Rachel ducked behind the conglomeration of thick and thin roots decorating the end of the tree, higher and larger than the bushes she and Tom had hidden behind. Acting like the foliage around the perimeter, the roots were easy to catch glimpses through when you were close to them, see through the holes and spaces between, but put some distance between the eyes and the coverage and it was difficult to differentiate anything but the roots. The ultrasonic waves from the sweepers would be unable to filter past the varying lengths and sizes and would skim over the information.

Rachel breathed through her nose to direct her air down. From her mouth, the breathing might move the roots and she didn't want to take the chance the movement would be picked up. Beep, beep, beep. Her heart pounded with the machines noise. She ignored the prostrate form beside her. He'd passed out.

Beep. Black boots moved closer. Feet, the only thing visible from under the bushes, combined with the image of the roots. Stepping in a weird two-step, down-up, down-up, nearer and nearer to Rachel. Down-up.

Movement distracted her from the approaching probes. Josh waved his arms fifty feet from her tree. What the crap? If he was here, where were her kids? She'd kill him – if he didn't get trounced by the men in black. He pointed toward her, at the threats and in the direction of the house. What? She couldn't move. The sweepers had reached her position. She froze. Shallow breaths. Short. If they didn't find anyone, would they search deeper? *Oh, hell, what if they found her?*

The screeching stopped. "Nothing's registering." The faceless voice barked.

A voice further away, closer to the SUV snapped through the cover. "Are you sure he came this way? Nothing is on the maps."

First voice, again, answered slower with hesitation. "No. I'm not."

A plunk like a dart shot from a tube. In the clearing, the man to Rachel's left fell to the ground. "Be certain." Clipped words from the second voice plunged Rachel into an icy sweat. He'd killed his man. Because he wasn't sure. Of all things holy, what had she gotten herself into? "You better be certain we get enough information from the people at the holding center."

Clenching her eyes shut, Rachel shoved her hands over her ears. *Wake up, you're at home. Wake up, you're at home. Nothing bad has happened. You're going to the grocery store with the kids today. Andy's beside you, holding your hand. The bed is soft and warm. What should you make for breakfast? Sausage, eggs, toast and hashbrowns. Lots of ketchup. Milk. Maybe orange juice. Do the laundry. Fold, put away. Help the kids clean their room. Andy and his projects.*

Someone pulled her hand from her ear. She gasped, jerked from escape.

Josh gazed down at her. "They're gone. We need to get back."

Rachel nodded and stood. She wasn't home. Andy wasn't alive. Her kids needed her. But the imagery had allowed her a small break. Her psych degrees were more useful than she'd realized. And she'd found something to fear. Maybe she was human.

Tom flopped in Josh's arms like a large ragdoll.

Josh sped through the forest away from the cabin. Around and around they went, stopping every three minutes or so to rest. Picking up on their mad dash into nowhere. After what seemed like years of maneuvering, they broke into the area from the north.

The setup from a different viewpoint surprised her. Everything was under cover of trees. She'd never noticed the clothing line had been strung up between two tall trees whose bows swept out to cover any clothing item she might hang. The raised gardens weren't made from wood, which when she approached from the incline coming down into the clearing looked like mole hills and had a random appearance.

Part of the house incorporated a large evergreen as a cornerstone and from the higher angle, not a window or door could be seen. Andy's brilliance at disguising the place captured Rachel's breath. The grieving process would be hard to begin when she couldn't decide if she was impressed with Andy's brilliance or angry for his constant generosity which ultimately killed him.

"Where are the kids?" Words she had forced down until they'd reached relative safety rushed from her. She swallowed. "Why'd you leave them?"

"I couldn't let you go alone. You may have a gun, but you mean too much to people here." Josh tilted his head to the house. "I tucked your kids into the master. Cole's in charge."

Heat infused Rachel's face. "Did you put up the laundry?" Her panties moved in the breeze. Trite question considering the situation, but at the same time her underwear winked at her. He didn't have any right pawing her undergarments.

He nodded, his gaze intent on her face. "I'm sorry. I was just trying to help." He didn't even have the grace to blush. Her panties!

Rachel's hands shook. Breathe. She stepped to the house, lowering her chin. "I know. Thank you. I just, well, I'm freaking out and you... well," where had her control gone? He spun her clothes onto a line and had to come rescue her from a situation she'd had under her thumb? Okay, maybe not that well in place, but she'd have snapped out of it eventually and made it back. Josh wasn't her husband.

Anger coursed through her. And to be fair, it wasn't Josh she was mad at. Andy was the target, but guilt was keeping her from acknowledging that to anyone but her spleen. Josh would have to do for the time being. She had to be mad, had to have an outlet for the adrenaline trying to get out of her nerve endings. She'd be in a fairer frame of mind, if she could get a moment free from the craziness swamping her world.

She motioned Josh into the front room of the cabin.

Rachel wrung a washcloth out and moved to wipe at Tom's forehead. Filthy and torn, his clothes had quality written all over them in subtle labels and tight stitching. Name brand sneakers minus a shoelace had lost their luster.

Cole peeked around the corner. "Mom, can we come out?"

"Yes, I'm sorry. Come out but stay inside. I'm not sure what's going on out there, but it isn't good." Danger was in the details. As long as they didn't have details, they wouldn't know they should be frightened. Rachel didn't know why fear gripped her, she just recognized its hold.

Josh stood beside her. "Do you think he'll be okay?"

"I'm not a medical doctor or a nurse, but it looks like he might be dehydrated, hungry, and tired. We'll let him rest and then we can talk to him." Rachel had never mentioned Brenda to Tom. He'd known her at least long enough to recognize the strong likeness between them.

~

Rachel waved to her kids and Josh in the clearing. "I'll be right back. I'm going to the top." She motioned toward the hill where the back of the house exited. Josh nodded and pulled Kayli and Beau out of their skirmish. Rachel couldn't focus on the fight and all but ran to the crest.

She reached the rock and threw herself to the bed of wild flowers at its base. And let her tears flow. And the wails wring from her body. She lost it. All her control.

The psyche games of recitation had no effectiveness. She'd tried, she had. All her training in psychology had focused on the control of fear, whether it was there or just a possibility, in dreams and consciousness, and she'd all but ignored the other mentality components. Grief. That was one she wished she'd covered, maybe as a minor degree.

No amount of psychology tricks would bring her husband back. Her children's father. She had nothing to hold on to. Her rock was gone. She sobbed his name, calling for him in the woods where he'd planned so much for them. "Andy." The world was falling apart and she had nothing. How was she supposed to stay strong for her children when he was gone?

Fear was one thing. Loss was another. She didn't realize she'd need to learn about one to understand the other. Her stomach and heart seemed to switch places. She hurt so bad. Her best friend was gone.

And where had Josh come from? She got it, the past, but Andy had put Josh in the area where she and the kids would be...

Andy knew she had nearly chosen Josh. What was he thinking? Had he been thinking? Or maybe he was secure enough in their relationship, he didn't worry about it?

She didn't dare think about her sister's plight. If she ignored it for the moment, maybe she'd harbor hope that someone in her life had made it. The possibility of Brenda's survival stopped her gasps and wails.

The pain receded enough to allow the thought of Tom Mason through. When he was younger, Tom struck her as tightly controlled. He reminded her a bit of herself. How he'd managed to make it to the woods testified of his strength of character.

They had to put the pieces of the puzzle together. Andy... she'd grieve for him better at a later time. But the pressure in her chest was lessened. She'd have a bit more stability when Andy's death sunk in for her kids and their grief culminated.

Rachel pushed off the ground and stood, brushing the broken blades of grass and pine needles clinging to her clothes. She had a patient to check on.

~

"Excuse me, Dr. Parker?" Tom had grown and his height had been hidden by his slumping. He stood an easy six inches above her.

Rachel tilted her head back. "Are you feeling better?"

"I am, ma'am. Can I use your bathroom?" He shuffled his feet.

Rachel pushed the chair away from the table. Leading him into the bathroom, she pointed at the shower stall. "Afterwards, feel free to take a shower. Everything you'll need is in the cabinet. I'll get some food."

She was dying for answers. Impatience could have been her motto, but she left Tom to his own devices. Who knew when he'd last had the chance to feel human. She'd grill him over dinner. His emotional controls had been food and drink. She'd need time to figure out his triggers. They changed as people grew.

A candle offered dim warmth. She and the kids had lined the windows with foil to block escaping light at night. Whoever the men searched for, they weren't looking for someone to shop with.

Shivering, Rachel wondered what animal would eat the dead body in the clearing. Northern Idaho wasn't short on wild predators, human or otherwise. She stirred the spicy, sweet anti-chili. Hers and Andy's recipe. They'd tasted it together over the years and made it better, spicier, chunkier with tomatoes and burger, green peppers and onions. Honey.

Water ran in the bathroom.

A toothpick pulled cleanly out of the cornbread in the oven.

The water shut off.

Rachel set the pottery dish on the table. At the door she hollered to the kids and they rushed into the room.

"Mom, I didn't think we were ever going to eat." Beau slapped the table and wiped his cheek. "Josh has been waiting all afternoon, too." He waved to the door and sighed.

"Josh? I didn't know he was outside. When did he get here?" She wiped her hands on a towel and waited for Beau's answer with a hand on her hip.

"About noon. Is your guest awake?" Josh stepped through the door and nodded toward the back of the cabin.

Rachel jumped. When would she get used to him popping up? "You have a bad habit of surprising me." She arched her brow. "He is. He'll be out in a minute."

The door opened to the bathroom. Cleaned up, hair brushed from his face, Tom could have been the kid next door who ran cross-country and waved each time he passed her house. He'd exchanged his dirty clothes for a fresh set and lost the shaky edge in his gaze from fatigue.

"Better?" Rachel glanced at her kids, careful not to stare at the changes in the man she'd known as a kid.

"Yes, thank you." He leaned forward, extending his hand to Josh. "I'm Tom Mason. Nice to meet you."

Where had she heard that before? Something in his tone when he said Tom Mason… he said it the same way as — "Were you the kid on the radio?"

He blushed. "You heard me? I didn't think anyone would."

"We didn't know what was going on until we heard your report. I didn't recognize your voice right away, it's been a while. I do better with faces." Rachel slid into her chair. "Sit down. We're just about to eat. Are you hungry?"

The mention of food widened his eyes. Tom rushed into the chair before Rachel could suggest where he sit. Hungry boy. "Where are your parents?" She scooped the aromatic soup into a bowl and set it before her guest. Subsequent dishes for the rest of them followed by corn bread and butter settled into place on the table.

Silence clouded the room. Rachel reached across her bowl and rested her hand on his shoulder. Ducking her head, she said, "I'm sorry. This isn't easy. When you've had some food, we'll talk." Pushing off the inevitable wouldn't help him, but Rachel didn't know if she could bear the thought of more loss, more pain. His mom had been funny and Rachel had enjoyed speaking with her. How much terror and trauma was ripping lives apart outside the protection of her woods? Inside?

How soon would the men in black come to find them? Would they? Would Brenda be okay? Or was she lost for good? She shoved her anxiety into a corner of her mind already full of other concerns and waved for everyone to eat. Questions tried to run from her mouth but she shoveled food in to block their escape.

Tom closed his eyes with his first bite. His comfort items. Food. Rachel glanced at Josh, glad to share the moment of helping another with someone. Lines at the corners of his eyes deepened with his smile. She broke eye contact and looked into her bowl where Andy's face watched her from the liquid.

Guilt adjusted the taste of the cornbread to a cement-like mass. Andy hadn't been gone long and already she was comforted by his best-friend's friendship. Friendship, nothing more, but still he was another man sitting in Andy's seat, smiling over Andy's favorite dinner. Okay, not his favorite, but one he liked a lot.

Rachel sighed and almost missed Tom's first words. "They're after me. I don't know why. I think my friends were killed a few months ago, but I'm not sure. I got away and saved Jenny from being shot and broke into your house and found Brenda. But I brought danger to them and now I don't know where they are or what I've done. I have no idea if my parents are alive, no idea if I can go home." He sniffed, his chin tucked to his chest. "I got Jenny kidnapped."

"Who's Jenny?" Rachel's throat tightened, cutting off the comfort she longed to give him. He was broken and so young. What could she say? What could she do?

"A girl from school. But I ran into her when the men chased me into the campground. Her friends were shot." He swallowed. The look in his eyes suggested she was more than "just a girl from school", but Rachel left it for later.

She covered her mouth with her hand. What the hell was going on when teenagers were shot in a family campground? "I'm sorry. I'm glad you escaped. Here, have some honey on your cornbread."

He raised tear-filled eyes to hers. "I'm sorry I broke into your house. We needed a place to hide and some food." Tom's gaze found his anti-chili once more and he mumbled, "Thought maybe if I saw you were okay, maybe you would be able to help."

"If I can help, I will." She brushed his hand with hers. "You don't have to be the adult anymore, Tom. Let Josh and I worry about the big things, okay?" How sweet that he was worried about breaking into her home. Her heart double-thumped with compassion for him. "Tom, listen. None of this is your fault. And I'm glad you got into the house. It means it's not being wasted by fire or something worse. I'm glad you met Brenda. I was worried about her. Now, you said they got Jenny *and* Brenda?"

He nodded, mid-scoop. "I don't know how they found us. But they did when we got to your house."

Rachel sipped her water to steady her nerves. Her sister. *Damn it, Brenda, you never did know when to do what you were told. Come to the property, not my house.* But was he certain they were after *him*? It wouldn't be the first time foreigners had searched her out.

She glanced at Josh over the rim of her glass. He watched Tom with kindness, no rancor or distrust on his face. Lowering the cup to the table, she peeked at her kids. Cole was the only one interested in what Tom said. Kayli and Beau picked at the cornbread with their forks, looking for more honey she hadn't stored enough of.

"What happened? Can you walk me through when you were discovered?" The truth would be hard to hear, but Rachel needed the information so she could formulate a plan.

He swallowed and cleared his throat. "Brenda said she saw something outside. We looked and nothing was there. She told us about this place, general stuff, and then yelled for us to run. They tear-gassed us, I think. I was the closest to the stairs, to the door, but it banged open and people were there, so I ran upstairs to the bedrooms. The girls were... screaming..." he swallowed again, his words working against him, "Someone yelled... something... I couldn't understand the language they used. I jumped out the master bedroom window onto a van parked in the driveway. Lights flashed in the house. The electricity went out again and the street light turned off. I jogged into the field across the street and watched from behind an abandoned barrel while they took the girls and left."

Shaky words matched the quiver in his hand. "A helicopter flooded the area with lights. I ran to Coeur d'Alene."

"You ran all the way to Coeur d'Alene?" Rachel dropped her spoon in her bowl. Awe laced her words. "That's like ten miles or so."

"Yeah."

"The Tom I remember didn't like anything that had to do with physical exertion. That's pretty far."

"Survival. I had to train myself to run." Another bite down. He left his story there. Rachel didn't want to know more at the moment. They'd carted off her sister and for what? Hopefully it had nothing to do with Rachel.

The group ate without talking. Spoons clinked on dishware and the occasional slurp from a cup broke the silence. Rachel didn't want to say anything. If she spoke, the tears would be loosed and hysteria would control her actions. She could hold it together. Besides, her kids were safe, right?

Okay, she'd lost her husband at a very early age and at the beginning of something terrible and the end of something lovely.

Why was this happening *now*? America had already had the crap kicked out of it with a maelstrom of natural disasters, why would another country cut them when they were down? Was the world against them?

Rachel's specialty was behavioral and causal psychology. She had multiple minors in abnormal psychologies, criminal interrogation and chemistry - biological, organic and inorganic. Instead of sciences, she should have focused on law and international affairs. Nothing made sense.

Empty, her bowl refused to release her gaze. She wanted to cry. Hard. But she needed to be strong for her kids. For Tom. But who was strong for her? Involuntarily, her gaze rose to meet Josh's.

He watched her with sympathy softening the lines around his lips and tilting his eyes down at the corners.

Suddenly, she was angry. She didn't want his pity. Rachel could do anything – anything! How dare he feel bad. Who did he think he was?

Rachel gave herself a mental shake. The anger was natural, good even, but counterproductive when pointed in the direction it wasn't meant to go. And where was it supposed to go? Certainly not toward her children, Josh or the orphaned teenager at her table.

She needed some perspective. "I have cookies, would you like some?" Rachel stood and removed the empty bowls.

Tom stood as well, picking up the plates and glasses. He followed Rachel into the kitchen and placed the dishes in the sink. "Thank you for dinner. I didn't realize how hungry I was."

"How long have you been trying to get here?" She welcomed a distraction from the route her thoughts traveled. Cookies stored in the pantry with milk were the perfect treat after the chili's spicy heat.

"Since your house? Over twenty-four hours, I think. It'd been a couple days since I'd slept."

"What can we do? I refuse to sit here and do nothing for Brenda and your friend. I can't." She spun to Josh. "I don't expect you to help, she's my sister, but I can't just sit here, protected from the hell out there." She waved her hand toward the window.

Josh turned his eyes toward Tom. "Do you have an idea of where they'd hold them?"

"No." Tom hung his head. The moment reeked of disappointment. He snapped his head up and gasped. "But I'm a member of ARRL and I have my portable radio in the pack."

"ARRL?" Rachel hated acronyms. *Just say it, already.*

"Amateur Radio Relay League. We have a few local leagues in the area but overall we work together during emergencies. We've never had anything of this magnitude," Tom snapped his fingers, "but when the earthquake took out Oregon all the way to Corvallis, we were able to get word to those further inland because of the ham radio connection. They work worldwide. We can even send files. Maybe there's someone out there who knows what's going on."

"Ham radio?" Rachel scrunched her nose. "Isn't that a hobby? I remember your dad was into that."

Josh laughed. "It's called amateur for a reason, Rachel. I'm game. In fact, Tom, I have a radio set up at my place. I meant to get lessons and figure out the jargon, but time didn't allow. You're welcome to try mine if you think you'd have more luck with a stationary setup."

Tom nodded. "Thanks. I could set up the portable I have in the field out there, but it needs a satellite and they pass overhead only every twelve hours. If I have to wait, it could take a day or two to track them. How high up is your station?"

"High."

"We can sure give it a shot." Tom squinted. "It'd shorten the searching."

"We'll go first thing. If we find where they're keeping Brenda, we'll see if we can get her out." Josh's confidence comforted the turmoil in Rachel's heart. Strength, which he had, would fix the problem. At least he promised they'd try. Made the biggest difference. Of course he'd never mentioned what they'd do, if Brenda wasn't being held… alive.

"Mom, I could help."

Rachel snapped her gaze to Cole. Angles were emerging through the meat of adolescence and the solid set of his jaw and slight downturn of his eyes hinted at Andy more strongly than ever before. His fourteen years had matured more in a couple of hellish days than the crap he'd endured at high school.

"Cole." Rachel moved to the table and sat down. She looked into eyes that could have been her husband's. "I know you can help.

I get that. But, Cole, I need you to be safe, more than I need Brenda home. Do you understand that?"

He nodded but looked away.

Who didn't want to be effective in scary times? Brenda was his aunt, his only aunt, but Cole was Rachel's only Cole. The only one. Her first born and she'd be damned if she'd sit by while he went off to find more trouble in a setting she didn't understand. It was one thing to face the world with all its temptations and trials, but something entirely different to face an entity that wanted to obliterate you from the earth. Cole would stay there. Her kids would be safe. No matter what.

Crap. Her ego was getting in the way again.

Josh cleared his throat. "Cole, that's awesome. But we're not even sure we can find her. Let's cross that bridge when we come to it. We might be facing an empty town out there. We don't know." He looked at Tom. "Unless of course you can remember anything we could use?"

"I remember a lot. But it isn't pretty."

Chapter 11

Brenda

Moans echoed from the paneled ceiling. Brenda moved her arms where she sat, testing for soreness. She and Jenny had fallen down the stairs at the house, landing on the men swarming into the front door. Hard. She couldn't have run, even if she hadn't tumbled down twelve steps into captivity.

Stagnant air pressed heavily on her limbs. Or maybe that was the person leaning against her. Little light penetrated the deep viscosity of the room. A high school gym? Squeaks echoed as people shuffled around, reminding Brenda of a Girl Scout sleepover long ago in junior high.

She must have a small concussion. Focusing was next to impossible. Careful not to jar any potential injuries, Brenda turned her head and glanced down at the young girl leaning on her arm. She recognized her, but from where? Pushing through the haze thickening with each throb of her pulse, the name... *Jamie? Jessie? Jenny? Jenny, that's it. Jenny. But where... Ah, Rachel's. Hopefully, Rachel was safe.*

The smell of burnt flesh curdled in the back of her throat. Her stomach growled in spite of the nauseating odor. When she'd left orthopedic surgery, she'd sworn to never endure that scent again. But fate, it seemed, hated her. And her nursing side was unable to sit still while sounds of pain wracked the closed in building.

Easing from beneath Jenny's head, she set the sleeping girl onto the ground where Brenda had sat. Brenda stood and stretched, noting any discomfort or twinges. Collections of people bundled together like bunches of grapes, ripe for the picking.

A partially hung banner declared the gym as the home of the "Fighting Trojans". So they were in Post Falls, Idaho in the high school which meant they'd been captured and taken to a cattle roundup while Spokane continued to burn across the state line in Washington.

How long would people survive the horrors being committed?

Brenda's dry lips itched. They'd crack soon and she didn't have any Chapstick. But her lips weren't giving off the burned flesh smell.

The clusters of people gave wide berth from a pile in the corner. Few flies hovered, but if whatever wound wasn't treated soon, there would be plenty more. Glancing once more at Jenny who hadn't stirred, Brenda picked her way over the sea of limbs and torsos to the corner. The smell increased, mixing with the smell of unwashed bodies.

Her eyes watered. Breathing through her mouth seemed the only logical way to keep from passing out. She slowed. Did she really want to help? She wasn't getting paid. The person was most likely dead anyway. What did she care about helping anyone? No one was checking on her. But still she pressed forward, stretching her hand out as she leaned forward. As much as she faked heartlessness, she'd never pull it off.

Charred strips of clothing camouflaged a pink mass below. She stumbled, her foot pushing the person's leg and causing a moan. *Oh, no.* "I'm sorry, are you okay?"

No answer. Of course, why would they answer such a ridiculous question. She knelt down beside the body and, with care, pulled the damp shirt, musty with sweat and stained red with blood, from the main part of the head, revealing a disfigured ear and the first half of a face. Brenda gasped, clenching her fingers.

"Andy?"

The man moaned. Brenda had never been so glad to see her brother-in-law in her life. "Andy, can you hear me?" Shaky, he nodded and struggled to sit up. Brenda slid her arm under his ribs and he squeaked. "Oh, I'm sorry. Are you that bad all over?"

Infection. Check for infection but there wasn't enough light. If she could get the wounds exposed, the flies might be able to lay eggs in any raw or necrotic tissue. It might be the only chance he had at survival. The filth of the other prisoners, at least in the dark, belied any suggestion of being treated well.

She had to figure out how to fix him. Brenda needed Andy, but not as much as he needed her.

His lips moved and a small sigh escaped. Brenda leaned closer, careful not to touch any part of him. The burns had no known limit and Brenda would be damned if she'd peel off anymore of his delicate skin. Delicate? She'd never attributed fragility to Andy. Big bad Andy.

"What'd you say?"

A whisper pushed past his lips. "Rach…"

"Oh, Rachel. I don't know where she is. I'm kind of glad she's not with you." She glanced over her shoulder, but turned back quickly. "How'd you end up in the fire? Why aren't they with you? I went to your house, and met up with some kids who'd broken in."

Andy smacked his lips like he searched for water, but came up dry. He had to be in serious pain. Rachel could barely make out his features, let alone the varying degrees of burn damage. She'd have to see clearly in order to pick at any crispy parts that had to come off. Maggots couldn't eat burned tissue with their soft mandibles and the small creatures were Brenda's only option for staving off infectious processes.

"I'm sorry, I don't have any water. Is there a part that hurts more than any other?" She swallowed.

He shook his head. "Can. I. Sit." He fought for control of muscles in his arms and legs that visibly spasmed and shook. Andy's condition was harder for Brenda to see than the pain and despair spread over the room like tar on a road.

"I'll put my hand under your arm, yeah, like that, and scoot you, yeah, like that. Okay. All set." He still resembled a pile of burned rags, but at least his head was above his heart which lessened the shock to coherent thought processes.

What she desperately needed included clean, boiling water, linens, thread, and gauze. Even iodine would be fantastic. And what she wouldn't trade for some Lidocaine and Marcaine.

Rachel moved her hand to Andy's top shirt. He stopped her with fingers on her arm. The damage free flesh surprised her and she froze. Maybe all of him wasn't hurt. That would make the debridement easier. She looked into his face.

Blisters, some popped and oozing clear fluid reflected the minuscule light seeping from the Plexiglas along the side walls. Bumps and swollen areas disfigured his face, but the slant of his forehead and angle of his nose were distinctly Andy and the burns couldn't hide that. Maybe the fire had burned away some of his ego, too.

Brenda sighed. Even during desperate times, she was still catty toward him and she had no right. Sensitivity. She needed to be more caring toward others. Taking care of the physical needs didn't constitute bedside manner. She'd been called in to the supervisor's office a few days before her trip south and reprimanded for her brisk manner.

She preferred to be called cynical. Brisk was rather mild. "Andy, I can't do much for you until I figure out what's going on. Can you wait here?" Brenda took his moan as agreement. There wasn't much else it could be. What would he do, say no? Then what? Hold her down and make her cough up morphine for his pain? He could barely breathe, let alone lift a hand.

Patting the ground next to him instead of his arm or shoulder – she had no idea what was burned and what wasn't – Brenda stood and turned to face the overwhelmingly large gymnasium. Packed. People were everywhere. Who held them? Maybe if she figured that out, she'd understand their circumstances a little more. Although attacking already devastated people gave quite a bit away on character and the possibilities were grim.

Brenda's chest hurt. Her sister was gone. Her brother-in-law was injured to a level she'd never seen before. And her niece and nephews... Tears threatened but she shoved them away. Stalwart, she tugged her professionalism around her and became Nurse Brenda, boss of the floor and hell to pay should any doctor or patient get in her way.

Captives to the right didn't move, Jenny somewhere in the tangled mass. To the left, moaning and squirming people appeared to be in more pain. Brenda squared her shoulders. She could do this. Triage would be the name of the game and she'd use what she had nearby.

Feet from the halo segregating Andy and the crowd, a trio clutched hands, eyes closed as if in prayer. Brenda's muscles ached. The more she moved the worse she felt. But she'd get through the room or fall down, only to get back up. If she didn't focus on something besides what was going on, she'd slip into insanity.

She approached the threesome and addressed the taller male. Soot and dirt disguised his skin color and red shot eyes peered from under a broken Mariner's brim. "Is everyone okay here? I'm a nurse. Do you need me to look at any wounds?"

He shook his head, casting his eyes down. A small woman turned her tear-streaked face to Brenda, her words audible if Brenda strained hard and focused. "We have children… missing. How do we find them?"

Brenda swallowed. Missing persons wasn't her job description. Truth be told, she had only come over to figure out what was going on herself. She wanted to lose it, too, cry over the ones she couldn't find, even the one she didn't want found. "I'm not sure. I don't even know *why* we're here."

The woman looked away and the small cloister shut off further conversation. Their backs formed a tight barrier between them and a couple sitting on the bleachers inches away. Dismissed, Brenda moved on to the next group.

Snarls commanded the mass of long hair on the first woman. She had pushed it behind her neck and tucked the ends into her jacket. The heat of the day and cool nights confused the need for a jacket. Even tangled, her hair was cleaner than the previous group and dirt didn't cover her or her partner's faces.

A touch to the woman's shoulder, Brenda smiled when both pairs of eyes turned to her. "I'm a nurse. Can I help you? Are you hurt?"

The woman nodded, her feverish eyes twinkling. "My ankle. We tried running, but I fell and he turned back to help me and…" Her words broke on a sob. She reached for her ankle and looked around the gym. "…they got us. I can't…"

The man pulled her closer, hugging her into his arms. Crinkles on his weathered cheeks declared happiness past, but pulled down at the dismal circumstances they faced. Brenda nodded. The woman lifted her leg and Brenda pulled the shoe and sock from a very swollen foot.

Brenda bit her tongue. Green flesh pulled taut across blue, purple, and mauve flesh, the ankle bone indiscernible under the engorged balloon of infection. But where was the laceration for the infection to get in? Without gloves, Brenda's caution raised to new levels of alert. The discarded sock would have to do as a simplified barrier between her flesh and the diseased.

She held the heel. A quarter-sized hole on the rear portion under the Achilles' tendon seeped a pink-green pus, eliciting a sickly-sweet odor wafting through the stench of too many people in too tight a place. How did she hide this? Without immediate antibiotics, the woman's lower leg would need to be amputated. Without antibiotics in the next day or so, the woman would be buried.

"How long have you been in here?" Brenda wiped at the wound with the wadded sock, increasing the flow of the fluid from the wound.

The couple looked at each other for the answer. The man spoke, his eyebrows pinched together as he considered his answer. "Three days now? Since the first day of the attacks. We'd run to the store to check on getting a generator. We need the fridge to run for our grandson's milk. Men in black were everywhere. We got out of our car and tried to run, but…" He motioned toward the gym, encompassing the situation with his sigh.

He seemed beaten, like he didn't think it could get any worse. Brenda hated to push him from the small amount of security he had left.

Smiling through terrible news had never been her forte. As a rule, she told all of her patients the truth, nothing hid in her blunt honesty, and most thanked her. But those situations had controlled care and medication on hand. Even flood-and-quake survivors had taken the truth easier. Even though they'd had a tragedy behind them, help had arrived. They could handle whatever came next with assistance.

But in her captive state? Brenda didn't know how much help she would be for those who didn't see an end in sight.

Brenda glanced into the eyes of the man. A conversation filled with regret on her side and sad resignation on his passed in their gazes. She opened her mouth to offer comfort but was seized from behind by rough hands. Spun around like a small doll, she gasped. The man holding her hid under a black hat. His eyes were blue as ice and hard, expectant. A small zing slid into her stomach.

He looked over his shoulder while his fingers bit into her upper arms. His grip edged on painful. "This isn't her." A melodic voice contrasted with the chiseled anger in his jaw. Who wasn't she? She angled her head to see behind him but weak sounds of struggling distracted her from his hold.

A voice, small in the crowded room whimpered, "Let me go."

Brenda whipped her upper body from one of his fists.

A man dressed in black inspected the lady's foot. Her frightened whimper rose to a squeal when he dropped it to the ground. Waving over his shoulder, he issued clipped words in what sounded like German but could just as easily be Austrian. He spun toward Brenda.

Shorn hair under a tight black painter-style hat added to the angry slashes of his features. His gray gaze cut from his squinted eyes and a cruel smile twisted his face into a horror mask.

Two different men, similarly dressed, pushed past Brenda and the apparent man in charge. One pulled the woman from her husband's grasp while the other pulled out a small pistol. Before Brenda could protest, the muzzle of the gun met the injured woman's temple and a small pop permeated the despair in the room.

Air in Brenda's chest escaped on a whoosh. The woman's partner cried out, his face dissolving into a mass of anguish. He clawed at her body, pulling her limp form onto his lap as he slid to the floor. Sobbing, he rocked her, back and forth, ignoring the guttural commands to release her. His arms like iron, he refused to let her go. Refused. Refused. Shaking his head no.

A collective groan swept the room. Others clutched together tighter, as if safer in groups.

Brenda's stomach twisted and she gasped against the feeling of a fist leaving her abdomen. Quit saying no, she wanted to scream at the new-widower. He shook his head against their demands.

Brenda glanced at the crowd of people. Why wasn't anyone trying to help? How could they stand by doing nothing? There were more of them than the men in black. The tilt of heads and shoulders screamed they'd had enough. Too much had happened to the survivors in the room. Guns were enough to keep even the strong subdued, but a personality beaten down and traumatized didn't stand a chance against the violence a gun promised. How long had they all been cooped up in their prison?

Swiveling her head toward strangled sobs, Brenda raised her hand. The same gun met the grieving man's temple while he was pinned down by hands wrapped around his neck. Another pop and the bodies slumped against each other.

Without thinking, anger pure and hot filled her limbs with courage she didn't understand, Brenda pulled from the man holding her. She rushed to the dead pair she'd offered to help. Kneeling beside them, death more painful to her than a wound or poor prognosis, Brenda's voice was surprisingly strong. "How dare you?"

She raised her tear-filled eyes, but met the gaze of her captor instead of the man who'd ordered them shot. What kind of a man would allow that to happen? His lips were tight, his jaw clenching and unclenching. But he studied her with eyes that had lost their cemented edge. She answered the question in his gaze with contempt riddling through hers.

Brenda pressed a finger to the neck of the woman then the man in a vain attempt to find some sign of life. Hope, even when the worst seemed inevitable. Finding nothing but warm pliable flesh, she bit out her words. "Why are we here? If you're going to kill us, then do it, get it over with." She stood, back straight, and raised her chin to challenge the man to send the next bullet rummaging through her brain.

The leader looked up from inspecting his fingernail. A tightening of his cheeks before he stepped close to her, his face an inch from her own. Burnt tobacco on his breath, while horrid, had a distinct difference in horrendous from the smell of the injured and dying. Both made her want to throw up but she wouldn't dare. She'd swallow whatever bile came up.

In a husky whisper, dark as the black irises pointed her way, he said, "I dare? I can do whatever I want. You're my test subjects and that is all. Like slaves." The accent added a silky slide to his words, like an educated Brit. But when he leaned back and eyed her head to foot and leaned in again, he was anything but civilized. "I can do whatever I want." He licked at a white blob of spittle in the corner of his mouth. Eyelids lowered in suggestion.

"We're not slaves. We're Americans." The sentences paired together bolstered her waning courage. Brenda wanted to run and hide under Andy's tattered clothing, pretend she was home, in bed, with Lee, bastard that he was. She stopped herself from playing the game she and Rachel had perfected growing up. Fear was fear and you had to face it. Rachel had learned to run. Brenda had learned to fight. She stood to gain some more ground.

The blue-eyed man slapped the leader's shoulder and tossed a comment in their shared language, dripping sarcasm. His words didn't need interpretation as his eyes raked her frame. A genuine half-smile pushed a dimple into his cheek, disarming Brenda. She flushed. Damn his hide.

The gray-eyed leader nodded, a chilling smile curving his lips. "Yes, you are American." He turned and spread his arms out as if to embrace the room, calling to the lost people in the gym. "Americans. You built your great country on the backs of others. The most powerful, yet you did so with slaves. You're numbered like cattle and you have so much land." He turned to Brenda and lowered his voice. "We shall whittle you down until your resources are all that's left." His eyebrow raised at the question she couldn't bring herself to ask, but she knew her face nearly screamed with expression. He nodded. "Of course. We are all over *your* country. You have no one to turn to. You'll be dead in days."

Abruptly, he turned from her and said to the blue-eyed man, "Daniel, I'm bored. Bring her for interrogation. She knows *something*."

Brenda didn't have the knowledge to analyze the psychosis in his words. Her sister had learned the pseudo-science while Brenda had decided on nursing. She understood the tissues, the flesh. Not the mind. But something had to be gained by saying it in English so she could understand. What? Fear?

Walking away, he flicked something onto the ground and kicked a leg out of his way. Other captives around the gym scuttled from his path. He ignored them.

Brenda watched, unable to face the man who'd held her and had been ordered to bring her from the group. He baffled her and she didn't do well with puzzles. Part of her wanted to shoot him, while another reminded her of the heat of his hands on her, even through the material of her shirt.

Think. If Daniel could watch others die at the hands of his own team, would he allow the same to happen to Andy? Most likely. Andy was nothing special to them. She was nothing special regardless of the meaning in his gaze.

Before she could consider strategy, Brenda met his eyes again, fear and anxiety pushing the words from her mouth in a speedy dribble of fear, laced with composure. "I'm a nurse. I can take care of these people so they won't be a bother." She glanced down at the bodies. "You don't need to dispatch anymore because they're sick."

He followed her gaze, considering her proposition. His hand stung her skin as his fingers slid down to her forearm.

Like a button had been pushed, tenderness filled his eyes, reaching for her across the inches separating them. The soft roll of his accent softened the quiet steely challenge in his words, low and meant for her ears only. "She would have been dead soon, anyway. She was green. And he wouldn't be worth anything, grieving for her." His explanation confused her. Did he mean to bend? Did he think she was going to capitulate? She wasn't into Stockholm's and understood the syndrome enough to watch for signs. And it didn't matter what he said, he wasn't the boss.

A different man, faceless in her efforts to not see him, coughed and shifted his feet. A line of sweat ran between her shoulder blades. What would happen if she left the room? What could she know? Why her?

"Come on." Daniel pulled on her arm.

Tightening her legs, she pulled against his pressure and allowed fear to screw up her features. "I don't want to. Please, sir, I can help these people."

His eyes softened further, matching his tone. The grip on her morphed and his thumb caressed her elbow. "The name is Daniel. I won't let you get hurt, but you need to come with me and watch yourself." He glanced at the handful of men surrounding them and lowered his tone further. "Don't provoke anyone and take whatever they give you."

Confusion halted her struggles. Turning from him as if to look once more on the dead couple, Brenda cast her gaze toward Andy's inert form. She'd go. But then what? She nodded. "Okay."

But her meek tone hid her determination to return. No man was going to cow her again. Lee failed and he'd been a poor excuse for a man. Any guy who still had to rape their wife couldn't be considered a *real* man – in her opinion. Daniel... well, he seemed to be made of tougher stuff, but she wouldn't beg again. No matter what.

Following behind Daniel, Brenda stared straight ahead. She couldn't face the people she left in the gym. Not after the people she'd tried to help had died. The remaining captives probably wouldn't let her help them now.

Another man, dressed much the same as the men corralling her, opened the gym doors from the well lit hallway. Brenda blinked. She'd acclimated to the low lighting, had grown comfortable in the relative cover of the darker confines of the gym.

She focused on as many details as she could. The hall was nothing extraordinary with boring, neutral colored linoleum surrounded by orange lockers, black and orange banners and streamers celebrating the pending graduation. Nothing special, yet each tile and corner seemed placed with care just for her.

In front of her, Daniel walked with military grace. The lines of his back and shoulders broad, trimming to a tight waist wrapped in utility belts. A gun grip winked in the lights at her from the small of his back. She averted her gaze, looking up. The black RΨP on his right lower neck screamed at her. She stumbled and shook, catching herself with an outstretched hand.

Rachel. How did Rachel play into the nightmare Brenda and the rest of the world was caught up in? Her sister had the same tattoo.

~

She couldn't snap out of the fog in her head. The Rhode Island Psychology Project had been few in number and traumatizing to every member. Brenda remembered when Rachel returned from the two-month-long trip. It was the longest Rachel had ever been away from her kids or her husband. She'd called Brenda for a ride home from the airport.

Brenda had stared out the windshield while her sister had curled into a ball and cried like a small child.

Brenda would never forget that night and how she'd felt like she'd picked up someone else's sister.

The distinct guttural edges of the leader's voice prodded at the vestiges of lingering daze in her head. She focused on his words. "Are you Dr. Rachel Parker? I'm not going to ask again."

She shook her head. "No." The man sat across from her. She'd at least been given a seat. Odd, she'd been left alone with him for the moment.

He'd commandeered the principal's office and stripped the walls and desk of memorabilia. The pile of pictures and trophies and miscellaneous items spilled from the corner under the window. He spewed cigarette smoke into the air and tapped the burning end of the cig onto the desktop.

"Who are you?" He raised his eyebrow and raked her with his gaze.

Hell no. "Who are *you*?"

He laughed. "Me? I'm no one of consequence. But you're looking for a name, aren't you? Lieutenant-colonel Gustavson." He leaned forward, his breath blowing the black and white ashes around the wooden desk. A knock on the door and he raised his head. "Lieutenant Bastian, enter."

Brenda refused to look around. She held her gaze on Gustavson's face, but felt the new presence come to stand behind her. "Sir, I brought the insignia you requested."

"Perfect." Gustavson's hard face broke on a smile devoid of delight but filled with anticipation. He returned his stare to Brenda.

"Your name?" He cut her off before she could begin. "Does she really look like Dr. Parker, Daniel?"

Brenda sat up straighter and interrupted their side conversation. "My name is Brenda Krous. I look like her because I'm her sister. Why do you want her?"

The man beside her inhaled sharply. He moved around behind the leader and watched her face. Daniel. He'd known Rachel. Somehow. They had the same tattoo in the same spot.

Gustavson laughed, the sound oily and sharp. "I want you to be difficult, Brenda. Certainly, I want answers, but I want this to be worth my time as well." He pulled a new cigarette from his inner breast pocket and twirled it between fingers with the grace of a pianist. "Dr. Parker is… shall we say, valuable for reasons I don't think are pertinent to this visit. Call it personal business, if you will. Regardless, I want you to tell me everything you know about her work."

Daniel's eyes narrowed. His nostrils flared. Brenda had the distinct impression he was angry. But she hadn't done anything. She needed to get back to Andy, to check on him. Check on the other people. Angering the captors wasn't the brightest route to those goals. But what did they want? She held up her hands, palms open. "I'm not sure what you want me to say? I don't know much about her work. I'm biological and she's psych. We don't understand the other."

"You mean to tell me, she never spoke of any of the tests or any of the jobs she took over the years?" He leaned back, comfortable in his role. "You think I'm going to believe that?"

She shrugged. The stale air in the small office stifled her. What was she doing? Fatigue and hunger combined and she snapped, "Look, I don't care what you believe. She hasn't had another job since Rhode Island two years ago. She's never been the same. She won't talk about it, won't even stay in the room, if you ask."

Daniel stood behind the lieutenant-colonel. He closed his eyes and ducked his head for a moment.

Gustavson held out his hand to Daniel. "Give me the brand, Lieutenant."

Daniel lifted his head and placed it in the outstretched hand. He glanced her way, for a moment, then trained his eyes on the wall opposite him. He clenched his teeth.

The hair on the back of Brenda's neck tingled. *What the hell did he need a brand for?*

"What did she say about Rhode Island, Brenda? Did she tell you about the tests she designed and tried on herself and others? Did she share with you her work for other countries?" The seated man shook his head, rolling the end of a stick the size of a skewer in his hands. Fidgety people annoyed her.

Thinking of Rachel the way he painted her was next to impossible. Brenda scoffed at her fear and at him. "Look, you need to investigate a bit more. I haven't been close to Rachel since that damn project – whatever it was. I never get to see her family and I have no idea what she's been up to, just the briefest information gathered between holiday and birthday calls. We used to be close. I don't think we have anything in common anymore." She bit her lip. Truth hurt and damn if she wanted to be in pain around the enemy. Brenda didn't care why they were doing what they were doing. The simple fact that she'd watched a man kill two innocent people and walked away ate at her.

"Do you know where your sister is?" He stood, slow, and rounded the desk to rest his hip on the corner. The stick in his hands didn't stop moving.

Something was important about the – what had he called it? – brand, but Brenda couldn't catch the meaning. She sighed. "No. I was at her house. You found *me* there, but not her. Obviously, we have the same information on her whereabouts."

"Assuming what you say is true I'm going to help you find something... in common with your estranged sister." He held the tip of the stick out to her. "Do you recognize that insignia, Brenda?"

Backwards, the RΨP didn't seem as intimidating. Brenda's gaze flitted from the silver quarter-sized end to Daniel's flushed face. What the hell was going on? She nodded, tilting her head back to refocus on Gustavson's hard features. He pulled a small stainless steel Zippo lighter from his pocket.

He fingered the rounded square and flipped the lid. A steady flame hypnotized Brenda. Was he seriously going to light up again? Didn't they teach about the dangers of smoking in Europe? Whatever kept him calm, she'd keep quiet. Daniel hadn't moved.

"Do you know what it stands for?" Gustavson rotated the stick through the orange heat. The oval moved and licked at the metal, looking for something to burn. Brenda couldn't look away, like a bad accident on the freeway. In a trance, she almost missed him jerk his head to Daniel who moved behind her seat. Gustavson's hands held her attention. His voice fell into a slippery moan, "It stands for Rhode Island Psychology Project. That's the psi symbol you see there in the middle. Didn't Rachel have one of these symbols tattooed on her neck?"

Brenda stiffened in her seat. What the hell was he getting at? Rachel never pulled her hair up unless her neck was covered. How did he know about the tattoo, unless he had one, too? She tilted her head and shifted her gaze upward. "Do you have one?"

"No, dear Brenda. I'm not smart enough to earn one. Daniel here, is, and your sister is or was, depending on her plight." He moved the flame around, the metal red as it troved through the heat. "I don't have any tattoo equipment on me and I'm not much of an artist, but I think you're smart enough to have the same mark as your sister. You can consider it a step towards reinstating your flailing relationship."

Brenda yanked her head back. What? She wasn't some animal to be marked. How dare he? Daniel couldn't stand for that. Could he? He'd been nice to her, like he would protect her, right? What Gustavson suggested was far worse than her getting shot in the head.

"I don't know what you're doing, but I don't know anything. Why would you do that? I'm not a psychologist. I wasn't there." Brenda bit back the whimper rising in her throat. He moved closer. Panic welled within her. She moved to stand, but arms, hard with betrayal pushed her down and pinned her to the chair.

"Don't take this personally. I can't find Dr. Parker, so I'm sending her a message. We'll call it a thank you and warning wrapped in a beautiful package. If you hold still and don't fight, it won't hurt as bad. Or so I've been told." He pushed on her head behind her ear and brushed the hair off her neck.

She'd never hated her size more. If she were Rachel's size, she'd be able to fight more effectively. Daniel didn't move a fraction when she struggled against his hold. She was strong, but the bastard was stronger. She froze. If she struggled, who knew where that thing would land, or even if he really meant to plant it. Daniel was just one more man trying to control – son of a BITCH! Pain shot up her neck and covered every nerve ending in her body.

A scream tore through her throat. Unable to disguise her agony, she bit her tongue, a coppery taste spilling into her mouth. Her eyes rolled back in her head. But she wasn't given the relief of passing out. Nope, not Brenda.

The acrid scent reached her nose at the same time the sizzle of her skin reached her ears. He pressed harder. Into the meat. Her scream escaped and somehow, the pain ebbed.

Nope, that was her bladder relieving itself.

~

Bursts of white flashed across Brenda's vision. The pain had morphed into a creature all its own and sat on her shoulder in the crease of her neck picking and pulling and pinching with razor sharp nails. She moaned.

The men had left soon after she'd wet herself. A different man altogether had flung towels through the door before slamming it shut again. She'd allowed herself to pass out. Judging by the warm saturation of her clothing, she hadn't been out for long. Minutes at the most.

She pushed herself up from the slouch she'd fallen into, her upper arms protesting where Daniel had held her down. Her chair creaked. She froze, looking down. She'd soaked the chair and down onto the floor. At least it had only been her bladder. Nursing had prepared her for worse, but thank heaven she didn't have to clean up herself much.

Strands of hair grazed the new wound. Brenda flinched. Her hair had fallen out when she'd been captured, but she needed a rubber band to pull it back. But nothing. She glanced at the door. No one stood sentry inside. Maybe the principal's desk had a couple in a drawer or something.

She wrapped her hair into a fisted mass with one hand while the other swabbed at the mess she'd made of her jeans with a towel. She left the floor alone. They wanted it cleaned, they could do it. She rounded the desk and fumbled with her free hand to pull the drawers open, every movement eliciting another round of hell to drive through her body. Who in the hell branded anymore? She wasn't a damn cow. Leave it to her to make jokes when she was upset. Like people who laugh at funerals. Or brandings.

A message and warning to Rachel, her ass! They could have written her something. Brenda would have delivered it. The second drawer down had a variety of rubber bands, paperclips, sticky notes and pencils. A pencil or a paperclip might come in handy. She tucked her shirt into her jeans and grabbed handfuls of the office supplies. Another glance at the door and she shoved the small items down her shirt.

Was it stealing if it was from someone who held you captive and burned you? She hoped so.

She snapped the drawer shut and twisted her hair up with the rough rubber. Now what?

A shadow appeared at the door. Brenda tensed, leaning forward into a defensive stance. Her collar rubbed the burn and she jerked upright. Dammit.

Bastian the Bastard poked his head around the door. He offered a sheepish smile. Seriously? "How you doin? Ready to go back?"

Brenda stared at him. Comprehension evaded her. Had he just asked her if she was ready to go in a Mister Roger's voice? She nodded dumbly and stepped forward to follow him. Her wet jeans chafed her skin.

Outside the door, the empty hall seemed different. Because Brenda was different. She didn't know how, besides physically, but her perception had changed. Rachel would have to explain it to her.

Daniel moved to her side and raised his arm like he meant to place his hand on her back. She jerked to the side, aware of the ache where his hands had been the last time he'd touched her. A pencil rolled against her skin and shifted on the other supplies.

He dropped his hand. "Is there anything you need to treat..." He waved in the direction of her neck but looked at her face. "That?"

She couldn't even see it, let alone know how to treat it. But Andy was burned and she had a feeling she needed more items for the other captives. "How much can I get of what I need?"

He arched his brow. "What exactly are you thinking?"

Brenda's empty stomach tightened. "I still want to help those people in the gym. You don't need to continue to kill them."

His blue eyes dulled. He shook his head. "I don't think I can help you. The lieutenant-colonel has plans for those people. I'm not in a position to interfere."

Position... "Then why did you promise you wouldn't let me get hurt?"

"I won't let you get hurt." He lowered his gaze to her lips. "I'll do my best."

Brenda's eyes widened. Had she stepped into the Twilight Zone? "Are you kidding?" She pulled her collar further from her skin and angled her neck. "What the hell do you call this? A hickie?" She snapped her head forward and poked her finger toward his chest. "You held me down. Explain that." Circumstantial attraction. That's what she'd call it. Why did she even care what his explanation was? He'd held her down. He wore the same uniform as Gustavson. A gun rode his waist. He was a captor. She didn't owe him anything and hell, he didn't owe her anything.

She rolled her eyes. The pain was turning into righteous anger and when Brenda got going, she didn't stop. "Forget it. I don't really care. I'm going to hold you to me taking care of those people. To do it, I need bandages, pain meds, petroleum jelly or antibiotic ointment and water. If you can get some food together, I'd suggest you bring that, too." Solid thuds from the soles of her borrowed hiking boots, echoed down the hall. She didn't need his escort to the gym. She'd find it on her own, if they'd let her go alone.

Looking back wasn't an option. What could he do? Shoot her? Yes. But would he? He'd proven he wasn't as nice as he seemed to want her to believe. How far was he willing to go? Her stomach forgot to care with her heart taking over. It triple thumped as a trickle of sweat inched its way down her chest. Great, urine and sweat. She was going to smell the best.

A click sounded over her footsteps. There it was. She was going to die. Her life didn't flash before her eyes. She didn't notice the temperature. Nothing really changed except she closed her eyes and wished she'd done things differently – made friends, been kinder, had a husband who loved her and wanted to take care of her and give her children. Anything more than what she had – which wasn't much.

"If you'll wait, madam, we can find some items in the nursing office." A scrape of a key sliding into a lock followed his words.

Brenda opened her scrunched eyelids and her eyebrows pinched together. She stopped and turned. Daniel watched her with exasperation and tolerance on his rugged face. Two men appeared behind him and stood guard outside the door he held open.

Brenda didn't question the turn of events. She'd hug her time on earth as a bit brighter and hope she could show him the same consideration while he gave her what she needed and not a moment longer.

~

"Thank you." Brenda couldn't look him in the face. He'd offered all types of kindness in the nursing station. The men who she'd assumed had been called to guard her had surprised her instead by carrying armfuls of first aid supplies to the gym.

The small pile of gauzes, oils, bandages, ace and Coban wraps, suture material, antiseptic and more at her feet felt like a victory against the invaders. Okay, so what if the enemy had supplied them? They were spoils of war. For a second, she'd worried he would ask for specific payment with the heat in his eyes matching the searing in her neck. Why not push him further? "How long until we get the food?"

He leaned in, an earthy scent heavy with oak and rain assailed her. She didn't look at him, but focused on a small tube of airplane glue two inches from her toe. His lips brushed her hair and he whispered, "The food will be here any minute, but you only get this one warning. Four of the bags will be untouched and they will be marked with a red slash on the corner. The rest of the sack lunches will have some form of poison in them. A different food will be affected in each bag. You're the only one who knows."

Brenda stopped breathing. Like he'd literally punctured a hole in her lungs and they no longer worked. Tears filled her eyes, blurring her vision of the medical items on the ground. He was gone before she could retort or ask if he was serious. Damn it. He had lulled her and just when she started to second guess his motives, he slipped in a twist that showed his real side.

The men had dropped the first aid items on the uncluttered floor near Andy. He hadn't moved since she left. Clusters of people had shifted and Jenny was nowhere in sight.

A quick scan of the gym failed to reveal Jenny's location. An ache started in her lower back. Jenny, one more worry to add to Brenda's list. Maybe the men had come and taken her. She was a pretty young thing and rape wasn't unrealistic.

She unloaded the office supplies as well, tucking them under the white wrapped packages. Hoping against hope, Brenda kicked the supplies closer to Andy and walked to where she'd left the teenager.

The crowd hadn't moved from that selective spot, but someone had tossed the initial fallen couple against the wall, their limbs mixed together. But where was Jenny? Had Brenda imagined her?

Look ahead, not back. She stepped over the leg of one of the fallen. She didn't look too closely at their faces as she passed. One wrong glance could break her resolve. She had people to help.

A large pallet of sack lunches arrived. Gustavson accompanied the large offering to discuss the plight of the remaining captives and their medical stability. The men tucked the rolling platform beside the bleachers and followed behind the leader as he circled the room with Brenda.

Haggling over each person like livestock was exhausting.

Her burned skin throbbed in anger with her close proximity to the taunting weasel of a man.

Overall, she'd been able to save the majority of the people in the gym. She'd lost three before they'd reached Andy. Simple quiet pops through black silencers. People had glared at her amidst gasps and muffled screams. Brenda had ignored them. Do not get too attached. Save as many as possible.

The movement of Gustavson and Brenda brought them full circle before moving amongst the ten or so in the grouping where Jenny had been.

Gustavson glanced into the corner and stopped. His guttural words clipped but lazy, boredom had set in a while ago. "Who's that?"

Fatigue vanished from Brenda's mind. This one mattered. The other people had taken their toll, but she'd been able to remove herself from the emotional impact with each bullet. But Andy... he was family. And what if he was too far gone to save. Damn, but she wouldn't give any less. In fact, their connection demanded she try harder.

She still didn't understand what they were looking for. His questions to that point had been pointed regarding background, education, value to the community. Brenda didn't know what he wanted, but she gave him everything she had. "He's my brother-in-law. I've already triaged him. He has burns, but with a little bit of rest and basic burn care, he could be the best of the lot. He's trained as a mechanical engineer and knows the hills and towns better than anyone." She bit her lip from spilling more like he has three kids, he's an ass but loyal at times. Nothing that wouldn't make him more appealing. If he wasn't attached, he'd be worth more. "Our families are dead. We're all we have." She might have just given a weapon to the bastard, but at the same time, it could be easily turned against him.

The leader stared at Andy. As if he hadn't heard a word she'd said. The moment dragged out. And out. Until finally, he nodded and turned toward the still inert forms, which was odd, because the rest of the crowd had awakened or stood with the sound of the gunshots and waited as they'd made their rounds.

He walked a few feet to the small group and pointed his finger like she was a dog ordered to sit. "Examine."

Brenda knelt to check the condition of the young body at her feet.

Nothing. No pulse, no breathing. No life. But how? She checked for wounds, but nothing screamed how the young boy had died. He couldn't have been older than twelve. Brenda shook her head and, still on her knees, moved to the next body, which was just... a body, empty of life. Through bangs covering her forehead, Brenda stole a glance at where she'd left Jenny slumped over another lifeless form facing the wall.

Brenda's breath hitched. Jenny hadn't returned. She checked the third, fourth, fifth, sixth bodies. All dead. All younger than twenty. Seven. Eight. She rounded the spot where Jenny should have been, the body could be her, but the hair was shorter than Brenda thought. She checked nine. Unable to avoid it any longer, Brenda rolled the shoulder toward her and bit her lip to keep from gasping.

A youthful face, but a boy's, stared at her. Jenny hadn't been among the people she'd checked. And Brenda had checked every body in the gym. Everyone.

The mystery of why the group was dead had to come before where Jenny had gone. Brenda's escort would demand an answer why and if she seemed worried, he'd suspect. Maybe. If she gave herself a moment to consider the truth, she'd realize she didn't know the bastard who wanted to kill everyone. She didn't know why the teenagers were dead. She didn't really have confidence that she could save Andy. Jenny was missing. And how the hell was Brenda supposed to be the only one to help all one-hundred-and-twelve people?

Nope. Brenda didn't believe in can't and if she didn't know, she'd learn. Survival demanded it and she'd be damned to give in so early. She was a friggin' American and these idiots were going to know it.

"Well? Any of them alive?" He pulled a box of cigarettes from his pocket and tapped it against the silver Zippo. Bastard. He lit a chimney and the gray smoke rose, round and thick against the angry backdrop of victims.

Brenda shook her head. Why speak when she had nothing to gain. Her pulse increased with anger which focused the sting in her neck. Damn him. And damn Daniel, too. She hadn't had to focus on the food debacle yet. How much could they lay at her door?

Gustavson shrugged. "Assign someone to discard the bodies." The man leaned to her and very slowly whispered, "You will be in charge. If anyone steps out of line, it will be your back. I do not tolerate failure." A smirk shadowed his face and he spun on his heel. Double-doors against the far wall closed behind him.

On her tour around the room, Brenda had noted each door chained shut with locks the size of softballs hanging from thumb-thick links of steel. There was no way out or in besides the doors the cattle herder had prodded her through earlier.

Where had Jenny gone? What did Brenda do with Andy? He was in the worst shape. The other three had already been shot. She had to choose someone to evacuate the bodies. It would have to be soon or the stench would be unbearable as the muscles relaxed and released the contents from their bowels. Maybe a few of the men could work the top windows open with cranks.

But what did she do about the food…

Brenda sank to the nearest available bleacher. The sheer amount of responsibility pushed and pulled. She hung her head.

"Pst." Brenda looked around. No one looked her way or even faced her. Great, she'd be the piranha, considered the traitor for working with the captors. They wouldn't see her efforts to keep any of them alive. Just the three shot where they lie. No, they'd see her talking to the man, poking and prodding them like animals and hear her describe their injuries and health like she discussed the humidity level of an April morning. She'd left with the bastards after all. Never mind she came back reeking like… well, like one of them.

She was imagining things.

"Pst." There it was again. For crying out loud.

"Brenda… Over here." Jenny's unmistakable whisper directed Brenda's attention under the bleachers.

Brenda stood and walked around the corner of the lowest step. Closed partway, the risers created a dark cave of narrow impassibility. Brenda looked beyond the chipped wood and steel framework. Into the black hole, she whispered, "Jenny? Where are you?"

Jenny poked her head out next to Brenda's shoulder. "Hey."

Brenda jumped. She pressed her hand to her lower throat, her thumb brushing the skin around her "mark". "What are you playing at? This is dangerous."

"I know. But I had to do something. The dead kids passed around some kind of pill and they all took them at the same time. They offered me one, but I slipped away before they could make sure I ate it." She held out her hand, displaying a brown pill the size of a candy-coated chocolate. "I don't want it, but I don't want to leave it where someone else might find it. You know?"

Brenda held out her hand. Holding the pill might prove to be the stupidest thing she could do, but to expect the young girl to carry that burden was more than Brenda was willing to do. A scuffle sounded behind Jenny. Brenda tried to see into the dark, tucking the pill into her back pocket. "Are there more back here?"

Jenny offered a small nod. "A couple, but there are more in the locker room."

The unbearable smell of chocolate chip cookies reached Brenda. She turned, feet from the food. Like zombies, the other people grumbled and moved toward the pallet, the Pied Piper scent pulling them forward.

She had a decision to make. Did she tell or not tell about the poison?

Chapter 12

Tom

He woke in a cold sweat. Images of bodies abandoned along the roads, cars littering the highways and fields, homes and buildings charred and flattened monopolized his dreams. He had to think about something besides the journey to Rachel's. His sanity depended on it.

A whimper from the back through one of the open doors echoed his worry and fear. He gripped the borrowed blanket in his hands and stared into the darkened room. The whimper grew to a cry and sounded like the younger boy was having nightmares.

Dr. Parker's gait was confident and reassuring, even in pre-dawn hours. Tom closed his eyes and absorbed the comfort she offered to her child through murmurs and whispered concern. For a second, he pictured his own mom, wiping his forehead and telling him everything would be okay.

He rolled to his side. Comforted, at least for the moment, Tom allowed the day's work to loom before him. Even if he wanted to chance facing the nightmares, Tom's interest in sleep left as ideas and possibilities worked their way through his mind.

The satellite hadn't detoured from its usual course. Ascertaining its position had been easy and Tom had told Rachel and Josh he didn't need a day or two to figure out the path. Tom would go to Josh's place after breakfast to attempt contact with someone… anyone.

He threw back his blanket and sat up. At home he'd run when he couldn't sleep. But when Rachel and Josh had consulted with him about the HumVee and the potential for further danger, they'd all agreed to keep close to the home fronts. But somehow he needed to stretch his legs, get the blood pumping and oxygen to his brain so he could think. Rachel had explained the Fight or Flight response. He had plenty of flight, but hoped he'd build fight.

Sliding into his jeans and runners, he tiptoed out the front door.

Dawn crept over the tree canopy. Goosebumps spread over Tom's arms and neck with a kiss of chill from the spring breeze. Cloudless skies perfect for the satellite crossing greeted him. Peaceful and serene, the clearing would be fine for running laps.

He loped into a jog, nothing too strenuous. How far could he get in the one-eighth of a mile clearing? Once around, past the door, pacing his steps with his breathing. Twice around. The morning breeze worked on his building sweat. Next lap, the rhythm ached and he'd found his gear. Four, five, six. Double digits soon welcomed him like an old friend.

What would happen to him, the city, the world? Where was Jenny? Getting a radio would add to his sense of security. Immersing himself in the ham world would garner feelings of productivity. Something his travel through Coeur d'Alene had stripped to bare metal.

Tom spun and reversed his direction, mixing up the scenery.

He turned the corner furthest from the cabin. And stopped cold. A shadow of a man stood beside a large Cedar tree, shoulders hunched. Tom's heart rate increased tenfold.

Josh stepped into the light. Tom's lungs regained control and he breathed in deep. His words fought for space in his throat. He gasped. "You're up early."

"I could say the same thing about you." Hands shoved in his pockets, Josh ambled out of the trees and joined Tom on the grass.

"Couldn't sleep." Tom's breathing caught up to the stress of the run. He folded in half and rested his hands on his lower thighs.

Josh stepped to his side and shrugged. "Well, why wait? Let's go check out the equipment and get it ready for the satellite."

"Okay. Let me change first."

Inside, Tom shed his jeans. He'd never jogged in denim before, but the stiff material hadn't impeded his run, only soaked up sweat like bread in a bowl of soup.

"Where are you going?"

Tom jerked upright. He blew air out on a whoosh. "Cole. You scared the hell out of me." He glanced over his shoulder. "Josh came early. We're going to his place to check out the radio and stuff."

Cole glanced down the hall and back at Tom. "Can I come?"

Pulling up short, Tom considered the question. And why couldn't Cole? Fourteen was old enough to be the man of the house, old enough to understand the danger, but not old enough to make any real decisions or cause any harm. "Sure. You might want to ask your mom." Tom motioned to the door. "Josh is waiting. I'll meet you outside?"

Cole nodded. His face unreadable.

In the brightening day, Josh lost all his sinister edges. "Do you need anything from here?"

Tom patted his backpack he'd slung on his shoulder beside the door. "Got everything I own right here." Sobering thought. He was defined by the material on his back which wasn't much in terms of possessions. He'd never owned a lot of "stuff" but what he had he'd taken pride in.

Josh's lids lowered. "Look, I know it's been hard for you. I can't comprehend how hard, to be honest. But you hang in there. We'll get this figured out and then we'll check on your parents. Alright?"

Emotion camped in Tom's throat, at the spot below his Adam's apple. If he swallowed, he might choke on it and if he didn't, he might cry. His parents. The worst part was he didn't know if they were okay or not. If they'd died and he knew, it'd be bearable, but no idea was worse than the worst case scenario in action. What if they were captured like Brenda and Jenny? Or were Brenda and Jenny dead?

His back to the door, Tom appreciated the moment Josh gave him to collect his composure. He moved to the side as the panel swung inward. "Ready?" Tom motioned to Josh and Cole to lead the way. It wouldn't hurt to have them in front as Tom continued to gather his control like small marbles scattered amongst the grassy blades.

Over his shoulder, Josh spoke to Cole, his voice cautious. "You ask your mom?"

"She knows where I'm at. Don't worry." Cole kept his head down. Something in the tilt of his head raised Tom's suspicions, but he kept his concern to himself. What business was it of Tom's to butt into Cole's issues with his mom?

From what Tom had gleaned, pretending to sleep on the couch while Josh and Rachel had talked at the table the night before, Cole's dad had died hours before they'd arrived at the cabin which meant Cole and Tom had something in common and, also, that Cole needed time to figure out where the situation placed him. Seventeen was hard, but Tom had hated fourteen. Cole was in for a time of confusion, especially without his dad. He'd need all the support Tom could offer.

The temperature cooled a degree every twenty or so feet as they climbed into the hills west of Rachel's homestead. Grass erased the footpath and Tom scrambled over a swollen, downed tree.

Josh veered to the left, and like ducks Cole and Tom followed. They turned left. Then left again and then left again, plodding parallel to the path they had been on before. A hundred feet up the steepening incline, Josh pulled the same trick but to the right four times landing forty feet over on the mountainside. Tom grabbed for rock outcroppings and small trees to hold on to as the hill rose sharp into the chilled thin air.

Paying more attention to the placement of his feet than where Cole was, Tom slammed into the younger teen's back with a grunt. "Sorry, man."

Over Cole's shoulder, Tom spied Josh walking to a rock the size of a small steamer trunk, indistinguishable from the similar chunks freckling the mountain. Grunting, he pushed the rock from a hole he shouldn't fit into.

Tom followed Josh's gaze, over the valley to Coeur d'Alene Lake and the city beside it. Smoke rose from various places, casting a grayish haze under the yellow sun. The seventeen story lake resort loomed in the distance, angled and charred like an abandoned old chimney. Nobody in their right mind would vote it "America's Best Small Town Vacation" spot.

Flashbacks of the streets as he'd struggled to get to the forest overtook him and he sat down on the lichen-covered slope.

"What was it like?" Josh sat beside him and Cole knelt at Tom's back. The question didn't feel prying, rather like an offered moment of release.

Goosebumps tightened across Tom's skin. The memories wouldn't be easy to contain if he opened the gates holding them in. He swallowed. "When I snuck across the fields away from the helicopter, I followed some cars heading into Coeur d'Alene. At a large intersection, cars weren't moving forward so people got out of their vehicles and walked. One man said he'd heard all the Red Cross shelters were filled in Spokane and so they were setting up a huge one in the Resort on the Lake."

Arms wrapped around his legs, Tom ignored the brisker wind whipping the hair at his temples and ears. "Going into crowded areas is stupid. I know that. It's one of the key elements they teach in Survival SOS. But I went. I followed. I couldn't help it." He drew in a shaky breath. The images swarmed him. "Our group grew from about a hundred to more than a thousand and then more. We reached the main street down by the lake. Kids. Old people. Families. People who didn't have anyone. Me…" His voice trailed off. Tom closed his eyes.

"The explosion hit in the center of the crowd. Bodies flew everywhere." An ache throbbed in his side at the memory. "I was closer to the water and was struck by a person's head —" he slapped his face, covering his mouth, "— a head! The hair tangled in my fingers." He shuddered. "I fell in the lake. Body parts surrounded me. I couldn't get out. I didn't know if they searched for survivors. I couldn't stay in there with all those dead people." A child had floated beside him. A beautiful hand, nails polished had drifted past on the waves from the impact.

"How did you get away?" Cole pulled Tom from the directness of the memories.

"My waterproof pack acted as a flotation device… I got it from one of those Survival 'R' Us catalogs. I rested my head on it and kicked my way out of the body parts, under the pier. Injured people gathered near the huge clock, making it way too easy for the soldiers to come in and round them up and cart them off like livestock." Pent up, the memories had tasted like acid, burning his taste buds and eating at his gums. But spoken aloud, sharing with others his burden, the acid released and softened to a harder version of Alka-Seltzer, distasteful, crude, and without flavor, but more bearable. Something he could stomach because he had to.

Josh's arm cradled Tom against his side. "I'm sorry that happened. You've seen a lot in the last few days. Nothing I say will make it better. It might be helpful to speak about this with Rachel." He glanced at Cole. "Don't you think? Your mom would have more experience with this type of thing, right?"

Tom looked over his shoulder at the young man who nodded and replied. "Yeah. She's worked for the FBI, CIA, and other freelance work, mostly government and rich people with fear issues. She's the one they call for behavioral analyses or control triggers. I know she does other things, but Dad always told us to go to her with our problems, said she'd have a more 'objective' answer."

Josh patted Tom's back, unaware of Tom's history with Rachel as a patient. "Alright. When we get this taken care of, you can discuss the incidents with Rachel, okay?" He glanced into the clear sky. "Let's get inside and get started. Who knows when they'll do a fly-by or other reconnaissance run." Rolling onto all fours, Josh led the way into the hole behind the rock.

On hands and knees for no more than three feet, Tom stood in a large foyer furnished with bean bags and green shag carpet. Flecks in the rock walls sparkled from the spare light bulbs set in the ceiling mere feet above his head. Sloping along the natural incline of the mountain, the room's vaulted appearance gave way to the abrupt addition of a man-made wall painted red.

"Hold on while I close this." Josh crawled into the space, his feet dangling from the opening. He grunted and a grouchy grind erupted into the room as the rock slid into place. He backed out and stood, brushing his hands on his dark jeans. "Okay."

Through a bi-fold door set in the red wall, Tom left behind any reminders of the dystopic atmosphere even Rachel's place couldn't dispel and entered a well-lit, well-designed house. Carpets, rugs, wood floors, kitchen sink, washing machine, oven, fridge, tables, and a television! furnished the spacious floor plan. Couches and chairs lined the walls and separated the dining and kitchen areas from the living space.

Cole pointed and looked at Josh. "Is that a Wii Station?"

Laughing, Josh nodded. "Go ahead. Have fun." He looked at Tom. "You?"

Tom shook his head. "Nah. I'd rather look at your ham radio. But, thanks."

Flipping some switches, Josh called to Cole. "We'll be in the next room. How long did your mom say you could be with us?"

"She didn't." Cole stared at the sixty-two inch screen hanging from the wall. He pointed his controller at the console and with rapid speed pushed buttons, scrolling through the game options.

Josh halted and cocked an eyebrow. He looked at Tom who shrugged. "What do you mean, she didn't? That doesn't sound like Rachel. What did she say when you asked if you could come with us?"

Cole paused his search. He slumped his shoulders. "I didn't ask. I left a note saying where I'd gone and said we wouldn't be gone too long."

Josh stepped toward the foolish boy. Tom flinched. Idiot. You didn't do something like that in the type of situation they were in. Even a small child knew that.

"What were you thinking? She's going to freak out. We can't just run you back down or even let you go by yourself. What is she going to do?" Josh leaned his head back. He sighed. "At least she knows you're with me." He pressed his fingers to his eyes.

Dropping his hand, his face tightened. "We need to get this done. Next time you do this, you'll walk back, dangerous or not. Understand?"

Cole didn't move. He must have sensed Josh walked on a tightrope between yelling his head off and maintaining his cool. Plus, if Tom read the kid's face correctly, he didn't want to lose the chance to play the video games all by himself.

In the back room, a station dominated the long wall. Buttons and panels called to Tom with a siren's song. "Do you have an amateur license? Or is this licensed as an amateur station?"

"No, well yes. Okay, here's the deal. I have all the equipment and it's licensed as an AS and I even have the AL but I'm not an amateur controller because I never took the exam to get the written authorization. It took too long. Do you?" Josh raised an eyebrow.

Tom patted his bag. "Yep. I have all that. I'm an officer in the local ARRL chapter. We have a few in the area, but my group is made mostly of people in wooded areas. We have – had – contests for calls and stuff. It's really fun. Even when practicing for disasters. If you need help studying for the exam, I'd love to help. I taught a few classes for my chapter." He looked down at his shoes. The laces had come undone. Now when had that happened? Offering a class at this time made him sound like an idiot. There were more important things to consider.

"Thanks, I'll keep that in mind." Josh pulled a chair from the main area. "Can I watch you?"

Tom sat in the seat. "Of course. It's your radio. Let's try it out, shall we?" He glanced at his wristwatch. "It's not quite time for the satellite to pass over. But we can do a local callout." Tom's hand itched to press the call button. Never used, it taunted him, red and shiny without fingerprints.

"Please, do whatever you'd like to do. I'm an observer." Josh settled into a chair and watched Tom with interest.

Excited to touch a radio, regardless of the unnerving scrutiny, Tom set his bag on the floor at his feet. Not far in case he needed something. He rolled his head on his shoulders and cracked his knuckles. From his pack he pulled a pencil and pad of paper. His dad had taught him to record everything transmitted on the waves, said or received. Most of his radioing he'd learned from his dad. Instead of playing ball like other fathers and sons, Tom and his dad Morse-coded with other hammers in the region.

He wished his dad was with him. Hanging onto ham radio would be a great way to keep him close. Pencil in his right hand, poised over the paper, Tom adjusted the microphone and pressed the call button with his left hand. "CQ. CQ. This is Pi Alpha Delta One-Seven. CQ. Over."

Josh waited until Tom released the button. "What was that?"

"CQ is standard call for 'is anyone available for conversation'. And Pi Alpha Delta seventeen is my call handle. I'm PAD17. Every year the number changes on my birthday and I run a lot so PAD has dual meaning. I'm also a note taker. It's really just because I had no idea what to call myself. Blame it on lack of creativity – I do." Tom offered a half-hearted laugh. He could play butt-of-a-joke. His call name sucked and he knew it, but he hadn't had much choice when his dad had asked him to come up with one on the spot. His dad, SHOT3, had all kinds of reasons behind his. But Dad had also had time to come up with the tough sounding name.

"Nah, I don't know what I'd use either. So what now?" Josh leaned forward and rested his elbows on his knees, watching the panels like they held the secrets to the attacks.

"Well, I'm going to do a repeating call if I don't hear anything in two minutes that will run on all the channels for whatever set time I choose rather than doing it manually." Tom pushed a few buttons, repeated the call into the mic, and set the loop for thirty minutes. "Someone will beep in, if they can talk."

Josh's eyebrows lowered. "What happens if it's a hostile breaking in?"

"There are codes the ham community uses for safety in case of that exact possibility. My dad used them a lot and while my handle was never approved for the codes because I'm under age, I heard them enough I can use them. In states of emergency, protocol isn't checked as much," Tom shrugged, "for obvious reasons."

"What about —"

A double beep sounded across the speakers and Tom held up his hand to Josh. A smooth voice, crisp in delivery, answered the call. "Pi Alpha Delta one-seven, I'll take your convo. What's your twenty? Over."

"He's asking for my location." Tom pushed the button and replied, "Take my CQ, what's your handle? And who does the Lady work for?" He released talk and to Josh, while he scribbled the notes in his journal, said, "Usually amateur radioists identify themselves with their handle. If they don't, it's someone who has no idea what they're doing or they don't want you to find out who they are. We'll see which one this guy is."

"Not to mention he's asking where you're at and knows nothing else."

Tom nodded.

The voice broke into the room. "Nancy Mary five-oh. Does the Lady work?"

Slumping into his seat, Tom didn't know what to say. He'd never heard the answer before, but he'd heard rumors of the replying phrase. "Crap, I don't know what to do."

"What? What was that?"

"NM50. It stands for North Militia and the provinces it covers are fifty. I've only heard stories about the militia call radios.

Had they only used the handle, I wouldn't believe them, but the replying question demands I answer as friend or foe. I think I…" He rummaged through his bag and pulled out his dad's convo pad, the familiar scratch of his dad's handwriting somehow comforting. Tom flipped through the first few pages, finding what he was looking for in moments.

Josh cut in. "Are they our militia or the enemy's? And isn't the militia bad?"

Tom sat up. "Good questions. I can't answer the first but give me a sec and I'll take a shot at the last." He pressed the call button, staring at the page. "NM five-oh, is the Lady part-time, full-time or contracting?"

"What the hell was that?" Josh flattened his hand on the shortened counter, eyes wide.

"I'm sorry, I know it's confusing. According to Dad's notes, part time suggests parts of the militia may be compromised, full time reports the militia is fully intact and seeking intel and contracting means they are speaking under duress."

Josh opened his mouth to speak, but the beep on the radio cut him off. "Full time. Are you contracted?"

Tom pressed call. "Not contracted at this time, ship is adrift but intact. Searching for secure channel. Please advise."

"PAD one-seven you are clear to channel Kappa Delta three-five-three. Code will be Nancy Mary of your province where you are currently located, not the province you're from. Once you're on, we will speak freely. Seventy-three."

Tom closed the call. "I'm transferring to channel KD353 to get into the militia's database. Once I get in, I'll be able to see the entire network and what's been happening. Do you have a laptop?"

Josh retreated to the rear of the room, returning with a standard thirteen inch processor. "Will this work?"

"Perfect." From his bag, Tom pulled USB cords and a headset. He plugged in and linked up, signing in with the information he'd received.

"How are you getting internet up here?"

"It's all based on data sharing. The signals and so on. The satellite helps, but this is standard transmitting. I'm not sharing files or anything, just traversing their site and discussing, like having a phone conversation while peeking at my smartphone." Tom clicked a few more buttons and NM50's voice clipped into the room.

"This is Major Dilbeck. PAD17 is SHOT3 with you?"

Tom shook his head, even though the major couldn't see him. "No, sir. He's not. When the attacks started, he was in town at his job."

Soft static preceded Dilbeck's beep. "I'm sorry to hear that. Do you have his convo pad?"

Convo pad? How did Dilbeck know about his dad's notes? Tom had been under the impression his dad kept notes because he was affected with a tinge of OCD. "What do you want with his pad, Major?"

"SHOT3 was intel for our Fairchild contacts. His notes have valuable information we can't afford to lose."

Josh's jaw could have come unhinged. Tom would have laughed in different circumstances at the comical expression. He turned away to focus on the pads in his lap. "I don't understand? Dad wasn't a member of militia."

"SHOT3 was recruited after the Ellensburg tsunamis. We met him at a Red Cross tent where he stitched up the wounded."

The map on the site showed Xs running along the new coastline and inland as far as Butte and south as far as Cody, Wyoming, where the Northern Militia's borders ended. Before responding to Dilbeck, Tom muttered over his shoulder, "Josh, do you have a printer?"

Josh enabled the cordless printer on a shelf and nodded. "Full color." He mouthed.

Militia? His dad? Impossible. Dad hadn't had a courageous bone in his body. He'd been stoic and bookish. He was straight-laced acting, even for someone in the medical field, and didn't like loud noises or stiff drinks. An odd match for the vibrancy of Tom's shiny mother.

Tom pressed the call button. "I'll need more proof you are who you say you are. Anyone could create a secure website. This is twenty-twelve, not nineteen-oh-two. Heck, my three-year-old cousin wrote an html code for his preschool last summer. Where's your proof, you're actually you?"

The stretch of silence had the feel of metal on metal, grinding and twisting. Tom avoided looking at Josh. It wouldn't matter his expression, Tom would start to laugh. He was the type to laugh at funerals and tell inappropriate jokes beside someone's deathbed. He didn't have a tact filter. His only saving grace was that he knew it.

"Here is my proof. If you're SHOT3's kid, you'll recognize the validity of this statement. The Northern Militia Fifty is a collection of the Army National Guards from the nine western states. We are state owned not federal and we don't prescribe to the anti-government propaganda. Not common knowledge."

Tom maintained his silence. He didn't know. Not for sure.

Dilbeck cleared his throat over the air and his voice acquired a husky tone. "Son, your dad didn't only work with me, but we spent time together researching and doing other information gathering. He was a good man and loved you and your mom. I hope he's okay and that he's wearing comfortable shoes. You know how he is about his shoes." He offered a soft chuckle that cut off when Dilbeck released the button.

Breathing a sigh of relief, Tom swiped at the tears welling in his eyes. Shoes. His dad's damned shoe fetish. He tossed his statement to Josh with a slight smile. "They're solid. Does that answer your previous question?" Button. "Major, I appreciate your candor. Thank you. Yes, I do have SHOT3's convo pad."

Palpable relief laced Dilbeck's reply. "Ten-four, PAD one-seven."

"Major, would you know where captives are being kept? If they're even keeping them alive?" He swallowed. Tom had always thought Jenny was cute and sweet, but finding out she was strong and practical increased his feelings for her. He really wanted to get her to a normal life again and take her out for pizza. He didn't want to consider the possibility that she wasn't alive any more. The world needed girls like Jenny in it. He needed her.

"Captives are being detained on the ground. What area did the capturing take place?"

"Post Falls, Idaho." If finger crossing didn't reek of second grade, Tom would do it. The seriousness of the situation mocked him with a strong neener-neener.

A handful of seconds passed and Dilbeck answered. "Anyone captured within city limits of Post Falls was taken to the high school. We suspect the gymnasium but their cafeteria area is large as well."

"Thank you, Major. Do we… have any word on Spokane?" Jenny could still be alive. Rachel's sister could be, too. What about Mom and Dad?

"Spokane is considered a nonentity right now, PAD one-seven. The pull of the multiple relief shelters was strong and most of the citizens in the area had gone into the city to get help. More attacks fell this morning on the buildings and the remaining hangars at Fairchild. Butte was attacked early last evening – their first round of attacks. Jackson, Wyoming; Reno, Nevada; Pocatello, Idaho and Boise were smothered yesterday with attacks and we haven't heard a squeak from anyone. You're the second one to make contact since the enemy attacked Fairchild and the bases in Arizona. I wish there was more I could tell you, but I'm in Montana, south of Kalispell about two miles west of Pritchard. I have to hold the communications open. There aren't a lot of us to spare with most of the garrison in the Middle East right now."

"We're not far from your location, Major." Tom didn't know what he could do, but they had information. They had to do something. To Josh, Tom said, "We have to do something…"

"Can you ask about the rest of the country?" Josh pulled fresh paper from the file cabinet beside the wall and loaded it into the printer.

Tom leaned in and pressed the button, more concerned with Jenny and Spokane than the rest of the country, but curious just the same. "Major, is there any word on the rest of the country? Are we getting assistance soon?"

A sigh flooded the room over the airwaves. "Disheartening. The east was hit with another earthquake up north and a Category Four hurricane slammed up the coast, ripping apart the remaining cities and towns. Invaders riddled down into the mid-west yesterday and I haven't heard the status. I'm sorry to say this, but America is getting torn asunder and no one is helping."

Tears stung Tom's eyes. Josh looked at his feet. Tom nodded, at no one in particular. "Yes, sir, thank you."

Frozen in grief for the great country being violated on multiple levels, the three men offered a moment of silence to gather their thoughts. Tom didn't know if he could speak, even if he wanted to.

Josh sniffed and pointed at the laptop. "How detailed does that map get?"

"I can't zoom in. It's just a basic marked up map." They had no answers. Nothing. They stared at the red Xs. How many had died at each Red Cross? How many were captured? Anger bloomed in Tom's heart. How dare they? Who, in their right mind, attacked America? Sure, the country had its problems, but come on, they had so much more going for them than other countries. Tom refused to sit there and accept it. He shook his head and straightened in the swiveling seat. "I'm not going to sit here. We need to do something.

Brenda and Jenny need us. We have to go get them. We can't just sit here and do nothing." Tom pushed the button, meeting Josh's eyes as he spoke. "Major, we're going in after the captives."

Josh nodded with Tom's words. His jaw tight.

"I'm going."

Tom spun in his chair.

Cole stood at the door, his arms folded, chin jutted. "I am. I'm going. I want to help get Aunt Brenda out, if she's okay. My dad would have done the same."

Tom's mouth went dry. He had no problem with Cole going, it was telling Rachel. He hadn't known her long as a mom, but what he did know resembled a mama bear he'd seen in the woods one summer. The bear had rushed him, feinting to move him along, running in spurts but never leaving the baby cubs more than ten feet away. Tom had had no problem running the opposite direction. Telling Rachel Cole was joining them would require more courage than actually going.

Josh walked to Cole. "Cole. This isn't a game. You don't get second lives and points for picking up mystery objects."

Tom shifted in his seat. He felt for the kid, he really did, but come on, did Cole really think Rachel was going to allow it?

Josh squared himself to Cole and spoke as if to a skittish horse. "Do you really think your mom is going to let you go after the stunt you pulled today? You left her a *note*, Cole, at a time when she needs to keep her kids close for peace of mind." Josh threw his hand in the air. "We're not even sure if she completely trusts *me* yet. And you just sabotaged that, with your move, she's probably thinking I put you up to it or at the very least that I went along with it." His voice lowered as the action involved him more and more in his head.

Shaking his head, Cole backed away from Josh. "Look, I don't care. I'm fourteen. I'm strong. I couldn't help Dad. I have to help *someone*."

Helplessness over his own parents pricked at Tom's eyelids. If anyone understood inability to help with the capabilities at their fingertips, it was Tom. He pinched the bridge of his nose, like he had a headache but brushed the tears away before anyone saw. Clearing his throat, Tom pushed himself from the rolling, spinning chair. "We don't have time for this. Let Rachel decide." He met Cole's gaze. "I think you should go along, if you're willing. But that's my opinion. We'll need all the help we can get."

Josh spun to face Tom, confusion on his face. Tom pointed toward the door. "Do you think it's been easy? Any of this? Getting away, escaping? No. For you, it hasn't really sunk in yet that there's a war going on and we don't even know who it is we're fighting. You live here." He bit back a tremor in his voice. "We lived out *there*. Our families are out there. We know it's real and sitting in a hole waiting for someone to come and help us is worse than being tied in a straight jacket. No one's coming to help us. They're all waiting for us to come help *them*!"

Chapter 13

Rachel

The heat was picking up, though in the mountains it reduced the sun's energy to samples distributed at a grocery store. Rachel pulled at the dandelion flower with care. If she could just get the roots out, maybe the plant would be intact to make a salad.

The leaves gave way. She bit her lip and tried again. Think about anything but the anger and frustration roiling inside. Try the next one. Okay, what would she do with the yellow heads? She had biscuit mix – dandelion fritters would be good.

A footfall sounded behind her, soft grass whispering with the movement. So help Cole if he wasn't standing behind her. Her movements became clipped and shortened. Damn kid.

"Rachel, I brought Cole back."

Her shoulders tensed. Josh. He'd been part of it, but she hadn't wanted to think about his role in endangering her son. Just when she was starting to trust him… With painstaking slowness,

Rachel stood and faced him, her husband's – no, her *dead* husband's – best-friend. "Where is he?"

Josh jerked a thumb over his shoulder and Cole stepped into view no more than ten yards from them. Rachel didn't move her gaze from Josh's face. But she was a mom which meant she didn't need eye contact to make her point. Low, like a cougar, she growled at Cole, "Get in the house. Now."

He hung his head, chewing on a fingernail. If she hadn't been locked in a battle of staring with Josh, she'd have commented on bad habits. As it was, she let it slide. He was in enough trouble.

The door shut. A small click left behind breathing as the only sound, as if even the birds feared what was about to happen.

Rachel controlled her breaths. Her heart beat was erratic and a flush had worked its way up her neck.

Tom coughed. "Excuse me. I need to use…" He sidled past Rachel and into the house, breaking the hold Josh's eyes had on her.

"What were you thinking? He's my son and you didn't even ask. What if something had happened? What if he'd been hurt? What if you'd been hurt and he couldn't get back here alone? And Tom… Nobody is here to watch out for him. How could you be so careless?" She inhaled deep.

His damned eyebrow quirked and a taunting half-smile enflamed her ire. "You were fine last night with Tom joining me at my house to use the radio. Why are you so upset now?" Rachel struggled to argue his logic under his penetrating gaze. The smile dropped. "Maybe you're upset because for once you weren't in complete control."

How dare he? She was not a control freak. Cole's absence had scared the soul right out of her. She'd seen his note too late for it to be calming. So many what-ifs had bombarded her brain. She sported a new migraine and the fresh air was getting to her. She pointed her finger inches from his face. "Don't twist this around on me. I didn't disappear with someone else's kid."

Josh wrapped his hand around her offending wrist. Rachel gasped. Hot, like fire but without the pain, his touch blistered her skin. The type of mark you couldn't see but you'd feel long after. He pulled her against his chest, his eyes searching hers. "Don't. I'm not going to fight with you. He's a big kid and now, he's the man of the family. Let him at least try to find his niche."

She and the kids hadn't been there a week, but it seemed like forever ago Andy had died and they'd lived in a normal neighborhood, slept in a house with stairs and rode a school bus.

"If you're not going to let him grow up now, you'll never be able to let go." His eyes saw her fear.

A hand's breadth separated them. She missed Andy's companionship. No grieving would be accomplished until she could cry on someone's shoulder. But it wouldn't be this man who told her to let her oldest son go. He didn't understand anything about her. She needed *her* man, not a man who used to haunt her nights with what-ifs.

She pulled free and turned to the house. Unable to meet his eyes, she mumbled, "If you haven't eaten, I've made brunch." Rachel didn't bother waiting for him. Her ego had been bruised enough for the day.

Inside, Tom and Cole sat at the table with a growing list between them. Pushing the discomfort between her and Josh aside, she smiled at Tom. "Good morning. Did you sleep alright?"

He shrugged and looked at her from under his bangs. "Sorry, Dr. Parker. I should have made sure Cole came in and talked to you." Tom nudged her son with his elbow and skewered him with his eyes.

Cole raised his gaze. "Mom, I asked to go with them. I told them I asked you and that you said it was okay." He returned his gaze to the sheet of paper and breathed his apology.

But… hadn't Josh been the responsible one for the letter? Heat scorched her skin to her hairline. She kept her back to the boys and Josh as she busied herself at the stove. She'd been certain her pride couldn't handle any further bashings, but apparently she had plenty of humbling to do. "Tom, please call me Rachel. I'm not your therapist here."

"It might be a good idea for you to consider treating him. On his way here, he saw some pretty horrific stuff." Josh's voice pretended nothing had happened, but Rachel imagined inside he gloated like a championship wrestler. She could think that, she was the injured party.

"Tom, if you'd like to go over some things, you know I'd be happy to sit with you. Just let me know, alright?" She gripped the spatula like going into battle.

"Kayli, Beau, time to eat." She poured oatmeal into bowls and set light buttered toast onto a large platter which she transferred to the center of the modest table. "Go ahead." Fingers became serving utensils. Everyone grabbed and loaded their plates. Rachel had started rationing according to Andy's chart on the wall. Some stuff would stay good awhile and some wouldn't. He had everything calculated out, how much, when and how.

Rachel smiled at the thought of her husband. At least her children were safe. But something wasn't quite right. Cole and Tom tossed covert glances at each other and in Josh's direction. She held her questions until they'd been satiated with food and nearly finished but not enough that they could escape by claiming to be done.

"So, what's going on? What are you cooking up between the three of you that I'm going to have to say no to?" Rachel sipped her cup of orange juice. "And before you say 'nothing', forget it. Just tell me now."

The boys looked at each other. Their hesitation annoyed her already irritated nerves. She sighed, a special sigh her children recognized as the last straw. Cole's eyes widened. He swallowed his food and hurried to answer her. "Mom, Tom made contact on the radio."

"Wow. Really? What happened?" Rather than irritating her, the statement got her attention. What did that have to do with being sneaky?

Tom jumped in and sketched the conversation. Engaged, Rachel forgot her anger. "Militia? Near here? That's terrific."

Josh scoffed. "I don't know that their news is exciting. Major Dilbeck reported the enemy is keeping captives alive."

Captives? Why would she care about… Brenda. "Where? What are they doing to them?" The smallest possibility that Brenda was alive was enough to hope. And hope after the last week was welcome like ice cream to a birthday party.

"The Post Falls captives are being held in the high school." Brenda had been caught at Rachel's home. The school was two blocks from her door.

Rachel couldn't sit still. She stood, clearing dishes and pushing her chair in, wanting to run to save her sister. Her baby sister. She needed to rescue Brenda. She had to be freaking out. Scared beyond measure. What would Brenda do without Rachel?

Snapping the lid on the butter, Rachel closed her eyes. Brenda was an adult. She hadn't relied on Rachel in years. Had barely been approachable since she'd married Lee. And honestly, her and Andy had clashed worse than Rachel had thought possible. Being around each other too long had been painful and soon they'd avoided each other which meant Rachel had missed out on her sister more. Andy hadn't had an answer for it when she'd asked him about it. Rachel had soon dropped the topic.

And to be honest and utterly fair, how much had Rachel reached out since Rhode Island? She'd even quit work to avoid reminders of that hell hole.

"What does that mean? Is the militia going in? Can they save her?" She directed her questions at the boys but spoke to the ketchup bottle in her hand.

"No. They can't go recover anyone because most of their men are overseas. There aren't enough service people in the area."

Rachel jumped. Josh was right behind her. Why couldn't he leave her alone? She needed space. She needed her sister. She sidestepped him and entered the pantry, arms full. Why couldn't things be normal? She shivered as she tucked the condiments into the fridge. The room was never warm and she didn't like to loiter in the dark chill, even though she didn't want to face Josh either.

But Josh had said the militia wasn't going to recover the captives. Why? She returned to the kitchen but kept distance between them. "What do we do? We can't leave her there."

"Mom, we want to go get her."

"We?" Was he joking? *No way.* Rachel swallowed the urge to scream.

Josh leaned against the counter. Nobody answered, but Josh watched her, as if waiting for her to come up with the correct answer. There was only one answer and that involved keeping her kids safe. No matter what.

"No, absolutely not, Cole. You're not going. I won't have it." She thrust her hands on her hips, her chin out.

"No? Do you think it's fair I don't get to do anything? You and Dad never let me do anything an adult would do. Or even what a teenager would do. I'm stuck at twelve. It's like you refuse to acknowledge I'm getting bigger. I'm fourteen, Mom. When Dad…" Cole choked on the word. "…disappeared was the first time you let me do something real."

Rachel stared at Cole, stuck in the truth of his words but scared to admit it. She turned and sat on a seat by the covered window. What would happen if she let him go? Worst case scenario? He'd die. Next worst, he was injured or captured. Best thing that could happen? He brought Brenda home and his self-esteem and confidence were exponentially affected.

And if he didn't go? Worst case scenario? She didn't see one, unless potential building rebellion could be counted as an outcome. If Cole reached sixteen and did what Rachel had wanted to do at that age, he'd turn and never look back. Brenda had been the only anchor she'd had. Rachel didn't want to push her children to drastic measures. The world was hard and getting rougher. Home was the one place they deserved to be safe and supported.

But could she support this?

Rachel refused to be her mother. She needed her husband. What would he say? What funny analogy would he offer to make her understand Cole's perspective. She glanced at Josh, but didn't find in his face what she needed, what would have been in Andy's.

Like an awl slicing and hacking at her heart, Rachel allowed herself to accept that Andy was gone and she had to make the decisions by herself. But she knew what Andy would want. And this time, he wasn't getting it. Cole needed to go. If not for Brenda, then for himself. But oh, the decision tore Rachel apart.

How could she grieve for a husband *and* a son? She wouldn't survive. And in that moment, Rachel accepted Andy's death. Her mouth dried up and her tongue felt swollen in her mouth. The signs of a long drawn out cry were coming and she didn't want to do it in front of the boys.

Josh claimed the chair beside her. She glanced up to find concern in his eyes. "Don't think you'll never see him again. He'll be with me. I'll do my best to not let anything happen to him. He can do this." His voice lowered. "You can do this."

Rachel appreciated his comments while she harangued herself for being a weak female. She'd rarely needed to lean on Andy, the hardest trials they'd ever faced included chickenpox and a possible outbreak of the bird flu. When she'd wanted to lean on

Andy, she usually did so because he was her best friend and it made her feel good. He comforted her. Plain and simple. Andy had been her rock. Her throat tightened. Damn it.

Listening to Josh's words of comfort strengthened her resolve to keep her kids safe, even from herself. She couldn't protect them from trials but she could protect their choices.

Obstinate, Rachel claimed a moment to lower her chin and think of the right words to say. She started slow, unsure where she might be headed. Hesitant to do what she'd decided. "Cole. Come here, please." He stood in front of her. Green eyes wide and worried, exactly like Andy's. She didn't want her husband in her head right now. She was too close to a breakdown. "I don't want you to go."

His eyes darkened as the pupils dilated. Fists clenched at his sides.

Rachel arched an eyebrow. "Let me finish. I don't want you to go, but I respect you enough that if you think you're old enough to do this, then I'm going to trust you."

Confusion relaxed his stance. Color returned to his white fingers. "You're going to trust me?"

"I think you know better than I do what you're capable of." She breathed in deep. Her heart lodged somewhere behind her right knee. "You'll never know until you try, right?"

Speechless, Cole turned toward Tom, Josh. He glanced at the kids sitting at the table and then back at his mom. Her heart didn't want to see him as a fourteen-year-old. A blanky in his hand and fuzzy blue pajamas had no place on his growing frame. For a moment, long and drawn out, Rachel wanted to grab him in her arms and force him into the cradle hold, like a newborn. He'd break her back, but he'd be with her. And he'd do what she said because Mother knows best.

"When is this excursion going to be?" Rachel avoided Josh's gaze. He was becoming a fixture in their lives and the acknowledgement was vastly annoying. Not to mention she needed someone to take her anxiety out on and he fit that role with a skewed sense of logic.

Tom spoke up, reminding her Cole wasn't the only minor going into harm's way. The poor boy didn't have parents to worry about him and here she was making a fuss over her son. How terrible Tom must be feeling. "We're going to leave before noon."

Noon. The hour loomed so near. "What's the plan? Are you going on foot? Do you have any idea where or even if there are traps or who the enemy is? They aren't Japanese. I doubt they're Arabic or Middle Eastern. They're white. Caucasian of European descent and this will make it that much more difficult to differentiate which side people are on."

"We discussed that with the major. He's only heard from one other hammer and they aren't sure who is attacking. Communication is sporadic between stations with the east coast going through another hurricane and more earthquakes and the middle states have another set of tornadoes flashing through. We're on our own." Tom shrugged, the shadow in his eyes much older than a seventeen-year-old should look. "We have to go soon. They could move the people any time."

People – Brenda. They could move Brenda any time and then who knows when the next location would be disclosed. She shook her head. Of course. The sooner they went, the less time Rachel had to rethink her decision. Better. Not easier, not enough time to prepare for it, but better. Let them go while their courage was still pomp and flurry. While Rachel was distracted enough by her mounting dismay over the loss of Andy that she couldn't do much about anything.

Rachel painted on her clinic face. "Figure out how long it will take. What you'll need. When I should expect you back. Plan for all of the possibilities."

"If it's okay with you, we'd like to take one of the quads. It won't leave you stranded to take one and we'll be able to cover more ground and maybe carry anyone that we're able to get out." Josh looked at his watch. "Boys, layer, hiking boots, hoodies. Make sure your clothes are dark." To Rachel, "Can Cole handle a gun?"

Rachel blinked. "Yes. Andy took him shooting and hunting all the time. But why?"

"Just in case." He threw a pointed look in her direction. Ah, Cole was big enough to shoot but not big enough to talk about? Double standards. As if Cole might chicken out at the thought.

"Cole can shoot if he needs to. Make sure he doesn't have to." Darting her message back with narrowed eyes and pressed lips. Two can play that game. And as a mom she played better.

What she wanted to scream, yell and whisper while pulling out her hair was "Why Brenda? Why us? Why Andy? My Andy… My Cole. Bring back my Cole." In her mind, she knelt in the grass and sobbed, releasing her anguish in sobs and wails. But outwardly, her grief was shuttered. She'd need to let Andy go.

She'd need to learn to trust again. Soon. Because one of her babies was running the family's escape route in reverse. Back to the danger. With a man who might expect her to trust him. Who had lost his best friend when she'd lost her husband.

The sooner they left, the sooner Cole would return.

Chapter 14

Brenda

Her back hurt. Not a small ache but the kind of pain that would grow into a spasm and she'd be wishing for a bullet to pop into her head. End her misery. But the misery was happening. The pain was real. Ignore the hurt in her back and the constant throbbing in her neck, people surrounding her were grieving and lost. Captured with a pile of dead that hadn't been moved. And Brenda had to assign someone to move them.

Had their captors counted? Was there a chance they didn't know how many had died? How many bodies lay there in that pile? One-hundred and twelve corpses she couldn't pull off, but was there a way she could get a few out? Jenny and thirteen others hid beneath the bleachers and in the locker room undetected, but for how long?

Gustavson had demanded she deal with the bodies.

Bastian had whispered to her the food was poisoned.

Now the scent of chocolate chip cookies wafted across the crowd and they moved like zombies to the pallet.

People were injured. She was wounded. But some of the victims hadn't eaten in four days. And hunger trumped injuries.

Brenda moved to stand in front of the pallet, the marked bags on the corner closest to Andy. Dang it, she needed to treat him, sooner rather than later. He'd get one of the bags. Jenny would get one. But then what? She wouldn't keep good food for herself. Not when she knew the truth.

A younger man, mid-twenties maybe, moved away from the growing group and reached for a paper bag. Brenda pushed his hand away. She shook her head.

He stood back, tossing a glance at the other people gathering around him. "What are you doing? That's food, right? You think you get to keep it all? We're starving."

Brenda nodded. "It is food." She coughed. "But… I mean…" What did she say? What the hell did she do?

"Then move. I'm hungry and my wife is hungry." He pushed her aside and grabbed two bags. Another person moved forward as well.

Brenda called out in a slow confident voice when she was anything but, "Then you tell your wife you're sorry she got poisoned. I can at least wipe the guilt of her death from my conscious." He paused and turned back to her, his head cocked like he hadn't heard her.

"Oh, yes, you heard me. Your wife? She's going to be eating food *you* brought her." Brenda moved toward him. She lowered her voice. "Those guards just told me the food they were bringing is poisoned. Not all of it, but some of it. I don't know what's safe and what isn't in each bag." She met the man's eyes. "Can you tell me what's poisoned in there?" She tapped on the brown bag, a solid crinkle sound carried over the hushed crowd. "Because I have no idea. And I'm not sure I would take that chance."

He shifted his feet and placed one of the meals on the stack. With exaggerated movements, he pulled open the top and peeked inside. From the bag, he pulled an apple, a peanut butter sandwich, chips, chocolate chip cookies, and a juice box.

While she decided what to do about the dead, she'd administered to the injured, saving Andy for last. No one had spoken with her except for the cursory reply to her questions. She moved to Andy, ignoring the group.

At least Andy had a reason for his stoicism. Each careful sweep of the damp, sterile gauze took away layers of dirt that had her convinced she would find third degree burns or worse with infection and who knew what else. But only first and minor second degree injuries greeted her gentle cleansing. His hands had the worst of it, blistered and red, but even those wouldn't be too horribly disfigured. Flinches and moans broke through his attempts to hold the pain's effects in.

Brenda made the move to his head and face. Bright red spots gave way to dark maroon crusts. Black and brown splotches and streaks decorated his skin and obliterated much of his paleness. The flicker of his eyelids flashed the whites of his eyes, stark contrast to the dark of the dirt covering him.

His forehead would be as good a place as any to start. She wiped downward. Andy groaned. In the wake of the gauze a new red trickle sprang forth. The laceration was deep and wide, a centimeter square at the least. Daniel hadn't given her needles but he'd supplied butterfly bandages. He'd cocked his brow at her request for super glue, but that had been given as well, two packages with five tubes each. The bastard might be smart but not in the sciences. He'd just given her an extremely versatile tool.

Andy's peripheral wounds wouldn't cause the level of disorientation he elicited. How many other head wounds did he have and how bad was the one she had already discovered?

"Can you hear me, Parker?" If he had a concussion, loud noises wouldn't help the recovery.

His movement was almost imperceptible. A small nod and a quiver of his lips attested to the amount of pain he had.

"I think you have a concussion, maybe more. I need to finish cleaning so I can see what we're dealing with. It may hurt. Iodine after that and that *will* hurt. I won't lie."

His lips moved. Brenda leaned closer. His lips moved again.

"What? I can't hear you."

Ears pressed almost to his mouth, Brenda held her breath.

"You never lie."

Brenda jerked back. Tears stung her eyes. She blinked them away. He would be okay. The brat. Making her worry.

Bringing up her lack of bedside manners at a time like that? Only Andy. But Brenda found she didn't really care. He would get better and then he could help her get out of the mess they were in. "I'm glad you're more alert. I need help." She glanced over her shoulder. People shifted their gazes between watching Brenda, the food, and the dead bodies. Brenda lowered her voice to a whisper. She put her mouth by his ear. "They've poisoned the food. There are four marked bags that are unpoisoned. What do I do? There isn't enough food for everyone in the four bags." She pulled back and met his gaze, sick to her stomach. "I can't let only a few eat while others go hungry, but at the same time… unh, I don't know what to do. You need to eat."

Pointing his finger toward the pallet, Andy murmured, "Tell them, all of it. Let them decide. I couldn't eat, even if I wanted to. The pain…"

Brenda nodded. Of course. Pain was debilitating. He needed water more than anything.

She patted the floor next to him. "I'll be back, then. I hope." She offered a weak smile. "I could stand to go without food a little bit, too."

On her feet, Brenda returned to stand beside the pallet. She pinched the marked brown bags with one hand and wolf-whistled with the other.

Groups approached, many eyes narrowed and brows furrowed with suspicion.

Over the grumbles rippling across the gym, Brenda raised her voice. "I was told these four bags haven't been tampered with. There are over a hundred of us, but maybe we can get a bit or a sip of something, if we share. If not, then we need to decide who will get the bags."

The man who'd taken the bag earlier pushed past an older couple. His shoulders were hunched and he led with furrowed brow and snarling lips. "Who decides?"

Brenda stood her ground. "We can do this democratically. Majority rules." She looked past him to the compacting group. "Three options. Take our chances with the unmarked bags and no one gets the non-poisoned food. Divvy up the marked bags. Or pick a few individuals to get the safe food." More eyes focused on her. "Think about it." She paused, which way did she want to go? Would they blame the decision on her… "Raise your hand if you think we all should get the unmarked bags." She leaned toward the belligerent man, "Can you count them to make sure we get the same number?" He tossed a quick glance at her and then raised his finger to count the slowly rising hands.

"I got twelve. You?"

Brenda nodded and swallowed. She didn't even know the exact number of people in the room. What if there were some in the locker room still? Was Jenny still under the bleachers? She wouldn't be counted. "Same. Okay, divvy up the marked bags?"

Hands rose in the air, more and more. The man helping count turned to her, his eyebrows raised. "I think it's unanimous, don't you?"

"So we have to split up four bags of food between a hundred or so of us? Some who haven't eaten in days? Is there any water?" This wasn't biblical times and there were no blessed fish around with loaves of bread. Sandwiches and chips. The basics and a paltry amount at that.

An elfin-like woman stepped forward, her pixy hair and petite facial features a deep contrast to the low sultry level of her voice. "There's water in the showers. They cut the water to everything in the gym, but the kids got into the locker rooms and there's plenty of water in there. I'm fine without food. The people who are hurt or sick can have my share."

Heads dispersed throughout the group nodded. But there had to be order somehow. Brenda raised her voice over the swelling aside comments and whispers. How had she been thrust into the leadership position, when all she wanted was to go home? "Let's have those who need the food or want the food on this side," she pointed toward the padded wall, "and those willing to go without against the bleachers."

Ten people found a seat on the bleachers while the rest formed a line to shadow the perimeter of the gymnasium. Brenda took herself out of the equation. Andy would need food. Jenny joined the bleacher group and two kids from where she'd hidden ran to the wall for the food. A bite, if that, would be passed to the people who had to have food.

Looking down the line, Brenda shook her head. So many people, older and young, injured and outwardly fine in appearance. While the large number seemed vast, the group was a mere sliver to the amount of people that hadn't made it into the containment areas. How many were still alive?

"Let's separate into four groups. Count off and then a bag will go to each one and you can share it as you'd like." A chorus of one, two, three, four rippled down the line. The ones collected under the basketball hoop and the twos followed suit on the opposite end of the court. Threes and fours joined at the half-court line.

She couldn't move Andy. But water. He'd wanted water. She could get him some. It'd be more important to get hydrated in his condition, anyway.

Surprisingly civil, the people moved for her as she walked across the rubberized floor to the locker rooms. The prospect of food acted as a healthy bonus toward congenial behavior.

Cup. How was she going to get him the water? Her hands? Come on. She pushed through the wooden door, the echo of her footfalls welcoming her away from the crowded public area. The room was empty. A few lockers stood open. Garbage cans led each line of metal cubbies. Glancing down, Brenda stooped and retrieved a partially crushed water bottle. Problem solved.

She filled the bottle but leaned against the cool tile wall. Just a small break. In the sudden silence, devoid of shifting people and moans, Brenda acknowledged the pain pulling her neck from her shoulder.

A mirror mocked her from the wall beside the door. If she got up to look at her injury, she'd be close to the door and might as well continue out. She waited another moment. Just one more. Maybe another.

Pushing herself off the wall, she sighed. Andy needed his water and her neck was killing her.

Lifting her chin and tilting her head to the side, Brenda pulled the collar from her neck. *Oh, no.* Blackened skin surrounded by puckered, swollen red flesh glared at her. Thin clear fluid seeped from the edges of the scab-like, quarter-sized burn. She'd have to patch it or the material of her shirt would irritate the wound further.

A scream rent the air, muffled through the walls and door.

Exhausted and past the "shockable" point, Brenda rolled her eyes. "No more. Seriously. What now?"

She shoved against the door which protested with squeaking hinges. Brenda scanned the room. Something was off, but what was it? Getting water and checking her burn couldn't have taken long.

Jenny stood on the corner of the bleachers, her hands clamped over her mouth, eyes wide. Brenda followed the path of her gaze. A man collapsed to the ground, followed by a woman two feet from him.

The downward movement of the captives pulled Brenda's gaze to the floor. She gasped. The number of people on the ground doubled the standing and more were dropping like baseballs. Something off? Hell, it was *wrong*.

Brenda ran to Jenny and shook her arm. "What happened?"

Shaking, Jenny sobbed between her fingers, "They portioned the food. Everyone got a bite-size chunk. And on the count of three they all ate it. Laughing. Celebrating. They've been falling down." She ended on a whisper. "So fast."

Poisoned. The bastard had told her the wrong information. She'd killed all those people. They'd trusted her and… Brenda tugged Jenny's fingers from her face. Speaking softly, she met the young girl's eyes, "Jenny, did you eat anything?"

"No. I wanted to, but I didn't." Guilt creased her brow. "What do we do?"

Brenda turned Jenny and pushed her gently from the bench in Andy's direction. "Go. Sit with Andy and don't watch. If it helps, plug your ears." Moans and groans, whimpers and small cries preceded thuds and shuffles as people fell to the floor.

She couldn't stop what was happening. But she could help diminish the effects of shock on the living.

The ten people on the bleachers had frozen, staring at the dropping crowd with mouths open and eyes wide. A man turned his head and dry heaved, his empty stomach relinquishing nothing. Brenda climbed the three benches. "Come over here. Don't watch. Hurry." She repeated her orders until they moved slow as frozen honey. She ushered them beside Jenny, into a protected area, slightly sectioned off from the remainder of the gym by the open stands.

She couldn't look. *Coward*, she berated herself. But what did she have to gain? No sound. Brenda squatted on the ground between Andy and Jenny. The ten people had paled. No one could raise their eyes.

Growing silence. Eerie.

Brenda pressed her hand to Andy's damp forehead. Clammy but not high enough for an infection. His breathing had grown shallow and his eyes closed. Jenny bumped against Brenda's elbow, her tremors forcing her to take a seat and shove her head in her hands. Sobs racked her thin, teen shoulders.

Oh, what Brenda would give to go into a closet and cry her eyes out. When had the world gone to hell-in-a-hand-basket? Everything she did turned out backwards and she wasn't used to that, being a nurse practitioner. Control was the name of the game and she helped calm people, save lives. Nothing had gone well. She'd lost… well, over a hundred by that point, a death count that superseded all the rest of her other deaths combined.

Jenny glanced up at Brenda and whispered, "Are they all… gone?"

Ten pairs of eyes glanced up at Brenda with Jenny's question which dropped into the silence like a rock in a metal bucket of water. Oh, to go back in time and remove the role of leader she'd somehow gotten stuck with. Brenda didn't want to look any more than the other people. She glanced over her shoulder.

No one stood. No movement. The food-poisoned people lay in organized piles of twenty-five or so, flanked by the young bunch of kids who'd eaten cyanide tablets. Limbs jerked but no conscious movement caught her eye.

Brenda faced the expectant, hopeful faces and closed her eyes, offering a soft shake of her head. Damn. Nobody lived. She didn't have a clue what to say or do. Lack of sleep, food and normal conditions took its toll. She couldn't get her brain to function and the survivors looked the same.

The control she'd held snapped. In a matter of nanoseconds, long strides delivered her to the door where she curled her fingers into fists and beat against the doors, screaming. "You bastards! Get in here and stop this! Aah!"

She slumped against the wood, flattening her hand and sliding down the surface to kneel on the ground. Sobs wrenched from her frame. Damn it. Her soul ached. Those poor people. Tears slid down her cheeks. "You assholes," she whispered.

Brenda leaned her forehead onto the cold handle. Think. She had to figure out what to do next. Nobody was coming to save them. If Brenda wanted out, she had to find a way.

If they didn't get rid of the bodies, they'd soon get sick. Gustavson or Daniel had said she had to assign someone to get rid of the bodies. Did anyone have the energy to do that?

Andy coughed, pulling her attention to him. He opened his eyes and watched her from parted lids.

He spoke, a whisper but stronger than before. "Where are we?"

Brenda dug through the medical supplies by his hip and pulled a fresh gauze square which she dipped into hydrogen peroxide. "We're at the high school by your house."

He searched the ceiling high above them. "We'd almost made it to Hayden. How did I get here? Are Rachel or the kids here?"

"I'm not sure about how you got here. Rachel and the kids aren't at this site. I'm not sure if they made it to your place. I don't know... anything." She couldn't believe how tired she was. Even the lies rolled off her tongue, coated in slurs and stutters. If her sister had made it anywhere, more likely than not Brenda would be unnecessary. But if she were worth anything now, why would they take the chance she'd eat the poisoned bags?

Unless. "What's going on?" Andy licked his chapped lips. "Did you tell anyone about the poisoned bags?"

Sitting back on her heels for a break, Brenda sighed. How did she tell Andy everyone was dead but a handful? "They lied to me." Blurting out the words was one way.

"What?"

"Daniel said the four marked bags were unpoisoned. I told everyone and we opted to dole out the contents to anyone who felt they needed something in their stomach. They're all dead. There are literally ten or so of us left. Ten." She hung her head. "I have to get rid of the bodies, but I don't... unh." Just a little bit of eye closure. A teensy amount of sleep. But when she closed her eyes, the bodies piled up in the dark recesses of her mind. She snapped her lids open. *Oh, hell.* "The bastards shot people right in front of me. I... I couldn't save them." Brenda swallowed the pain she'd been able to bury the last handful of hours. Did she complain about the brand on her neck... not to Andy. He had more burns on his body than her little bitty burn could stand up to. Regardless how "small" it was, she still needed to cover it. The stinging tug when her shirt moved had become a form of Chinese water torture, except she'd welcome a splash of water.

Shock and disbelief riddled the air. Andy stared at his foot while Brenda rechecked his wounds. How did one recover from hearing what she'd dropped on him? Was there a grieving process for that? Death you could deal with. Sickness, marriage, loss, financial need, even disasters and attacks you could find a way to cope with. But how did you accustom yourself to the *anticipation* of those things?

Brenda snorted.

"What?" Andy raised his gaze to her face, questions mixing with dirt and blood.

She sucked her teeth. "I was thinking about anticipating terrible things. Reminds of when Rachel tried explaining fear to me a long time ago. She'd always been adamant that if you had fear for something then that thing ruled you. I always..." Ruled by something you feared. Her exhaustion disappeared.

Andy pushed on the ground and tried to push himself up, but grunted with the effort. "You always what?"

Brenda reached out and lifted him under his armpits – the only place fire never seemed to reach. "You always what?" Brenda pressed her hand to her forehead. "Remember when Rachel came back from Rhode Island and she had that odd tattoo?"

Andy's jaw tightened under the crinkled skin. His eyes narrowed. "Yes. They'd made her take the mark to remind her of what she'd worked on, like a secret society or something. She's never been the same." He leaned back into the wall and grimaced when his shoulders made contact with the cement block structure. "I hated that thing. Reminded us and we didn't want to be reminded."

"Yeah. Well," Brenda leaned forward, shoving her neck into Andy's line of view, "they gave me my own version."

He blew his breath out. "Oh man. Brenda, I'm sorry. Did they burn that in? Were you awake?"

Pulling back, Brenda shrugged. "Yeah, but… it's nothing like your wounds." She wiped at a different puncture wound on his skin two inches from the first. She ignored Andy rolling his eyes. "I think you fell on something with nails or bolts. These are uniform. Do you remember anything?"

He closed his eyes. "Fire and climbing inside a house to push out two teenagers. The house fell in on itself. I think I threw myself under the bed to keep away from the roof. The bed had to be a rod iron frame. Hot as Hades. I don't remember how I got out. The fall was fast. I don't even recall landing."

Brenda nodded. "Adds up to a concussion. Sometimes you remember and sometimes you don't."

"Excuse me." A soft voice behind them pulled Brenda's attention from the small world she'd locked herself in with Andy. The familiarity between them offered comfort unavailable in the hell she'd been locked in. Brenda had blocked out the chaos, even if for only a moment.

One of the girls, about Jenny's age, stared at the bags of food. "Do you think they're all poisoned?"

Brenda had had the same question. If Daniel had lied about the other bags, could he have purposely switched the information? To in fact poison the people that Brenda "valued" above all the rest? Because isn't that what most people do, give the "best" to the ones they love? Brenda was a nurse and didn't work that way.

The pallet hadn't moved since the bags of death had been handed out. Bags of Death... Like a Stephen King novel. Brenda really was losing it. She stood and approached the pile of lunch bags with hesitation. Could it be? A real chance untouched food existed in their midst?

Ripping open the brown paper of the top bag, Brenda glanced at the Uncrustables, peanut-butter and jelly sandwiches with the crusts removed. The packaging hadn't been tampered with. In the four marked bags, the sandwiches had been handmade and wrapped in baggies. In her bag, the milk, while warm, hadn't been touched either. Chips were individually packaged while the chips in the other bags had been in clear, fold top sandwich baggies.

Brenda turned to the small group of survivors. Because of their sacrifice not to eat, they were still alive. Some of them had watched loved ones die. Dirt covered a couple from head to foot like they'd rolled around in it while they slept. Dust bunnies and cobwebs clung to hair and shoulders. Slumped and without fight, defeat wiped the hope from their faces.

"Okay, I'm not sure, but I think some of this food might be okay to eat." Nothing sparked on their faces.

A man with arms the size of dodgeballs busting from his tee-shirt winced. "I don't want to die like that." He jabbed his thumb over his shoulder, unable to look toward the piles of death behind him. Brenda couldn't help but allow her gaze to stray to the jumbled bodies. She shivered.

But they needed something and if there was a chance… "I'll try some." Even if it was poisoned, Brenda needed food. At that point, she didn't really care. Her stomach was eating itself and next it would eat the organs around it. She'd be better one way or the other, food in her stomach or dead. But anything had to be better than where she was at that exact moment.

She pulled out a sandwich and inspected the packaging. No holes or small tears that she could see or feel. A glance at the rest of the group increased her courage, not much, but enough to open the wrapper and hold the food in her hand. Each person leaned forward, the shift in the circle palpable. Their eyes widened.

Raising the bread to her nose, Brenda sniffed. If it was rat poison, then it would affect her with a headache. But they needed a hole to get the granules inside the bag and she hadn't seen any. Yeasty. Oh, for the love. She closed her eyes. Just do it. Take a bite. And before she could rethink it, Brenda tore the sandwich in half and stuffed one in her mouth. Go big or go home.

Chew. Chew. Swallow the half-macerated, half-dry peanut butter and grape jelly sandwich. She couldn't open her eyes. For a second she was afraid it was a chemical reaction, until she realized she was just plain scared. Her empty stomach protested the sudden onslaught of food while welcoming it at the same time.

Okay, she was still breathing. Her heart rate hadn't changed from the strong, fast, freaked out pace it'd held since her house burned down. A slight clamminess to her skin was the only difference, but that was more likely due to the nerves from the moment. Saliva returned to her mouth and she stuffed the rest of the sandwich into her mouth. Hell, too late now anyway and she was still hungry.

"Brenda? Are you okay?" Jenny's hope raised her voice a few octaves.

Opening her eyes, Brenda wiped at the crumbs clinging to her dry lips. "Surprisingly. At least the sandwiches don't seem to be poisoned."

Andy coughed and spoke, his voice stronger, "The Brenda I know would have faked like she was dying just for a laugh."

Smiles came a little easier with food in her stomach. "Some other time."

The older man to Jenny's left pointed to the bags. "Do you think they're all safe?"

A woman, tears in her eyes and tracks down her cheeks shook her head. "But they're all dead. How can we eat when they just died? Right here? Acting like nothing happened." Her voice broke on the last word.

Brenda's smile softened and her stomach clenched around the meager offering. "I know. It isn't easy, is it? Imagine how I feel... the men lied to me about the food. I believed them and all those people are dead because I wanted to share instead of keeping the bad food for myself." She let the reality sink in. "But I'm not going to roll over and let those bastards win. We need to find a way out of here. I'm not going to live like this until they succeed at wiping us out."

Only two of the people nodded, the rest stared at the bags. "Obviously, we're too hungry to plan anything. I think the sandwiches are probably safe. I checked the packaging first."

Nobody waited for further encouragement. The sounds of rustling bags filled the small area they sat in. Brenda pulled open another bag and reclaimed her seat beside her brother-in-law.

She'd only be able to offer the soft stuff anyway. His mouth might be burned from breathing the oven-like air. He was lucky there hadn't been any bronchial swelling or lung failure from the smoke-damage. Dime-sized, the bite she offered Andy wouldn't hurt him and would barely make a dent in any hunger, but it was a start.

While Andy took his time chewing the small morsel, Brenda looked over the remaining Americans. Four women besides herself and eight men. No one over forty. The woman with the tears didn't touch a bag, but continued to look toward the dead inhabitants.

Brenda tore off another piece. She had to figure out a way to get rid of the bodies.

Death from poison wasn't pretty and she didn't know how much had been used with how fast acting it was. Desperate people wouldn't notice an odd taste. The bodies, though. Ugh.

"What's the matter?" A crease between Andy's brows looked like folded plastic with the sheen of the burned skin. His burns reminded Brenda of hers.

She tore another chunk. "They told me I have to get rid of the bodies, but I don't know how to get rid of… so many." The white bread held her gaze. What could she do? "Do I tell them?"

"I don't understand what's going on… "

Brenda turned to the group and forced herself to look up from the food in her lap.

Bruised, his face half swollen and shirt torn, a man in his late twenties held up a hand like he sat in first grade, a sandwich in his other.

Open bags filled the spaces between them. Brenda didn't want to live on PB and Js, but she didn't have the courage to try anything else. She sighed. "I don't either. But I think these… um…I was told to get a group together to get out the bodies, and I'm thinking that 'group' is going to be us." She waved her hands around their small collection.

"I don't want to move dead bodies. Not those or my aunt's." The man crossed his arms and tucked his hands under his elbows, his sandwich eaten in two bites.

If she couldn't whine, then hell if someone else could. "I don't either. But here's what we have to do. First of all, suck it up. Things get worse before they get better. And we might have only one chance to escape and it might be moving the bodies." Brenda couldn't look at the prostrate group past the boundaries of the survivors. "Don't look at the bodies. Focus on me one more second and then you can finish eating." She spoke lower, her tones reaching the members as they leaned in. "We have to get free or we're dead. Do you understand? We have to."

The nods reached her but the tears on their faces burned. She pointed over her shoulder and called out, "I'm sorry. I wish we didn't have to do this. I'll figure something out. Any ideas would be greatly appreciated."

~

Hell. Hell on earth. Watching people die and then sitting amongst their dead bodies.

Worse? Not all of the poisoned were dead. Almost, but not quite, and their pain-filled whimpers sliced through the silence and echoed throughout the gymnasium.

Brenda hadn't conjured up the courage to ask if any of the survivors had watched a loved one die. She didn't want to know. A glance over her shoulder revealed one of the men she'd shared a sandwich with approaching a writhing woman on the floor. Crap.

"I have morphine for them. Would you mind passing it around? I need to finish cleaning his wounds." Brenda passed the breakable capsules to Jenny. Brenda had reached her limit and used Andy as a cop-out to send a teenager to do a terrible thing. But she couldn't. She couldn't.

A Charlie horse clamped the palm muscles in her hand as she clutched a verified clear spot on Andy's arm. She hummed under her breath to relieve her mind from the torrential cries bearing down on her, all around. Finally, she gave in and prayed those suffering would die soon. Die now.

"I know this is hard for you." Andy's words broke through her self-induced bubble. She focused on his voice and watched his face. "I've teased you about being abrupt and uncaring, but the truth is, I know you're a very good nurse. I've seen it. And now I've experienced it. Thanks for bandaging me and fixing the wounds." He offered a grimace Brenda accepted as a smile.

"I'm not very good. You were right. Everyone was right. I just don't believe in sugar-coating things. Rachel was always good at that. Delivering news in a way that made you think it was all flowers and jewels, even if what she reported was schizophrenia or sociopathic syndrome." Brenda's sister, the perfect Rachel. "I tell it like it is and most people don't understand that."

"At least they understand what's happening. Imagine the mind games the enemy would have us wrapped in then."

Mind games. Rachel had said something about that once. "Andy, do you remember when Rachel left for the east coast?"

"Yeah, she came back warning us against using fluoride or eating Twinkies." He laughed.

"No," Brenda shook her head, "not the food, remember when she had those nightmares?"

"What nightmares?" Andy pressed his lips together, enhancing the cracks and scaling skin.

Brenda looked past his shoulder to the wall. She could focus on the static of the cement bricks. Easier to think without the trauma of his burns facing her. "Rachel used to call me in the middle of the night, crying, and saying things I used to think was nonsense about testing she'd had to design on what broke the human spirit. 'Broken humans' she'd called them. I can't remember who 'they' were, but she couldn't sleep for weeks, maybe months. I took that graveyard shift and she stopped calling me." Why had she cried? "Something about kids with parents and siblings. When I'd finally gotten her to calm down, she'd shut me down before I could ask more about it, said it was in the past and that she didn't want to think about it. What if this was the kind of thing she'd helped design?"

"Rachel?" Andy looked into his lap. "I don't think she could come up with something like this. Not the Rachel I married."

"Andy, Rachel can do anything. Anything. The second you stop giving her credit, the second she loses her respect for you. Don't do that. And stop protecting her from everything. She knows things you'll never wrap your engineer brain around." If she could slap him without damaging his nerves, she would. Damn him. He'd always treated Rachel like she was a fragile princess and it drove Brenda nuts. And more than a little jealous.

Andy lifted his gaze to her, the steady focus unnerving. "You sound like you might like her."

Brenda jerked her head back. "Of course I like her. She's my sister. Why wouldn't I like her?" Couldn't accuse Andy of reading her mind.

He shrugged, his gaze unwavering.

"What?" And why wouldn't she like her sister? She loved her.

"Things have been kind of tense for a while. Haven't heard from you for a time."

"I need to check…" She released his arm, her fingers stiff and unyielding. Standing, she didn't know where to go.

Quiet. A stolen whisper here, a half sob over there. Brenda's pulse quickened. Heaviness in the room as the remaining people left their bodies. Her countrymen. People she could have seen at the store or passed on the road. Poisoned like rats because the captors had bravado for everything but doing the job themselves. They weren't even there to witness who lived and who died.

Wait. They didn't know. Hadn't checked. She squeezed the shoulder of the fellow survivor. He held a woman who shuddered in his arms. Brenda couldn't focus on the dying woman or what she meant to the man.

The nurse in her screamed for justice. The spirit in her ached for revenge. What could she do? How did they help these people? How did she help herself with them? An idea played at the edges of her mind, on the fringe of shock and disbelief.

A woman pressed the eyelids closed of a younger man laid across the free-throw line of the basketball court. Hanging on the wall a "Go Trojans!" spirit poster striped like a tiger watched the action. Days ago kids had filled the gym for PE, maybe in between classes, and now it served as a jail for people who shivered into death as the poison attacked their nervous systems. *Don't think about it, Brenda. Focus. If you fail, they will fall apart.*

She returned to Andy, determined to hold her emotions inside a vault locked away in the forest. If she could get free with all the living, maybe then she could search out her grief and release it. Whatever may be left.

Squatting beside him, Brenda whispered behind his ear. "I think we'll have to use these to get out."

"Use what?" Andy glanced from her face to the bodies.

"The dead people. We can say we're ready to transport them. Or we could hide under the bleachers. Or we could try to slip out the side doors. Or the windows. I don't know. But we have to do something. We can't trust anymore food that comes through. We're going to get sick if we stay in here with the corpses much longer. Something has to change and it can't be more deaths. No one will make it past another trauma." She turned her gaze to Andy's face. The fire could have done more damage than the burns on the side of his neck. His ear was the worst on his entire body, but she'd glued it where it'd burned through the delicate skin and while it would be closer to his head, he'd still have it. Fortunately he could still hear and hadn't lost any feeling in his skin or eyes. "Andy. We have to get out of here before grief cuts through the shock. Once that happens, they'll be worthless and we'll have to leave them."

"Could you leave them? Even if you and I could get out, would you leave them to whatever fate is planned for them?" Andy's voice carried.

"Don't leave us. We'll do whatever. We can do it. Their deaths can't have been in vain." A gaggle of five of the survivors huddled together feet from Andy and Brenda, bent half-way in the fetal position with their arms crossed over their stomachs, loss stripping their individuality. One aching mass.

Brenda approached the group. "I don't want to. But if we don't figure something out soon, we'll be too sick to do anything, or they'll make another move against us, or you guys will become incompetent in most everything but breathing. Some of you won't even want to continue without your loved ones. Right now you're in survival mode, but when it wears off – and it will wear off – what then? What good will you be?" The remaining five returned from the floor.

"Don't leave us. Tell us the options and we'll figure it out." One of them said, but how could Brenda look closer than that? If she looked too close, her heart would break and she would lose her edge.

Tossing a glance at Andy, Brenda nodded. "Okay, but you'll need to choose fast and you all have to agree. I can figure out the details, but only after you choose." She waited for their nods. The worse thing? She knew what they would choose and she didn't want to do it. "Options are, one, some play dead and we move the living as well as the dead out of the gym and wherever they plan on the bodies going. Two would be to move bodies but run as soon as we're out the doors which could open up a slew of gunfire we can't guarantee will hit or miss. Three, hide under the bleachers and hope they think we all died. And four, well, I don't have a four, but I can come up with something that doesn't involve staying here and waiting." She watched them take in the choices she'd supplied. "I'll give you a minute to talk it over and when I come back, we need something. Ask yourselves what the risks might be and how much you're willing to risk to get out. I can't guarantee it's any safer out there, but at least we won't be fed rat poison."

She turned back to the group as they eyed each other. "And one more thing. If you're thinking of maybe sticking it out here, hoping they won't do anything more, check this out." Brenda ripped her collar down, the untreated burn damp around the edges. "They branded me for the fun of it. I didn't know anything, but I still got burned."

Tension toppled onto the group's fear. Decisions with consequences far beyond their scope of understanding loomed in immediacy. Option four was to stay and Brenda had offered the possibilities with that choice as well.

Guilt and sadness swamped her. She tried to offer a consoling smile, but found she had no consolation to offer.

Beside Andy, she struggled to hold in the exhaustion warring to claim her. Sleep? Only a word, a noun, a verb, but something she so desperately needed like oxygen. If sleep made its way onto the Periodic Table of Elements, would its letters be Zz?

"I'm letting them decide." She glanced at the group deep in discussion, eyebrows lowered and hands gesticulating at waist level. Andy didn't answer. Meeting his gaze, Brenda allowed her nonchalance to slip. "Andy, one way or the other we have to get out of here which means we need to find out if you can walk or what your limits are. Do your legs hurt? Are your feet injured?"

He shook his head, the effort to speak evident as he swallowed. "Hands. Leave me."

His hands. Dang it. How could he move the bodies if he couldn't do much with burned palms and fingers? Brenda would be able to help him up with his arms or under his armpits, but not much. Andy wasn't a huge man but he was taller than Brenda and a solid fifty pounds of muscle heavier. The math wasn't hard to figure out.

"I'm not leaving you here. Rachel would kill me. We need to figure something out. Think, Andy. You need to get to Rachel and the kids. What can we do to help you?" They had no access to crutches or a wheelchair, nothing that could remotely be used to at least get him out the doors and away from the range of guns. Unless… "Hold on. I know which way they'll go, but I'm going to speed things along."

Brenda returned to the group. "Did you make your decision yet?" Twisted expressions met her search. Of course they hadn't. Brenda had seen adults come in to her hospital with the inability to comprehend the consequences of drinking and driving or unprotected sex. The captives wouldn't be able to grasp the concept that no matter what they did some of them would most likely die. They were in shock and showing it.

She didn't expect them to know which choice would be the lesser evil. The lesser gamble. Statistics she understood, but she'd never been good at gaming. Hopefully her luck was different when it mattered and she stood to lose lives not dollars.

She spoke loud enough for Andy to hear. "I'll choose for you. We're going to have some of us act dead and the rest will move the bodies. We have roughly twenty or so still alive. Our weakest survivors will be the… dummies and we'll mix them in with the crowd. Two people need to carry one person. We'll have to make multiple trips each to get everyone out. Some dead bodies will go out first in case they choose to check them. I'd hate to get anybody killed because we planned poorly."

Brenda's stomach ached. "I'm sorry. We need to get going. If you have loved ones, move their bodies to the back of the group so we don't have to move them. I don't know how much time we have before they come back."

They nodded in jerky motions. One girl looked over her shoulder. "I think everyone is… gone." She bit her lip and turned back to Brenda.

The dying. Poisoned. How had things gotten this far? Trapped and poisoned like rats. Dehumanizing.

"I'm sorry. I have nothing more for you guys than that. I wish I had thought of the possibility. I just… didn't think they'd try to kill us." Excuses offered to people who couldn't defend themselves with her intentions. "Go round up what you need. Let's get started."

Walking the few feet to Andy, Brenda finally had something to focus on. "I'm going to have you be the fourth or fifth evacuated. That way you'll have someone to help you but you can still lead the others as they come out." Brenda fell to the rubbery wood floor and shoved her head into her shaking hands. "Andy, what am I doing? I can't do this. I'm not a leader. I'm not someone people follow. Deciding for others? I'm a nurse practitioner. I handle the sick, not escape plans. What if more people die because of me?"

"Who's died because of you?" His whisper cut across her low cries.

"Over eighty people, here in the gym. Can't you see them? Unh… I didn't think he would lie to me so blatantly. I didn't think. I was too happy to get the food and supplies." Brenda refused to give in to the craving to soak in her own tears, allow the release sobs would bring.

"Don't be ridiculous. Nobody elected you to be the food tester, the nurse or doctor of this place. You had to jump up and do what you did because no one else could. Their deaths are not your fault. It's theirs." He lifted a blistered hand and pointed to the exit. "We need to get out and there aren't a lot of options. You're providing us with something. We'll take it or die. Do you think they're going to keep us alive after the stunt you uncovered?"

Why would he be wrong in the whole mess of horrors they'd been subjected to – what made their circumstance special? "Do you think other people are being held? In other places…"

Her brother-in-law nodded. And Brenda decided maybe he wasn't so bad after all. Not many people would admit to the possibility of the worst without a whole lot of words to explain it away. She appreciated the simplicity of his answer. She didn't want excuses, she wanted knowledge. And action. And escape. And damn, if she wasn't going to get it.

Resolve bolstered her emotions, shored up her energy and blasted away the tiredness. "Let's do this. I'm sure we don't have much time."

Everyone poisoned enough to die was dead. Brenda walked amongst them. An hour, maybe more, for the rest to suffer from the ingestion before succumbing to its effects. The living gathered in the corner beside Andy. Whispers and glances cast around, they tried to avoid looking into the bowels of the gym at the remains of loved ones and others they'd never known.

Brenda had to choose the bodies that would go out mixed amongst her charges. Somehow, someway, they'd become her wards. The people she was responsible for, regardless of what Andy said. The weight pulled at her and again, her stomach clenched. When she got out of this, she needed a toilet and bad.

A tall man caught her eye. In death, he gripped the fingers of a woman. Damn. Brenda recognized him as the one who'd wanted to take a lunch to his wife. She turned from their twisted fingers and faced the mass of victims.

The people she chose to take out first, she marked by crossing their right arm over their abdomens. Hard to miss if one looked for it, but spread out enough over so many bodies, no one without the information would pick it up. She and the few who would move them needed lighter bodies or their strength would be sapped. Some of them hadn't eaten in days.

She approached the group, nerves clanging over the sounds of shifting life in their feet and whispers. "Ready? Because this is going to suck."

Nervous laughter covered a few sobs and gasps. Brenda clucked her tongue. "I know, this is terrible. You want to grieve. But we need to survive first. Grief is a luxury at this point. Hold it in. Control it. Once we get out, and I promise we'll get out, you can cry and scream and get revenge. But right now, we need to act." Twelve would have to do the moving. Looking around the group there were only eight that were smaller, most of them girls. Andy would have to be moved and he wasn't light, but the guys that made up the other half of the group looked to be capable and angry.

Anger she could mold and direct. Anger would do.

She pointed. "You and you will organize the bodies. We'll do four dead ones first. Then, Andy, over there, next so he can be our watch as we move the rest. We'll move another dead, then a live one. And alternate as we go so that the last one is you." Brenda pointed at the smallest girl. "I'm sorry to have to end with the smallest. But we'll have more energy at the start and can't be dragging at the end someone heavier when we still need to run."

Brenda met Andy's gaze. "You think?" He nodded and she scanned the group. "Is everyone okay with this? Say now so we can reorder the plan. Or even say if you don't want to be in on it. You don't have to leave. I promise. You can stay here." She doubted herself. Even she was allowed doubt. "I could be wrong. You might be safe here. They might have been weeding out the weak. Or…"

"Or looking for ways to get rid of us. Looking for ways to torture us." Andy's voice hinted at strength, even through the frail thread he offered to the group. "Brenda, you're not wrong. And you know it."

She tucked her chin. How did she answer that? She wanted to scream at them she was scared as hell that they were going to be caught. That she didn't know what to expect. That maybe, just maybe, they were all going to wake up and this was just a terrible nightmare. But no, she wouldn't do anything of the sort, because she had smothered the pandemonium sparking in their eyes. No way would she do anything to restart the coals.

"Everybody's in? Okay, one last warning. When they come in to let us take you out, you can't move. At all. You're dead. They might kick you, spit on you, slam guns on you, whatever, but you must not move. If you move, you'll really be dead. Do you understand?" The chosen dummies nodded their heads. Brenda wanted to shake them. Did they really understand? Did they?

"Separate. Let's try to get this done in ten minutes." A white corner of gauze packaging poked from beneath Andy's knee which reminded her. "Does anyone have a backpack or bag?"

A battered bag passed from hand to hand. Brenda grabbed hold and nodded. "Perfect. Thank you." A dead person could have donated it to the cause along with their life. She forced the thought from her mind.

While the group organized as Brenda had instructed, she packed up as much of the medical supplies she could fit. She wouldn't be allowed to take them out but if she packed them on top of Andy under a coat and try to pass him off as a larger male, she'd be able to have them on hand. She hadn't told him what she planned yet, but he'd agree it was smart thinking. She hoped.

"Brenda? We're ready." Jenny touched Brenda's shoulder, her voice low. "Andy is in place and we used some extra clothes to cover up the others better including their faces. Are you ready?"

"Thanks, Jenny. I need this packed tight against Andy underneath his jacket, please." Brenda looked to the doors. "I'll go tell them we're ready."

Jenny took the bag without comment, but her eyes pleaded for answers and offered sympathy. Brenda faced the locked exit.

What would she say? Would they come? She'd banged on the door and nobody had answered. What if they didn't answer? Hell, what if they did?

She'd avoided thinking about this part of the plan, thinking she'd wing it because she didn't know how to counter maneuver. Like chess. She always chose white because white usually went first.

Think like she played her knight against the rook. What would she do? She stepped forward. People claimed poker face, but it was better to say chess face. If you were a sneak attack or an aggressive player, passive offensive or conniving, you had to hide your strategy in your thought process, in your words, mannerisms. Chess. She could do this. But the urge to spit in Daniel's face might be hard to overcome.

The doors had no windows. Her knock echoed in the small space beside the opposite bleachers from where Andy had holed up. Beside the water fountain. Brenda didn't even want to chance drinking from the metal basin at that point. The bastards might have managed to tamper with the water as well.

She waited. An expectant hush hung over the gym. After another moment, she flattened her hand and wailed on the wooden panel until her palm felt bruised. Not more than fifteen seconds later, Gustavson, accompanied by two foot soldiers dressed in black and blank expressions, appeared. A minion, his hair short and his eyes clear, unlocked the door. He turned and stared at her.

"What?"

Brenda motioned to the supine forms spread around the dim gym. The lights hadn't been turned on. Plexiglass windows showed shadows and shifting light, but no bright sun to hint at morning, noon or evening. "I think a virus struck us. The majority of the people are dead. We need to get the bodies out of here. I have a detail ready to do it, but we can't get out." Innocence contained clarity in her features. If he knew she suspected poisoning, he'd be on alert, but if she played her cards right, he might think he'd gotten away undetected and would be complacent for a while longer.

He nodded. "We'll be out in five minutes." The door clicked shut in her face and a jingle of keys called from the other side.

Five minutes. Jogging to Jenny, Brenda repeated the time for the group. Five minutes. What was she forgetting? What could she do to further protect them? Improve their chances? They had to get free.

But where would they go? When everyone got out, or even a fraction escaped, where would they go?

Brenda rubbed her forehead. A migraine shaped and nudged, cutting into the soft space behind her eye. She'd never been fond of responsibility and here she'd taken on a whole whale load. What was she supposed to do? Too many questions with too few answers. Screw it. From that point on, she'd do her best and hope and pray the consequences weren't too severe.

Four minutes.

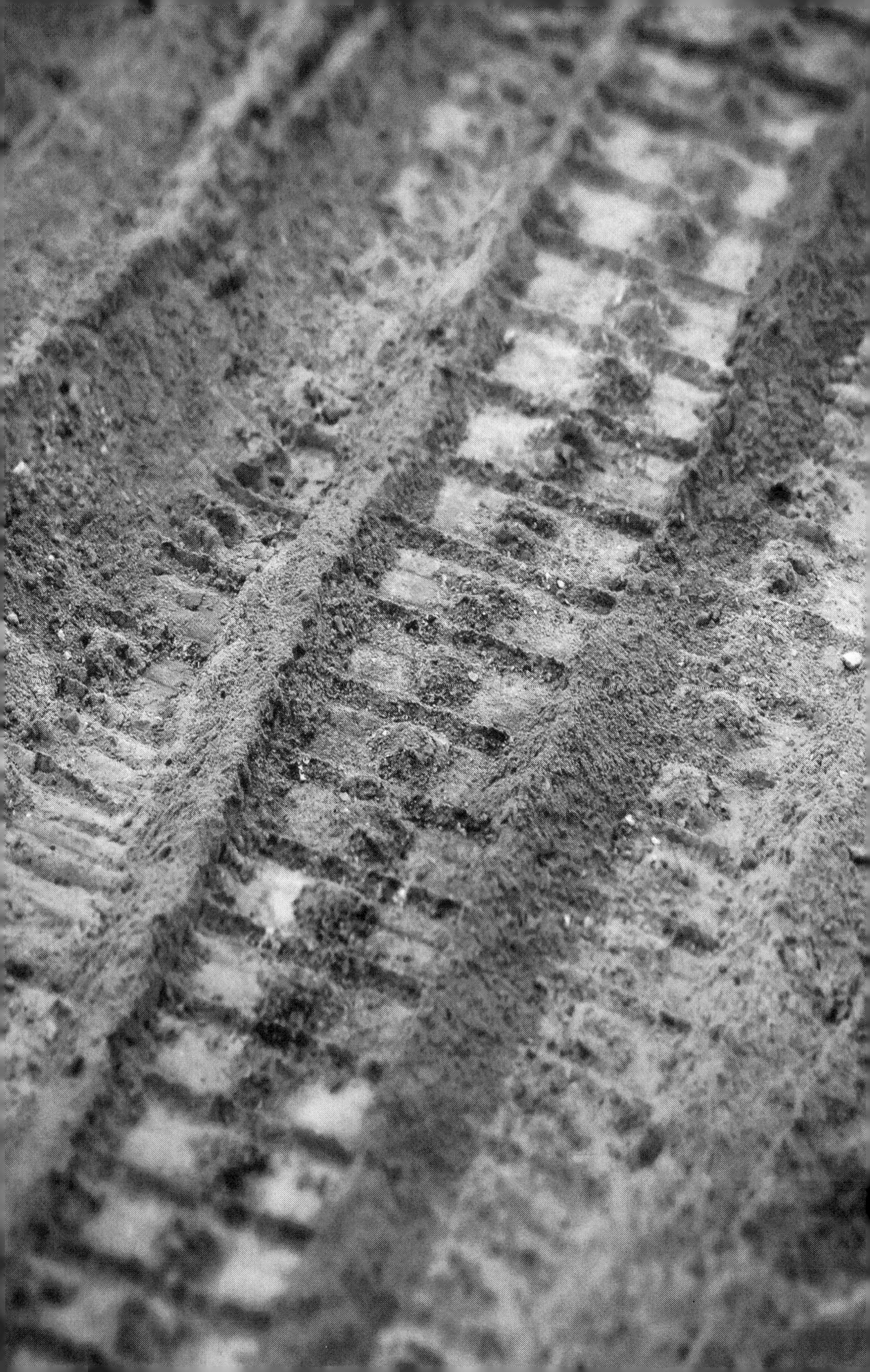

Chapter 15

Tom

Cole claimed the first shift in the rough-riding trailer. The going looked rocky.

Tom was grateful for an opportunity to ask Josh questions without Cole hearing.

Hard to believe Rachel had allowed Cole to join them on the rescue mission. "Do you think Rachel has a control issue?" *Crap, Tom, sometimes you speak before thinking, well done.*

Josh laughed. "I guess you could say that. Andy used to come up and complain about how much she babied her kids, bit too much sometimes, and never let them come up for more than a day or two without her. You have to hand it to her, though. If nothing else, she got her kids away from the city and to safety. The woman has her priorities straight."

"Is she really a government psychologist?" The idea scared the hell out of Tom. People who worked for the government didn't have protection against brainwashing. No privacy. Nothing private. He didn't like the sensation of ant feet running up and down his spine when he thought of it. She'd been his therapist. What had she handed over to Big Brother about him?

The back of Josh's head moved. His voice lowered. "No. She's a freelancer, so never actually employed by any one branch of any government or military. Andy didn't know much more than that, but he refused to let her sign up with any specific branch. He didn't want to move from the area."

"Has she worked for others beside ours?" Now that was a nightmare. What the hell had that lady been up to? She'd been in control when he'd known her, but the person she'd become seemed made of ice. Not many emotions played across her face or in her voice.

"Yes. I'm not sure which ones, information was always classified. But she once told Andy that she'd never contract outside of the States again. We apparently still follow some ethical and humane guidelines. Many other countries lost their grip on humanity a long time ago and do testing on orphans and homeless people. Psychology is such a loose science that while you can prove the affects of biological testing, you can't prove or disprove the cruelty of mental abuse."

Tom swallowed. Josh painted an ugly picture Tom didn't want to face.

Rocky slopes gave way to a grassy trail. Tom didn't want to return to the city. He didn't want to see the dead mingled with bombed buildings. At Rachel's it'd been a mirage, an oasis from the terror ripping the countryside apart. His reprieve hadn't been long enough.

A bump jostled the supplies they'd packed and secured with elastic tie downs. Heavy metal rested against the small of Tom's back, a comforting threat. If he pulled the borrowed piece out, he'd damn well better be ready to use it.

"Do you think there are a lot of survivors?" Maybe his parents had made it in Spokane. Right then, they too could be stuck in a high school in the city, housed with food and clothing, protected from the bombs.

But if the map on the militia's site was accurate, the buildings in downtown Spokane up to the base had been little more than rubble, not much different from the travesty left behind by a flaming tornado.

Josh's reply barely carried over the rumble of the engine. "I don't know, Tom."

Be honest. Tom wanted to yell and scream, but men didn't suffer in public. They bottled it up and corked it, tossing the container in the corner with their bumps and bruises to be stored away until there was just no more room. His storage overflowed and he was running out of places to chuck the feelings. Emotions. Damn.

Josh slowed the quad. A hundred feet separated them from the freeway on-ramp and the road to the Old Highway. The freeway had an open vulnerability whereas the Old Highway, lined one side by the deep lake and the other with trees, would provide great cover and options for slipping away. The windy road would take a bit longer, but the lower chances of being caught were too appealing. Josh angled the tires and they coasted down to the potholed pavement.

Undercover of the forest and beneath the overpass, Josh parked the four-wheeler. "Okay guys, we need to discuss a few things before we go any further." Sliding off the vinyl seat, he stood to face them, grave finality stamped on his features under the slight shadow of beard and rim of his hat.

Tom glanced at Cole who waited as if he'd expected some sort of pep talk or discussion.

"Tom, you remember what it was like when you were attacked. Cole, you escaped before you could see any real damage. I'm not discounting what happened to your dad, but I am saying that you didn't see bodies, you didn't see actual death in front of you." Josh looked off into the trees, as if the words he wanted sat on a limb deep in the shadows and if he could just pull them out, Tom and Cole would be appropriately warned.

Josh took a deep breath. "I've never been in a war. I've never seen death but from what Rachel told me, this isn't going to be easy or fun. We will see people, dead, alive, in pieces. Random things will stick out to us and weaken us. We have to hold it together. The second we grieve for the dead or dying is the moment we will become lost and lose our purpose. Which is to bring Brenda back. Our sole goal of going out here is to get Brenda." He nodded at Tom. "And maybe your friend, Jenny. But that's it. Ignore the other people. Ignore them. It's not going to be easy, but I want you to do this. Do you understand?"

Tom nodded his head. An ache in his shoulders testified his anxiety. He wasn't looking forward to this. He'd already escaped hell and now he was running back into the flames.

"I'm serious. This will be ugly. Keep your firearms at the ready and don't hesitate to shoot. We have no idea who the enemy is or what they look like." Josh nodded and then paused. He loped to the trailer and spoke to Cole in small murmurs and silent nods. Josh patted his shoulder and jogged back to the quad and climbed back on the seat.

Tom called to Cole, before the engine started, "Do you want to switch?"

Cole shook his head. "Nah, I'm good. Thanks." Leaving Tom feeling more than a little relieved.

Josh turned the motor over and eased onto the empty highway. The road's black pebbled surface passed beneath them, smoother than the mountainous trails. Tires hummed with increasing speed.

A shotgun blast resounded across the smooth lake. Birds scattered from the treetops. Tom ducked, his breathing hitched. He clenched his hands on the back of Josh's coat. "What the hell?"

On the road ahead, a man in black cargo pants and camouflage jacket postured with his weapon aimed loosely in their direction.

The brakes groaned in protest as Josh stopped fast. Tom stiffened against rocking forward into Josh.

"Who goes there?" The man spit to the side, his squinted eyes never straying from Josh and Tom. "I'm not afraid of shootin' yous. I won't miss neither."

Josh muttered to Tom, "Crap. He talks like a redneck but that's easy to do if you watch John Wayne movies."

Tom watched the weapon become steadier and surer in its aim as they failed to answer his question. His dad had always laughed and said you could tell an Idahoan by one true tic. "Ask if he voted for the latest honest democrat."

Josh didn't hesitate. "Did you vote for the honest democrat?"

"Shit. Those two words don't belong in the same sentence. You must be a communist." He raised his gun to his shoulder. "Democrats don't belong and neither do commies."

"NM50 sent us." Tom yelled over Josh's shoulder.

The barrel lowered. If possible, the man's eyes narrowed further. "Eh?"

"Dilbeck. We're on a rescue mission. The attackers are collecting captives and storing them at the high schools." Tom's breathing had quickened. The tense moment gripped him. Was he saying too much? Why hadn't Josh stepped in?

"Lieutenant Dilbeck's still in the NM?" The barrel lowered a centimeter.

"He's major now."

The man dropped his gun completely and waved them forward. "No, son, he's been major, that's the test to see if you really know Major Dilbeck." His hick affectation dropped and his sloppy manner crisped to a stiffened back and straight shoulders.

"We're trying to get to Post Falls. Do you know what the situation is?" Josh motioned to the smoky haze lingering over the western horizon.

"We're on our way to Coeur d'Alene and Lake City high schools to see what we can do there. I'm not sure how many foot soldiers are on soil, but we've been instructed to be prepared for any action." He offered his hand. "David Farnham."

"Josh Hughes. Nice to meet you. You said 'we'?"

David pursed his lips and a shrill whistle pierced the air in a three-beat pulse. Six similarly dressed men secreted from the trees along the road line, coming to stand beside the street. David nodded in their direction. "This is my regiment. We were all on leave when the attack came and met in the lower Fernan area. Dilbeck said he'd been contacted by one other radio handle, but he didn't tell us who. We have family in the schools. We hope."

"Us, too. Does anyone know about Spokane? Are there any survivors? Do we know who is doing the invading?"

Tom glanced at Josh. He'd omitted they were the handle. But why?

Farnham tilted his head. "The worst part? We think they've been living among us for a while. Some of them, informants, turned on us right on the heels of the earthquakes and the tsunamis. I heard the airspace was cleared for aid and instead we got bombed. Washington wasn't even ready. I think they've called back some of our troops from other countries, but embassies are being attacked and the east side just had a nine-point-one earthquake rip through Pennsylvania. America's hurting and no one's going to help us… but us."

"You're better informed than we are." Josh offered a laugh that suggested a question needing an answer.

"Could be. But I didn't know Post Falls had captives, too. Do you need help getting them out? We could swing up to our schools and then loop back to yours." David raised his eyebrows.

Tom swallowed. Farnham and his group seemed like an okay band, but something wasn't sitting right. He couldn't pinpoint what the problem was, but distance between the two groups wouldn't be a bad thing. He cleared his throat, but only loud enough to carry the few inches to Josh's ears.

"I appreciate the offer. The only problem is, we don't know how long they're going to keep the captives in the schools or even if they'll be kept alive." Josh shifted in his seat and cast a glance over his shoulder at Tom and Cole. A warning in his eyes kept them silent.

"What's your handle on the ham? We can contact you with any information we get or vice versus." Tom spoke up. Move. They needed to get moving.

Farnham pointed at a smaller member of his group. "Hambone over there is the radio geek. He uses HIT33. We rally through him. What's yours?"

HIT33? They couldn't be the Hate IT Coalition out of Hayden. HIT had moved onto the Aryan nation compound a few years after it'd been confiscated and sold. The main handle at the compound had picked air fights with Tom's dad over positional descriptions and technique. He'd even gone so far as to report Tom's dad's airwave activity to the FAA.

Tom spoke before Josh could offer theirs. "FOUR19. I'm the radio man. We'll listen for you. Let us know if you need anything."

Josh took the hint and started the engine. Farnham and his mates waved them away. Tom swore he could feel their gazes on him well past the turn in the road.

"FOUR19? As in a minute before marijuana time? Are you serious? That's not your handle, anyway. What if they come up with something?" Josh didn't turn his head.

"My buddy's call handle before he died. HIT33 is a handle from Hate IT."

"Really?" Josh tilted his head, but facing forward his expression was hidden from Tom. Had he known what Hate IT was?

"They caused a lot of problems for my dad and me on the air waves. I even had to change channels when they'd get on for a while because of the harassment. They complained Dad was in on the conspiracies to govern and control." Tom gripped the metal rack he sat on. "I'd never understood it. He hated government. Thought we'd all be better off without one and just have a Lord of the Flies existence."

"But even they had…"

"I know. But Dad liked ideals. He didn't care about the logistics unless it was *his* reality. One time, he wanted a patient to have a weird diagnosis so bad, he actually rigged the tests to read something different. While the patient wasn't hurt, Dad had a lot of fun testing and diagnosing what it could be."

"Is your dad a doctor?" Josh rounded the next corner and pushed the engine to pull them up a long, steep-graded hill. The speed steady but ground-covering.

Is? Or was? "Yeah. Doctor of osteopathy. One of the few in the area."

"Nice. If Farnham is Hate IT, do you think they're going up to cause problems for the captives or the captors?"

"Captors. It fits that their families are up there. The compound is in Hayden but that doesn't mean everyone lived there. Lake City and Coeur d'Alene schools covered a large district." What had been the real problem? Did he care what Farnham was up to? "They tend to do the opposite of smart. Loud mouth and brash.

I'm surprised you don't know more about them, living as close as you do."

"I'm more of an introvert. Actually, it's funny, Andy was my only friend for the last few years."

The hill leveled out and slanted downward. A cemetery eerily untouched beside a shredded restaurant had an ambience of hope in the devastation surrounding it. Swiss-cheesed, the road would never be managed properly with a car, even a small one like a Volkswagen or Festiva. The four-wheeler would press its luck if it didn't stick to the wider portions.

Josh locked the brake and shut off the engine. A bird chirped in the sudden silence. Pink and white flowers grew in the crack of the sidewalk feet from Tom's boot. Rubble and dirt pushed around the lean patch, drawing Tom's gaze to encase a pile of dirt, pavement, and a red sports car in a sandwich resembling a club, layered just so. Stuck to the bumper, a red circle proclaimed "No More War" in white letters.

No more. Like they really even knew what war was like. An odd odor mixed sugary sweetness with bitter sour egg. "We need to move, Josh. I smell gas."

Josh sniffed, brushing the dirt off his hands as he rose from checking something under the four-wheeler. "Yep, that's natural gas. Climb off. We need to push until we're out of range."

Tom climbed down and Cole copied, stretching even as he positioned himself behind the rear wheels. Popped in neutral, brakes off, the four-wheeler rolled smoothly along the flat surface, past demolished buildings and cars, intact offices and houses whose landscaping was untouched.

Cole gasped and pointed. A pale hand protruded from under the jagged pieces of a door. Smudged skin with painted nails. A small ring on the pinky finger. The boys couldn't look away. No way could a body be attached. The panel was only large enough for a cabinet.

Josh pushed forward. "Come on, guys. That won't be the last one you see. Look at the road and don't focus on anything else."

But the deeper into town they pushed, the more cluttered and chaotic the devastation became. A stroller pinched between two buildings. A bar and grill's awning had collapsed and covered debris from a fire that had gutted the insides. A condominium, stripped of its northern corner, resembled a pop icon whose skirt had flown up over a grate. Kitchens, dining rooms, and bedrooms gaped from the shorn opening.

"We need to go up this road." Tom puffed. He was in shape but the quad was a beast. The stupid thing had to match a small car in weight. "We're almost to the resort. We don't know where they kept these survivors." The lake. Oh, Tom would have a hard time getting close to a body of water again. Even baths would remind him of body parts bobbing against him.

"I think we're far enough away from the gas leak. Let's get out of here." Josh swung his leg over the seat and started the engine.

Tom looked at Cole. "Do you mind if I ride in the trailer for a bit?"

"Nope." Cole, pale beneath his tan, switched spots with Tom.

A pat to the side of the wagon, Tom settled in amongst the food and supplies they'd tucked under a large tarp. Josh pulled forward and Tom welcomed the sway and jolt of the unsuspended wheels. Anything to get his mind off the last few days.

Chapter 16

Andy

Damn the pain. The burns didn't sting as bad as they should compared to the hole in his side or the pounding in his head. He'd distracted Brenda from looking too closely at him, pretended his only wounds were outside of his clothes.

If he had let her know how bad he really was, she'd never have agreed to a risky escape plan. She'd be under some false hope that they'd all make it through the next trap.

Boots slapped on the gym floor. Andy breathed shallow through his nose. The shirt they'd covered his head with smelled of blood and urine, not the scents you want to breathe in and out while drenched in your own fear.

Set up as the fifth body to leave, Andy was the first live one to go out. As soon as distance separated the group from danger, he was going to make Brenda fix the hole in his side with the medical supplies she'd padded under his clothes, if they weren't too saturated in blood.

The "live" people moved but very little as they waited for directions. A guttural voice, low with a heavy German accent, barked to Brenda, "There are more bodies than we agreed. You can't take out this many. It will take too long."

"What? These are the dead. Please let us get them out. We don't have to bury them." A pause. Andy fought not to hold his breath. He didn't want to gasp when he started breathing again. She continued. "You could help us. We could use a few of your men." Another voice murmured.

The toe of a boot connected with Andy's upper hip. Blackness swirled before him, in the holes of the shirt and back out. All of his self-control and some he borrowed from the dead person's shirt held in the scream kicking its way up his throat. A voice disembodied, floated above him, scathing in contempt. "Why would I carry filth for you? You're worthless."

"I didn't mean any disrespect. But if you're going to complain about the time, you could help and it'd go faster. Or you could let us get on with it. We'd be done by now." Brenda's kahonas were impressive, but if she weren't careful she was going to end up dead.

"I'm sure you won't mind if I check they're really dead." A hammer clicked. Andy tensed. Was the gun aimed at Brenda?

Bam. The gun went off. A vibration buzzed along the floor. Who were they shooting? No one made a sound. Andy couldn't close his eyes if he tried. Under the cover of the shirt, his gaze roved, searching for answers. What the hell?

Another gunshot. A bit closer. Andy's pulse raced. Another one. Closer. He had to see Rachel. He'd change things. Spend more time with the family. Hang with his kids more. Help around the house. A hammer clicked. So, close. He'd tell Josh the truth. Tell Rachel. Let them know what he'd done.

"Are you going to shoot every single one of them?" Brenda was annoyed. Not an ounce of fear. Was the gunman shooting the wall or something? "Because if you are, we can put these ones down until you're done. This is taking longer than if one of us moved them all." She sighed.

"Maybe you are protecting this one, eh?" The bullet left the barrel.

Andy bit his tongue. Damn.

"Yep, you got me. I wanted to leave that one intact for the funeral service. Now what am I to do?"

The boots walked past Andy, thudding across the room, humming through the flooring. "You Americans and your sarcasm. Do you think you're funny? I could kill everyone in this room. You are alive because *I* allow it." Brenda kept her mouth closed in the pause filled with threat. "Get these bodies out of here. We will watch you. Daniel, you stay here and keep these pests under control."

Andy forced his muscles to relax. Rigidity wouldn't help as his fellow captives tried to move the dead. He waited for a click. Another boot. Some hint he needed to guard against incoming pain.

His sleeves pulled at the shoulders and his pants at the waist. Andy's feet were left to drag and the tug across the ground yanked at his waist band, searing his wound. Bounce, jostle, bounce, step, bounce, drop, bump, drop, trip, bounce, jostle. The pain was indeterminable. He couldn't breathe.

Get him a damn boot! He'd rather be kicked again.

"Dump it over there." And lacking aplomb, his carriers did as instructed. His tailbone hit first and the drop to his shoulders throbbed to join his concussion. What the hell?

Weight of a leg crossed his and another arm slapped across his chest. A little chilled, the body was dead and Andy fought to control his gagging reflex. Lying beside a dead person was one thing, touching and mingling with another was one he didn't want to do.

The shirt hadn't been removed and the stench crowded him, covering him in someone else's fear. The cool breeze tickled his exposed uninjured ear and teased him with freshness. He had enough fear of his own, damn it. And emasculation didn't sit well with him. Fright wasn't a familiar emotion and he didn't want to deal with it when he hurt. His head switched places with his stomach.

Andy yanked the shirt off his head. He rolled to his feet, avoiding his hands and grunting at the ripping pain in his side.

"What!" A guard, feet from the pile of bodies, stepped back, his mouth wide and round as his eyes in a mixture of horror and surprise. Fingers clutched at his holster.

Devoid of any weapons, Andy threw his body at the man, clobbering him in the abdomen. Wrapping his arms around the guard's waist, Andy held on and ignored the nausea and pain pulling him toward a black hole in his mind.

On the ground, the stronger man rolled to the top, struggling against Andy's wounded desperation. He slugged Andy in the shoulder, then froze. And keeled over. Jenny lowered a large rock to her side, horror evident as she registered what had happened.

"Good. Job." Andy gasped through the pain. He pulled at the man's belt and withdrew the Glock, checking for a bullet in the chamber. "Can. You. Get. Me. To. Tree?"

Jenny nodded and grabbed him from behind under the arms and yanked as he scuttled like a weak crab. Five feet and he leaned against the rough bark of an evergreen. Smelled like Pine, crisp. He closed his eyes and expected to see Cole loading up another cord onto the back of the truck for the cabin. Chainsaw in Andy's hand. To get there again, Andy had to hold it together. If he wanted Rachel and his kids, then he damn well better straighten up.

Tight facial wounds helped hold his eyelids open and if he stared at the doors across the field he could focus with less dizziness. Less was good. Nerves attacked him, left over from his desperate struggle with the prostrate man, and his hands wavered. The gun clicked a bit in his shaky grasp.

Andy glanced at Jenny. She might not have noticed that he was acting like a coward and not like a leader. Brenda was the leader. How she'd gotten them out of there was a miracle, or magic, or both. Only three had gotten out, though. Jenny, Andy and another girl not much bigger than Jenny.

He watched the doors and moved the gun up. A head and then one more emerged from the doorway followed by hunched shoulders as they carried the next body.

At the rate they moved, it would take all day, but if they could get everyone out, it'd be worth it. But how did they hide the downed guard? Taking so long, the other guards were guaranteed to become suspicious and they would investigate only to find a bunch of prisoners alive and attempting a breakout.

Brenda hadn't planned further than getting beyond the walls. Each pair of people doing the carrying would need to make another trip or more into the gym to get everyone out. Brenda was staying inside until the last one had gone, in case... well, just in case. Andy hadn't offered to take her place. He'd have to do what he could from where he sat.

"Jenny, you gals are going to have to go back in."

She bit her lip. "I know."

"I don't want to." Trembling, the other girl's lip shook with emotion. "I want my mom. I want to go home." A large tear rolled down her cheek.

"I know you want to go home. I do, too. But there are still a lot of people in the gym that need help getting out. We need you to go back one more time. That's all. It could be worse." But could it? Doubt crept into the hole where his courage and valor were stored. What would they do with the people they saved? Let them die in the woods? Send them to a militia lifestyle? They were American and that entitled them to a different level of lifestyle. But in war? Was this war?

What else could it be?

"I need you to go back in." Andy was at a distinct disadvantage. She looked down on him and didn't see anything more than a weak injured man which didn't lend to his leadership role.

She scoffed, glanced at the people coming closer and ran into the woods without looking back.

Andy shook his head. Great. How many would do that until only a few were doing all the work or none?

Jenny's shoulders slumped with the girl's flight. "I'm sorry. She didn't quite understand what was going on. She thinks it's a hostage situation and cops are waiting out here to save us."

"Nobody is waiting." Sad to say. "But me."

Jenny offered a small smile. "And me." The others trudged across the last thirty feet. From the side of her mouth, Jenny whispered, "Do you think anyone is looking for us?" She glanced at him for his answer. Andy didn't know what to say. He didn't have a reply. To give in to the hope that someone looked for them would admit that maybe someone was out there who had made it through the attacks and the abductions.

And then someone would have to be brave enough to face the unknown and come back into the fray for people they couldn't be sure were alive. As the disappearing girl proved, there weren't a whole lot of brave people left in the world.

But taking hope from a young girl all alone wasn't his style. "I'm sure they'll be here to help us in no time. Just wait, someone will rev over that hill any second." And pigs will fly out of his ear, but if the girl had more optimism in her bleak present, who was he to squash it?

The next set arrived and dropped the real dead body on the ground and groaned. Andy watched the guards, distracted as he counted the seconds between deliveries. Too many. They'd never get everybody out. The lead captor would grow suspicious enough to act.

Buzzing ran through his ears and aggravated his concussion, or maybe his concussion caused the hum. Except it grew louder and the three other people in the clearing stared away from the building. And just as fast as it came, the sound cut.

Jenny clustered with the others, pointing and whispering. Andy couldn't peek behind the tree without causing exorbitant amounts of pain shafting through his insides. Recognition widened her eyes. She stepped forward and then took off running.

Andy swiveled his head left to right to see around the trunk, but the only clarity he received were the sparks in his head pushing for the black. Someone Jenny knew was coming, but would they hinder or help in the cause?

Voices grew closer. He recognized one, but before they crossed the line he gave over to the syncope kicking him down.

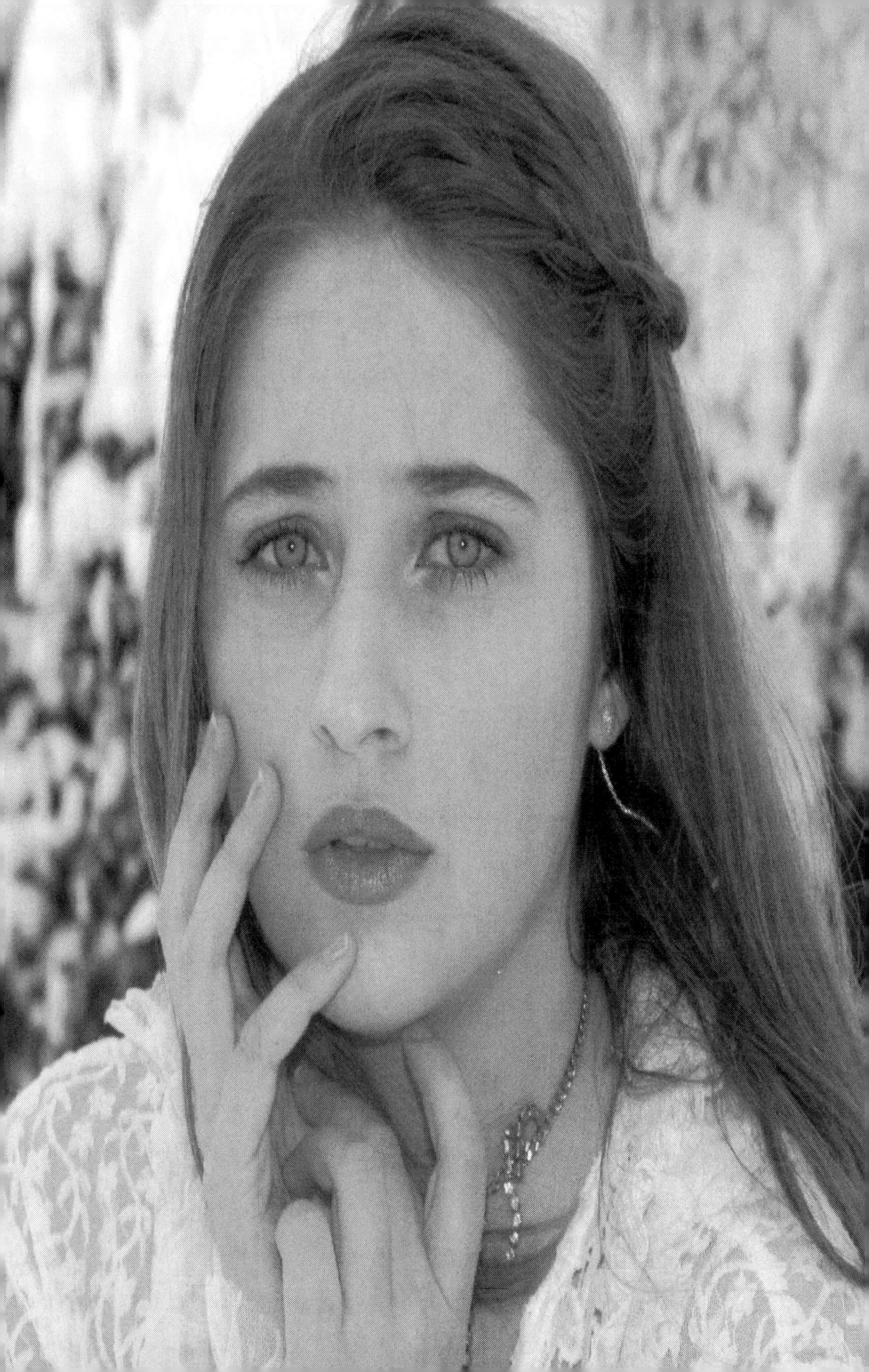

Chapter 17

Brenda

They needed to move faster. Gustavson was getting restless. He'd passed by, giving her the once over four times and his glances were becoming more invasive. Did he think he could see beneath the grime and blood that covered her? If he had the capability to see into her, he'd recognize red loathing and white vengeance. But like most men in positions of tyrannical power, he wanted to lord it over her more. The fighter in her wanted to beat him at his own game, before he attempted anything, but the other captives needed her to do all she could to gather them more time.

She cleared her throat. Lee had asked her to do degrading acts all the time and had guilted her into them more often than she cared to admit. Maintaining stoicism, even when dead people were shot in the head, was a talent she claimed. Brenda had almost lost it when the man was two bodies away from Andy. And he'd called her bluff but had shot another dead one. Thank Heaven, she'd called out when she had.

Gustavson stopped beside her. "Did you need something, mon frère?"

"Have you ever heard of Stockholm's syndrome?" She held her voice low, between them. But a flush crept up her neck, hopefully adding to the effect she tried to create.

"Stockholm's? No." He watched her chest. Sometimes she had hated Rachel for the slimmer build, less rounded curves. But other times, gratitude over her more shapely form filled her. As the man perused the lines of her body with his gaze, she was grateful once more. Her shape would have more impact if she didn't reek of urine, blood, and sweat.

Husky, her voice demanded he meet her gaze with his. "Stockholm's is when the person being held lusts after the captor. He becomes her protector and she becomes... his." Corny, she'd roll her eyes but...

The man's pupils dilated and he tossed a glance toward the other men supervising the body removal. Daniel stood to the side and watched Brenda with Gustavson, as if he suspected she was up to something but he wanted to see it play out rather than interfere.

Brenda breathed in deep to lift her chest a bit and pressed her hand, fingers splayed, across the tear in the top of her t-shirt, pulling the material down enough to display flesh most men salivated over.

She'd caught his attention and damn but she'd hold it. Through stray strands of hair, Brenda glimpsed another set of bodies leave the gym. Keep going. She tilted her lips with a pout that beckoned, while attempting to add a touch of innocence. All she wanted to do was punch the bastard and run. Think Scarlet O'Hara.

Crossing her arms in front of her, creating a deeper cleavage, Brenda leaned closer to the leader and widened her eyes. "I've heard it's quite common. What do you think?"

A shuffle at the door drew his attention and Brenda worried she'd lose the ground she'd gained. He barked a question in another language and received a short reply. Brenda rested her palm on his arm. He tensed. "Is everything okay?"

And snap. He slapped her into place. She bent over with a hand on her face. But she had his attention along with a stinging cheek. "That's none of your concern" She bit back her smile. Like dealing with her husband. The games she could play. At least the zone was a comforting one. Men like that were all the same. If she acted like he'd hurt her, he'd be satisfied but move on. But if he could be convinced she'd liked it, things might go her way… or roundabout.

He watched her and not the activity by the door. She returned to her spot in front of him. Lifted her chin and arched her brow. "My concern or not, I'm asking." A bit of backbone would intrigue him, he'd want to hit her again, but he'd hold back to see how much attitude Brenda would dish. Of course there was a psychobabble term for it, but Rachel was the shrink in the family. Brenda was the trampy nurse… Lee's bitch, he liked to call her.

Yay for her, she could act the part.

He played to her, interested in her reaction. Brenda braced herself for the next contact. He'd most likely be the man who'd hit harder and harder to see if he could break her. Which could be painful, but Lee had discovered Brenda didn't break.

"Are you testing me? I'd love to give you to *them*." He arched his brow and glanced pointedly at the spot on her neck he'd branded.

Ignoring the meaning in his gaze, Brenda smiled. "Whatever. I could test you, but what good would it do me? If you want to share me, okay." Brenda shrugged, but prayed hard the bodies would get moved. How would she extract herself from guards intent on doing what their leader wanted? Most likely he was a voyeur. Disgusting. Brenda had to get out too, and had no idea how. "But I'm much better with just one." She leaned forward and planted her lips full on his, the bottom lip thicker than the top.

He yanked her hair. She couldn't cry out, his tongue had claimed her mouth. A low wolf call echoed through the cavernous room and comments, while in a different language, had the same meaning that they did in English.

He bit her lip and pulled back. Copper exploded on her tongue. Bastard had made her bleed. Her hand itched to reach up and wipe her face. Eck, if she made it out alive, she'd wash her mouth with bleach and then maybe some Ajax.

Cold and calculating, the eyes on her didn't convey anything but satisfaction. Frick.

Shots – one, two, three. Guards fell. Others ran for cover but they'd been distracted enough to move into the entryway by the door between the bleachers. They had nowhere to go and dropped like drunks in winter.

Daniel had disappeared.

Fingers like crustacean claws clamped around the nape of her neck. He angled her body in front of his and murmured as if he caressed her with his words. "You play well. If I go down, you go with me." He backed them further into the gym, headed toward the doors. But bodies lay like tinsel over the basketball court. His foot caught on one and he tripped, dragging her with him. The fall jarred her, twisting her ankle, pain shooting up her leg. She'd be bruised by the next day, if not sooner.

Footsteps pounded into the gym, irregular as they avoided the bodies. Brenda scrambled from his hold, pieces of hair stuck in his grasp. A separate wave of pattering feet left the gym.

Crawling from the leader, Brenda fell onto a dead person. Gustavson's hands brushed her calves and she kicked in the vicinity of his face. "Run, guys, run! Get out. Hurry." About eight bodies clamored to stand and rush out. Screams and cries heralded their escape.

The man clutched her ankle. She couldn't break free.

She looked back, oblivious to the newcomers. Who cared what they fought for. She didn't. If the man touched her again, she'd regret it – may not survive it. His fingernails cut into her skin like daggers. *Focus, Brenda.*

He pulled her closer, wrapping his other hand higher up her calf, digging in, a feral light in his eyes. She yelped.

Nothing was sturdy. She grabbed at arms and legs of the dead under her, but the bodies moved as he pulled her back, sliding on the smooth surface. What the hell? Why couldn't she get free? Someone help! She rolled to her back and loosened his hold enough to break free. The rage mixed with delight in his eyes struck more fear in her than waking to find her house on fire.

He glanced to the doors and back at her. Steely eyes promised revenge. Gustavson scraped at her lower leg with his nails and pushed her away. Standing, he retreated through the doors furthest from the chaos.

She stared after him, chilled. Her fingers numb. Someone needed to chase him down and beat him with a sharp stick. The bastard was going for help. Had to be.

Daniel. Brenda turned and scanned the gym, searching for his tall form. He'd be dangerous, if he infiltrated any local groups. He didn't have an accent at times and could blend in. And what if he continued to search out Rachel? Brenda didn't know how to help her sister, if that prick caught up with her.

Help? She needed help. All kinds. Not the kind Gustavson would bring, but maybe what he ran from.

Brenda limped across the gym, gaze darting between the leader's escape route and the men who had charged in, bullets flying. At least the others had gotten out. But Andy, had he made it? Jenny?

"Aunt Brenda?"

"Cole? What are you doing here?" She caught her breath and wrapped an arm around her oldest nephew, who didn't look like a nephew should. His jaw angled sharp from the chin, bold and masculine like his father's. Brenda would term him an "old" fourteen.

"I came with Tom and Josh, Dad's friend. Tom said you were captured and we found out where you were held. So we came for you." Cole led her to the door. The mid-afternoon light was brighter than the scratched, clouded Plexiglas roof panels had let on.

"Did you see your dad?" She searched the groups around the bodies spread across the grass yards. Andy had been the first live body out, where was he?

Cole shook his head, his eyes bleak. "Aunt Brenda, Dad died in a fire the day of the attack."

"Cole, your dad is out there in that group, right now. I promise. He was in there with me. He's burned and has a severe concussion, but he's alive." She squeezed his hand hanging over her shoulder.

He turned eyes that could have been Andy's toward her, lit with hope but shadowed with fear. "I saw the house fall."

"I cleaned his face." She pulled his arm from her shoulders and nudged him to the tree line. "Go. I'm still a little shaken from everything." He searched her face, but his body angled toward the group. "Go. I'm right behind you."

Brenda bit her lip from the pain in her leg. The asshole must have damaged some muscle or tendons. Her ankle burned and a Charlie horse was building in her lower calf. Her cheek throbbed as she inventoried her injuries. She reached up and touched the swollen area under her eye. Damn, that one was going to bruise big time.

Heavy footsteps rushed to fall into step beside her. "Rachel? How did you..." Blue eyes traced her face and Brenda blushed. Tall, almost Paul Bunyan in build, the man stared down at her, concern and confusion pushing off him in waves. Maybe it was the lack of freckles, or the difference in size, or maybe even the significant difference in body shapes that snapped the facts in front of him. He blinked and backed up a step. "I'm sorry. You look… you must be Brenda. Rachel sent us to get you."

Large men could be mean men. No matter how attractive they might be. Lee was reason enough to stay away from men in general, the main reason to avoid attractive men. Like snakes. But this one's eyes didn't seem snakelike. Sincerity added softness to what Brenda suspected would be lines and angular planes on a masculine face. Her vision was blurring. Gustavson hit harder than she'd thought.

"I am. Of course she did. And you are?" Wariness was her armor and the man's confusion turned to professionalism.

"Joshua Hughes. Longtime friend of her deceased husband's. I have a place by the Parker's. I've been helping Rachel during this hard time."

For the love, did Rachel have every man in love with her? She wasn't even widowed for an entire week and she had a man rushing to do her every command. Sick. "Well, she doesn't need to mourn any more. Andy's up there by the dead. He was the first one out. You passed him as you came in."

Surprise wiped the empathy from his gaze. "Will you excuse me?"

She nodded. The pressure in the air relented as he jogged the last twenty feet from her. A man with a presence that could suck the oxygen from her body was not the best guy to have around.

Brenda joined the emotionally charged group, her limp hampering anything resembling speed. Cole knelt beside a body slumped against a tree and shouted at Joshua.

"Tom, you made it to Rachel." Brenda pressed a hand to her head. "I'm sorry. I should have known you did when I saw Cole.

We're all tired." Among other things. She lowered her voice and angled her head closer to his. "Most of these people went into the gym with families intact, but had to watch their loved ones die. They'll most likely crack soon."

"One already did." Jenny joined Tom and Brenda in their small huddle. Tom's smile caught Brenda's eye, a bright spot in a sea of darkness. His happiness swelled Brenda's heart.

"Jenny. Tom scuffed his foot, his confidence waning. The butt of his gun poked from his belt.

"Tom. Thanks for coming for us." She reached for his hand and held on, tossing a glance at Brenda. "I think we should move away from here. The bodies are causing issues for people."

"Was anyone injured during the shooting?" Brenda performed a visual triage of the standing people. Her gaze slid to Cole and Josh kneeling by the tree. Boots protruded from the space between them. Where was Andy? She crossed the distance, leaving Tom and Jenny to follow or stay. She didn't care. Andy had to be… "What's going on?"

Joshua shifted to rest his feet on his heels. Andy's unconscious face came into view. Cole turned tear-streaked cheeks toward Brenda and it clicked. "Excuse me." She pushed the tall imposing man out of her way. He moved, but not because she was strong enough to budge him. He, too, grieved.

Brenda pressed her fingertips underneath Andy's tucked chin. A faint but thready pulse thudded through her fear. She yanked her hand from his skin and pointed her finger in each person's direction as she called on them. "Tom, pull Andy's feet until he's flat on his back. Joshua, I need water from the faucet in the gym. Cole, go with him in case he needs help with returning guards. Jenny, I need material – a shirt, pants, anything to wrap around his hands." They scrambled to do their assigned tasks.

What had made him pass out? His burns weren't that severe. The concussion? Maybe, but he'd made it to the tree from the pile and by the looks of things, he'd commandeered the gun of the outside guard. Brenda scanned him, head to toe. Nothing. That she could see.

Tom pulled and flattened Andy on the grass. "Tom, we need to lift up his shirt and maybe pull his pants off." Water from the drenched grass soaked through her borrowed jeans as she knelt beside his form. She worked the buttons of his flannel and pushed the panels to the sides. Tom pulled on the edges of the t-shirt underneath, revealing long-john material underneath.

Brenda muttered, "Jeesh, Andy, how many layers do you have on?" Reaching under his tee to yank up the long underwear from his side, Brenda's fingers stuck to his skin. She pulled her hand back, streaked with red. "Oh, crap. We need to roll him."

Tom pushed Andy her direction until he was on his uninjured side. Pushing his arm above his head and arranging his top leg to act as a kickstand and keep him from rolling forward, Brenda pulled the rest of his clothes out of the way. Wood splinters speckled the edge of the hole in his side. She pressed around the periphery, nothing oozed. The abrasion matched the shape of a rounded square the size of a large man's hand.

The medicine pack she'd hidden with his body rested on the ground where they'd rolled him from. She nodded toward the bag. "I need some gauze, iodine and a popsicle stick."

Tom rummaged through the bag, holding a hand on Andy's hip to keep him steady. One by one, he handed over the items. Brenda, grateful for the moment to think about what to do, took them without a word, lost in thought. Wooden stick in hand, Brenda poked the ravaged flesh.

The biggest concern was if the perineal was ripped or torn. She couldn't fix anything if it was deep into the abdominal cavity. No thread, needle or sterile environment. Around the torn edges, the skin looked angry and red. But the damage didn't seem to surpass the muscle and fat layers. Solid heat worked its way through his clothes. Febrile, the heat would never abate with the multiple pounds of material trapping it in.

Infection. Redness, fever, and irritated wound all pointed toward something Brenda could normally suggest an antibiotic for. But pharmacy hours weren't an option. Nothing was open. And if a pharmacy wasn't open, no one would be inside to mix the meds.

A warm hand squeezed her shoulder. Startled, she looked up into Joshua's face.

He held out a thermos. His voice, soft and rambly, melted around her. "The water. What else can we do?"

What could he do? What the hell could *she* do? Rachel had sent these men, one of them her oldest son to get her sister. It didn't matter what Brenda needed to do, she'd do it. She and her sister had to get to a point where they could be happy again. And the only way Brenda could initiate the adjustment was to do everything she could to return Andy to Rachel intact.

"He has an infection, needs food, water, and antibiotics." She looked around, the open space broken up by a few randomly spaced trees leading to a thicker but small wooded area. "And a safe place to rest. This won't work."

Joshua knelt beside her. "We have a four-wheeler with a wagon. I can load Andy into the trailer and pull him, but I have no idea what to do with the rest of these people. There are too many to travel together safely. I don't know how many of the enemy are out there."

Brenda chewed on her inner cheek. Nineteen scared refugees with the desertion of the first girl. Dead guards. Dead people. Injured Andy and who else? Danger around every corner. And they had no idea who to trust. And Gustavson was out there. He'd escaped. He'd all but promised to come for her, find her. The throb in her cheek testified to his brutality.

Daniel was out there. Even worse.

Overwhelmed, Brenda closed her eyes. Break it down.

What did she need at that exact moment?

Safety, shelter, food, water, antibiotics.

What did she have to do to get those items?

They needed to move Andy and the people to, where?

The woods? The hills? Wherever, they needed to move. So many people could easily find or make shelter fast when they found where they were going. Food and water would be a bit harder to find, but not impossible.

No, the impossible or improbable task would be the antibiotics. She had no idea how to get them, unless they walked to a Walgreens or Wal-Mart and broke in for supplies. But wouldn't they be guarded or protected? A Costco would even be worth a lot in a situation such as the one they found themselves. Looters wouldn't last long as they'd be killed or captured.

She opened her eyes to find Joshua studying her. "I can't believe how much you look like Rachel."

"You're not the first to tell me that." Brenda applied an eight-by-eight inch gauze to Andy's side. "Andy needs antibiotics. Here's my proposal. We need to get out of here. Let's split the group into smaller chunks. We'll have them rendezvous at a specific spot and then move as an entire unit the rest of the way into the National Forest. I don't care where they go after that, but they'll need someplace."

"I bet the National Guard will take them and they're not far into the hills from Rachel's place. Let's head out. Once we get there and get Andy settled, me and the boys can search out antibiotics." Josh stood, offering his hand to her. "I'll bring the quad and load him up. You tell them what we're doing."

Like they had kids and she was going to tell them to get ready to go to the store or something. "Okay." She'd take his direction. He probably had food in his stomach and a rested mind. Brenda had a small amount of one and none of the other. She recognized her rationality had disappeared a few hours ago. Come on, it had to have, she'd tried seducing the man who'd branded her.

Joining the segregated groups in one large collection, Brenda waited for a break in the mumbling to call out for everyone's attention. Some huddled against each other, tears mapping their faces. Others stood alone and stared into space. No one looked at the bodies. Brenda had to get them out of there. Shock was an ugly ailment and once started, hard to reverse. Recovery was the only way out. Getting recaptured wouldn't allow time to recuperate.

"Hey, everyone, listen up." Heads swiveled her direction as she cut through the uncertainty they all shared. Bodies pressed closer. "We need to separate into groups of four or five. Each group is going to head in a different direction. We'll meet on the other side of Coeur d'Alene." Brenda spoke over the murmurings. "It shouldn't take more than five or six hours to get there, but you can't take your time. Get there so we can head into the forest. We think there might be food and shelter the National Guard can provide. But first we have to get away from the danger."

"But the guards are dead. What else could hurt us?"

Brenda tried to see the person whose voice suggested they were in the clear. When she failed, she spoke in the general direction. "You think those guards are the only ones who did this? They might have captured you here in Post Falls, but there are more cities and towns and a whole lot more of them." Two girls on the edge of the group sank to their butts and sobbed. "I know. It's scary. But let's get out of here before they come and make our fears real."

Another voice called into the worried silence, "I don't want to leave my parents."

Another. "I don't want to leave my son-in-law."

"My brother's here."

Brenda shot a glance at Joshua who had reached the quad and was backing it to the edge of the clearing. Why she searched him out, she didn't know, but she needed help and he was a responsible – she hoped – adult who'd shared in the idea with her. No help while he dealt with Andy.

That's okay. She could do it. She'd almost seduced the leader of the enemies. Not much else was worse. Brenda shuddered. Lovely. Her tongue sought out the tender spot on her lower lip.

"Break off. I want to check on everyone first before we go. Make sure you're ready for the trip." And they didn't do much but stare at her as if waiting for a magic wand to whisk them to safety. "Hey! Do you understand this wasn't a fluke? They will come back. We didn't even get all of the guards. At least two got away. Who knows when reinforcements will come? I'm not staying. I suggest you leave as well."

The urgency in her tone broke them up. Bands of three to as many as six separated like oil drops in a bowl of water. Not one would stand too close to the fallen bodies. If they didn't get out soon, bees and flies would find their way to the area to pester the dead *and* the living.

Five bundles of frightened people waited for her. Each one with their own fears and grievances.

"I don't want to walk that far."

"Will we be caught?"

"Can we have a gun?"

"Should we raid the school?"

"What else could they do to us?"

"I want my mom."

And so on. Brenda's heart ached for them even as she nodded and commented on the good ideas brought forth.

A boy wore flip flops, the cheap plastic kind. Brenda pursed her lips. "Sorry, honey, you need shoes. There is no way you're going to make it into Coeur d'Alene and then the woods in those. You need to find some more."

"Where?" He held out his hands.

Brenda grabbed his wrist, mindful that he didn't mean anything by his ignorance, but she directed his attention to the bodies and winced. "I'm sorry. But you won't make it and they don't need them anymore." Just the suggestion was enough to bring on a wave of nausea and upset stomach. What she wouldn't give for some Pepto Bismol. Hell, a sandwich of butter and bread and apple juice. Fresh, cold apple juice. She needed to throw up and the nausea wasn't going away.

The boy's lip quivered. Brenda didn't expect anything less. His parents, friends, other family members may be in that pile or in the collection of dead still inside the gym. But under different circumstances balking at necessities would be fine – even accepted, yet the trap they were caught in was not. "I'm sorry." Tough love would be more effective than easing him through the process. She considered fetching the shoes for him, but she wouldn't help anything with that maneuver. They needed to get going and travel to Coeur d'Alene.

She looked to the groups. "Okay, we have five routes to town." Brenda pointed at each group and assigned directions, naming the streets they would need to take. "Poleline. Prairie. Seltice. Atlas to Kathleen. And we'll take Highway 53."

"You're going with the quad? That's not fair." Mulish mouthed, a girl eyed the four-wheeler with longing.

Jenny stood beside Tom and Joshua at the end of the wagon. She glanced at the complainer and back at Brenda. "Why isn't it fair?"

The girl squared off to Jenny and tossed a red mop of hair out of her face. "It's not fair because your group has four people and wheels. My group has three and no idea where we're going."

"It's the other side of Coeur d'Alene. The fire department playground. You can see it from the freeway. How can you not know where that is?" Jenny planted her hands on her hips and jutted her chin. "I'm from Spokane and I know where it is."

But the red head was right. It wasn't fair that Brenda was opting to send some young people out into the countryside alone with little more than directions on where to meet. They didn't have weapons, and those that did, may or may not know how to use them.

Brenda gave in before Red could retort. "Alright. I'll go with your group, but we're doing it my way or I'm skipping out to join my original group." Brenda held up her hand to the protest written across Jenny, Tom, and Joshua's face. "No, it's okay. You need to get Andy out of here. The sooner we can get him home the better."

She met the gaze of each member in each group. "Band together. Rely on each other. If you get caught, we won't know it and I can't guarantee they won't try something else to hurt you. At the playground you'll wait in the trees on the hill. Don't go onto the playground, it's too open. You'll know we made it when you see the fire helmet smeared with mud. Stay there if you don't see any, unless you're being pursued. If that's the case, get into the forest as fast and as deep as you can." Brenda walked to her new group. The red hair girl, a twenty-something long-haired and goateed boy, and another girl whose mousiness added an overstated vulnerability Brenda wanted to groan at. Raising her voice once more, Brenda met Joshua's eyes. "If you haven't reached the playground by dawn, I'm going to assume you're not coming. It's early afternoon now. Don't play around. Get there. You can rest when you're safe."

Each group milled for a moment, then moved toward Greensferry, the common street connecting to the majority of each of the routes. Brenda had assigned Highway fifty-three to the quad. They'd roll it out fast, if they could stay free of detection. But she'd added herself to the Hayden group which meant she had to bust it out to go north and then south again, essentially backtracking. Three weak and whiny kids weren't the best traveling companions.

Something about the breadth of Joshua's shoulders suggested he'd be a good one to travel with. Or maybe he wouldn't. He was after all male. But he'd be protection in case of an ambush. Wait a minute, she was capable. "Hold on, guys." Brenda approached Joshua and pointed at Andy lying in the wagon. "Can I take the gun he has?"

"He doesn't have a gun." Tom's eyebrows knit in the center.

Brenda moved to Andy and pulled the butt of the gun from the armpit where Brenda noticed it during her exam. She'd let it be, but now she needed it and Andy wouldn't have any use for it.

Joshua nodded. "Can you shoot one?"

Brenda raised her eyebrow. "Want to be my target?"

He shrugged, but a smile flitted under the dark blond whiskers. "We'll see you at the playground. And Brenda," his voice lowered to deliver the words to her ears alone, "I came all this way to bring you back to Rachel. You better be there at dawn and you better be in the same condition you're in now."

Or what? He'd flay her with his blue gaze or knock a bruise onto her unblemished cheek? She didn't know what his gaze threatened, but she hoped it was a promise and not for pain. Wow, she was a tramp. A trampy nurse. She needed to stay away from men – the captors, abusive husbands and hot knight-in-shining-armors.

Brenda didn't bother with the niceties of introductions when she rejoined her group. "Come on." She glanced back once at the rev of the four-wheeler cutting through the clearing of dead and departing.

She hoped she'd see them again. The few miles stretched between her and the meeting place and overwhelming defeat loomed ahead. She wouldn't let hopelessness suck her in. Brenda would make it, if for no other reason than to prove to herself that she wasn't a useless girl.

The fresh air couldn't seem to push the odor of death from her nostrils. Short of shoving pine needles up her nose, she'd probably be dealing with the smell for a while.

She pressed her palm to the body of the gun. Shoot. She could do it. Maybe.

~

If Megan didn't stop whining, Brenda was going to aim her firearm and plug her mouth with lead. Between Mouse, the name Brenda had chosen for the nondescript girl because Brenda couldn't hear what she'd said her name was, whimpering every few steps and Raven smacking on a piece of his hair, Brenda was close to going crazy. She'd very willingly surrender to the enemy at that point, if only she could find an enemy.

Daniel was looking better and better.

They'd trekked north up Greensferry, passing smoking foundations and blackened car husks. Dodging from shadow to shadow, they hadn't seen anyone, friend or foe.

The length along Prairie greeted them with tedium. Prairie grass whispered in the slight summer breeze. Such a pretty day, like Mother Nature didn't give a damn their world was falling apart.

Suburbs popped up here and there, separated from the open space by fences and pressed trails. Firs and pines offered cover in clusters every fifty yards or so. Dark clothes didn't camouflage well against the yellow and brown ground. But they had nothing to work with and didn't dare stop at the random farm houses they passed. Americans were usually armed and if the home owner wasn't there prepared to blow a trespasser off their feet, it didn't mean the other guys weren't.

The other three lagged behind. Mouse and Raven leaned on each other. Two animal names, weird. Brenda continued to glance back to make sure they kept up. She had no idea why.

If they didn't want to survive, why the heck would she care? Megan, on the other hand, stomped and pouted, alternating the attitude with whining and complaints that she didn't get to go on the quad and why didn't she have a gun? When she sped up to "lead" the group in front of Brenda, Megan would glare over her shoulder, and then trip or stumble to which the crying would start anew. Brenda would brush past. And the cycle continued, never ending.

"My feet hurt. I'm stopping." Megan yelled. Brenda looked over her shoulder. Megan crossed her arms and stuck her thin bottom lip into the air like a shelf, spindly legs spread. Hm. She resembled the stick figures Beau drew when Brenda used to babysit him.

"Um. Us, too." Raven mumbled around the wet clump of hair he'd wrapped around his finger. He and Mouse halted a few steps behind Megan, eyes downcast.

Brenda sighed. "What? You need a break? We just took a break. We have to keep going to make the time. Joshua and the others that know where we're going won't wait past dawn."

"No. I don't care. I'm done. I'm not following you. We're not following you anymore."

"But we're almost to ninety-five." Why was Brenda fighting? Let them stay. She'd travel faster and make the meeting without the baggage. "You made me come with you. Why? So you could challenge everything I say? How'd you make it this far?" She traveled faster than them with her limp.

They didn't answer. Megan stared past Brenda's arm. Two blocks and they'd be there. The sun suggested dinner but the ache in her legs screamed she'd walked forever. How long did she wait? What was Brenda waiting for? *Forget it.*

"Fine. I'm leaving. Last chance to join me." Five, four, three, two, one. Brenda returned to the path she followed, glancing up and down Prairie for signs of danger, other life, anything. The only movement came from the corner of a yard sale sign flipping against the telephone pole it was stapled to.

Cool in the heat, the breeze was welcome. Brenda clenched her hands. She'd joined these idiots when she could have been on the quad, moving toward a goal that was within range. What the hell was she supposed to do alone? She'd lost the dirt bike when she'd been captured and a car or truck would certainly gain someone's attention.

A small blessing, the attack could have come during August, the hottest month in the northwest. Dry as a wishbone, the sun pressure-cooked a person who wasn't swimming or sitting in air conditioning.

She tried to keep her footsteps from morphing into trudging. She'd walked for so long. *Stop it, Brenda. You sound like Megan.* Shoulders lifted, chin up, she bent her arms and pretended she was on a speed walk challenge with a girlfriend from work. The boots were the wrong shoe, the jeans uncomfortable in the knee, but the change in outlook ate the ground beneath her feet.

The sound of a two-stroke engine, most likely a dirt bike, most likely a year or two older, roared from the north. She'd never forget the definitive high pitched whine as the throttle engaged. Her husband had always ridden two-stroke bikes. Brenda preferred four.

In full bloom, a purple lilac bush offered thick plumage to hide behind, under or in. She chose the former.

Feet from the front porch of a double-wide trailer, Brenda stood indecisively between the roughened, worn steps up to the shot out, splintered door and the bush. An orange square, the size of a sheet of notebook paper, had been stapled behind the house's address numbers. In bold block letters spread across the top "REGISTERED GUN OWNER" declared the home both compliant and carrying. A detailed list of the arms in residence followed as well as government disclaimers.

Brenda had never registered any gun she owned, warned by Andy a few years back that doing so would only bind the gun owner rather than helping them out. The bullet holes speckled the front door, the wood siding, and the screen. Glass had disappeared, probably shot out. No gun holes came from inside.

The whine grew louder and Brenda identified multiple two-stroke engines revving in a pack well before they came into view. Red, orange, green, and blue bikes roared to the intersection closest to Megan, Raven and Mouse. Gloved hands pointed toward the walkers.

Foolish refugees hadn't moved since she'd walked more than a block away. Brenda glanced over her shoulder. Ninety-five was so close. Maybe she could make it. Maybe the bikers were friendly. Maybe Megan and the others didn't have anything to worry about. Maybe the bikers were the help they needed. Brenda stepped to the side of the bush. Maybe they'd have access to antibiot —

Three shots rang out in quick succession. Brenda ducked behind the branches of the bush, her hand pressed to her mouth. Holy crap. They were dead. Without a chance. Brenda had the gun for the group and she'd left them alone.

The engine whines moved her direction.

Her breath caught. What the hell was she going to do? No more trees around and the house would be an obvious place to hide. Another house, twenty feet away, had been partially destroyed in a fire. Brenda had no other choice. She snuck into the bush, balancing on the thick trunk-like branch system. Twigs scratched at her exposed face.

Leaning against the largest of the branches, Brenda scraped her neck brand against the rough bark and had to bite her lip to keep from screaming. She broke out in a fine sweat.

The riders pulled to the intersection, feet away. Brenda closed her eyes and chanted in her head like they could and would do what she thought. *Go. Drive on. Go.*

They cut their engines. Voices remarkably close lilted with French accents and sounded about her age.

"That was awesome. Do you think we'll see anymore? I haven't been able to shoot much." The man's husky voice irritated Brenda with its curly Rs and strong Ls.

Sounding like a mockingbird, a woman replied, "Lieutenant Bastian will be expecting us by the freeway. How many did he say escaped? Ten?"

Daniel. He *had* gotten away. And he was looking for the escapees. Did he search for her? Or Rachel.

"I couldn't hear him over the engines. We'll say we just shot nine. He's not going to argue. He's the one that let them get away." Austrian accent? How many nationalities were in the mix? A ladybug skittered across her wrist. Dang it, Brenda hated bugs. Hate with a capital H. She closed her eyes. If she focused on the conversation and holding on, she'd be able to ignore any new creepy crawlies… beetles, centipedes, caterpillars, ticks – oh, crap, ticks. Her neck itched and throbbed. Maybe something was moving through her hair.

She lost the conversation between the bikers. Bugs, maybe bees, or… no… spiders. She could do the outdoors, beat off mosquitoes, but hell if she could deal with bugs so close. She breathed in slow, releasing it on a silent whimper. *Bugs are better than bullets. Bugs are better than bullets.*

Screw what they were saying. She didn't care. They were going to the freeway. Okay, she wouldn't go that way. Big deal. Wait, someone had mentioned the house.

"I'm pretty sure we got that one. Didn't Lieutenant-Colonel Gustavson shoot in with the shotguns yesterday?"

"Yeah. The screaming went on forever." The last speaker laughed the words. How did someone laugh while speaking? Brenda's hand itched to rip his face from his head. How had her countrymen been reduced to sport?

"We don't need to check it than. I'm getting bored just riding around." The Mockingbird-girl's voice hardened.

The weight at the small of Brenda's back tipped at the belt. She opened her eyes and grabbed for the butt of the gun she'd forgotten in the tension of the bikers' arrivals.

And slipped from the trunk.

Through the leaves, the image of five heads swiveling her direction decided her next move.

Gun already in hand, Brenda shot through the leaves. She'd never been the best at hitting the exact center of a target, but she wasn't shooting to kill, just maim… bad. But at the same time, not too bad, she was a nurse after all.

The gun gods smiled on her aim, but frowned at the riders' luck. Each one fell to the percussion of a shot. Bikes piled on each other, landing on the people amidst screams and cries.

Brenda emerged from the limbs, grateful to be free of any possible bugs and fighting the shock tingling in her limbs. She'd shot people. Her.

Damn it. She wasn't going back into a gym to watch others die and she'd be damned if some punks from another country were going to ride around on dirt bikes to shoot her like game on the run. It was her land and she was the one who needed the rides.

Empowerment. Four bullets. She had four left in the clip. Gun leading the way, she followed the metal barrel to the pile of pain and motors on the pavement. Ignored the blood she'd spilled. She had to be able to face her actions, but not at the moment. She might have to shoot again and wouldn't be able to, if she was thinking it through.

The first body closest to the curb had taken one in the chest. Red covered his sweatshirt. Fatal wound. She moved to the next one, a woman. Butch hair, dark liner around her open eyes. She clutched her chest below her clavicle. Brenda pulled the gun from the ground beside the fallen woman.

A man lay across his bike, an exit wound in the posterior portion of his abdomen. Yuck, gut shot. Brenda gave him wide berth. His bike crushed another body, legs the only evidence someone was under it. Hopefully that person was dead, because underneath the bike was not the best place to be stuck. Engines were hot and burned fast and without mercy.

The last man, a few feet from the group struggled with the pump action on his shotgun.

Fear laced up Brenda's spine and sparked over her nerves with a rush of adrenaline. His fingers slipped from the flat black metal. A foot closer and Brenda breathed. His right arm, drenched in maroon, jerked against his attempts to control it. The bullet must have shattered his shoulder.

His light brown eyes met hers. *Damn it, he was just a kid.* Brenda bit her lip. Fingers tightened on the cannon in her hand. His cheeks, spotted with slight pink bumps, hadn't seen a razor yet. Not that day. Not ever. The uninjured arm shook. Lower lip quivering, he muttered something in a language she didn't recognize, motioning toward her, bloody fingers slick on the gun. He spoke in a tone that could only be used with a curse and he tossed the gun to the side, tossing his arm into the air. Sweat covered his face in clear drops.

What did she do? Her primal instinct was to shoot him. Get the hell out of there. But he was a kid. But it was her or him. She pointed the barrel at his head. This close, she couldn't miss. She centered between his eyebrows. Forefinger tense on the trigger. Four shots. She hadn't needed another one for the others.

Kill him and take his bike. Kill him. Take his bike. Kill the kid. Kill. *Brenda, pull the damn trigger.* She whimpered and dropped her arm.

He groaned and a dark spot spread across his lap.

Brenda motioned to his bike. "I'm taking it. I don't want to shoot you. Don't make me." She rounded the body of the bike. A Yamaha 250. Dang. A bit big for her. *Oh well.* Watching for movement or aggression from any of the possible survivors, Brenda pulled hard on the bike. The beast was heavy, but adrenaline powered her arms and she lifted the bastard upright.

The boy slumped to the ground. Should she get another gun? Take his shotgun? She didn't have any extra shells. And did she dare release the 250 after she'd put everything she had and then some into getting the bike up? She still had four bullets. That had to be enough.

She slung her leg over the seat, pushed up and then slammed her foot down on the kick start. The beautiful engine roared to life, the sound of her freedom. One more glance at the pile of death and trauma she'd caused, she shifted and pushed off into first. Second. The wind in her hair. Finally, the smell of death was gone.

Chapter 18

Rachel

Beau sat beside her on the couch. He tucked his small fingers in the crook of her elbow. *Not again. Don't ask again.* "Mommy, when will Daddy be back?"

Don't sigh, Rachel. Don't get exasperated. Don't sigh or yell. Or cry. "Beau, remember Mommy told you this already? Daddy fell in the house fire. He's not coming back. He's dead." Matter-of-fact wasn't getting through to him. Omitting her emotions hadn't helped. Kayli applied the term "dead" to her dad but she didn't really understand what it meant.

Rachel looked at her daughter standing by the foil-covered windows, painting trees on the silver surface with food coloring. "Kayli, come here, honey." Her daughter set the tube down and wiped her fingers on a washcloth. She sat beside Rachel on the futon, opposite side of Beau.

Could she do it? Was it okay to mourn with others looking on? How much of an effect would her grief have on them? Emotional displays were appropriate in situations of this type but to what extent?

Kayli's expectant face, mirrored by Beau's, knocked the breath from Rachel. Crap, she was institutionalizing her children's life experiences. Who cared if she looked like an idiot while she blubbered? Her kids couldn't grieve because she wasn't and they didn't know what to do. Coping with situations was a learned trait and she was teaching oh so well... for a robot.

A sob escaped her. She wrapped her arms around their seemingly frail shoulders. "Guys, Daddy's not coming home. Ever. He's dead. He's gone. Do you understand? He is gone." And the reality broke down her protective walls. Yes, she could accept it. Her husband was gone. Her love. The man she had planned forever with, even into the end with. He was dead, burned. And she had their children to take care of.

Kayli's green eyes, so like her dad's swam. Beau buried his face in Rachel's side. She closed her eyes and leaned into the stiff back of the makeshift couch. They'd come a long way in a few days. Had it really only been less than a week?

Her children's bodies comforted her like teddy bears.

Was that... no. Her eyelids flew open and her gaze sought the handgun resting on the side table. The quads weren't two-stroke. She and Brenda had been raised around dirt bikes and that was definitely a two stroke motor roaring into her clearing. She squeezed the kids' shoulders and stood. "Stay here, guys. If you hear gun shots, lock yourselves in the master." She flinched at their small answering whimpers.

Rachel grabbed the piece and pushed the tinfoil from the corner of the front door's window. A blue bike, a Yamaha, leaned against a tree trunk on the west side of the clearing. A figure darted into the shadows. Rachel held her gun at her side and twisted the knob.

Rachel opened the door without a sound and stepped through, watching the spot where the figure had disappeared.

"Rachel?"

She froze. A trick. It had to be. Her sister was here? She couldn't ride a 250. The bike was too tall for her. "Brenda? Come out, I can't see you."

Rachel's hands shook. She tucked her gun into her belt and moved to meet her sister. Brenda emerged from behind a tree. Matted, her dark hair twisted into a bun and secured with a stick. Dirt clung to her skin with fierce tracks leading from the corners of her eyes as if she'd cried going fast into the wind *and* standing still.

But Brenda didn't cry.

Rachel continued to inventory her sister as Brenda stepped closer, cautious. Her eye was swollen and discolored and her lip had the look of a split, overripe grape tomato.

Limping.

Rachel reached out a hand and pulled Brenda into her arms. "Oh my word, Brenda, what happened? Are you okay? Where are the boys? I sent them to get you." No one else was in the clearing and outside of their conversation no other sound filled the air.

Her sister had lost weight. Oh, Rachel'd missed her. And if her little sister had made it, the boys would be along shortly. Relief joined the riot of emotions swirling in Rachel's heart.

Brenda squeezed Rachel's waist. "Can we sit down? I'm tired."

"Of course." Rachel motioned her into the cabin. Holy crap, Brenda had made it. "Kayli, Beau, Aunt Brenda is here." The kids still cried, but excitement mixed with loss and they raced to hug their aunt. A brightness where there'd been nothing. Thank Heaven.

Brenda greeted her niece and nephew with a weary smile. Blood had splotched her shirt and spattered the side of her cheek. Rachel waited until Brenda settled on the futon. She was brimming with questions and gratitude. The two emotions warred within her and she blinked the moisture from her eyes. She hated all the mushy stuff and so did Brenda, but really? Her sister wasn't dead out there, but it looked like she'd been through her own form of hell. "Kayli, Beau, can you guys run into my closet? Aunt Brenda needs a new shirt and pants, please. She'll want to change after she takes a shower."

Sighing, Brenda sat forward. Her lips barely moved. "We don't have time for that."

"What do you mean?" Rachel sat across from Brenda. Shock. Her sister had to be in shock. She'd recommend some relaxing techniques, hot shower, foo—

"Andy needs antibiotics. I couldn't get to the meeting place, but if Joshua brings Andy here, thinking I'm out there, he may or may not head out to get medication and not know what he's looking for. I need to go."

Confused, Rachel held her hand out, palm down. "Wait. You said Andy. You meant Cole. How did he get an infection this fast? He hasn't been gone that long." The mistake was cruel to Rachel's lacerated emotions.

"No. Andy. He has a huge laceration on his stomach he didn't tell me about. A concussion and second degree burns all over." Brenda met Rachel's gaze. "Oh, that's right. I'm sorry, Rach. I know it's hard when you think one thing but find out the opposite is true."

"What's true?" Kayli's gaze ping-ponged between the women, her arms filled with clothing.

Rachel pointed her finger at Kayli but directed her comment to Brenda. "No. This isn't funny. Don't say it unless you're absolutely certain."

Brenda's unwavering eyes held Rachel's gaze, freezing her soul with hope. "Rachel, Andy is alive. He's with Joshua, Cole, and Tom on the quad. I had to separate from them. Couldn't get to the meeting spot this morning. They should be here fairly soon… if they're coming."

"Daddy? Beau! Daddy's alive." Kayli dropped the clothes on the ground and ran back through the hallway, her squeals soon matched by Beau's excited cries.

Andy. No way. Rachel had watched the house fall. He'd disappeared in the flames. She'd driven away, thinking he'd died. Her love. *Oh, Andy.* She smothered her mouth with fingers aching to grab him and cradle him to her.

But no. Even if she could hold him close, he wasn't okay. He had an infection because she'd *left* him. His life was in danger because Rachel hadn't stayed to check. Guilt… ah, an emotion she was familiar with.

"Don't think of it that way." Brenda's voice lowered and she shot a meaningful glance at Rachel.

"How can I not? *I* left him there, and he was *alive*." Rachel brushed her damp hands over her jeans. "What do we need to do?"

"I'm returning to town. Any pharmacies could have the medication he needs. I just have to get into one. Joshua would have come with me, but it might be better if I don't wait." Brenda leaned forward and rested her head in her hand. Fingers from her free hand twirled a loose strand of hair. Her nervous tic. Her left eyelid drooped, just a bit, indicating fatigue.

How could Rachel let her little sister go back out into that? Whatever *that* was… But her husband was alive. With an infection. And if Brenda didn't go, Rachel might have to deal with the grieving widow role all over again.

Once again, she had to choose to let someone do something unsafe for the greater good of someone else. Another person that meant the world to Rachel. Who mattered more? Could she quantify her feelings? Qualify her love?

In a field study, she would associate the amount of maneuvering to the fight or flight mechanism. Rachel stayed safe, out of the way of danger, blaming her inability to go-and-do on the necessary attendance of Beau and Kayli's only living parent. She sent others out to do the dirty work. Like a queen bee. Safe. Unharmed while her child and sister went out into danger.

"I'll go." Rachel and Brenda's gazes clashed, both shocked at the words that had jumped from Rachel's mouth. "I'll go. I can't have you go out there in the condition you're in."

"What about the kids?" Brenda glanced toward the newly returned children who hung on their every word.

Rachel's stomach ached. At that point, she wasn't doing them any good. "You'll stay here with them. I know how to calculate the meds, you just tell me what ones to get."

"You can't go out there, Rachel." Brenda brushed the hair off Kayli's forehead. She kept her eyes down for a moment and then jerked her gaze up. "I met Daniel."

Rachel screwed up her lips and scrunched her brow. "Who?"

Brenda's eyes hardened and she slapped her thigh. "Daniel Bastian. He certainly knows you. Made sure I match you *and* him." She yanked her collar down and the clear definition of Rachel's tattoo could be seen in the blackened grooves on Brenda's white skin.

Flinching, Rachel self-consciously rubbed where her mark was. A tattoo had been hell. What had a brand in the same spot been like? Genuine tears warmed her eyes. She lowered her hand, which she hadn't realized she'd raised. "Brenda, I'm sorry. But it couldn't have been Daniel. Daniel's dead. And he'd never do that. I'm sorry. Are you okay?" She shook her head. "No, he's dead."

"Wow, sounds like the story of your life, Rach. Think your husband's dead and he's not. Find out someone you worked with, who obviously hasn't forgotten you, isn't dead either. He's alive. What's next? He held me down while his boss did *this* to me." She rearranged her shirt, a large hole in the chest falling just short of exposing the top of her breasts.

Chin jerked back, Rachel breathed through her teeth. "You sound a bit defensive. I didn't make up his death. The head psychologists kicked us out after an accident in the middle of some of the designing sessions. He said Daniel and two others were dead." Daniel had died. She'd been left alone. He'd been the only one who'd understood, who she'd connected with and had held her above the drowning levels of fear during the tests. When they'd designed the settings for the procedures and then subjected each member of the group to the tests, she and the other psychologists hadn't factored in what it meant to have someone to return them to a level of hope after each day of testing. Once Daniel had been removed from the equation, her hope had been easy to diminish.

They'd never told her she was going home in two weeks. Those fourteen days had been interminable.

"I don't know how to assimilate this, Brenda." Rachel pushed her hair off her face. She avoided meeting Brenda's eyes, but couldn't help glancing at the crease where her sister had been burned. Daniel, dead or alive, had nothing to do with her. Andy being alive mattered. Daniel didn't. Right?

Brenda leaned over and tapped Rachel's knee. "They're playing games, Rachel." She arched her brows and tilted her head.

"Games?" Brenda could only mean the psychological ones. Why else would she think Rachel would care?

"Bad ones. Poisoned close to a hundred by simply telling me the wrong information." Brenda's pupils dilated. "Shot others. I don't…"

Rachel motioned to the bathroom and bedroom. Her kids didn't need to hear the details. "Kayli, could you get some shoes, too, please? Beau, grab some towels and soap, please. And I bet Aunt Brenda is hungry. Can you grab the sandwiches I made earlier?" The kids left and she directed her attention to Brenda. "And? What happened?"

Brenda's breath caught. "Almost everyone died. We had to…" She choked and swallowed. "Watch. We had to watch as people died. Family members died in front of their loved ones. Friends watched friends die. He shot people in front of me, in front of the others. I argued, but…" Wiping her hands down her face, Brenda shook her head.

"Daniel did it." It wasn't a question. Rachel didn't want to hear what Brenda said. But she had to. "Did *they* watch?"

Brenda whispered, "No. They pulled me out and questioned me about you, branded me, and then gave me medical supplies for the people."

Hell. Nova Scotia all over again. "Are you *sure* no one watched you?" The games only worked if Daniel watched, observed. There wouldn't be any point to any of it, if they didn't have a way to document information. He'd been with her at most of her consultations as he was recognized as the foremost expert in his theory of valuation versus physical reactionism.

"We didn't see anyone. If they'd watched, they'd have known we were staging some of the live people to act as dead ones. We were supposed to get the bodies out."

"Did anyone know you thought it was poison?" Damn it.

"I told them the other dead bodies in the gym were making us sick, too. Killing us." Brenda twisted her fingers in her lap.

Rachel nodded her head. Good. Part of the experiment involved gauging the reaction of fear in the victim when they suspected everything and everyone as their potential predator. Daniel wouldn't have allowed testing to proceed without some form of detailing the findings.

Her nightmares had returned to haunt her, but Rachel wasn't going to wake up and realize it was just a dream. Not this time.

Chapter 19

Andy

Flames ate up his sides. No wait, pain burned up his side. He'd been burned and it seared in a different way. Josh had said something about staying quiet. Stay quiet and they'd be back for him. Andy couldn't remember who "they" were.

Rachel. She had to be worried sick about him. The kids. He cracked his eyes open to find scant light filtering through leaves enveloping him in his hiding spot.

Josh. How had his best friend found him? He'd said something about Rachel sending him. And Cole. Andy's oldest son had been there, but where had they gone and what had Rachel thought about seeing Josh again. Did she remember him?

What the hell was Andy thinking? Of course Rachel remembered him. Josh had *almost* been the choice she'd made. Andy had been certain she'd already chosen and he'd lied. Like a dog. Convinced Rachel Josh had impregnated a girl in his econ class. She'd bought it. Married Andy. But their first year had been rough. Andy had cut Josh from his public life, keeping him a secret. He'd never come clean to his friend or his wife. Why should he?

When Josh had convinced Andy to buy the land, Andy had honestly thought there was no way his family would ever need to use it. He'd made it a hobby, inventing ways to get off the grid. Enthusiasm for conspiracies had overtaken Josh and his excitement had been contagious. But Andy had returned somewhat to reality when he'd gone home to his family.

If Andy had actually considered any of it a real and direct possibility, he wouldn't have put his wife in the same path as her "long lost" possibility. Or better yet, he would have come clean to the two of them, purged his lies, and let the chips fall where they may.

Then Rachel had pulled back from him and the kids after her return from Rhode Island. Andy spent more time with Josh and consoled himself with the possibility she wouldn't care one way or the other. He'd avoided telling either of them. It wasn't immediate.

Andy couldn't risk losing Rachel. He needed her. But at the same time, he needed Josh. Halves of himself shared with two important people who might actually prefer each other over him.

Crap. And Rachel had believed him to be dead. How fast had she turned to Josh? How fast had Josh gotten into Andy's spot? Damn it. Wait, that wasn't fair. Or was it? The pain scratched his state of mind.

Andy lifted his head, leaves rustling with each movement. Had Josh and Cole covered him with fresh plants and abandoned him? Time blurred, marked by the throbbing in his side and the fog in his head. He relaxed back on the ground. Focus. Don't think about Rachel, and Josh consoling her. Or their children.

Josh had said they'd be back for him. He'd be back. Andy may have dropped the ball being a friend, but Josh had never let him down. He wouldn't this time, either.

Grinding his teeth together, Andy muffled his groan. His side hurt, but what the hell, the guilt hurt worse.

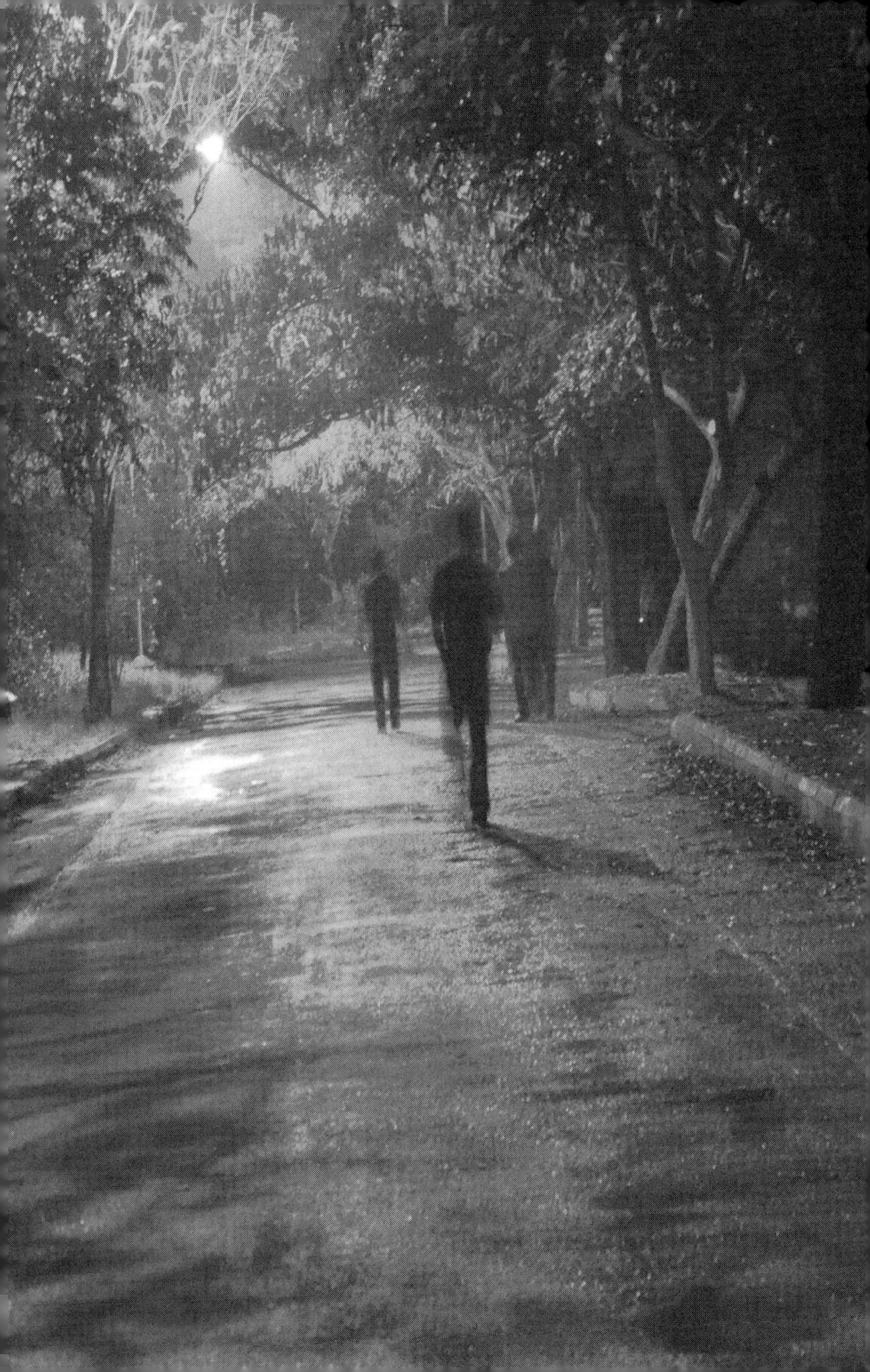

Chapter 20

Tom

A stitch in his side pulled with each gasp. Josh, Cole, and Andy had headed north on the quad. Tom and Jenny had run south. But being tired hurt Jenny's running pace and she fell behind, slow enough Tom walked beside her, looking behind them every few seconds.

Gasping, Jenny stopped and doubled over. A sob cut through her hard breathing. Tom placed his hand on her hunched back. He didn't know what to do. She needed a break, a real break – with food, sleep and water. But they needed to get as far into the forest as possible and as it was, they had another five miles or so to go before they started the hard trek north.

She wiped spittle from the side of her mouth and stood up, resting her hands on her hips. "I'm. Sorry. So. Tired."

Removing his hand wasn't an option. He patted her back. "I know, Jen. I don't want to push you but we have to keep going. Only a bit further and we can stop, okay?" Tom pointed toward the shale shed-off a hundred feet ahead, cutting through the tree-covered path like an avalanche had torn down the side of the mountain in the middle of May. "I promise. Get past the shale and we'll find somewhere to hide. Less than two-hundred feet. That's all. Not even a football field."

Jenny nodded, lowering her chin and moving into a rambling gait. Her feet barely left the ground but she was moving forward. Tom held her elbow and propelled her further. He'd carry her, but with the uneven terrain, he'd just as likely fall and do more damage.

Twenty feet down. Sweat had saturated his shirt. The butt of the pistol hidden underneath stuck to his skin, pulling free with each lean-and-look over his shoulder. Jenny's arm was cold, like her body was abandoning the extremities as it struggled to survive.

Forty. Fifty. Sixty. An avalanche had cut the forest off the face of the mountain with rock and mud. The open space sliced off any chance of seclusion, even the boulders too flat to hide behind. If they could get across the mere fifty feet or so of shale, they'd return to the safety of the forest. Just across the shale.

One-hundred feet. Tom jerked Jenny to a stop on the edge of the shadowed tree line. She slumped against him, her eyes half-open.

The trail disappeared. Two feet into rocky debris it petered out, covered by the rocks. Tom slid Jenny's inert form to the ground. He'd have to carry her, but he couldn't find the trail. He'd have to pick his way across first, scout it out.

Jenny curled into the tree roots he rested her in. He pulled the warm metal from his waistband, the surface slick with sweat. The pistol was lighter and the butt shorter than any of his dad's guns. His palm didn't recognize the weight.

Adjusting his footing over the protruding levels, Tom skirted the large light brown and gray splintered boulders. The path was there, just not used consistent enough to pattern in the footsteps of others.

Each step a different length, height. He felt like a mountain goat. Glancing over his shoulder, Tom stopped. He'd traveled further than he'd expected by watching his feet and not looking ahead or behind. The light slash across the mountainside separated Tom from Jenny. But the going had been easy and with Jenny's light weight combined with Tom's desperation to get out of there, it should pass even quicker the second time.

He could sit for a second. Breathe. Jenny was fine. She hid in the shadows of the trees where he'd left her. Tom only had a few feet to go to reach the safety of the forest on the other side.

Rock falling caught his attention. Tom spun to face the scuttle coming from above.

Nothing but a few rocks sliding down the face on a bed of dust.

Heart pounding, hands shaking, Tom backed into the nearest forest line. What the hell. He was skittish. The going might be perfectly safe, but how did he get up the nerve to travel back the way he'd come. A nearby fallen log served as a great bench to drop onto. He placed his elbows on his knees and cradled his head in his hands. And set his gun beside him in a crack of the wood.

When had he lost his nerve? Somewhere at the lake? Or maybe as far back as his house. He'd powered through and hadn't looked back. But the adrenaline piled up around him, cast off with the lack of need.

He rubbed his wet eyes and drew in another shaky breath.

"Tom."

Tom was going crazy. He'd just hallucinated his dad was calling to him. Either he was hallucinating or ghosts traveled through the woods.

"Hey, son. How you doing?" Heavy fingers gripped his shoulder and Tom fell back over the rounded edge of the log. *Holy shit.*

"Dad? You're alive. Oh, thank goodness." Looking up at his dad, Tom lost control over the tears he hadn't known he was holding. He couldn't breathe. "How… is Mom here?" Tom craned his neck, but nobody stood behind his dad. Confused, Tom looked closer at his dad then shrank into the struggling ferns at his back.

A squinting tic clenched his dad's right eye. A sharp pull on his left lip offered a grimace he tried passing off as a smile. The man was his dad, but not.

Tom's mouth dried up like a sponge under a hot lamp.

Dr. John Mason was spotless when everything around him was falling to hell. Not a grain of dirt could be found on him. His glossy black boots devoid of dust on a dirt trail. How was it possibe? A white button-up shirt tucked into sleek black dress pants complete with a "new" sheen to his glasses. Maybe Tom really was seeing a ghost.

"No, your mother didn't make it. I…" His dad shook his head and reached his hand out to Tom. "Tom, where's the pack I gave you?"

Tom took his soft hand but let go as soon as he gained his feet. He stepped back from the image that was more mirage than real. He didn't let on that Jenny was on the other side of the shale. Something wasn't right. He'd seen too many of his dad's "faces" and the one he showed now had nothing but deception engraved in the deep lines around his eyes and in grooves lining his mouth from his outer nostrils to his chin.

John's silver-lined sandy blonde hair hinted what Tom's would be in the future, if he made it that far.

Don't look, Tom, don't look. She's safe for now. He focused on his dad. Conflicting emotions tore at him. On one hand he wanted to run to his dad and let go of the responsibilities he'd held onto. On the other, he'd been through too much in the last few days to not understand the old adage "if it looks too good to be true, it probably is".

Sharper than before, John's words hissed across the feet between them. "Tom. Hurry. Where's the pack?"

Tom fell back a step into a flee-or-kick-ass stance. His dad was a short man but bulk filled his clothes and he could eat Tom under the table. Tom shook his head. "I don't have it with me, Dad. I left it at my friend's." A glance over the doctor's shoulder didn't reveal anything.

John jerked his head toward the other end of the shale-covered path. "*Whose* place? You never went to any friend's house, Tom. They've been watching you. And when you logged on-air, they knew they could get you into town." He raised his hand and ran his out-of-character elegant fingers through his hair. "Damn it, Tom. I told you to stay off. Remember? I said your handle wasn't old enough. Why'd you go launching the codes from my convo book? They know you have it now. There's no 'out'. You have to give me the book." His eyes hardened. "Or I'm dead."

A glance, out of Tom's control, slid across the rocks lit by the rising sun and revealed Jenny sleeping in the lap of the tree. Safe so far. But what was the catch? What was so special about John's codes? He had to know something thought to be valuable. "Who wants you dead? Or the book? Seriously, what is going on?" Tom sidled to the side, deeper into the forest, away from Jenny.

"Where is it, Tom? Did you leave it at the house? Somewhere along the way? I need it. Now." John moved one menacing step toward him.

Tom froze and stuttered. "Dad, I left it at Dr. Parker's. She helped me out." Not the entire truth, but—

"Dr. Parker? Rachel Parker? You gave her my book? Damn it, Tom. You're as naïve as your mother was." The doctor pulled a hand down his face, weariness in the sudden slump of his shoulders.

Was. The word stuck out with a bombshell of meaning attached. Tom matched his dad's stance but shoved his hands into his pockets. He'd left his pack on the trailer of the quad. But now that his mom had been reduced to a "was" existence, Tom didn't much care about the convo pads and what his dad imagined they held.

Thick with shadows, the forest beckoned him to run. But from his dad? His dad had never hurt him – but how many patients had he been negligent with because he wanted more excitement at work? Tom wasn't naïve. That was his problem. He had too much suspicion to believe others, even his own father.

He could outrun his old man. His dad had bulk but not enough of it was muscle. Three, maybe four, steps and he could sprint the other way. A foot fell into position.

"They know who she is." The flesh on John's cheek ticked.

Tom froze. "Who?"

Dr. Mason smirked at his boy. "You know who I'm talking about, Tom. The doll across the way. Sleeping. They're watching me and they got a bead on you when you met up with them earlier. You'll need to meet with them, come up with a plan on getting the convo book for me."

Turning, Tom stared across at Jenny's unprotected form. What had he done? He could've... leaning forward, Tom blinked. Shadows surrounded Jenny, and they weren't shaped like trees. Men had found them.

"You've had enough time, Mason. Did you get it?" Footsteps crunched down from the rocks where Tom had searched for movement before.

The man's mossy oak cover fell over his semi-automatic rifle. He looked to the sky and backed under the trees. Farnham pulled the hood from his head and nodded Tom's direction. "Tom. Your dad told us you were sympathetic to the cause."

Did he recognize Tom from before? The straight-leg posture would be hard to miss, but his darty eye movements and husky voice sealed the memory for Tom with a scoop of black tar.

Tom cleared his throat, hoping his heart didn't bump out of his chest. "Yes, sir. But I don't have the convo books with me. I could take Jenny and go get them. She needs food and water and sleep. Where can I meet you?"

John held up a hand. "Now just a minute, Tom. Farnham, Dr. Parker has the books. Tom's been holed up with her. If you want inside information, get Parker. Tom can take you to her place. She knows more than she lets on."

Farnham turned his gaze to Tom. "Is this true? Did you leave your information with Parker?" He sneered the name, disgust curling his lip and tightening his jaw.

Tom nodded. "But I can get them back." He wouldn't take the bastards anywhere near Dr. Parker. She'd been good to him for so long. Helped him.

Farnham looked over his shoulder at Jenny and his men, and then back to Tom. "No, we'll take Jenny *or* your father, you get the other one. When we get the book, you'll get back the hostage. We need that book, Tom."

John jerked his eyes from Tom to Farnham.

Hostage? Farnham had claimed to be on the side of the militia, the government, but instead had some if not all of the men in the Hate IT coalition at his disposal. Tom didn't know what the "cause" was, but if it didn't keep Jenny or his dad safe, it wasn't a cause he had a lot of hope for.

He had to choose. John's face had paled with the man's statement and he dropped his hands to twiddle at his sides. Jenny wouldn't be any better off. She was a hot little thing, and Farnham had a look about him. But John was his dad and Jenny was just a girl.

Movement past Farnham's shoulder caught Tom's attention. Jenny woke up and one of the men started yelling at her. She cried out and looked around for Tom. The man raised his hand and brought it down across her temple. Jenny crumpled to the ground.

Tom broke from the small group with his dad and Farnham. He bounded onto the shale, slipping here and there with each step. He stopped midway and looked behind him. His dad and Farnham hadn't followed, looked in fact as they were held behind the dark line by an invisible wire. Turning the other way, Tom balanced on a large flat rock the size of a tire and watched the men around Jenny. They, too, didn't move from the protection of the foliage.

In the open, Tom was left alone. No Jenny or dad, true, but no threats or ultimatums. He wouldn't need to go back to the forest for the pressure of a choice.

Nobody moved. He had to make a choice. His dad. Or Jenny. He couldn't stand there forever. Or could he?

Tom shook his head. Of course, he couldn't. Jenny and his dad needed him. He had to choose.

A roar shook the mountain. Tom spun around to look up at the peak covered in gray and white smoke. And the rocks tumbling toward him. He ducked as a stray flat rock targeted his cheek from the eruption.

Now what the hell did he do?

Chapter 21

Brenda

"I don't understand any of this." Brenda twisted a lock of her hair around her finger. She'd removed her wedding band long ago, but the faintest tan line mocked her. She'd been waiting for Josh to show up since she'd pulled into the clearing. But the draw had to be fatigue and concern for her nephew. Nothing else. She'd done the married thing, the attraction thing, and it hadn't worked out. At all.

Kayli and Beau sat in timeout on opposite ends of the couch, arms crossed and shooting glares at each other. Rachel rolled her eyes. "I know you don't. But if you really saw Daniel, your 'brand' is a message with more meaning than he let on. Gustavson is hunting me for something and Daniel is warning me. But I don't understand for what."

"Daniel didn't brand me. Gustavson did and he had entirely too much fun doing it." Brenda shook her head. "And what do you mean tests? With Daniel? What, like games or something?" Her neck itched, like talking about her brand made it exist more exactly in that one moment than any other time. Her sister had acquired a far off glaze in her eyes when Bastian's name had dropped like a rock between them. She hadn't refocused more than a minute or two at a time. Brenda snapped her fingers in the direction of Rachel's face. "Seriously, Rachel, what the hell?" Brenda glanced at her niece and nephew. Language. Like they even cared.

"No. I mean, yes. Not games, per se. We designed a series of fear inducing activities which actually were safe, beyond safe, but the activities allowed us control because the subject *thought* there was something to fear." Rachel looked around the room, her fingers fidgety and her damn knee bouncy.

Brenda quirked her eyebrow and smirked. "You're saying you can control me with the suggestion of something to be afraid of?"

Rachel twisted her own wedding band and nodded. "Yes. Establish a fear, strong enough to threaten some form of stability or value in a person's existence."

"Who were your test subjects?" Science needed experiments to prove theories. Fear was nearly incalculable. And Brenda didn't think rats would fear suggestions.

Her sister pursed her lips and looked down. Brenda leaned forward. "You're kidding me. You tried to qualify and quantify an emotion that has no constant trigger or escape? What the hell were you thinking? On yourselves? Dang, Rachel. Why?"

"I can't just play with people's minds. We thought that if we designed the tests, we could control the outcome, see just how bad it would affect the subjects – us. But we lost control of the settings about two weeks in and the only thing holding us together was that we knew we weren't alone. The leaders maintained the boundaries we set, but started jacking with the peripherals – what was at stake, the values of each fear, reassigning stages of fright until we couldn't define if what we were feeling was fear or just anxiety."

Rachel smiled, the expression startling Brenda. How off to speak of horrible tests that retrained your emotions and yet smile about it.

"You can't define fear?"

"Oh, I can define it. Better than any textbook out there. I can identify it in others and I know how to treat it, but I'm not sure when I, myself, feel it. Or when it's appropriate to be afraid. Things... bug me, make me uncomfortable, but my values have been altered. Now all I care about are my kids." Rachel tucked her chin. "It's not something I can explain easily."

"Bull." Brenda slapped her hand on her thigh. "That's crap and you know it. But all that aside, they weren't scaring people with threats, Rachel. They were killing people. Dead people can't feel fear. So your tests can't be key here." Sometimes her sister's intellect was amazing and sometimes Brenda didn't have to wonder why she chose such an easy major. She leaned into her seat and looked at the ceiling.

"Well, if Daniel *was* there, then that's exactly what they're doing. The application, though..." Rachel stood and waved her hand at the kids. "Beau. Kayli. Timeout's over. Stop fighting, please." Both children ran from the room. Rachel stared after them, a far off look on her face. "They're starting. The denial process is first, but the anger is the worst."

"Of grief? But Andy's not dead. He's alive."

Rachel spun and faced Brenda. "For how long? You said he was infected. Well, he's not back yet and I don't have antibiotics on hand. I'm getting cabin fever here with nothing to do."

Studying her sister, Brenda admitted that Rachel had more of a haggard appearance than Brenda at the moment. A ponytail replaced her normally smooth maintained style. No makeup, none. Her dry lips stood out like a slash of mauve on her pale skin pulled taut across her cheekbones. Rachel always had been a doer.

Sleepiness gummed up her mind and Brenda found herself staring at the darkened corner in the ceiling above the kitchen. She clenched her eyes shut then forced them open. "When do the kids go down for bed?"

Rachel opened her mouth to answer, but a shout from outside cut her off. Brenda stood and followed her sister to the door. Was it Josh?

He rushed into the clearing, bent at the waist, arms pumping. Josh waved his arms and slowed to a trot. His breathing ragged, he gasped but pushed past them into the living room. "Close. The. Door. Lights."

Rachel shut the panel and Brenda flicked the switch in the wall. Mid afternoon sunlight seeped through the screen of the window off the dining table. Rachel leaned across the seats and slid the foiled panel closed. Minimal light to see by. Less distraction for Brenda. She'd better not sit or she'd fall asleep.

Josh gathered his breath, leaning on the door. He looked at Rachel. And what Brenda had assumed was sweat on his cheeks, flowed like tears from his eyes. She stepped closer. But he didn't glance her way. His gaze was trained on Rachel. Brenda held her breath. One more. Not another one.

Rachel raised her hand to her throat and shook her head. Josh nodded. The conversation between them in silence until a whisper tore from Josh. "I'm sorry."

Rachel sobbed, but clamped her hand over her mouth.

Brenda's gaze darted between the two. She had no idea what was going on, except Andy, Tom, Jenny, and Cole weren't with him. "Josh, where is everyone?"

He turned his attention from Rachel to Brenda. *Finally.* He shook his head and his voice came out raspy and uncertain, like he couldn't believe what he said and he was testing out the words. "We made it. To the park. But a branch of the militia we'd run into on the way to the school intercepted the groups we were meeting. I went down to check out what they were doing, left everyone with the quad. They were asking for volunteers, recruiting. I said I'd be right back and returned to the quad. I... I sent Tom and Jenny down a different trail and stashed Andy so I could deal with Farnham. When I turned back to talk to Cole, ask him to hide until I'd..." He swallowed. "He wasn't there. He'd gone around and joined Farnham's group. Told them about the quad we had. Farnham took the quad at gunpoint. I grabbed mine and Tom's packs and stashed them in the woods so I could run back." He ran his hand down his face and fell silent.

Rachel sank to a kitchen chair. Brenda had hit her limit of comprehension. But she pushed through the fog and walked to her sister. "We need to get Cole and Andy. And we need the antibiotics. What about Tom and Jenny? Do they know how to get here?"

Josh straightened and slumped in the chair opposite Rachel. "Tom knows. I'm not worried about him. He's resourceful. I can find Andy again, but I need the quad. There's no way I can pull him that far by foot. He'd be dead for sure if we made it back, or be begging me to kill him." He glanced at Brenda. "I don't know what to look for with the antibiotics. Can you go?"

Brenda might not understand psychology but she knew the body. And hers was done. "I can't go anymore. I need rest. I haven't slept in days." She pressed a hand on her sister's shaking shoulder. "But Rachel can go. I can tell her what to look for and she needs to do something. I'll stay with the kids and get some rest. Maybe you'll beat Rachel back with Andy, Josh. Which you'll need me for anyway." She closed her mouth against the nausea joining the fog. She'd been up way too long. "Josh, can you go now?"

He nodded and stood. "I need to grab some supplies from my place, then I'll be down to grab the quad. I hope to be back by tomorrow afternoon, at the latest." Josh stared at Rachel who continued to focus on the table. He turned to Brenda, as if seeing her for the first time. He grazed her arm with his fingers, making her elbow burn. "Thanks. Really." He stuck his head out the front door and looked around before darting back into the clearing.

Brenda shut the door and claimed Josh's vacated seat. She grabbed her sister's free hand, stopping her index finger from the insistent tapping. The nail was chewed and cracked. "Rachel?"

"What about Cole? I need him back. He's my son. Andy will be alright. But I need Cole to come home. He must be so scared. He's only fourteen. Brenda. I need my son back." Her voice cracked.

The confession ripped at Brenda. Of course her sister was worried about her son, but Brenda hadn't realized how much. "Can you get the medicine? Andy needs that, honey. Then we can worry about Cole. They're not going to hurt him. I promise." She was making guarantees that she had no control over and Rachel knew it. But she seemed to grasp the hope Brenda's words offered.

She raised tear-filled eyes to Brenda. "I think I remember fear, Brenda."

Of their own accord, Brenda closed her eyes. She couldn't recall a time in the past few months where fear hadn't been present. And now Rachel had an inkling of what fear was like again. Just in time for the real terror to begin. "Don't let it control you. We can beat it."

"I don't know if I can." Rachel wiped at her wet cheeks. A pounding on the door pulled her from her thoughts. She stood and opened it.

Josh fell through, landing on his side. Blood ran from his shoulder. A loud buzzing followed him through the entryway. "They're bombing the mountains."

~~~

Stay tuned for Book #2 of the *Into the End* series – *Through the Flames* –and **discover why allies = all lies**.

Go to www.brpaulson.com and sign up for the Survivor newsletter for chances at giveaways and more information on Paulson's writing.

About the Author

B.R. Paulson finds crazy in the everyday. Do you have what it takes to turn the page?

Find Paulson's other titles at
www.brpaulson.com

Printed in Great Britain
by Amazon